"I'm like Luk

Del continued, "He doesn't ~~want~~ ~~me,~~ but he's got a buddy. Han Solo. Grady's like Han Solo. He's my buddy."

Tara tried not to flinch. "You have a dad."

Del's face went stubborn. "He doesn't want me. And I don't want him. I don't need him. I got a buddy."

She wanted to tell him that his father still loved him in his own way. It was a lie, but she believed it was a lie he needed. He was too young to deal with the truth. As the movie's theme music welled up, Tara's heart sank. What were her choices? Let her son sit like an automaton in front of the television screen? Or let him fall even further under Grady McKinney's spell?

For Grady could cast a spell, a strong one. She was close to being snared herself. Del was clearly starving for a man's company. And so, perhaps, was she.

ABOUT THE AUTHOR

Bethany Campbell was born and raised in Omaha, Nebraska. One of the best things about growing up in Omaha was that, like it or not, every schoolchild was herded at least once yearly through the city's sumptuous Joslyn Art Museum. Omaha also had a great central public library, not far from Joslyn. As a geeky teenaged bookworm, Bethany spent many a happy Saturday afternoon exploring both spots.

In college she majored in English and minored in art. Her first three ambitions were to be a cartoonist, an illustrator, or a writer. Later, as a freelancer, she worked for several greeting card companies as a writer and doing rough art. She sold her first romance novel in 1984 and has won three RITA® Awards, three *Romantic Times* Reviewer's Choice Awards, a Maggie Award and the Daphne du Maurier Award of Excellence

Bethany loves to hear from readers. Please drop her a line through her Web site, www.bethanycampbell.com.

Books by Bethany Campbell

HARLEQUIN SUPERROMANCE

CRYSTAL CREEK titles

Home to Texas
Bethany Campbell

HARLEQUIN®

TORONTO • NEW YORK • LONDON
AMSTERDAM • PARIS • SYDNEY • HAMBURG
STOCKHOLM • ATHENS • TOKYO • MILAN • MADRID
PRAGUE • WARSAW • BUDAPEST • AUCKLAND

ISBN 0-373-71181-6

HOME TO TEXAS

Visit us at www.eHarlequin.com

Printed in U.S.A.

"Make new friends, but keep the old;
One is silver, the other is gold."

To Carol Dankert Stoner, who is pure and solid gold.

CHAPTER ONE

GAVIN CHANCE STARED AT HIS SISTER in disbelief. "You sold the *horses?*"

"I didn't sell Licorice or India," Tara said, her gaze dropping.

She'd kept her son's pony and her own horse. But the other three animals had been sold a week ago. She'd wanted to cry, seeing them taken off, but she had run out of tears long ago.

She sat with her brother in his hotel room at a small table covered with a linen cloth and set for lunch. His visit was a surprise—he had flown to California out of concern for her. Tara had only picked at her salad, and Gavin had pushed aside his sandwich, half-eaten.

Tara looked out the picture window, but instead of seeing the skyline of Los Angeles, she saw her pretty little ranch outside Santa Clarita. Like the horses, it must be sold. There were already two prospective buyers. Soon her home would no longer be hers.

"But *why?*" Gavin demanded.

Tara kept staring at the skyscrapers. "We need the money."

Gavin swore and threw his napkin down, rising from the table to pace the gold carpet. He was three years older than Tara, an exceptionally tall man, whip-lean, with thick, sandy hair. Despite his rangy build, he had an artist's face, with a sensitive mouth and dark, expressive eyebrows.

He jammed his hands into the pockets of his cargo pants. "I mean why didn't you ask *me* for money?"

Tara toyed with a silver fork. "Del and I will get along. We're tightening our belts, that's all."

Gavin came back to the table, pressed both hands on it and leaned toward her. "You've sold your horses. You're selling the ranch. Good God, Tara. I'd have helped you. You know that."

She laid the fork aside with exaggerated care. Her brother was a rich man—on paper. In real life he was risking all he had trying to develop not one, but two model communities.

Though the first, in Hawaii, was still under construction, Gavin and his partners had taken a dizzying chance on a second. They'd bought a huge tract of land in Texas, paying millions for it. They would pay millions more for its development. Their plans were as ambitious as they were original, and the gamble was enormous.

So Tara had not told her brother all that was happening to her. Gavin had been in Hawaii, desperately trying to finish that project. He hadn't been to the mainland for months.

When they talked on the phone, she'd held back things. He had, she believed, enough burdens of his own. And she had her pride, her independence. Too much of both, Gavin had often said.

Now he glared at her in frustration. "You mean Sid still hasn't given you one damn dime in child support?"

"No," she said, her voice calm. She'd taken Sid to court. It had done no good. She could have him jailed, but the thought made her sick. How could she do that to Del?

"Does Sid ever come to see Del? Does he use his visitation rights at all?"

The questions hurt. Tara looked away from Gavin and out the window again. Her husband had left her and their son for another woman, a younger and very jealous woman. For her he'd given up everything: his home, his honor and, most shamefully, his son. Del, not yet five, was shattered.

Tara shook her head, unable to speak. Gavin leaned in closer to her, but she wouldn't meet his eyes. "Sid's still acting crazy?"

She pressed her lips together and nodded. She studied how the smog made the tops of the tallest buildings hazy, how it turned the sky murky.

"Is that why you sold the horses? Because he won't help?"

She hedged the question. "Partly."

"And the ranch?"

"I have to be practical. I don't know what's ahead. We were living beyond our means. And—and—"

Gavin groaned in anger and frustration. "Don't tell me. Is Burleigh making trouble again? About visitations with Del? About custody?"

Burleigh was Sid's widowed father, Del's grandfather. An imperious man, he'd disowned Sid over the divorce, but he blamed Tara for letting it happen. Del, he claimed, was now his only living kin, and he had a right to have a say in the boy's life. A big say.

Burleigh Hastings was powerful and, when he chose, he could be as disruptive as a hurricane. He was vice-president of a huge and prosperous company, and he loved control, control of things, control of people. Tara was certain Burleigh was the reason Sid had turned out as he had, and she feared his influence on Del.

"He's out of the country right now," Tara said. She was grateful for his absence, but knew that she and Del were inhabiting a false and limited calm. It was as if they were in the eye of a storm.

"But he'll be back," Gavin supplied. "Demanding his 'rights.' He'll scare Del and confuse him and do all he can to undermine you."

"Yes. He will." She was resigned to it. "But I'm prepared to ask for a restraining order against him if it comes to that."

"He'll make your life hell. Where is he? How long will he be gone?"

"He's in the Middle East. A big government contract. It seems they needed a 'forceful' personality there. It'll tie him up for two months, maybe three. I'm talking to a lawyer. I need to be ready for him."

Gavin knelt on one knee by her side. "Tara, you should take Del and get out of here." He took her hand between his. "Out of Los Angeles. Out of California. Away from this crazy situation."

She shook her head. She had to face facts. "There's no place to go, Gavin. My job is here."

Tara had grown up with horses and now she taught riding at Santa Clarita's Kane Stables—both regular classes and those for special needs students. She loved her job, and she was good at it. But she was also more than a little frightened. There were rumors of cuts in programs and staff.

Gavin pressed her hand more earnestly. "There're other places. Other jobs. And there's one that's perfect. I know California's always been home, but let it go. Look what it's doing to Del. What it's done to you. You don't look like my Tara anymore."

Her throat locked and her mouth went dry. Del was becoming an unhappy, nervous child, and she—she wasn't sure what she was becoming.

Gavin reached into his back pocket, flipped open his wallet and shoved a photograph in front of her. "What happened to this girl?"

She tried not to wince. The photo was a close-up of her, snapped a few years ago at a friend's wedding. She wore a wide-brimmed white hat, tilted low to emphasize her eyes. They were dramatic eyes, an unusual clear gray, the irises ringed by darker gray.

Her hair fell past her shoulders in loose waves. Her makeup was skillfully applied. The photo showed an elegant, even stylish, woman—she was tall, long-legged and slim.

But now that woman was gone, hidden away. Even today, meeting Gavin here in his hotel, she hadn't dressed up. After Sid had left, she'd thrown her makeup away and defiantly left her face plain, letting her freckles show.

Sid had once loved her wealth of auburn hair, shot through with red and gold. Now she had pulled it back severely and pinned it into a tight roll. She wore black slacks and a loose black blouse. She tried to look drab, and she had her reasons, but she wasn't sure she could put them into words to Gavin, or even to herself.

So she looked at her picture and saw someone who was both familiar and utterly foreign. She said, "Gavin, I just haven't felt like—"

"Like what?" he asked, one hand still grasping hers.

"I've had so many other things to do." She shrugged. The explanation sounded lame even to her.

He tucked the photo into his wallet and slid it back into his pocket. He put his thumb and forefinger under her chin and raised her face so she'd have to meet his gaze. "Tara, we have an offer for you. A job. It's perfect. You were made for it."

She cocked her head, puzzled.

"The land we bought in Texas used to be a dude ranch. Most of its buildings got torn down. But the house and lodge still stand. We want to make them the center of a special section of our development. I want one part of this project to be an equestrian community."

Her eyes widened. An equestrian community? Gavin had spoken of such a place for years. Each house would have enough acreage for one or more horses. There would be a bridal path accessible from every yard, pastures and a communal stable.

Gavin said, "We want to refurbish the lodge, make it into a recreation facility for the community as a whole. But first fix up the house. It's solid, but it's been empty for months and there's been some water damage. How about it? Think you could fix up an old house?"

She smiled in spite of herself. They'd grown up doing exactly that, time after time. Their parents had made a career of buying run-down farms and ranches and transforming them into sound, neat horse outfits. Up and down California they'd moved, from one spread to another.

Tara had loved the challenge. The family always began by camping out in some dilapidated house. There'd been a special excitement in that, like being pioneers. She'd loved the process of restoration and the satisfaction of seeing it done well.

"A house?" She was intrigued.

Gavin nodded. "The house would be your first priority. We want one wing set up for me when I'm in Texas, with rooms for corporate guests. The other will be living quarters for the stable manager. And that, Tara, would be you. The stable needs to be built. You'll have your say-so in its design. Could you deal with that?"

She looked at him in disbelief. She'd always wanted to run a stable; she had firm ideas of how it should be done. As for building, she and Gavin had entertained themselves for years by planning the dream stable. They had built it in their minds and constructed it in conversations and sketched it on paper.

"You're kidding," she said, because she didn't know what else to say.

"No. I'm not kidding. But you'll have to go to Texas."

She felt light-headed at the prospect, and her stomach was full of butterflies. "Texas is a big place. Where?"

Gavin looked more solemn than before. "Just outside a little town called Crystal Creek. About an hour from Austin."

She couldn't imagine it and laughed at her own incomprehension. "I don't know a soul in Texas."

"You know me," drawled a low, familiar voice. "I grew up there. I got people there. They'll watch out for you and Del."

She whirled to face the second man. He'd been silent so long, and her conversation with Gavin had been so intense, she'd almost forgotten his presence. It was one of her brother's two partners, Cal McKinney.

She stared at him as if he had just magically appeared in a puff of smoke. He was tall, but not as tall as Gavin. He was wider in the shoulders, and he carried himself like the rodeo cowboy he'd once been. He was a devilishly handsome man with thick brown hair and long-lashed hazel eyes.

In his late thirties, he still had a boyish air, even more so when he smiled and showed his dimples. He showed them now. "You're perfect for this, Tara. You know it. Gavin knows it. I know it. And Spence goes along with us."

Spencer Malone was the third partner. She knew him, but not nearly as well as she knew Cal. And Cal, bless him, was generous to a fault. So was Gavin, where she and Del were concerned.

"I—I couldn't do it. And you'd just be doing it as a favor because Gavin thinks I need to get away from here. I—"

"No." Cal's smile faded. "You're doing us the favor. Didn't you study design in college?"

"Yes." Her major was design, her minor equestrian studies. It might seem an odd combination to some, but to her it had been as natural as breathing. It was she, not Sid, who'd done most of the renovation on the little ranch outside Santa Clarita. Sid couldn't read a blueprint or pound a nail in straight.

Cal said, "Serena and I've seen your ranch. You did a top-notch job on it. I know that's true 'cause Serena tells me and that woman's got taste."

"In everything but husbands," joked Gavin.

"Especially in husbands," Cal shot back, grinning.

Cal moved to the middle of the room. He and Gavin were both horsemen, but Cal, Texan to his marrow, always dressed the part. His boots and belt were hand-tooled, his sky-blue shirt Western-cut.

He said, "Here's our plan. I'm gonna have a ranch on the western edge of this land. Spence wants to build the main community section, small estates in sync with the environment. But he doesn't start until the equestrian section's finished."

Gavin moved to Cal's side. "Cal and I have to get to Crystal Creek, meet Spence, finalize some things. Then I need to get back to Hawaii. When I'm done there, I'll come back to Texas to keep an eye on the start of main construction. You fix up the west wing of the house for me. Who knows what I like better than you?"

Tara looked at these two men and was staggered by their generosity, fascinated by their offer, yet at the same time wary.

"Texas is a long way off. It's a long way to take Del."

"I told you," Cal said. "I got people there. My daddy's just retired and is off gallivantin' for a while. But his cousin Bret's managing the ranch. Big Bret. He'll be right next door. My sister and brother-in-law are there. You'll love my sister—she's horse-crazy as you. Serena and I have friends there, too, and they'll help you out. You got my word on it."

Tara was still uncertain. "No. It doesn't feel right. I'm not the little match girl. I don't want to take charity. I don't want to go imposing on people I've never met. I—I—"

"You're scared," Gavin said. "Once you would have jumped to go. But Sid and Burleigh have knocked the starch out of you. You're afraid to take chances."

Confusion disappeared in a flash of indignation. "I am *not* afraid. Our parents *raised* us to take chances."

"Then what's the matter? You don't think you're up to it? Loss of confidence?"

"Certainly not!" she retorted. "Restore a house? A lodge? Get a stable put up? Damned straight I could do it."

"You really think so?" he asked.

"Yes, I do. Yes, I *could*," she said before she knew the words were out of her mouth.

"Well, then," Gavin said, as if in philosophic resignation, "That's that. Cal, how fast you think we could get her set up there?"

"Under ordinary circumstances, two or three months. But put my sister on the job—four weeks, easy."

Gavin narrowed his eyes. "And Sid won't try to stop you. You know that."

To her sorrow, she knew.

With a certain slyness, Cal said. "Texas law's different from California law. It'll put another obstacle in what's-his-name's path."

Burleigh, she thought. And any move that slowed down Burleigh was a good one.

"It won't be easy," Gavin warned. "There was a flood that did considerable damage downstream. Most construction workers are tied up there. Labor'll be hard to find."

"Lynn'll help her." Cal shrugged as if the matter were already resolved. He glanced at his plate, sitting empty on the desk, then at Gavin's. "Gavin, if you don't want the rest of that sandwich, can I have it? Tara, what about that salad?"

Did I just agree to go to Texas? She asked herself, dazed. *Yes. I think I did.*

Numbly she passed her salad bowl to Cal. "How can I settle in Texas in only a month? Things would have to be done at warp speed."

Cal picked up a fork and speared a cherry tomato. "Just leave it to the McKinneys, darlin'."

Gavin gave him a sardonic glance. "Texans. Always bragging."

"Well, you know what they say," Cal answered. "If it's true, it ain't braggin'."

CAL HADN'T BEEN BRAGGING.

Exactly one month later, Tara was in Crystal Creek, Texas.

She sat, temporarily alone, in the kitchen of a kindly, cheerful stranger who was not quite a stranger—Lynn McKinney Russell.

Today Tara and Lynn had met face-to-face for the first time after a frantic month of e-mails and phone calls. Tara had smiled and chatted, asked and answered questions over coffee.

The whole time she'd pretended that all of this was normal. She'd pretended that she was the most confident woman in the world. Inwardly she still wondered how in hell she suddenly found herself halfway across the continent, a California girl in the heart of cowboy country.

She stole another glance out Lynn's kitchen window to check on Del. He was playing lustily on a backyard jungle gym, almost wildly. After all, he'd been cooped up in the truck so long. His black-and-white terrier, Lono, released from his cage, happily chased about the yard.

This morning had seen the last leg of the journey. Tara had driven from Dallas through Austin, then to this little town and to Lynn's house. Lynn had already done a hundred kindesses for her and Del, and she had welcomed them like family.

Del was clearly happy and excited because he had, for a while at least, what all only children most desire, a playmate.

A little black-haired boy, Jamie, also about four, clambered and swung on the bars with him. The other boy's mother, ripely pregnant, watched them. Her name was Camilla, and she was Lynn's next-door neighbor. She stood with her arms crossed over her round belly, smiling at the children's antics.

Tara sat in Lynn's cozy breakfast nook, a mug of coffee warm between her hands. From the oven wafted the spicy scent of a casserole. Lynn had insisted that Tara and Del lunch with her, and afterward Lynn would lead them to the house Tara had seen only in photographs and old blueprints.

We're almost there, Tara thought, watching Del hang by his knees. *We're almost home.*

Except it's not home. It's not remotely like home, taunted an inner gremlin of uneasiness.

Near Los Angeles, the hills glowed with such a vibrant, vital green that they seemed to shimmer like emeralds. Palm trees nodded and swayed, their fronds sensitive to the sea breeze.

The hills here are stony, arid. The trees are bare. They're twisted into strange, low shapes.

Shut up, she fiercely told that treacherous voice. Hills were hills, dammit, and trees were trees. Home was where you made it, and by all that was holy, she vowed she would make a home here.

What she needed to worry about wasn't the scenery, but if the Texas move could really slow down Burleigh's plan to be the dominant force in Del's life. She had sent him a letter on the day she left. She hoped it would take a while to reach him. When he read it, he would not take it kindly.

She took a sip of coffee and straightened her spine defiantly. If he wanted to fight, she'd fight. If he wanted to maneuver, she'd outmaneuver.

"Found it," Lynn said, bustling back into the kitchen with a fat, leather-covered photo album.

Lynn was petite, and she moved with an efficient briskness and an athlete's grace. Her hair was swept up into two pert ponytails that made her look like a teenager, not a woman with two grown stepdaughters and a ten-year-old son.

She sat down on the banquette beside Tara and began flipping through the album's pages. Lynn giggled. "Cal would kill me if he knew I showed you this. Ha! Just let me find it..."

Lynn paused, pointing with amusement at a snapshot. "This isn't it, but look. The gang of usual suspects."

Tara looked and smiled. After her long journey, it was good to see familiar faces.

There, with their arms around each other's shoulders, stood a trio of tall men, mugging and grinning for the camera. One was her brother, Gavin, another was Cal, and the third was Spencer Malone. The Three Amigos, Inc.

Lynn gave Tara a wry look. "But the real hoot is a shot

I took last month. The last time they were all down here together.''

She turned the page. The same three men stood on a nearly barren lawn. They wore ludicrously large, sequined sombreros, and they held up margarita glasses in an exaggerated toast.

"Idiots," Lynn said, but she said it fondly. "That's the day they signed themselves into debt up to their necks. Recognize where they are?"

In the background only a portion of a house showed. Built of native stone, even that small section managed to look both elegant and on the edge of ruin. Boards barred the door and the windows gaped blankly.

Tara swallowed. She knew the place from other pictures. This was the house she had been sent to save. It was where she and Del would live, perhaps for a long time.

Again she peeped at Del, dangling by his arms from one of the jungle-gym bars. She'd known for his sake and her own, that they needed to be far from Los Angeles. But this far?

Lynn turned pages, paused and tapped another photo. "This is me and both my brothers."

Tara looked at a slightly younger Lynn, her arms linked with those of two young men in Stetsons, one serious, one laughing. The laughing one, of course, was Cal. The more solemn one Tara had only heard about: Tyler.

Lynn's finger moved to another picture. "And this is my whole family together."

Cal had regaled Tara with stories often enough that to her the McKinneys were already the stuff of legend. As the founding family of Crystal Creek, they had cast their fate with that of the Hill Country.

Lynn pointed out a handsome older couple with a young girl. "This is my father, J.T.," Lynn said fondly. "And our stepmother and little sister. Daddy just retired. The three of them are in Paris now. Believe me, it's very hard to imagine Daddy in Paris."

She smiled, then sighed. "This is Tyler again. And his wife and two girls. They've gone out to Napa Valley for the year. They're trying to see if they can handle two wineries—one here, one there."

Lynn shook her head pensively. "And Cal's in Mexico, selling his brewery. Everybody's so…far away. It's the first time they've all been away at once. I feel—abandoned."

Tara bit her inner lip, knowing how it was to be truly abandoned.

Lynn's expressed grew abashed. "I shouldn't complain, heaven knows," she murmured. "And I'm not really the *only* one left. Daddy's cousin's here. He's a cousin, but he and Daddy were as close as brothers, so he's almost like an uncle. Big Bret. We called him that because Mama also had a cousin Bret, and he was short, so he was Little Bret. Big Bret's managing the Double C for Daddy. I've got a picture here—somewhere."

How different it must feel, thought Tara, to have roots deep and strong in one place. Her family had moved eleven times while she was growing up.

"Here he is," Lynn said, smoothing the page flat. "Big Bret. Looks like Daddy, doesn't he?"

Tara studied the man. In his fifties, he gazed into the camera grimly. He did not look like the sort who changed his mind or gave his affections easily.

Yet if affection didn't show in his unsmiling face, it showed in how his arms draped the shoulders of two younger men. Although they stood close to him, their expressions were as joyless as his.

"His sons," Tara said, knowing it must be so.

"Yes." Lynn's voice was quiet. "This isn't the greatest picture. It was taken just a little while after my aunt Maggie's funeral. She really was the glue that held that family together. Without her, it's become a bit undone."

She squared her shoulders, forced a smile. "You'll meet him soon, Big Bret. He's your neighbor, and he'll be a good one. This son—"

She indicated a handsome, boyish young man with angel-blue eyes. "This is Jonah, the youngest. I'd kill for eye-lashes like that. He came to the Double C to finish his dissertation. A sweetheart. But all he thinks of is books and cows."

Jonah, Tara mused, was so handsome he was perilously close to being pretty. He was not as interesting as his brooding dark-eyed brother.

"The other one," Lynn said, "is Lang. He'll be here soon. He's kind of at loose ends now. He's getting a divorce."

She must have seen Tara's face tighten in control. She quickly changed the subject. "There's another brother. Grady. But you won't meet him."

Tara looked at Lynn with mild curiosity. "Why not?"

Lynn's smile was indulgent. "Grady's the one with the Gypsy in his soul. We're afraid he'll never settle down. I wish he would. Of the three brothers, he was always the most…"

She paused, bemused.

"Most what?" prompted Tara.

"The most fun to be with," Lynn said thoughtfully. "The hardest working. Maybe—it's a hard call—the smartest. The easiest to talk to. The hardest to understand."

She shrugged, patted the album cover and smiled. "Whatever. Ready for lunch?"

BRET MCKINNEY WAS GOING about his business in all innocence when he was ambushed by a godlessly seductive nightie.

All he'd done was open a closet door in an unused bedroom of the Double C. There were other clothes in the closet, but it was the nightgown that sneak-attacked him.

Then Bret realized that there was a crowd of nightgowns and negligees. They hung tauntingly empty on their satin hangers, and they reminded him of how long it had been since he'd been with a woman.

Bret slammed the closet door shut in panicky haste. He

felt guilty, like an inadvertent Peeping Tom. Whose intimate, gauzy stuff was this? Did it belong to his cousin's wife? One of his nephews' wives?

For the first time in years, Bret felt the stirring of a long dormant sensuality. He'd thought such feelings were dead, and he hadn't mourned them. He meant to be faithful to his wife's memory. He was a man of iron discipline, and he'd made up his mind.

It disturbed him that his body had rebelled against his mind's dictate. He stepped to the window and stared out at the miles of rolling Texas range.

Bret still missed his wife, Maggie, dead two years now. He had severed himself from his job in Idaho in part because he could no longer endure the ranch house so painfully haunted by memories of her.

Bret's plan had been to come back to Texas to learn to live alone and like it. Fate, however, had decreed that solitude was not an option. First, his youngest son, Jonah, had announced he'd join him.

Bret hadn't minded this so much. Jonah was a good man with cattle; he was serious and he was quiet. He helped work the ranch by day and wrote his doctoral dissertation at night. He was no trouble and made no demands. It was *almost* the same as being alone.

But now Bret's middle son was on his way to the Double C, tangled up in money and marriage problems. At thirty-one, Lang was too damned young to be having a midlife crisis, but that wasn't stopping him.

Bret shook his head in frustration. Lang was due tomorrow, which was why Bret was checking out the room. It was why he'd opened the closet and been bushwhacked by the nighties.

Well, the things would have to be moved, that was all. Lang didn't need a closet full of female finery to taunt him.

Bret left the room and strode down the hall to the kitchen, from which floated an aroma of Tex-Mex beef and spices. He would ask Millie Gilligan, the Double C's housekeeper, to move all that frippery somewhere else, *anywhere* else.

He found her in the kitchen, stirring a pot of chili. She

was an odd little gnome of a woman, restless and given to strange pronouncements.

Mrs. Gilligan was almost as new to the ranch as Bret was, and J.T. had cautioned him about her. "She's the best we could find. She's a great cook and a fine housekeeper. But, dammit, I think she might be a witch."

She indeed might be, thought Bret, for she would stir her pots, dropping in pinches of this and sprinkles of that, and produce foods that seemed too delectable to be created by a mere mortal.

"Mrs. Gilligan," Bret said gruffly, "I need your help when you've got a minute. My son will be using the back bedroom. There are some women's…things…in the closet. Could you move them someplace else?"

Mrs. Gilligan squinted at him wisely. She had eyes as green as bottle glass and wildly curling gray hair. "I'll see to it," she croaked. "We'll make him comfortable. Even the finest phoenix needs its nest."

Whatever the hell that means, Bret thought. "Yes. Well. Thanks."

He paused. "Mrs. Gilligan, about my son—I don't know how long he'll stay. Looking after an extra person…you're sure this is all right?"

"The more the merrier, or so the wind blows. I'll tend to the closet." She left, her gait somewhere between a scuttle and a scamper.

Bret sighed harshly and stared after her. How old was she? Fifty? Sixty? Eighty? He couldn't tell. At least he doubted if anyone would gossip he was sleeping with his housekeeper. Wiry little Millie Gilligan seemed as sexless as a pipe cleaner.

Jonah came in the back door, quietly, of course. More leanly built than his father, he also stood taller, nearly six foot three. He had dark-lashed blue eyes like Maggie's, intelligent and sensitive. Sometimes looking into those eyes ripped Bret with pangs of loss. *She's still here,* he'd think. *In him.*

Jonah gave Bret his serious smile. "Hi."

"Where've you been all afternoon?" Bret asked.

Jonah tipped his brown Stetson back to an incongruously rakish angle. "Riding fence," he murmured.

Bret nodded in approval. Riding fence was a common stockman's job, but Jonah never minded humble work. No part of ranching was beneath his interest. He was going to make somebody a hell of a manager.

"Anything new?" This was generally a useless question to put to Jonah, because he always muttered, "Not really."

But today a troubled look crept into Jonah's eyes. "New neighbor's moving in."

Bret frowned. As if he didn't have enough to do. "The woman?"

Jonah shifted uneasily. "Yeah. Slattery told me." Slattery was the foreman.

"Well," Bret said impatiently, "what did he say?"

"She's here, that's all," Jonah said. He shrugged out of his denim jacket and hung it on a peg beside the door. He went to the refrigerator, took out the milk jug and poured himself a full glass.

"We should pay her a call," Bret muttered, not looking forward to it. "Cal asked us to look in on her, make her feel at home."

"You go," Jonah said, then drank his milk the way some men chug beer.

Bret gave a sigh of frustration. Jonah went out of his way to avoid women.

Bret would go alone. He wanted to honor his nephew's wishes. He knew the woman was the sister of one of the partners, but nothing more.

The only clue he'd had was Cal's request to be friendly to her. "Help her if you can. She's had a tough time."

Bret had been too discreet to ask what kind of tough time, and Cal had been too discreet to say. Well, maybe Bret would saddle up, ride over and get the job out of the way. He was not by nature a sociable man, and with Lang boomeranging back on him, he felt less sociable than usual.

"Might as well do it and be done with it. Maybe I'll saddle up that big bay gelding—" Bret began.

Jonah's blue eyes narrowed. "Somebody's coming up the drive."

"It can't be Lang?" Bret said and shook his head dubiously. "Too soon."

Lang had said he couldn't make it to Crystal Creek before tomorrow evening.

"No sir," Jonah said, still staring at the driveway. Something like real joy glimmered in his eyes. "It's Grady."

Bret felt a stab of displeasure. *It can't be him. He wouldn't have the guts...*

But hiking up the driveway came a man in faded jeans, a blue work shirt and an open denim vest, lined with sheepskin. He wore a black Stetson pulled down over his eyes. He carried a scuffed duffel bag and walked like somebody who'd hiked a long way. Yet he somehow still managed a swagger.

Bret would know it anywhere, that air of lazy swashbuckling, that easy strut. His face went rigid as he watched the too-familiar figure approach the house.

Wide across the chest and shoulders, the man was a solid six feet tall. Although the day was chill, he wore no outer covering but the vest. His shirt was grease-stained, his black hat was dusty and he needed a shave. Still, he sauntered up to the back porch like a prince.

It's him, all right. Grady.

With a shriveling sensation in his stomach, Bret looked on his eldest son for the first time in two years. He forgot the new neighbor. He forgot any promise to Cal. He even forgot Lang. All he could see was Grady, mounting the stairs like trouble itself getting ready to cross the threshold.

Lord in heaven, Bret thought with sorrow and bitterness, *just what have I done to deserve this?*

He had come to Crystal Creek to be alone. But now, as if directed by malignant forces, all three of his sons were descending on him. He had welcomed Jonah. He was determined to be hospitable to Lang. But what ill wind had driven Grady to his door—the only one of his sons who was truly charming—and truly worthless?

CHAPTER TWO

TIME AND WEATHER HAD CARVED the country around Crystal Creek into an uneven land of great hills and valleys. Some of these hills were massive enough to be called mountains, but most were low and rolling.

In some places, great sweeps of rock covered the earth, like a flow of pale, hardened lava. Soil was thin. Only what was strong could survive here.

Yet the landscape had stark beauty. Even in mid-November, the scattered oaks and elms fluttered golden leaves, and the sumac and soapwood bushes flared up from the ground like scarlet torches.

But most of the trees were the scraggly, twisted ones that Lynn said were mesquite and their branches were nearly bare. They looked tough enough to suck nourishment straight from stone.

Ahead, the flashing red of Lynn's taillights signaled that she was turning from the highway to a dirt road. Tara followed. The road led up and was so badly rutted that her truck rattled and swayed. The way grew steeper and rougher, jolting her bones.

Then, suddenly, the road leveled off, and the two trucks were halfway up a hill big enough, to Tara's mind, to qualify as a mountain.

And there *it* was—their house.

She had seen pictures, but she was not prepared for the impact of the real thing. It was, she thought, magnificent. Magnificent yet sad, because it had been both neglected and abused. But she had come to change all that.

The house was a long one-story sweep of limestone that glimmered so brightly in the sun it seemed almost white. It angled into a wide V shape so it could command views of the valley beneath it and the tall hills rambling into the distance in the west.

It had once had decks and sun porches, but they'd been torn off, leaving bare patches of concrete and raw slashes on the face of the stones. Concrete blocks, stacked unevenly, formed three jerry-built steps to the back door.

An enclosed walkway attached the house to a triple garage. A vandal with a can of red spray paint had scrawled graffiti on both stone and wood. Tara bit her lip in resentment, already feeling protective toward the house.

"What do those words say?" Del ask, squinting at them in curiosity.

"Nothing," she said. "Foolishness."

Among the obscenities and insults, one message stood out: Fabian Go Home!!! Brian Fabian was the man who'd recently owned the property. It was he who'd had the porches torn down and most of the outbuildings razed. Gavin had told her the outline of the story, but not the details.

Lynn parked in the graveled driveway, and Tara pulled in behind her, pebbles rattling under her tires. Both women got out, and Tara unfastened Del from his seat. "Is this our new house?" he asked in a small voice.

"Yes," Tara said. "And it's going to be a very nice house."

He stared uncertainly at the ruined porches. "It's broke."

"Yes. But we'll fix it."

She went to the back of the truck and unlocked the door of the kennel box. Lono bounded out, sniffed the ground with enthusiasm and lifted his leg at a cactus. He was clearly pleased with the surroundings.

Del was not. He frowned in worry. "Why'd somebody write on our garage?"

"Sometimes people do bad things. I'll paint over it."

He didn't seem reassured. He put his thumb into his mouth, something he did when he was tired or anxious, and she could tell he was both. For once she didn't tell him not to suck his thumb. Instead she picked him up, and he leaned on her shoulder, yawning in exhaustion.

Lynn nodded ruefully at the defaced garage doors. "Sorry about the graffiti. Sam was going to paint over it last Sunday, but we had an emergency. All three dogs met a skunk. Yuck."

"It's all right," Tara said. "I'll take care of it. You've done more than enough for us."

"You may not feel so charitable when you see your decor." Lynn rolled her eyes. "It's only a mix of cast-offs and garage-sale bargains."

Tara patted Del's back and smiled. "It'll be fine."

She'd sold most of the furniture she'd had in California. She didn't want the memories.

But the few good pieces she'd kept were coming, and their books, kitchen things, odds and ends. The man at the moving company said it was such a small lot, he'd have to squeeze it onto a truck headed that way with other loads, other stops. In the meantime, their possessions were in storage and might not arrive for weeks.

Tara didn't mind. She'd lived in nearly bare houses before. She'd told Del it would be like camping out. He'd thought it sounded like fun—then.

Her horse and Del's pony, their saddles and tack, would be brought by a man who moved horses for his living, Garth Gardner. Tara had known him for years and trusted him implicitly. But he, too, had a full schedule, and the horses were not due to arrive for almost a month.

When Lynn learned all this, she'd insisted on furnishing the house temporarily, even if the furnishings were few and haphazard.

"You're going to feel like you're living in a thrift store." She gave a sigh. "Not even a good thrift store."

She tunneled into the back pocket of her jeans and

brought out a jingling brass ring. "Well, are you ready? Here they are, the keys to the castle."

"I'm ready." Tara took them, and they felt as weighty as her responsibility to her son. And to her brother.

AT THE DOUBLE C, Grady half limped up the stairs of the back porch.

He'd walked a long way and had picked up a stone bruise.

But he forgot the pain as he reached the top stair and his eyes caught the familiar vista of his uncle's rolling land. J.T.'s spread looked good to him, mighty good.

The hills loosed a throng of memories that tried to force themselves into Grady's mind. He blocked them expertly, as if they were gate crashers trying to storm an inner place he'd long fought to keep private.

Grady didn't like to think much about either the distant past or the far future. He'd tried to live like a bird in flight, soaring in the present moment—but it had been harder to do of late. And he had to admit this particular present moment wasn't so good, pride-wise.

Suck it up, he told himself. His father wouldn't be happy to see him, but he'd take him in. Somebody had said that, right? *Home is where they have to take you in.*

So he raised his fist and knocked at the door. He gazed at the countryside from the top of the porch. And he remembered in spite of himself.

How many years since he'd chased Lynn McKinney up these very stairs, brandishing a garter snake at her? And she'd stopped on the top step, wheeled around and bloodied his nose—for scaring the snake. God, he'd been fond of J.T. and his wife and three kids. He'd thought the Hill Country would be home forever.

Don't think of that. Don't think of those days.

He started to knock again, but the door swung open. His father stood there, staring at him like he was a freshly delivered bad surprise. He supposed he was.

"Hi, Dad," he said. A smile sprang to his lips because

in his heart he was glad to see the old man, even if the feeling wasn't mutual.

He hadn't set eyes on his father for two years, not since the funeral. They'd had words then. They'd had few since. Grady phoned once in a while, but the old man never had much to say. Well, two years was a long time, and Grady had never been one to hold a grudge.

As for the old man, although he looked perplexed and displeased, he didn't actually look *old*. He looked a lot better than he had at the funeral, where he'd been worn and ashen as a zombie. He looked strong again, like his old self.

So Grady nodded in approval and said, "You're looking good." He meant it.

His father's dark eyes looked him up and down. They had a spark of their old fire. "To what do we owe this honor?"

Grady cocked his hat back. "I heard you were in Crystal Creek. I was passing through. I was going to stop and see you." He grinned. "But my truck stopped about eight miles before I did."

"Oh, hell," his father said and swung the screen door open with a sort of stoic resignation. "Come on in."

Grady entered the kitchen, lugging his duffel bag. The scent of spicy beef hit him like a whiff from heaven. "Lord, that smells fine," he said. "Am I invited for supper?"

"I suppose," Bret said in the same weary tone.

"Good to see you again," Grady said and offered his hand. Bret took it and initiated a contest of who could squeeze the hardest. Grady let him win, dropped his duffel bag to the floor and turned to Jonah, who stood by the window.

For a second Grady's heart took a strange, flying vault. Looking into Jonah's eyes was like plunging backward in time and staring into their mother's eyes. Nostalgia pierced him like an arrow through the chest.

"Little brother," he said with genuine affection and embraced Jonah. Good Lord, the kid didn't look like a kid

anymore; his even features had lost their last trace of boy-
ishness.

Jonah accepted the embrace awkwardly. Like their father,
he was embarrassed by emotional displays. But unlike their
father, he was not judgmental. Once you were in the circle
of Jonah's affection, the devil himself couldn't pry you
loose.

Jonah mumbled, "Good to see you."

Grady disengaged himself and punched his brother's
shoulder affably. He faced his father again. "Okay if I spend
a couple nights? I don't know how long my truck's gonna
be out of commission."

"I suppose." Bret's mouth was grim. "Where you heading this time?"

"A spread down in Florida," Grady said. "Via New Orleans."

"What's in New Orleans?"

"That's what I aim to see," Grady said, keeping his real
reason to himself. He gave his brother's shoulder another
punch. "You want to come, kid? Those French Quarter gals
would love you."

Jonah's handsome face darkened in a blush, but he
smiled.

"Jonah's got a job here," Bret said emphatically. "A
steady job. *And* his dissertation to finish."

"Dissertation." Grady eyed Jonah with playful pride. "A
doctor in the family. How's it goin'?"

"Okay." The same little smile stayed, playing at the corner of Jonah's mouth. He seemed truly pleased to see Grady.

Bret wished he could feel the same easy pleasure. But his
emotions were rent in two as he studied his two sons, the
youngest and the eldest.

He wondered how he had gone so right with one, so
wrong with the other. There was Jonah, as dependable as
gravity, marked for certain success. And there, on the other
hand, was Grady.

Grady wasn't as tall as Jonah, and his good looks were

more rugged. His hair was almost black, his skin was tawny, and his eyes, like Bret's own, were as dark as strong coffee. When he flashed that killer smile of his, weak women melted. Hell, even strong ones melted.

And Grady liked to melt them. He was used to it. He had charm, and Bret believed it was his undoing. Everything had always come easy to him, so he had never had to apply himself to anything.

Grady was in his prime—thirty-five years old—and he had not accomplished one blasted thing in his life. The fates had given him every gift. He was smart—his test scores in school had proved it. But he'd dropped out of school when he was seventeen and hit the road.

Look at him, Bret thought, fighting down his disappointment. His son's jeans were faded and dusty. His boots needed a shine. His shirt had a black smear down one sleeve. But the hat, as usual, was tipped to a cocky angle. That hat told the world, *I don't give a damn. I never have. I never will.*

Bret stared at his firstborn, thinking, so much potential; so little accomplished. It had broken Maggie's heart, though she would never admit it. "He'll settle down someday," she'd always say as if she could believe it.

Grady had not even made it home in time to see Maggie before she died. Oh, he had his excuses, of course, like always, but not being at Maggie's deathbed was a lapse Bret could not forgive.

After the funeral, Bret had rebuked him bitterly, but his son wouldn't bow and accept the blame he so justly deserved. When he'd left, Bret had been secretly glad to see him go.

Now he was back. Acting—and this was Grady's special gift—as if nothing had happened. Oh, he could charm the pants off a duck if he tried. He was even making Jonah talkative.

"Yeah. Lang's coming home. He should be here by tomorrow night," Jonah said.

"No kidding?" Grady grinned. "I'll be danged. Perfect timing. It'll be old home week. Is he bringing Susie?"

"Just h-himself," Jonah stammered.

"Susie left him," Bret said, more sharply than he meant to. "Now she wants half of everything. He'd just put the earnest money down on that little horse spread. He'll lose it."

Grady's dark eyes flashed. He snatched off his hat and slapped it against his thigh. "Hellfire and monkey turds! How much bad luck can one man have?"

"Plenty," said Bret.

Millie Gilligan came walking into the kitchen. She stopped in the doorway, eyeing Grady as if he were something strange and out of place, like a green grizzly bear.

"*You're* not the one," she said to him.

Grady, his face still flushed with anger, stared at her without comprehension.

"He's not the one what?" Bret demanded of the woman.

"He's not the one you said was coming," she replied, something akin to censure in her voice. "He's not the one you expected."

Now how in the hell did she know that? Bret wondered, but he didn't have time to think about it. "You're right. Tomorrow my middle son comes. This is an unscheduled visit. Mrs. Gilligan, this is my oldest son, Grady. We'll need a place to put him up tonight. Grady, this is Mrs. Gilligan, the housekeeper."

"Pleased to meet you, ma'am." Grady all but bowed to her. "Are you the little lady responsible for the savory brew I smell?"

She peered at him, uncharmed. "You were swearing in my kitchen."

Grady blinked. "Beg pardon, ma'am. I'd just heard some bad news."

"Ahh. You'll soon hear more," said Mrs. Gilligan, not taking her glass-green eyes off him. "But for every yang, there's a yin. Many an accident happens, and many an accident will, or maybe it's fate in a fright wig—who's to say? I'll go fix you a room. Don't swear in my kitchen. Nobody swears in this kitchen but me.''

She turned and left, and the three men stared after her. "I'll get more?" Grady asked, dumbfounded. "More bad news? Accidents? What'd she mean by all that?"

As if in answer, the kitchen phone rang.

THE INSIDE OF THE HOUSE YAWNED immense and nearly bare. It smelled of dust and mildew. Yet Tara's heart sprang up in love for it, in spite of the must and shadows.

A cathedral ceiling, beamed with oak, soared over the front rooms. No wall divided the living and dining areas. Instead they flowed into each other, separated only by a free-standing fireplace of gray-white stone.

Still carrying Del, Tara followed Lynn through the rest of the house. The west wing contained a guest room, a sitting room, an enormous master bedroom and a bath fit for an emperor. A large office came with a modestly sized library room and its own half bath. Except for its dusty fixtures and shelves, this part of the house was empty.

Lynn's and Tara's footsteps echoed eerily on the slate floors, and Lono's toenails went *tap-tap-tap*. He happily sniffed the strange new scents. Del, breathing heavily, was falling asleep, his head on Tara's shoulder.

This wing would be Gavin's private living quarters when he came, and Tara was already having visions of how she could make it rich and full of comforts for him.

The east wing, which would be hers and Del's, held three good-size bedrooms, each with its own bath. The rest of the space had been engineered into a boggling series of spacious storage closets.

True to her word, Lynn must have hit every yard sale in Claro County. She'd pulled together enough used furniture and appliances to provide bare essentials for Tara and Del— and then some—even a washer and drier. She'd had all the utilities turned on and a phone installed.

Two of the east wing bedrooms each had a single bed with faded but clean bedclothes. Each had a somewhat battered dresser. Del was growing heavy in Tara's arms, so she lay him down on the bed in the room that was his. Next to the bed stood a scuffed toybox spilling toys.

"Stay," she told Lono quietly. The dog wagged his tail and leaped on the bed, turned around twice, then curled up snuggling against Del's side. The look on his face said, "Don't worry. I'm here."

Tara gazed down at her son. "I won't shut the door. He has—dreams sometimes," she whispered to Lynn. "If he wakes, I want to hear him."

Lynn nodded. She went to the dresser and switched on a chipped little lamp shaped like Donald Duck. "This used to be Cal's," she said with a smile. "I think he'd like knowing it's here."

The two women moved softly down the hall. "I'm surprised he can sleep," Tara said, looking back over her shoulder.

"He and Jamie played hard." Lynn turned right from the hall, heading for the kitchen. "Come on. I put a couple of wine coolers in the fridge. Let's drink a toast to your new house."

The kitchen's original appliances were gone. Next to the sink squatted an old three-burner stove. Beside it, an equally ancient refrigerator hummed and gargled, as if to prove by its noise that it was on the job.

Lynn swung open the creaking door, withdrew two bottles and uncapped them. From the cupboard she took a pair of mismatched jelly glasses and, with a flourish, filled them. She handed one to Tara, and they clinked the glasses together in mock solemnity.

"To your new house," Lynn proposed. Each took a sip.

Then Lynn tilted her head and regarded Tara over the rim of her glass. "What do you think of the place? Are you depressed beyond words?"

"It's wonderful," Tara said sincerely. "And a thousand thanks for all you've done."

Lynn tossed a dubious glance at the card table and wobbly chairs she'd set up in the kitchen for mealtimes. "Cal said you've done this before? Lived with nothing but the basics?"

Tara nodded. "My parents did it almost a dozen times. Believe me, we really roughed it a few times. This is luxury in comparison."

"This was a beautiful house once, and it can be again. I have the feeling you're the one to make it happen. Want to look at the main living space again?"

Tara nodded. Together they drifted through the door and back to the central living area. Lynn had created a makeshift office near the fireplace and facing the western bank of windows. She'd used a sturdy wooden table for a desk and had found a handsome old-fashioned oak swivel chair to complement it.

Nearby, she'd put a pair of cushioned lawn chaises and a cuddly looking beanbag chair in front of the small television. She'd even hooked up a VCR and placed a basket of videos beside it.

She'd put another box of toys by the television: cars and action figures and Thomas the Tank Engine characters that her own son had outgrown.

Of all Lynn's acts of kindness, her kindness to Del touched Tara most. She was so grateful that she could not find words, and her throat knotted.

But Lynn acted nonchalant, as if readying a house for a stranger was all in a day's work. She looked up at the oak-beamed ceiling. "This place was well-built, that's an advantage. And another is that it wasn't empty long. Only since June."

But her expression changed when she moved to one of the big windows overlooking the valley. Her calm brow furrowed, the corners of her mouth tugged downward and she shook her head. "Fabian. He nearly ruined it all—damn him."

Tara, moving to her side, followed her gaze. Gavin had sketched out Fabian's story with professional detachment.

But Lynn simmered with emotion, and Tara saw why. Beneath them, the landscape was different from the rest of the Hill Country. The valley was as desolate as a wasteland. A huge hole gaped in the earth as if a meteor had smashed into the ground, destroying everything around it.

"This used to be a gorgeous vista." Bitterness tinged Lynn's soft drawl. "That's why the Harrises built their house here—they owned the dude ranch. They were going to build out on the edge of the property, but they couldn't resist this view…now it looks like very hell."

The valley stretched out bare, bulldozed and eerily lifeless. Lynn's tone changed to sadness. "In spring there used to be a carpet of bluebonnets down there—acres and acres, so beautiful you couldn't believe it. And other wildflowers. Seas of them."

Tara studied the dead and barren land. "Will the flowers come back?"

"It'll take years. Unless our brothers reseed it." The thought smoothed her brow, made her smile. "If I know Cal, he'll want to."

Tara nodded. *So would Gavin.*

Lynn pointed to the huge raw-looking pit. "That's where that fool Fabian tried to put his lake. He never should have picked that spot, but he had to exploit the flowers. Bluebonnet Meadows he was going to call it." She squared her jaw in resentment. "Well, the bluebonnets are gone. And so are his cheesy model homes."

"Gavin told me," Tara said softly. Fabian, set on his grandiose development, had tried to create an enormous artificial lake. But autumn rains had drenched the county, breaking his dam, and a wall of water had swept the valley, devastating it.

Lynn pointed to a featureless bulldozed area. "The first

thing Three Amigos did was route the water back the way God intended. They had to bring in people from Dallas to do it. They'll fill in that lake bed when they can get enough equipment here. And good riddance.''

A chill prickled Tara's bones at the sight of so much folly. ''Gavin said that's why it'll be hard for me to get labor for a while. That the flood destroyed so much downstream that everybody's working there.''

''I've found a few people to tide you over,'' Lynn said. ''But yes, Fabian caused damage, especially down at Baswell. Thank God the land's not in his hands anymore.''

''If people resented Fabian developing this land, won't they resent Three Amigos doing it?'' Tara asked. It was a dark thought, one that had nagged her.

''But this is different,'' Lynn said, raising her chin. ''Fabian wanted to put over a *thousand* houses on this land. They only want a few hundred. And to keep the land as natural as possible.''

''If they can pull it off. It's going to take time, work—and money.'' Tara was still worried over Gavin's money, although he assured her the Hawaiian property was starting to bring in money—a lot of it.

''They'll make it work.'' Lynn clearly refused to doubt her brother. She changed the subject.

''You're going to be isolated out here. I'm glad you have a dog. Is he a good watchdog?''

Lono wasn't a big dog, but he had a terrier's protective and fearless heart. He'd fling himself into the midst of a pack of jackals for loved ones. ''He's the best.''

''Good.'' But Lynn looked thoughtful, almost haunted. ''But eventually you're going to have a lot of men out here on construction. And you'll be the only woman. You can't be too careful. Once I was…''

Her voice trailed off, as if once more she had wandered into a topic she'd rather not speak of. Tara examined the emotions fleeting across Lynn's mobile face. ''Once you were what?''

"Nothing. There was some—trouble. This roughneck—never mind. Sam'll loan you a rifle if you don't have one of your own."

Tara had spent time in wild country when she was growing up. She knew guns were sometimes necessary, but she also had an instinctive hatred of them. "No, thanks. But if I change my mind I'll let you know."

Lynn looked Tara up and down as if she liked what she saw. "Do that. And call me for any reason. I mean that. Most of my family's gone, and I'm not used to it. I'd *love* to be needed."

Then Lynn glanced at her watch. "Oops, Hank's going to be home from school soon. I need to get cracking."

Tara walked her to the back door. She touched the other woman's shoulder. "Again, I can't thank you enough. You've made me feel I'm very lucky."

Lynn grinned. "No. Hole in the Wall seems back in good hands at last. I think we're the lucky ones."

Tara hoped so. But as she watched Lynn drive off, the word repeated itself ironically in her mind. She was alone with her son in a strange house in a strange region.

She wondered what Burleigh Hastings would say to see his grandson in such a run-down house overlooking such a desolate view. He would claim she was insane to bring him here.

I can't worry about him. Not now. There's too much else to do now.

She rolled up her sleeves so that she could get to work.

GRADY FELT LIKE FORTUNE'S FOOL.

The weird little housekeeper had been right. More bad news came, and it came by phone. Accidents, she'd said.

Please understand that accidents happen, Jervis Jensen had pleaded with Grady. *Please, please understand that.*

Jervis owned Jervis's Towing and Auto Repair. When Grady's truck had broken down, he'd hiked into town and asked Jervis to haul it in. Though Jervis was a rugged man in his fifties, on the phone he'd sounded as if he was going to cry.

An accident had indeed happened. Jervis's assistant had been towing Grady's pickup into Crystal Creek. Jervis swore that he had been doing this task safely, gently and with all possible tender, loving care. Then something occurred that no one could have foreseen.

Both the tow truck and pickup were sideswiped by a tanker carrying yellow grease to a rendering plant in Waco. All three trucks went into a ditch, and the seams of the tanker ruptured. All three were deluged with used canola oil.

"I know how you feel—I really do." Jervis's voice was dangerously near breaking. "Thank God nobody was badly hurt. But *my* truck's ruined, too. Do you know how much a tow truck costs? The woman at the insurance company is boggled. She's just boggled. She never heard of such a thing. You do have insurance, don't you? Please say yes."

Numbly Grady said he had only minimal insurance. He hadn't meant to keep the truck, but to sell it in New Orleans. It was an investment, a vintage 1956 Chevy.

"The tanker company's saying it's my driver's fault. It's not. I'll have to sue, and so will you." Jervis said in a choked voice. "I vow there will be justice done for this."

Grady hung up, stunned. He'd sunk most of his money into buying and restoring the truck. But he'd had an offer for it and would have made a sweet profit on the sale, enough to have kept him in tall clover for the next year or more. Now what?

JONAH DROVE GRADY AND BRET to the scene of the accident. Grady felt a numbing sense of surrealism. The Crystal Creek Fire Department had sent two dump trucks filled with sand to soak up the oil in the ditch. Grady's pickup had yet to be pried from under the glistening, dripping tanker. The whole countryside stank of old French-fry grease.

Grady truly didn't know whether to weep or to storm up

and down the highway, raging and shaking his fists at the sky. Since he couldn't decide, he simply stared. The truck had been beautifully restored. Now probably only parts could be salvaged, if that.

"You know, I think this could only happen to you." Bret shook his head in disbelief. "Why were you driving such an old junker?"

Grady said nothing of the truck's true worth. He had long ago tired of trying to explain or justify things to his father. Now the truck looked only like what it was, a congealing wreck.

Jonah's face was pained with sympathy. But then, all of a sudden, he began to laugh. And laugh. And laugh. Grady couldn't help it. Although he was filled with something close to despair, he laughed, too. Until tears came to his eyes.

"IT'S REALLY NOT FUNNY," Jonah said that night. They were in a pink bedroom full of ruffles and teddy bears. It was where Mrs. Gilligan had quartered Grady, his bed a pink canopy with side curtains.

As he lay stretched out on this innocent confection of a bed, Grady wished he was back in the sleaze and tinsel of Las Vegas.

Jonah sat by a dressing table with a skirt on a white wrought-iron chair with a pink velvet cushion. He had his leg crossed over his knee and a somber look on his face.

"I mean," Jonah said, "that cooking oil's bad news. When it spills, it's worse than fuel oil. A guy at the university said it was actually harder to get off a seabird's feathers."

Grady put his hands behind his head and stared gloomily up at the pink canopy. The buyer in New Orleans had cussed him out over the phone, calling him a stupid son of a bitch for not taking out more insurance. Grady had counted on his skills as a driver and a mechanic to get him safely to the Big Easy. He'd counted on his luck, too, but it seemed to have run out.

His insurance wouldn't cover the oil damage to his truck, nobody was admitting liability and it looked like he was going to have to join Jervis Jensen in suing the tanker company. A lawsuit could drag on forever. Grady was marooned. Thirty-five years old, nearly broke and back living with his father. His depression felt bone-deep.

"Change the subject, will you? Whose room is this? It looks like something out of a damned fairy tale. I keep expecting the Seven Dwarfs to troop in."

"It's Jennifer's. J.T.'s daughter by his second wife. They're in Paris."

"I never met them." Grady remembered only J.T.'s first wife, Pauline, and their two sons and daughter. He supposed J.T.'s sons had done better by their father than Grady had by Bret.

"Where's Tyler?" he asked moodily.

"California. His father-in-law died. He and his wife have to decide if they're going to run the winery he owned out there or come back to the one they started here."

Either choice sounded plenty cushy to Grady, but he didn't have an envious nature. He let the thought pass. "What about Cal? Still doing fine?"

Jonah nodded. "He and his two partners just bought the old Kendell place. The one that got turned into a dude ranch. Sank a *lot* of money in it. Taking a big chance."

Grady turned his head and frowned at his brother. "Sank money in that spread? It wasn't anything special. What do they want with it?"

Jonah gave an indifferent shrug. "Couple of different things. Part of it'll be a development. Try to pump new life into the town."

"It needs it." Grady stared at the pink canopy again. After Vegas, Crystal Creek looked like Podunk, U.S.A. Once he'd thought it the finest spot on earth. He'd learned a lot since then.

Jonah said, "They're fixing it all up. They sent some woman here to be in charge of fixing up the house and lodge."

A woman. Grady's spirits rose slightly. "What's she like?"

"Don't know," Jonah said. "She's got a kid. She must have money. She's sister to one of the partners. Lynn knows her."

A rich woman with a child? Scratch that possibility. Grady had had his fill of rich women. And kids were always a complicating factor. He'd trained himself to avoid complications. He sighed in resignation. "And how's little cousin Lynn?"

"She's good," Jonah said. "Married. Family. Keeps her horses here. She's the only one of 'em around right now. Cal's down in Mexico selling assets or something." He paused. "Seems funny being in their house."

Grady cast a gaze around the pink room. "You're telling me."

Both men were silent for a moment. Grady said, "And it seems weird, J.T. having a different wife. How long was he single?"

"Five years."

Grady mused on this. "Mom's been gone two."

Jonah said nothing. Sometimes he could talk about their mother, and sometimes he couldn't. It was like he was still sorting out his feelings about her death. So, in truth, was Grady. She'd always believed in him.

Grady asked, "You think Dad'll ever get married again?"

Jonah stared at the carpet and shook his head. "I don't think he even considers it."

Grady wondered. His father must have had a sex drive once, or he and Lang and Jonah wouldn't be here. Yet he couldn't imagine it. No, Bret would spend the rest of his life being true to his wife's memory. Once Bret got a notion, he hung onto it like a bulldog.

Grady settled more heavily against the ruffled, rosy pillow. "Too bad about Lang and Susie."

"Yeah."

"Why's he coming here?"

"No place else to go, I guess."

"What's he going to do?"

"Work for Dad."

Grady set his jaw. "I'm going to have to find a job, too. I'm not going anywhere without wheels, but I've only got five hundred bucks and a lawyer to pay."

Jonah's expression became uneasy. "I don't know that Dad can hire all three of us. I mean, the ranch needs fewer hands in the winter, and he felt funny about giving Lang a job."

"Oh, hell." Grady squared his jaw defensively, "I won't even ask *him.* It'd give him too much satisfaction. I can find a job on my own."

"Not much doing around here. Except over where Cal and his buddies bought. There'll be some construction and stuff soon."

Grady tossed him a mild look. "Hey, Professor. I've done construction. I'm not too proud to do it again."

"I don't look down on it," Jonah countered. "I've done my share of grunt work."

"Yeah, kid, I know." Grady yawned. He'd already made up his mind. Tomorrow he'd go over and talk to the rich boss lady from California.

He didn't know what he'd say to her, but inspiration would come to him. It always did around women. She wouldn't know what hit her.

CHAPTER THREE

DEL DREAMED HE WAS LOST on a dark planet. Shadowy craters pitted the bleak landscape, and three red moons hung in the sky. He was all alone, his heart pounding so hard it hurt.

Behind him, he heard noises rustling wetly in the depths of the closest crater. He turned and saw what he always saw: a terrible set of tentacles reaching up from the darkness. They whipped and twisted toward him.

He wanted to run to safety, but couldn't; there was no safety. Out of every crater, jungles of tentacles rose, writhing and glistening in the red moonlight, and they lashed, slithering toward him from every side.

Slime creatures! Surrounded by slime creatures! A dripping tentacle shot out and seized his ankle. A second wrapped around his shoulders in a crushing embrace.

He screamed while he could: *"Mom! Mom! Mom!"*

His eyes flew open and blearily he saw what seemed to be his room—but wasn't. The familiar yellow night-light, shaped like a star with a smiling face, gleamed reassuringly.

His Buzz Lightyear curtains hung at the window, shutting out the night. His Buzz Lightyear bedspread covered him. His own yellow toy chest stood in the corner with his name stenciled on it in red letters.

But Del realized this was *not* his room. The walls were pale and dirty, the furniture was all wrong, and Lono was not in bed with him. *I've been kidnapped by slime creatures! I'm in slime creature prison!*

He took a deep breath and screamed again with all his might. *"Mom! Mom! Mom!"*

Then his mother was there, warm and kissing and hugging. Her hair was loose and tickled his cheek like a nice friend he had known forever. Her flannel nightshirt was soft.

Sleepiness was in her voice and the way she moved. "What's wrong, honey? What's wrong?"

"Slime creatures," he moaned. "They caught me. They changed my room. They took Lono."

She smoothed his hair. "There are no slime creatures."

She *always* said this. As great as she was, for some reason she didn't believe in slime creatures. Still, she could always chase them away. She just couldn't *keep* them away.

"They got Lono," he repeated, trying to convince her.

"Lono's right here," she said. And Lono himself leaped onto the bed, gave Del a sleepy kiss, then turned around and lay down next to him.

"Where was he?" Del asked. Had Lono, *faithful* Lono, tried to trick him? What was happening?

"He came to bed with me," his mother said. "Let me fix your covers."

"Why'd he do that?" Del demanded.

"Sometimes you kick in your sleep."

"He's supposed to stay with *me*." His voice wobbled with fear and a sense of betrayal.

"He's with you now." His mother tucked the covers more firmly around him. "Everything's fine."

"They changed my walls," he argued. He felt almost safe now, but groggy and grumpy and as if things were still very wrong but he couldn't put it into words.

"We're in a different house, that's all." She smoothed his hair again. "I put up your curtains and your own sheets and bedspread. Your toys are here. We'll paint these walls so they'll be just like your old ones."

"Paint them *now*," Del insisted. Suddenly he hated these walls. He blamed them for everything.

"It's three o'clock in the morning. We'll paint them tomorrow. I promise.'' She kissed his forehead. "Go back to sleep.''

"I'm afraid." This was true. He was afraid of the walls, he was afraid Lono would leave him again, he was afraid to go to sleep because the creatures were probably waiting to slither back and slime him to death.

"Okay. I'll stay with you." She settled down, soft and snuggly, beside him, one arm around him in protection. He wrapped his fingers around a soft strand of her hair because it made him feel better, like a magic charm.

Although he wasn't supposed to, he put his thumb into his mouth. He settled more deeply into his pillow. It wasn't just the walls; this whole place wasn't right. It was Texas, and he hated it, and with all his heart he wanted to go home.

By THE COLD, RATIONAL LIGHT of morning, Tara regretted her rash words. She didn't have time to paint Del's walls. A hundred other tasks screamed to be done. But she had made Del a promise, and she would keep it.

Of course, Murphy's Law was operating full force. Everything that could go wrong was going as wrong as possible. The woman Lynn had hired to help Tara phoned to say that she wasn't coming after all.

Mrs. Giddings said her husband drove a tow truck and had been injured in a terrible accident yesterday. He had a broken right wrist and could not do one single thing for himself. He was helpless as a newborn baby.

Furthermore, he'd had to be scrubbed so hard at the hospital to get the canola oil off him, he was as raw as a butcher's bone.

"Canola oil?" Tara echoed.

Yes, and the man was traumatized by the whole accident, as well. "He's all shook up," said Mrs. Giddings. "He's itching like a man on a fuzzy tree. I told him, 'Albert, you have become an Elvis song.' I can't leave him alone like this."

Tara sighed and looked at the kitchen walls, which, like

all the others, needed to be scrubbed before they were painted. She'd already washed Del's with a mixture of water and vinegar.

A man had been scheduled to come at eight to put up a temporary paddock and stalls for the horses, but he hadn't shown, either. Although the horses might not arrive for a month or more, Tara wanted everything ready for them. Del had cried when they'd left the pony behind. Putting up the stalls and paddock would prove to him that they were coming.

In the living room, Del, settled deep in the beanbag chair, watched a video of *Peter Pan*. This worried Tara. If she let him, he'd watch videos day and night. Yet she could not send him out to play. This was wild, unknown country, and he could wander off as soon as she wasn't looking.

She decided to call Lynn to ask for guidance. "I'm sorry," Lynn said. "I don't know *where* Joe Wilder is. He swore to me on a stack of Bibles that he'd be there at eight o'clock. I'm really sorry, Tara." Then she added, "It's *hard* to get help around here."

Well, Gavin said it wouldn't be easy, thought Tara, gritting her teeth.

Lynn went on, "It took Daddy and Cynthia forever to find a housekeeper for the Double C. As for Albert Giddings, well, he was in this really bizarre accident yesterday. Oh, I know! I'll call the Double C and—"

Tara heard the sound of an engine in the driveway, and her heart took an optimistic leap. "Somebody just drove up. Maybe it's Joe Wilder."

"He's a little fat man," Lynn said. "With bright red hair. He drives a beat-up white truck. He'll introduce himself as 'Fat Joe.' You'll see."

Tara peered hopefully out the window. The truck was not white, but sleek, shiny and black. A man got out, slamming the door. He was not little and fat and red-haired. He was tall. He was dark. He was—Tara swallowed—sinfully handsome.

He walked toward the back porch with an easy, narrow-hipped amble. Her heart speeded up. "I don't think this is Fat Joe."

She saw the stranger mounting the jerry-built steps. Lono, hearing the sound of his boots, barked insanely. He hurled himself at the kitchen door, his neck hair bristling, his voice rising an octave and a half.

"Good Lord," Lynn said.

Above the wild barking, a knock sounded loudly at the door.

"Hang on, will you?" Tara asked. "I have no idea who this is."

"Absolutely. You make me nervous out there all alone."

Tara set down the receiver on the marble countertop. She seized Lono firmly by his collar with one hand and unlocked the door with the other. Lono barked even more frantically.

She swung open the door. On the other side of the screen, the stranger swept off his Stetson. The sun gleamed off hair as black as a crow's wing. His white shirt set off his tanned face and dark, dark eyes.

"Hello, ma'am," he said. "I'm Grady McKinney—"

Lono's shrieks became a piercing, hysterical yodel. "Excuse me," Tara said, struggling to subdue the dog. "Lono, down! Quiet!"

Lono quieted himself to a mere rumbling snarl, his teeth bared. His neck hair bristled more fiercely, and he was tensed and ready to spring.

The stranger grinned, an engaging blaze of white. *Good Lord,* thought Tara. *There's enough wattage in that smile to light the whole state of Texas.*

Hat still in hand, he said again, "I'm Grady McKinney. My father's manager over at the Double C—"

She tore her gaze from his face and looked at the gleaming truck. Now she saw the crest painted in gold on its door: two overlapping C's within a gilded wreath. Her eyes went back to his, as if by magnetic attraction.

"Y-you work at the Double C?" Grady? This was the

one Lynn had said she *wouldn't* meet. Or had Tara misunderstood?

His gaze was bold, warm and slightly wicked. "No, ma'am. I just got in from Nevada. You're Mrs. Hastings, I believe."

Lono growled more horribly, his body shaking with suppressed rage. "Yes. I—I'm Tara Hastings."

He put his hat back on and tilted it. "We have mutual friends, I think. My cousins. Second cousins, actually. Cal. And Lynn."

Her breath felt trapped in her throat, but she managed to say. "Lynn? I'm on the phone to her right now."

That smile again. *Oh, Lord, he has dimples. Just like Cal's.*

He said, "That so? Tell her hello. I'll be over to see her soon."

"I will," Tara said. "Just what can I do for you, Mr. McKinney?"

He hooked his thumbs on either side of his belt buckle. His belt was slung low, the buckle large and silver. It was engraved with a large cactus reaching skyward. *How phallic,* thought Tara in confusion.

He looked slightly rueful. "Frankly, Mrs. Hastings, I'm sort of marooned at the Double C. Meant only to be passing through, but I lost my truck in an accident. Borrowed this one from the foreman. I heard you just moved in and thought maybe you might need a hand. I'm a dependable worker, and I could use a job."

He could use a job? Tara stared at him slightly dumbfounded. No, this would not do at all. He was far too goodlooking. He was a McKinney, but unemployed? Something must be wrong with him, seriously wrong.

He seemed to see her doubt. "It's been my experience that when people move, they need help. My father and brother'll vouch for my honesty. So will Cal and Lynn, I reckon."

She considered this. "What exactly do you—do, Mr. Mc-Kinney?"

"A little bit of everything, ma'am. I'm a sort of jack-of-all-trades." He nodded at Lono. "I helped train guard dogs once. That fella's little, but he's a natural. Hello, boy. Good boy. Good dog."

Grady McKinney had a low, rich, lazy voice, and amazingly, it seemed to quiet the dog. Lono stopped showing his teeth. He no longer strained at his collar. His growl lowered to a halfhearted grumble deep in his throat.

"What was your last job?" Tara asked.

"I worked with horses. Andalusans. In Nevada."

"Andalusans?" she said, impressed in spite of herself. "What did you do with them?"

"Handled them, worked them out for Caesar's Palace. Before that I crewed on a yacht out of Sausalito. Before that I did construction in New Mexico. I got some letters of reference if you'd like to see 'em."

Grady reached into the back pocket of his jeans and drew out a long yellow envelope.

He's a rolling stone, remembered Tara. *That's the problem.* She looked him up and down, trying not to be distracted by his sheer male appeal. He was confident, friendly, clean-shaven, and his white shirt was ironed to perfection. His boots were worn but polished.

She put on her most professional air. "Let me talk to Lynn."

"Fine." His smile was close to cocky. But charming. Too damned charming.

Tara dragged Lono to the phone, though the dog was now wagging his tail tentatively.

Tara turned her back on the man and picked up the receiver. "Lynn, there's a man here who says he's your cousin Grady. He wants a job."

"Grady?" Lynn practically shrieked his name in delight. "That's just what I was going to say—I'd call the Double

C and find out if Grady could help you. I just heard he was back. Grady's the handiest guy in the world.''

Tara lowered her voice. ''You mean I should hire him?''

''Is a bluebird blue?'' Lynn laughed. ''Grady can do anything. Your problems are solved.''

Tara gripped the receiver more tightly. ''He's—trustworthy?''

''Absolutely. He's held down some very responsible jobs. My aunt Maggie used to keep us filled in on what he was up to. He's a fascinating guy. He's just got itchy feet.''

Tara repeated it mechanically. ''Itchy feet.''

''It's his only real flaw. He won't stay put for long. But while he's here, grab him and cherish him.''

Tara dropped her voice to a whisper. ''If he's so great, why's he have to knock on a stranger's door, asking for a job? Nobody sent him, right?''

''He probably heard you'd just moved and figured there'd be work. And he's also probably too proud to ask his father for favors. Big Bret's a good man, but with his sons, he's—demanding. Bret's very structured. And Grady, well, Grady's a free spirit.''

''How long do you think the free spirit will stick around?''

''Who knows? This mess about his truck may take time to straighten out. Tell him to give me a call. Grady—I can't believe it. And tomorrow Lang comes. They're *all* going to be at the Double C.''

As Tara hung up, her heart beat hard and her palms were moist. She wiped her free hand on the thigh of her jeans and went back to the door.

Grady McKinney stood staring up at the sky. When he heard her approach, he turned to her. ''You talked to Lynn?''

Tara had control of herself again. She was not a woman easily addled, but she was confounded by her own reaction to this man. It was just that he was so unexpected, she told herself.

Careful to keep Lono inside, she opened the door and stepped out on the raw boards of the porch. She was disconcerted by the gleam of sexual appreciation she saw in his eyes. He was attractive, sure of himself—perhaps too sure—and probably used to conquest. If he thought she was susceptible, she'd knock that idea out of his head fast.

She gave him a cool look of assessment. She held out her hand with a no-nonsense gesture. "I'll see those references."

He gave her the envelope, then stood, his hands resting on his hips, watching her skim the letters. "I hope you'll find that my papers are in order," he said. She didn't miss the sarcasm, and it needled her.

But he had almost a dozen letters. One from the Parker Ranch in Hawaii, two from yacht captains, others from a startling array of people: a building contractor, a horse rancher, a security specialist, a stock manager.

"You don't seem to stay in one place long," she said, an edge in her voice.

"As long as I stay, I work hard," he answered.

She thought of Del's room and the walls that put him at the mercy of his nightmares. "Can you paint?"

"I worked for a painter in Sacramento. Yeah. I can paint."

She thought of the fencing supplies lying in the mountain pasture up the slope. Lynn had had them delivered and waiting. But Fat Joe Wilder, the man hired to put them up, was a no-show. "Can you put up fencing? Temporary horse fencing? Set up portable stalls?"

"Done it many a time," Grady said. "No problem."

"I've got a lot of restoring to do on this house. Can you mend roofing? Do cement work?"

"All that and more."

"And how long could I count on you being here?"

This was the first question that seemed to throw him. A shadow passed over the confident face. "I could promise you a month or two, I reckon. By then I hope to be on my way."

A month or two, she thought. *A hardworking man could get a lot done in that time.* She took a deep breath. "When could you start?"

"Right now, if you want. You won't regret it, I promise you that."

Your problems are solved, Lynn had said. Tara thought hard, conflict still roiling deep within her.

But the prospect of a man who was strong and skilled was too tempting. She kept her voice brusque, almost cold. "All right. You're hired. Today I want you to paint my son's room."

He nodded. "You got the paint?"

"No," she said in the same tone. "I need to go into town and get it. Go home and change clothes. You're going to get dirty before the day is over."

He touched the brim of his hat in salute. The gleam came back into his eyes. "I've never been afraid to get dirty, missy."

She stiffened involuntarily. Was he being suggestive? She'd put him in his place double quick. "Call me Mrs. Hastings. Be back in an hour. Don't be late."

"I'll be here," he said. "At your service—*Mrs.* Hastings."

He sauntered back to his borrowed truck. He climbed in, backed up and touched his hat again in farewell. As he drove off, she thought, *I hope I haven't just made a really, really stupid mistake.*

THE WOMAN WASN'T WHAT HE'D expected, Grady thought, driving back to the Double C.

She was from California, so he'd figured blond. Her brother was rich, so he'd figured, she'd be thin as a bean sprout, with diamonds rattling around her bony wrists. He'd thought she'd look brittle and expensive. It wouldn't matter if nature had made her pretty or not; money would make her seem so. She would be as rigorously groomed as a prize poodle.

Wrong on all counts. Her hair was russet, not blond, pulled back from her face, and she wore no makeup. It was as if she didn't want people to notice she had beautiful hair, a beautiful face.

At first glance, she'd seemed plain. At second glance, she had a kind of simple, almost elegant prettiness. And at third glance, she was stunning.

Best, she was stunning without trying. Her freckled skin was so perfect it was like delicately flecked silk. The mouth was full and well-shaped and innocent of lipstick. The nose was straight, the eyes a peculiar cloudy gray with darker gray around the irises. She'd been dressed in jeans, riding boots and a plaid flannel shirt with the sleeves rolled up.

At first, she'd seemed bewildered to see him. And then he'd been sure he'd glimpsed a spark of sexual interest in those smoky eyes. Hey, from a woman like that a man would gladly accept a sensual invitation.

But she'd canceled it. If he'd caught her off guard, she'd jerked back on guard with a vengeance. At first, a charge of eroticism had leaped between them. But she'd made it stop, as if she'd thrown a switch and shut down the current. She'd become so cold and businesslike that a lesser man might have felt frostbite.

But so what? She'd hired him anyway. Was *Mrs. Hastings* a snob, letting him know she wasn't about to slum with a lowlife like him? Or was she basically cold? Was she one of those frigid, ungiving women? Or had she been hurt? Well, whatever the answer, she was easy on the eyes. He'd watch her.

He drove back to the Double C, borrowed a tool chest and post hole digger from the foreman, Ken Slattery, and swapped him the black truck for an older model. Grady hadn't seen his father this morning, and there was no sign of him now. "Gone into town," Ken said.

Grady went to the pink bedroom and found that Millie

Gilligan had washed and ironed all his clothes, including the ones he'd thought had been clean. She'd even patched the knee of his oldest pair of Levi's.

He'd awakened early this morning to shine his boots, but before he could get out the back door, she practically wrestled him down and stripped off his shirt so she could iron it. "I delight not in wrinkled raiment. Scabby donkeys scent each other over seven hills," she'd muttered. She'd demanded to iron his good jeans, too. Then she'd scrambled him the most delicious eggs he'd ever eaten.

Now he went into the kitchen to thank her for doing his laundry. She only repeated her strange pronouncement. "I delight not in wrinkled raiment."

He asked if he could make himself a sandwich. Her answer was sharp and to the point. "No. Sit."

She said it with such authority, he sat. Without saying another word, she packed him a whole lunch in plastic things with lids and put them into a sack with a thermos of coffee and a bottle of spring water.

She was an odd little thing, but kindhearted in her way.

The kitchen was fragrant with the scent of freshly baked chocolate cookies; they smelled ambrosial. She wrapped a cookie and put it into the sack. She looked at him with glittering eyes.

"North, south, east, west. It's not only the chick that needs his nest," she murmured. "To take the woman by the heart, take the child by the hand."

Startled, Grady said, "Say what?"

"I wasn't talking to you," she said, almost snappishly. "I was singing. An old, old song."

GRADY GOT BACK TO TARA'S HOUSE before she returned from town. He looked more critically at the place. Jonah had said it was in rough shape. The kid had put it kindly.

Structurally the house seemed sound enough, but the place had an air of having been assaulted. He looked at the graffiti on the wall and garage doors with loathing. He'd get rid of that ugliness.

As for the other damage, porches had been ripped off, the patio torn up. An outdoor spigot dripped forlornly. Grady wasn't a man who liked being idle. He found the water main, shut off the flow and hauled the toolbox out of the pickup.

Just as he was screwing the faucet handle back in place, a gray panel truck drove up. He stood up, a wrench in one hand, wiping his other on the thigh of his jeans.

Tara Hastings parked and got out. A little kid, thin and blond, hopped out on the other side. Except for his blond hair, he resembled his mother.

The kid acted shy at facing a stranger. He put his thumb into his mouth as if the act could somehow protect him. Grady had a gut instinct that the kid was deeply unhappy. He felt a surge of sympathy for him.

"Del, take your thumb out of your mouth." Tara said it almost mechanically, as if she'd said it hundreds of times. Del pulled his thumb away. By his furtive glances at his mother, he seemed already planning on how he could slip it back.

Tara struggled to get paint cans out of the truck. Grady went to her side and took the heavy cans from her hands. His hard hand brushed her cool, smaller one. She didn't blink or react in any way.

"Thank you." Her voice was clipped.

"This your boy?" He nodded toward the child, who stared at him with wary eyes.

"Yes. Mr. McKinney, this is Del. Del, this is Mr. McKinney, the man I told you about. I hired him to help us." She kept the same brisk tone. Hoisting an armful of hardware-store bags, she made her way up the back stairs and fumbled to get her key into the lock.

Grady took the key from her so smoothly that she didn't have time to protest. With a flick of his wrist, he unlocked the door and swung it open for her. "I've had your water off,'' he said. "To fix that spigot. It was leaking. I'll turn it back on.''

"Thank you,'' she said in that maddening cool way. "It seems like a sin to waste water in country like this.'' She set her sacks on the counter and unpacked them with snappy efficiency.

The dog danced around them, and this time he didn't bristle or bark at Grady. He sniffed at Grady's boots, the legs of his jeans, then looked up at him, bright-eyed and wagging his tail.

"Hi, boy,'' Grady said, and stooped to pet him. The dog fairly wriggled in delight. Grady scratched, petted and stroked him, but at the same time stole a look around the interior. The boy, Del, silently slipped into the living room and switched on the television. A video was already on the player, and the screen blazed into color with a ticking crocodile chasing Captain Hook.

Del sank down in a worn beanbag chair, gazing transfixed at the screen. He popped his thumb back into his mouth and sucked it solemnly. Grady rose, and Lono went to join the boy in the living room.

Grady put his hands into the back pockets of his jeans as he looked at the neglected living room. The woman and the kid were really camping in this house. No frills, no luxuries and the necessities were a hodgepodge of secondhand stuff.

Again she surprised him. Someone like her, living like this? It made no sense. She should be staying at a suite in a hotel, sending her pricey Austin decorator out to manage this mess.

She hadn't dressed up or put on makeup to go to town. *What you see is what you get,* her bare face and plain clothes seemed to say. But she couldn't disguise her natural grace.

"What do you want me to do first?'' he asked, looking her up and down, trying to figure her out.

She gave him a perfunctory glance. Her eyes had long, sooty lashes, barely tinged with auburn. They seemed to look through him as if he were barely there. She started sorting the equipment on the counter.

"You said you could paint? I need my son's room painted. That robin's-egg-blue. With cream trim. It's the first one down the hall. On the east side. There are tarps in the garage."

He studied her profile. With her gaze downcast, her face seemed surprisingly delicate, almost vulnerable. His curiosity was growing.

"Those garage doors. I could cover up that spray paint first."

"No. First, my son's room. It's most important."

"All these walls look like they need cleaning," he said. "It smells like mold. It leaked in here, right?"

She didn't answer him directly. "I cleaned Del's walls this morning. His room has the least damage. You'll find a ladder in the garage, too."

"If there's much patching, it's going to be a two-day job," he cautioned. "The patching compound needs to dry—"

"I got the fast-drying kind. Paint, too," she said. "I'll show you the room, then let you get about your business."

"You'll be here if I have questions?" he said. What he really wondered was if she'd be around while he did her bidding.

"Yes. I've got plenty to do." She turned from the counter, but didn't look at him. She tilted her pretty chin up and kept her voice icy. "There's your equipment. Excuse me now. I want to get to work on the living room. So I'll need water. I need it *now*."

He raised an eyebrow at her tone. But she'd clamped her mouth into a grim line and was ignoring him. She grabbed a bucket and a stiff brush from under the sink. He cast an appreciative glance at her derriere, knowing she'd be offended if she saw him do it. That only sharpened his appreciation. Then he went out to turn on the water.

When he came back in carrying the tarps, he caught a

glimpse of her in the living room. She sat with the kid before the TV, her arms around him, her cheek pressed to his. The boy was clearly close to tears. Her face was earnest and unhappy as she tried to comfort him.

"I know how hard Scotty laughed at the crocodile last time," she said, rubbing his back. "I *know* you wish Scotty could be here. But he can't, sweetie. He's in California."

The intensity of her concern caught and held Grady. She was no longer the aloof creature he'd first met. She radiated love and a kind of desperation to protect the child from whatever troubled him.

She held him tighter. "I know you're lonesome. But you'll make friends here. You'll get to like it, you'll see. No, sweetie, don't put your thumb in your mouth."

Then she saw Grady, and her face paled, her expression going defensively blank. She looked away, but hugged the child more warmly. "Let's just sit here and watch the end together," she murmured and kissed his forehead. "You and me, babe."

The boy said nothing, but he didn't look as sad as before. Grady went into the back bedroom, revising his opinion of Tara Hastings. Coolness and control were not her true nature.

No, she was fighting fears, not only hers, but those of her child. He sensed something had gone badly wrong in their lives, and she was bound and determined to put it right again—especially for the boy. More for the boy than for herself. He sensed a kind of gallantry in her.

She clearly loved the kid; he had seen that in that brief scene in the living room. And she would protect him with her life. She was scared of something, but she was resolute, and she had valor.

A complex set of emotions stirred deep inside Grady. He didn't know what they were or what shape they were taking. He only knew they were foreign, and he had no name for them.

CHAPTER FOUR

TARA YEARNED TO GO BACKWARD in time and start the morning over. She wished she hadn't acted so high-handed with Grady.

True, he was a flirt, but she'd dealt with flirts before. True, he was handsome and masculine as hell. But the world was full of handsome, sexy men, especially where she'd come from in California.

Why was this one different? He'd stricken her breathless, heated her blood and shaken her thoughts. Then, because her response shamed her, she'd taken it out on him.

She had forbidden herself to have sexual urges. Some of her reasons were complex, but one was simple. In California, Burleigh Hastings had had her watched. When he learned she was here, he'd do the same. She would walk the straight and narrow path.

Grady had the air of someone who'd departed from that path long ago. He probably had a series of flings that stretched from Texas to Tasmania.

But whatever his faults, he was a demon worker. From time to time, she stole glimpses of him as she passed Del's room.

Like a magician, Grady had spirited Del's furniture and toys into the spare bedroom. With uncanny speed, he'd unscrewed switch plates and hardware, detached the light fixture. He taped what needed to be taped, patched what needed to be patched and covered the floor with the tarps. He did it all without wasted motion.

Tara had made it clear she wanted him to stay out of her

way, and he did, almost supernaturally well. At noon, when she fixed Del lunch, Grady went out on the makeshift back porch and ate out of a paper bag, alone.

When he came in, he asked her if he could give the cookie in his lunch to Del.

Del looked at Tara, then Grady, then the cookie. Tara doubted he would take it; strangers made him bashful. But the cookie was beautiful, large and chocolate, with darker chocolate frosting, and Grady offered it with such simple generosity, that Tara found herself urging, "Go ahead, sweetie," and Del accepted.

He bit into it, and his eyes widened. "This is *good*," he said. After he finished it, he slipped off to follow Grady. This amazed Tara. She moved softly to the bedroom door and peeked inside.

Del, chocolate crumbs on his chin, was looking up at Grady with scheming interest. "Can you bring me more cookies like that?"

Grady was starting to paint the last wall. "I can try. A lady gave it to me. I'll ask her if she's got more. I can't promise, though."

"What lady?" prodded Del.

"The lady who works at my father's house." Grady smoothly rolled on the sky-blue color. "Her name's Millie."

Del frowned and pondered this. "She works for your dad—like you work for my mom?"

"That's right, champ."

"Do you live with your dad?" Del asked.

Tara saw Grady's brows knit, as if he was choosing his answer carefully. "No. I don't live with him. I'm just visiting."

"We don't live with *my* dad," Del volunteered. "He left us for another lady. She can't make cookies, though—"

Good grief, Tara thought in humiliation, and sprang into the room to stop any further revelations. She seized her son's sticky hand. "Del, don't bother Mr. McKinney. Come with me."

But Del was a child with great powers of concentration. He wasn't about to have his line of thought derailed. "She can't do much but lay by the swimming pool in her bik-bik-bik—"

"Bikini?" Grady supplied helpfully.

Tara wished to die, to shrivel up and blow away like the lowliest bug.

"That's it." Del sounded relieved. "In her biknini."

Pretend he didn't say that, any of it. Squeezing Del's hand more firmly, she tried to draw him away. "Come and wash up. Then you and I and Lono'll go for a walk."

Del tried to tug away. "Me and Mr. McKinley are *talking.*"

Tara's grip tightened. "Mr. McKinney and I. I said don't bother him. He's trying to work."

"He's no bother." Grady seemed absorbed in his painting. He didn't say anything else, for which Tara was grateful.

She injected false cheer into her voice. "Come on, Del. Let's explore. We haven't really seen much of this place."

"I don't want to see more of this place," Del said with a wounded expression. "I don't *like* it."

Grady turned and gave him a mild look over his shoulder. "You don't? I did when I was a kid. I used to love this place."

"I want to go back to California." Del strained harder against Tara's hold. "Texas is no good for nothing." His heels were dug into the tarp as firmly as if he had spurs.

Tara gritted her teeth. She didn't want to yank the boy away as if she were a tyrant. But neither did she want him rebelling against her.

Grady, drat him, came to her rescue. "California's fine. So's Texas. Now, why don't you mind your mother? A walk sounds good. There's lots of stuff to see around here."

"Like what?" Del demanded.

"Like you can go to the creek." Grady had stripped off his chambray work shirt and his muscles rippled under his white T-shirt. "You can see animal tracks. Coyotes. Mountain goats. Wild pigs. I used to find arrowheads in that creek. Once I found a dinosaur tooth there."

"A dinosaur tooth?" Del's eyes widened in fascination.

"Only once." Grady dipped the roller in the paint. His tanned biceps flexed and his chiseled wrist moved expertly. "Still, you never know what you might find around here. Nope, you never know."

"How *big* a dinosaur tooth?"

Grady paused and held out his thumb and forefinger three inches apart. "About yay big. Now. Mind your mom. Go see what you can see. Or I don't ask the cookie lady for any more cookies."

Del's decision was quick. "Come on, Mom. Let's look for dinosaur teeth." He practically dragged *her* from the room.

"You probably won't find one the first time," Grady called after them genially. "You have to go back and look again and again."

Tara threw him a parting look, trying to say *thanks.*

Grady's dark eyes met hers. He smiled as if to say, *happy hunting. I meant it. You never know what you might find around here.*

ALL DINOSAUR TEETH STAYED HIDDEN. But Del did find a broken deer antler, a perfect squirrel skull, a wishbone, a small blue feather, an enormous black feather, approximately seventeen pebbles that looked as if they might be diamonds, a dead fish and a live toad.

He wanted to take everything back to show Grady. Tara said he could take all except the fish and the toad. She used the time-honored excuse that if they carried off the toad, it would miss its mother.

Lono, whose greatest passion was rodents, chased a ground squirrel, a rabbit and some sort of bounding rat. He tried to dig up a mole, barked at a garter snake and studiously avoided confronting a lone Canada goose that patrolled a section of the creek, looking possessive and militant.

All in all it was a successful walk, although Tara ended up carrying all the rocks, tied up in the scarf she'd worn. For the last hundred yards she also had to carry Del, who'd worn himself out.

Grady must have seen them from the bedroom window, for he came out to meet her. A chill haunted the air, but he'd put nothing on over the T-shirt. It was flecked with blue paint. "Hi," was all he said to her, then took Del from her arms. Grateful, her arms aching, she let him.

He turned all his attention to Del. "What'd you find, champ?"

Del was blinking sleepily, but he tried to tell Grady of his treasures. He proudly showed the broken antler.

"Wow," Grady breathed. "That's a fine one. You'll want to save that."

Del fumbled in the pocket of his denim jacket and produced the skull. "And *this*. My mom says it's a squirrel."

"Then it must be." Grady nodded with conviction.

"This blue feather—"

"Ah. An indigo bunting."

"And this e-nor-mous black one—"

"Vulture. Outstanding."

"No," Del insisted, fighting a yawn. "It's a *eagle* feather."

"You could be right." Grady wiped a smudge from the boy's chin with his thumb. "Could be. Eagle."

Del lost his fight and yawned. "And all these rocks that might have diamonds in them—"

"I used to bring those home myself. Mighty sparkly."

"Mom says they're not diamonds." Del sighed. "They're quart crystals."

"Quartz," Grady told him. "That's right. That's why they call it Crystal Creek."

"Not diamonds?" Del sounded disappointed.

"Quartz is good, too," Grady reassured him.

Del sighed more deeply in resignation. Then to Tara's surprise he laid his head on Grady's shoulder. The gesture touched her, yet it also sent a ripple of wariness through her. Del seldom trusted people this fast, and she wasn't sure why he'd taken to this man so quickly.

But she said nothing. She shifted the scarf filled with pebbles to her other hand. The wind had loosened her hair, and she felt it blowing, untamed, around her face. Her cheeks tingled from the cool, fresh air.

Del's eyes fluttered shut, and he fell silent, breathing deeply. She said nothing for fear of rousing him. Grady, his hair ruffled by the breeze, also stayed silent. He walked beside her as if she wasn't there, keeping his eyes on the house.

He held Del as if he had often carried a sleeping child. They mounted the steps and she held the door open for him.

They communicated by glances, not words. She darted a look toward the hall. He nodded. She led him to her room and again met his eyes. She looked at her empty bed. So did he, and then at her again.

Too conscious that they were together in her bedroom, she nipped at her lower lip and shook her head yes. He lowered the boy to the faded bedspread. Del sighed, stirred, then sprawled, limp with sleep. His grasp on the antler weakened. It fell silently to rest beside him on the mattress. So did the two feathers, the blue and the black.

Tara picked them all up and set them on her dresser with the wrapped pebbles. She did not want to look at Grady again. She stepped out into the hall, and he followed wordlessly. She could feel him watching her.

She didn't let herself meet his gaze. "Thanks. He was getting heavy."

"I could tell." His voice was low.

"I should get back to work." She'd tried to sound brisk. Instead she sounded breathless.

"You don't want to take off his jacket or shoes?"

"I'll wait till he's sound asleep."

His hand was on the doorknob to her room. "You want this shut?"

"No." She could hear Lono lapping thirstily from his water dish in the kitchen. "The dog will want to go in and out of the room. And I need to hear Del. Sometimes he has—bad dreams."

"Oh." He left the door ajar. "I'm almost finished with his bedroom. What do you want me to do now?"

I want for you and me to get out of this narrow hallway, she thought. *It's too close for comfort.* She could still feel the chill from outside radiating from his body.

Uneasily she moved to the living room. "I ordered a temporary paddock and stalls." She pointed out the window. "The hardware store delivered them, up in that meadow. Can you set things up?"

"Sure. It's only a two-wrench job. Where do you want it?"

She moved to the table and pointed at a map. It showed the original layout of Hole in the Wall. Grady stood right behind her and looked over her shoulder. "The dude ranch had the paddocks here." She pointed out the spot on the map. "When you walk out there, you'll see the outline of the foundation of the stables."

"Yes." His breath tingled her ear, and the back of her neck prickled. The vibrations from his body no longer seemed cold, but warm.

She tried to ignore it and pointed to a second map. "This is the way the property is now. I've thought and thought about it. They had it right. The stable *should* go there."

"Why's it gone?" he asked, still just as close, just as disturbing.

"It didn't suit the man who bought the place. That Fabian person. He had almost everything torn down."

"And it's your job to put things back together?"

Yes. She thought of her life and Del's shaken into pieces. *It's my job to put things back together.*

She put her finger on a dotted line. "The fencing goes here for the time being. The stalls here. I have our horses coming in a few weeks. I want Del to know we're ready for his pony."

She moved sideways, out of the almost electric aura he radiated. "So the sooner it's done the better," she said with more authority than she felt.

"You want to step outside and show me, just to make sure?"

She welcomed the chance to shake off the closeness of the house. His presence was too powerful; the enclosed space seemed to sing with it.

"Yes. But we'll have to be quick. I don't like leaving Del alone."

"I understand."

They both looked out the window, saw the golden leaves falling swiftly from the oaks, the elms. The sky had turned gray. He turned to her, eyed her thin jacket. "Wind's coming up. Will you be warm enough?"

She crossed her arms, a defensive gesture. Against the growing cold? Or against him? She didn't know. "I'll be fine."

"Let me get my shirt."

She didn't want to wait. "I'll meet you outside," she said.

GRADY SHRUGGED INTO HIS SHIRT and buttoned it, standing again by the same big window. He watched her striding gracefully down the slope toward the site of the old stable.

He put on his hat and went after her, leaving the dog in the house to guard the sleeping boy.

He heaved the toolbox up from the ground near the faucet, grabbed the post-hole digger out of the truck and followed her to the big plateau where she waited. The wind had grown stiffer, and although it didn't bother him, she huddled deeper in her denim jacket.

Her hair, so severely controlled, so perfectly in place before her hike, was growing still more tousled. More strands had slipped from the silver barrette and danced, multicolored, in the breeze.

Her oval face, left so carefully uncolored by any artifice, was burnished by the cold. Her cheeks were pink, making her unusual eyes seem more vivid. Her full mouth looked riper.

He thought, *I wish I had a picture of you like that. Hair like autumn, eyes gray as the clouds. Like you came right out of the clouds, part of the sky itself...*

His own fancy shook him. He was not given to poeticizing. Still he looked at her and thought, *Some man left you? He was a fool.*

He said, "Some guy pulled down a perfectly good stable? He was a fool."

"He wanted something else," she said, and he wondered if the words applied to her ex-husband as well.

"I hate to see good things abused," he said. "I hate to see them wasted."

He studied the play of her hair in the wind, wondered what it would feel like if he touched it, then cautioned himself, *Slow down, boy.*

The look in her eyes grew far off, her expression stoic. "What's done is done," she said. "We deal with it."

She exhaled, burrowing her hands more deeply into her pockets. "So. Let's pace the outline of the fence. Then I'll let you get to your job, and I'll get to mine."

"Sure." He fell into step beside her. "What kind of horses have you got coming?"

"An Appaloosa." She kept her eyes on her boots as she paced. "And a Shetland pony."

He found this interesting; he always found horses interesting. But there were other things he wanted to know. He jerked his head in the direction of the house. "The painting.

You bought all the right stuff in town. You knew what you were doing.''

The unspoken question was *you've done this before?*

He didn't know if she'd answer, but she did. ''We grew up with our folks doing it. Buying one place after another. Fixing it up. Moving on.''

He tried another angle. ''Cal? You know him well?''

She gave him the briefest of sideways glances. Her smoky eyes had the strange power to fascinate and shake him at the same time.

''Yes. Well.'' She seemed lost in thought for a moment. Then she looked at the sky and said, ''I'm sorry I was so unfriendly to you earlier.''

The remark threw him a bit off balance. ''I didn't notice,'' he lied.

''Yes, you did. You took me by surprise.''

I could say the same for you. He stole a glance at her profile, the straight nose, the long lashes and the untrammeled hair.

She stared off at the far horizon. ''People will ask you what's going on over here. What's becoming of this property. Each of the partners has a different vision. But they're working together. My brother's going to establish an equestrian community. It's part of a bigger development. All of it committed to preserving the integrity of the land. I don't know much more than that.''

He stopped, and she stopped, too. He pulled his hat farther down over his eyes. ''An equestrian community? For people who own horses?''

''Own. Or lease. People who want enough space in the country to live and have a horse or two. Or who live in Austin but want to keep horses. To have a weekend getaway and place to ride.''

''And your brother's put you in charge of start-up?'' he asked. It was a big job for a woman, especially for one recovering from a bad marriage, but Tara was not an average woman.

She nodded and started walking again. "He's played with the idea for years. So that's the story. I oversee reconstruction on the house and lodge. We've got to get the stable up and running. In Austin, architects and landscape architects are planning the rest of it."

He kept pace with her. "Do you want me to keep quiet about it? I mean, folks are bound to be curious. But it's your business and your brother's."

"No. There's no need for secrecy. People will know soon enough." She paused, her eyes sweeping the hills, then settling on the house. "I've got to go now."

"Yeah. Well. I'll move Del's furniture back in before I head home."

"Thanks." She said it without smiling. She turned from him and walked away with long, sure steps. She did not look back.

It was after six o'clock, and Del, full of energy after his nap, had decided to shadow Grady. He was an interesting man who did interesting things.

He had put up almost a whole fence where no fence had been before. He could take the light fixture out of the bedroom ceiling, then put it back. He'd turned the dirty walls a clean and comforting blue. He was strong enough to move even a big dresser, and that's what he was doing now.

"Why'd you put tape on the walls?" Del asked. "Did they have a boo-boo?" He stifled a snicker.

"You don't fool me." Grady shoved the bulky steel dresser into place. "That's a joke. Ha. A pretty good one."

"It is." Del laughed and fell on his bed, still giggling at his own wit. "So why'd you tape them?"

"So you don't smear paint. The brush smears the tape instead."

Del thought about this. As he thought, he wriggled down to the end of the bed and rolled over on his back, staring upside down at Grady. "Are you going to paint the whole inside of our house?"

"If your mother wants me to."

Del hung a little lower because he liked the funny feeling it gave him in his head. "Will you paint anything outside?"

"If she wants."

"Will you do whatever she wants?"

"Just about. I suppose." Grady pushed the dresser the final inch so that it was even against the walls.

"Will you come with us on a walk tomorrow?" Del was getting dizzy upside down, so he rolled over on his stomach. "Maybe you could help me find a dinosaur tooth."

"Nope. Your mom pays me to work. Taking a walk is play."

"It's *kind* of work," Del reasoned. "It is if you walk so far you get tired."

His mother came into the room. She carried his Buzz Lightyear curtains, hanging on the rods. "Infinity and beyond!" Del intoned Buzz's motto and stretched out his arms, wriggling his fingers. Grady straightened up and wiped his face on his forearm.

Del looked up at him. "What's infinity? And what's beyond it?"

"Mmm," said Grady. "Good question. Ask your mother."

His mother gave Grady a funny look. Del sat up on the unmade bed. "Mom, what's infinity? What's beyond it?"

"I'll have to ask your uncle." She stood on tiptoe and started rehanging the curtains.

Grady moved to her side. "Need help?"

His mother was having trouble, but she said, "No, thanks. I can manage."

"Then I should get back to the Double C. What do you want me to do tomorrow?"

"The windows need washing. The rest of these walls have to be scrubbed and painted. There's that leak in the roof. The garage doors. And there's a terrible pile of junk way out back. It needs to be hauled or burned."

Grady watched her struggle with the curtain rod. Then he

stepped up and with one sure moment, snapped it in place. "Fine. I'll be here."

Del watched his mother's eyes grow wider. Grady came to the bed and ruffled Del's hair. "See you tomorrow, champ."

Del decided to follow him to the back door. So did Lono, who had been lying on the bedroom floor, quietly observing.

"Bye." Grady waved as he got into his truck. Del stood, his thumb in his mouth, and watched until the taillights disappeared down the mountain.

Lono, too, watched, slowly wagging his tail.

His mother came into the room. "Sweetie, close the door. And please don't suck your thumb."

Reluctantly Del closed the door and withdrew his thumb from his mouth. "He's a nice man. And he *likes* me."

Del looked up at his mother. "Why doesn't Dad like me? What did I do wrong?"

Then his mother was on her knees, her arms around him, hugging him tight, almost too tight. "You didn't do anything wrong. Not at all. You're perfect."

But Del didn't understand. It was too puzzling. If he'd done nothing wrong, why had his father gone away? And why did he now have a new little boy, one that he was keeping?

THAT EVENING DEL WAS MOODY after Grady left. He sat in front of the television, watching videos, and didn't want to talk. Tara was worried what might be going through his mind.

Yet when bedtime came, he fell asleep with surprising ease.

Perhaps, she thought, he was still tired from their long trip. And perhaps he felt more relaxed now that his room was the familiar sky-blue that had always meant home. Tara marveled that mere paint could create such change so swiftly—

No, she corrected herself. It wasn't just the paint. It was also the man who'd done the job.

Grady puzzled and disturbed her. Yet how could she not be grateful to him? She remembered him in his paint-flecked T-shirt, holding Del in his strong arms, the wind stirring his black hair. She struggled to thrust the image from her mind.

She sat at her makeshift desk in the living room, trying to study the ranch's original plans. But her thoughts kept drifting back to Grady McKinney.

The phone rang, startling her. She answered it quickly so it wouldn't wake Del. "Well?" Lynn's voice had a mischievous lilt. "How'd he do? My hunky cuz?"

Tara's back straightened defensively. *Hunky. Yes. Unfortunately, yes.* She had a guilty feeling of having been caught out. "He's—a hard worker."

Lynn laughed. "A hard worker and a bright guy. Give him a problem, he can figure out a solution. When he quit school, I was heartbroken. I thought he was throwing away his life. I guess he was trying to find it instead."

"Um," Tara murmured. With false casualness she asked, "He dropped out of college? What was he studying?"

"Oh, *no*. Not college. He quit *high* school. In the middle of his senior year. Big Bret was fit to be tied."

"High school?" Tara frowned. She'd met her share of drop-outs and would-be dropouts with her special needs students. Grady didn't seem to fit the pattern.

"They'd just moved to Idaho. Grady hated it there. He started cutting school. When Bret found out, they clashed. Grady just left. He hitchhiked back to Crystal Creek. But then moved on. He'd go back to Idaho to visit, but he never really lived with his family again."

Tara nipped at her lower lip. She remembered how painful it was to change schools; she and Gavin had been forced to do it often. Gavin, too, had been rebellious at times. "That's a shame."

"I've always really liked him. He's one of a kind, and

most of the family accepts him as he is. Poor ol' Bret's the only one with a problem.''

Her words pricked Tara's curiosity. "Why 'poor Bret'?"

Lynn sounded regretful. "Bret's a nice man who's always played by the rules. He can't understand anybody who doesn't play by them. And Grady's turning up unexpectedly flummoxed him.''

Tara grew more intrigued. "Flummoxed? How?"

"It's always bothered Bret about Grady. He tried hard to be a good father. When Bret came back to Crystal Creek, he thought he'd raised his sons and done his duty as best he could. But now, one by one, they're coming back, and I think Grady showing up's the last straw. Bret feels like a failure as a father. I saw him this afternoon. He seems sort of poleaxed.''

"But lots of adult children move back with their parents these days," Tara offered. She wished she'd had such an option. She and Gavin had scattered their parents' ashes at Big Bear Lake. Then they'd held each other and wept. Their mother and father had died when their commuter plane crashed in the Coast Range Mountains. That was seven years ago, before she was married, before there was Del. And it was, she realized, the last time that she'd let herself cry freely, without feeling ashamed or weak or angry.

Lynn said, "Bret can deal with Jonah. But Lang's hit a rough patch, and Bret's concerned. As for Grady, the way he lives has always been a burr under Bret's saddle. But I'm talking too much. Sam's gone tonight, the girls are gone, and I'm babbling on just to make some noise in this big old house. I'm sorry. I guess I'm just lonely, frankly.''

"I understand," Tara said. She understood all too well.

"Look, you can meet them all and form your own opinions. The *real* reason I called is that I want to have a get-together Friday night at our place. To welcome you and Del officially. Nothing formal. Your family, ours. Bret's. A few other folks. You can get to know your neighbors.''

Bret's family? That meant Grady, too, of course. She felt a ripple of excitement that was both pleasant and ominous.

It was one thing to see each other as hired man and boss lady. What would it be like to be treated like equals, to meet each other simply as a man and a woman?

CHAPTER FIVE

BY THE TIME GRADY GOT to the Double C, Bret and Jonah had already eaten. But Mrs. Gilligan warmed up chili and cornbread and fried some Mexican vegetable cakes dipped in batter. It was a meal fit for a god.

He was devouring a gigantic wedge of the most delicious lemon cake he'd ever tasted when his father walked in. Bret poured himself a mug of coffee and sat down across from him, his face as craggy and unreadable as Hill Country granite.

"I talked to Lynn this afternoon. She said you went to the new neighbor. Asked for work. You might have told me."

The cake went tasteless in Grady's mouth. "I needed a job. I got a job," he said tonelessly.

"You just knocked on her door like a hobo?"

"No." Grady looked his father in the eye. "Like her neighbor's son. Like Cal's kin. And Lynn's. Lynn put in a good word for me."

"And the Hastings woman—she hired you?" It was as much a challenge as a question.

"She hired me. You got a problem with that?"

"Lynn says she's a nice woman. That she's divorced. Has a kid."

Grady took another bite of cake and nodded. "She is a nice woman. He's a nice little kid."

Bret crossed his arms over his burly chest. "Don't go messing around with her. I know your ways. You think it's fun to play around, then be on your merry way. But *I* have to live next to her. Don't go do something to make her regret the sight of me.''

Grady gritted his teeth and reached for his coffee mug, remembering why he'd left home all those years ago. He made no answer to his father's remark because it deserved none. He didn't grant him so much as a shrug.

Bret crossed his arms even more tightly, his hands clamped under his armpits. ''Lynn wants us all to come over to her place Friday night. If you decide to go, I want you to keep your place. As is fitting.''

Grady took a swallow of coffee, wishing it was straight bourbon. He knew what his father was thinking.

Bret didn't want him to go to Lynn's. In Bret's eyes, Grady was a common laborer, a drifter so down on his luck he was reduced to odd jobs. And he was a womanizer, to boot.

''I should 'keep my place,''' he said evenly. ''That's an interesting way to put it. I'm not ashamed of what I do. I give an honest day's work.''

A muscle twitched in Bret's cheek. He looked as if he was about to order *See that you do, dammit. Don't let her think a McKinney is a slacker.*

Grady tried not to let it get to him. He'd held responsible jobs, plenty of them, and plenty of times he'd had a healthy bank balance.

When something more interesting beckoned, he went. What was so wrong with that?

When he was seventeen, he'd made such a fool of himself over a woman that he'd forever sworn off the stupidity of falling in love. Nothing wrong with that, either. It had kept his life free and simple.

But he didn't want to argue, so he changed the subject. ''Have you heard from Lang? I thought he might be here by now. When's he getting in?''

Bret looked stormier than before. ''I don't know. He's been detained.''

''Detained?'' Grady frowned. ''Why?''

"He was driving through New Mexico and called Susie. She's with her folks in Santa Fe. She wants to try to patch things up. He's gone to see her." He made a sound of disgust.

Grady's jaw dropped. "He's going to take her back?"

"How do I know? He doesn't know himself what he's going to do."

Bret took a swallow of coffee and grimaced. "That damned woman."

Grady tried to be philosophical. He thought Susie was silly and shallow, but he didn't think she was evil. "Well, if they can work it out—"

"They'll never work it out," Bret snapped. "He's a rancher. All he's ever wanted to do is raise quarter horses. Just when he's got everything pulled together, she quits on him. She's not a rancher's wife. She never will be. He never should have married her. Bah!"

Grady raised an eyebrow. He'd always suspected his father disapproved of Susie, but he'd never known Bret's feelings about her were so strong. Still, Lang was like Bret, a one-woman man. He'd loved Susie from the moment he'd seen her.

Grady said, "So, who should he have married?"

Bret made a gesture of anger and frustration. "Somebody like—that Hastings woman. Lynn raves about her. She sounds like everything Susie isn't. And she's a horsewoman besides."

Lang and Tara Hastings? The thought jarred Grady. It pained him to realize she *would* like a man like Lang. Lang was steady, faithful, serious. He knew what he liked best in life, and he stuck to it. He wanted roots and welcomed responsibility.

Bret, having found an idea he liked, hung on to it with his usual tenacity. "Maybe he'll see the light—finally. Maybe this'll really be the end of it. His instinct was to come here. Maybe there's a reason for that. This Hastings woman made a bad marriage, too, Lynn says. *She'd* appreciate a good man when she sees one.''

Grady could think of no reply. He wondered what Tara saw when she looked at him.

He doubted if it was what his father called ''a good man.''

FRIDAY MORNING WAS SUNNY and bright, so warm that Tara opened the kitchen windows and back door to air out the biting scent of disinfectant. She'd been up since 6:00 a.m., cleaning walls.

When Grady pulled up in his borrowed truck, her heart beat abnormally fast—*stupidly* fast, she scolded herself.

Del pushed his empty cereal bowl aside, shoved back his chair and rushed to the screen door. He would have run outside barefoot if she hadn't snagged him by the back of his pajama shirt.

''Grady's here!'' he cried, hopping in excitement.

Tara couldn't deny it—she, too, was excited to see Grady McKinney. But her excitement was of a different sort than Del's—a dangerous sort. She'd hoped to keep her sexuality in permanent hibernation. Now it was stirring into wakefulness, and she could not lull it back to sleep.

Lono stood on his hind legs, forepaws against the screen. As the truck's door opened, his ears perked up. His tail began to wag.

Grady got out. He moved with that same easy, almost arrogant grace. He wore a blue work shirt, the long sleeves rolled up to the middle of his forearms. The shirt was only partly buttoned, showing a white blaze of T-shirt beneath.

He'd pushed his hat back to a jaunty angle. She watched the play of his shoulders as he hoisted the toolbox from the truck bed. He ambled toward the house, carrying it as easily as if it were a child's lunch box.

When he saw her and Del and Lono looking at him through the screen door, he grinned. That white smile, with its deep dimples, gave Tara a flutter deep in her stomach. He waved, and Del waved back wildly.

"Hi, Grady! Hi, Grady! Hi, Grady!"

Lono's tail flailed like a mad metronome. Tara raised her hand and waggled her fingers slightly, almost against her will. In answer to Grady's smile, she couldn't keep back one of her own, small and shy.

She unlocked the screen door and swung it open. Lono bounded out and began doing the Lono dance around Grady's boots. He pranced and capered and wagged.

Grady petted him, which made the dog lay his ears back in pleasure and then lean against Grady's legs in a near swoon. Grady laughed. "I wish I got welcomed everyplace this way." He stroked Lono's back a final time, rumpled his ears, and stood.

Tara backed up so that she wouldn't accidentally touch him as he entered the kitchen. She held her breath as he passed her, Lono again gamboling around his feet.

Del tugged at his sleeve. "Hi, Grady. Look at my pajamas. They got rocket ships on them. They're going to infinity and beyond."

Grady looked him over nodded appreciatively. "Awesome."

"Did you bring me a cookie?"

"Del!" Tara, embarrassed, put her hand on his shoulder. "Don't—"

"It's okay," Grady said, dimpling again. "We made a deal. Yup, sport, I brought you a cookie." He glanced at the kitchen table, with its dishes and pitcher of orange juice. He raised an eyebrow questioningly. "You finished your breakfast?"

"Yes," Del said, still clutching his sleeve. He made a face. "Even the prunes. Mom makes me eat prunes. She says they help me make poopies."

"Del!" Tara's face burned, but Grady chuckled deep in his throat. "Your mom knows a lot of interesting stuff."

He turned to Tara, merriment in his eyes, and she blushed more hotly. "Is it okay? To give him the cookie?"

"I—I guess so."

He reached into the pocket of his work shirt and drew out the cookie, wrapped in waxed paper. "Here, champ."

Del took it eagerly.

"Say thank you," Tara told him.

"Fank oo," Del said, his mouth already full.

"You're welcome." Grady tousled the boy's blond hair, then slipped a sideways glance at Tara. He really did have, she thought, the darkest brown eyes she'd ever seen.

"What are my orders for the day, boss lady? Start with painting the kitchen? Or patch the roof?"

"Start with the shingles." Her voice came out falsely bright. "I need to do the dishes and fix lunch ahead of time. Then you can paint in here. Think you can get it done in one day?"

He gave the room a thoughtful glance, then nodded. "If I can start in here before noon—maybe. I can get it close to done."

"If you go on the roof, can I go with you?" Del's mouth was smeared with chocolate, and the cookie had vanished.

"No way," Grady said, but his voice was kind. "You have to be old enough to grow whiskers to go up on a roof like this one. It's steep."

"What's 'steep'?" Del asked.

"Steep." Grady put his hands together at an angle to show him. "Like that."

Tara touched the boy's back. "Go, go wash your face and change your clothes. I laid them out on your dresser for you."

"I can dress myself." Del thrust out his chest proudly. Then a frown puckered his brow. "Except for my shoes. I can't tie my shoes yet."

Grady flashed his grin. "That's why cowboys wear boots. So we don't have to tie our shoes. Okay, go mind your mother."

Del sped off in his blue pajamas, Lono cantering at his heels.

Grady turned to Tara and pulled his hat brim to a more serious angle. "I hear you're invited to Lynn's tonight."

Her heartbeat dashed into high speed again. She did her best to pretend that tonight hadn't been on her mind. "Yes. I guess we are."

"My family's invited, too," Grady said. "Including me."

She smiled with false indifference.

"Would you rather I didn't come? I'll stay away if you want."

The question made her blink with surprise. "If you have other plans—"

"I don't. I thought you might feel awkward. Having to socialize with the hired help."

She lifted her chin. "I won't feel anything, one way or the other." Because that sounded a bit snobbish, she added, "You're hired help, but you're good help. And you're also my—our neighbor."

The corners of his mouth turned up, almost mockingly. "And I'll try to be a good neighbor. So, neighbor, what are you doing today? If I can ask?"

She shrugged as if she felt perfectly normal. "I keep scrubbing walls. Then I'm going to pry up the linoleum in the laundry room. I don't know why they didn't put slate there, too. Maybe I'll put down tiles."

Grady frowned. "Tearing out flooring's not a job for a woman. I'll do it."

"I've done it before. I'm pretty strong."

His eyes swept her body, head to toe and back. "I can tell you're strong. You just shouldn't have to do that kind of work. And all this scrubbing." He gestured at the kitchen walls. "You don't even wear rubber gloves. You'll ruin your hands."

She smiled wryly. "It's too late. They're already ruined. Do these look like the hands of a lady?"

She held up a hand, turning it so he could see the rough

skin, the broken nails, the scars. Her ex-husband had always criticized her hands. "Why don't you stop working with those damned horses so much," he'd say, "Why don't you get a manicure?"

But Grady raised his hand as if he meant to take hers. The movement was so slow, it was hypnotic. Her breath seized in her chest.

Both of them watched his hand rise toward hers as if it had a will of its own, and he had no control to stop it. And she seemed to have no power to move hers from his approaching touch.

They both watched, spellbound, as his fingers approached hers. The action lasted perhaps only two seconds, yet seemed to stretch out as though in slow motion.

Then both Tara and Grady snapped back to reality. He mustn't touch her. She mustn't let him.

His hand jerked back and fell to his side. She snatched hers away and clenched it tightly against her waist. He eased back from her. She did the same from him. She dropped her gaze guiltily.

But he said softly, "Yes. To me they look like the hands of a lady."

She clenched her hand more tightly still, not meeting his eyes. She did not dare. Something was happening here, whether she wanted it to or not.

Then she thought of Burleigh Hastings. She made her voice businesslike and cool, even cold. "We'd better get to work," she said and walked away from him, not looking back.

GRADY STRADDLED THE CREST of the roof, prying up a worn shingle. He felt confused.

Grady was not used to confused emotions. He considered himself a simple, direct guy who tried to live in the moment, although the last few years—again he had to admit it—it had been getting harder. The last two days had been damned near impossible.

He was thirty-five years old and back living with his father. His only prospect was a long, money-eating lawsuit. He had a thousand interesting memories of the past, but no idea of the future except that suddenly it looked empty. His father was making him think it looked pointless, as well.

Grady, who usually avoided complexity, now found himself in the middle of it. It was unsettling as hell. And so was his response to Tara.

He thought he understood women. He knew when a woman wanted him, and he usually knew why. He'd trained himself to choose relationships that promised to be brief, sexy—and uncomplicated.

Tara Hastings was anything but uncomplicated. She was a class act, who could have been beautiful as a supermodel. Instead she played down her looks and dressed like a tomboy. Today she wore old jeans, a brown and black plaid shirt and scuffed riding boots. Her face was bare of makeup, and she'd pinned her extraordinary hair back in a tight knot.

Yet if she'd looked any lovelier, he'd have fallen down at her feet and died for her. Why? Because his father had said she was off-limits? That she wasn't for his kind, but rather somebody like Lang? Forbidden, she instantly became that much more desirable.

No, he told himself; that might be a part, but only a small part. When she'd held up her hands, he'd seen no ugliness at all. He'd seen character. He'd seen—what did artist types call it?—a work in progress.

Her hands were roughened and flecked with a dozen small scars. They were the hands of a woman who did things, made things, saved things, and he'd wanted to touch them. He'd wanted to touch *her.*

He hit his thumb with the hammer and swore. What was *wrong* with him? He never did stupid things like that—it was as if his own hands were set on betraying him this morning.

He gritted his teeth, repositioned the nail and tried to concentrate on hitting it right this time. He hit it with precision and just the right force, but his mind went back to Tara as if hijacked.

He dug his heels into the sides of the roof as if spurring a horse to take him away from his own thoughts. What had happened in the kitchen was just plain *weird.*

He'd wanted to feel his flesh against hers. That was basic enough. And she'd wanted it, too. He wasn't a fool; he knew desire when he saw it.

He also knew trouble. This was not a woman to trifle with. This was the kind of woman that could get under a man's skin. And if he'd seen desire in her eyes, he'd also seen reluctance—even fear.

She'd been hurt, badly, and she didn't want to be hurt again. He could see himself getting involved with a woman like her, but, dammit, he didn't *want* to get involved. They both knew better than to start anything.

But for a moment, the temptation had been stronger than him, and stronger than her, too. He'd started to reach for her. Those few seconds seemed like eons in which wanting battled with common sense. For an instant, desire had been more potent than he could control.

But for what? he demanded scornfully. Just to take her hand in his? If a sexual charge that strong had leaped between him and his usual sort of a girl, they would have been rolling around in the sheets within minutes. Or possibly on the floor.

But she wasn't the usual sort of girl. He hit his thumb again. *Damn!* he thought. *Damn, damn, damn, damn.*

FROM THE HEIGHT OF THE SUN in the sky, Grady figured it was about ten-thirty when he finished patching the roof. He gathered his tools, the spare shingles and descended the ladder, moving as lithely as a cat.

He'd had a long talk with himself up on the roof. He'd decreed that he should just put up a mental wall between himself and Tara. He'd had enough of feeling uncertain. It wasn't his style.

So up there in the bright sunshine, he'd banished all shadows. He'd put up his mental wall stone by stone, then topped it with accordion wire. He'd blocked her out. He took the last step, felt the earth beneath his boots and decided it was good to have both feet back on solid ground again.

He pushed open the screen door to the kitchen. Tara, her back to him, had the refrigerator door open and was bent over, rummaging for something on a lower shelf.

Her rounded bottom filled out her faded jeans perfectly. As soon as Grady saw those tempting hips, the wall he'd built against her tumbled down in a welter of useless stones. The barbed wire turned into a wisp of smoke and disappeared.

Hearing the door open and close, Tara straightened and turned around with two red apples in her hand. She bumped the door shut with her knee.

Grady swallowed and knew he was going to have to fake indifference; he couldn't conjure up the real thing. He was so drawn to this woman it shook his whole belief system.

"Finished with the roof?" she asked. Her striking eyes settled on him. Some of her hair had escaped the prison of its tight knot. Silky auburn strands framed her face.

"Yep," he said, setting the toolbox on the counter. "Where do you want me to put the rest of these shingles?"

"Just leave them there," she said, moving to the table. "I found the box in a storage closet in the garage. It was lucky nobody threw them out."

She put the apples into a brown paper bag. He guessed she was packing a lunch for herself and Del. She nipped her lower lip, as if she was nervous. It was a humdinger of a lower lip. The upper was mighty fine, too.

He imagined that plushy, tempting mouth beneath his own.

"You're lucky, all right." He studied the way freckles dusted her nose.

"You got the job done quickly." She folded the paper bag shut and didn't look up at him.

"I don't do everything that fast." It was a suggestive thing to say. He couldn't help it. He thought it, he said it, then wished he hadn't.

He knew she caught his meaning, because color crept across her cheekbones, but her expression stayed controlled, unreadable. "I still have walls to scrub," she murmured. "I'll be out of your way, and you can get to work in here."

In the living room, Del was in his beanbag chair. He was watching another video, this time *Pinocchio*. Beside the boy sat the dog, its head cocked, looking like the dog in the old RCA Victor ads. It was good for Grady that the kid was there. He was a pint-size, but powerful, barrier between the two adults.

Tara picked up the bag and set it on the end of the counter closest to the door to the living room. She gave Grady a guarded look. "How does that roof seem, looking at it up close?"

"Just okay. Not great. It should see you through the winter. In spring you'll want to think about a new one."

"I suppose you've been a roofer in your time?"

He smiled slightly. "Yeah. For half a year in Nebraska."

She nodded in her composed way. "But you won't be around here by next spring. You'll be long gone by then."

"Yes, ma'am," he said truthfully. A lawyer named Belyle was filing a suit for him and Jervis Jensen. With luck, when the suit was over, Grady would have money in his jeans again and be on his way. "I hope so."

She nodded, picked up the box of shingles and started toward the door that led into the double garage. He made a move to help her, but her body language warned him off. She said, "The painting things are in that pantry closet there. I guess you know what to do."

"I guess I do," he answered, watching the sunlight fall through the window and glint on her loosened hair.

What I need to do is keep my hands off you, he thought. *Unless you want it otherwise. Do you? Do you?*

She said nothing. She went back to her own work and ignored him completely.

TARA TRIED WITH ALL HER MIGHT to ignore him completely, but she couldn't.

Once in a while she stole a glance at him. His attention seemed focused on his work, but not tensely, and though he worked quickly, he did nothing in a sloppy way.

She saw him unscrew every switch plate, his wrists and fingers moving with a watchmaker's precision. He did intricate things to small wires; he laid down masking tape with surgical exactness. Then he could turn around and move the bulky old refrigerator or stove as easily as if he were swinging a dance partner.

When Del's video was over, he drifted to the kitchen. "Can I help? Can I do that?" he kept asking Grady. "What are you doing now? Why?"

"Del, come back. Don't bother him. He's working."

She said it more than once, but Del always replied, "I know. I want to *help* him."

This time she beckoned to him. "Come help me. I'll get you a sponge."

Del was not tempted. "What you're doing is boring. I don't like the smell. I want to work with Grady."

"He's no bother," Grady said unhelpfully.

She bit the inside of her cheek in frustration. *"No,"* she said. "Del, come back here." And then, although she could have kicked herself for it, she added, "Come watch another video."

Del turned from the kitchen, looking dejected. Grady shot her a short, critical glance, as if to say, *Is that what you use the TV for? A baby-sitter?*

Del shuffled through the videos without enthusiasm. At last, he picked one: *Bob the Builder.* Tara helped him put it into the player. "I could help," Del said with glum stubbornness. "I could help fix this place." He recited Bob the Builder's slogan, "Can we fix it? Yes, we can!"

"That's right," she said, kissing his cheek. "We *can* fix it. And we will. You'll see."

She sounded more confident than she felt. Once again she thought of Burleigh Hastings, casting his shadow over their lives even from the Middle East. She feared how he would react when her letter about moving reached him.

With help she could restore the house. Make it whole and strong again. But could she do the same for her boy?

CHAPTER SIX

DEL'S VIDEO CAME TO AN END, chirping its theme music. He rose and, before Tara realized it, had stolen to the kitchen door to stare in at Grady.

"Can I paint, too?" Del's voice was plaintive.

Tara whirled to call him away, but Grady was already answering. "Not unless your mother says so. She's in charge."

Del sighed and turned to Tara. "Mom," he said with maximum pathos, "Can I paint with Grady? I'll be careful."

"No. It's time to eat," Tara said, all briskness. "I made us a picnic lunch. We'll take a walk, then eat." She set down her scrub brush, wiping her damp hands on the thighs of her jeans. "Go wash up, and we're off."

Del's face brightened, but he didn't move. Instead he leaned into the kitchen. "Hey, Grady! We're having a picnic. Want to come with us?"

Oh, God, prayed Tara. *Please let him say no.* She couldn't see Grady, so she glared in his general direction.

But his voice went lazy, with an undercurrent of laughter in it. "Sure, champ. Fact is, I know a good place for a picnic. Close, too. Called Robber's Ridge."

"Robber's Ridge?" Del sounded intrigued. "Were real robbers there?"

"Yup. Well, one robber. A horse thief, he was."

Del's eyes widened. "What happened?"

"I'll tell you when we get there," Grady promised. "That is, if your mom says it's okay for me to come along. Actually, I made a mistake. I should have told you to ask your mother before you invited me."

You slick devil, Tara thought.

"Why?" Del demanded.

"It's manners," Grady said smoothly. "To get along in the world, a man needs manners. Always ask your mother if you can invite somebody."

Del frowned, but spun to face Tara. "Mom, it's okay if Grady goes on a picnic with us, isn't it?"

Grady stepped into her sight line, and his gaze met hers. He smiled seraphically. The afternoon sun poured through the kitchen windows, gleamed on his dark hair and made his T-shirt seem blindingly white.

Against that snowy shirt, his skin looked all the more bronzed. He'd been painting trim. A cream-colored smear streaked one hard forearm, another highlighted the edge of his jaw.

"Just this once." She made the words clipped.

"Just once?" Del acted wounded. "Why?"

Tara, cornered, said, "Because I say so, that's why. Go wash your hands."

Del scampered away and the dog ran with him, leaving her alone with Grady. "I don't appreciate that." She put a fist on her hip. The stance was assured, but her heart hammered against her breastbone. "You practically invited yourself."

He shrugged. "I didn't invite myself. Your son did. And I told him he should ask you first."

Tara lifted her chin. "*After* you'd already said yes. And got him all excited about this…this…Rustler's Roost."

"Robber's Ridge." He set aside his paintbrush and folded his arms. This made his muscles do interesting things, and she tried, desperately, not to be interested.

She tilted her chin higher. "This will not be fun for me. And this will not be how things continue to operate."

He rubbed his chin. "I'm not doing it for fun. I want to talk to you."

Tara was instantly on guard. "Talk to me? About what?"

His expression went serious. And he said the two words that always struck her to the heart: "Your son."

THE SKY, FLAWLESS AND BLUE, seemed to stretch on forever. *To infinity and beyond,* thought Tara.

Grady led them upward, over the stretches of limestone that patched the rugged ground. Sunshine spilled down, a breeze played capriciously and birds sang from the mesquite trees.

Though the climb was not steep, it was winding and unpredictable, quirking back and forth between stands of trees and rocky hillocks. But Grady moved as if he knew the way by heart.

Lono ranged ahead of the little party, sniffing ecstatically, running in zigzags, his tail wagging. Del adjusted his backpack and looked up at Grady. "Did you play here when you were little?"

Grady grinned. "All the time. Me and my brothers and my cousins."

"How many brothers you got?" An only child, Del was insatiably curious about such things.

"Two. Watch your step. There's a gopher hole."

Del eyed the hole without interest.

"Where are your brothers?" Del persisted. "Are they grown up, too?"

Grady gave him an odd smile. "They're grown up. Yep. Right now one's in New Mexico. The other one's at the Double C. With my father."

Tara silently kept pace with the two of them, glad to let Del talk so that she didn't have to. Grady had slipped his work shirt back on, but hadn't buttoned it. It flapped behind him in the breeze like a short, sky-colored cape. He'd shortened his long stride so that Del could keep up with him.

Whenever Grady glanced to check on Tara, she made sure to look elsewhere, down at the rocky ground, up at the azure sky, out at the far-flung horizon. But mostly she watched the interplay between man and boy.

"You and your brother live with your father?" Del's brows drew together in puzzlement. "Even though you're big?"

Grady shrugged and pulled the brim of his black hat lower. "We're just visiting. Sort of."

"What happened to your mom?"

Tara almost told him not to pry, but she clamped her lips together and stayed silent. Grady, with his easy way, didn't seem to mind the boy's curiosity.

"Our mother died," he said, looking up at the crest of the hill. "Just over two years ago."

"Were you sad?" Del stared at him in concern.

"Very sad. We all were. My brothers and my father, too."

Del seemed to ponder this, his forehead wrinkling. "But your mother was old, wasn't she? Is that why she died?"

Once again Tara forced herself to stay quiet.

Grady skirted around the tall spines of a century plant. "She'd seem old to you. Yes."

Del frowned harder. "My mother's not old."

"No," Grady lifted him over a boulder. "She's not."

"So she won't die," Del reasoned. "Will she?"

"Oh, no," Grady said, as if he had perfect foreknowledge. "You shouldn't worry about that at all. She'll probably last for years and years."

Del blew air from between his lips as if relieved. "That's good. 'Cause I wouldn't want to live with my father." He shook his head with conviction. "No, I wouldn't. Do you like living with your father?"

A crease appeared between Grady's brows. "It's all right. He has a housekeeper who can really cook. She made those cookies I gave you."

"Is she your stepmother?"

Grady laughed and helped Del over a fallen tree. Then he vaulted it himself. "No. I don't have a stepmother."

He turned and offered his hand to Tara. Stubbornly she shook her head.

"Don't worry about me. I'm in good shape."

She climbed over the trunk easily. It was no harder than mounting a big horse, and he watched her legs with wicked interest.

She'd meant only to say she was doing fine without his help, but he eyed her with appreciation. "Indeed, you are, ma'am. Very good shape."

He's incorrigible, thought Tara.

But then she noticed that he and Del had stopped on a long, uneven outcropping of limestone. They had reached the top. She climbed the last few steps and stood beside them.

"Look," Grady said. "You can see clear to the Double C. See that funny round mountain? That's called Thunderball Mountain. My cousin Cal got bit by a rattlesnake there when he was a kid."

"Really?" Del was immensely impressed. "Did he die?"

"No." Grady shook his head solemnly. "But the snake got sick as heck."

Del's mouth fell open and he stared at Grady with such puzzlement that the man laughed. "That's a joke, champ. No, Cal was fine. The snake got mostly boot when he bit."

Del grinned in comprehension. "Two jokes. Boot when he bit."

"Better a bite in the boot than a fang in the foot," Grady said solemnly.

Del snickered. "Better a bite on the boot than a f-f-f—"

He couldn't get the rest of the tongue twister out and started to giggle. "But a boot in the butter is better than a b-b-b—"

Tara, glad to see him so carefree, put her hands on his shoulders, squeezing them affectionately. For this moment, she almost forgave Grady.

"Is this it?" she asked him, looking at the vista of rolling foothills that swept to the edge of the sky.

"We're here," he said. "This is it."

She inhaled deeply, and the air was so fresh, so clean, it half intoxicated her. The breeze was stronger here. It teased loose strands of her hair to play freely around her face. She didn't care. In the distance the Claro River was a ribbon so silvery it reminded her of Christmas tinsel. "It's a beautiful view."

"Yes. It is." But he wasn't looking at the landscape when he said it. He was looking at her.

THE PLACE WAS MUCH AS GRADY remembered. The great hill was like a prehistoric beast whose stony backbone arched highest at the point where they stood. Its sides were patched with stands of trees and thickets of brush.

Even here, at the summit, a grove of hardy trees had persisted against the frosts of winter and the lash of summer storms. With a start, Grady recognized the biggest, a cedar gnarled by years of high-sweeping wind.

He hadn't thought of this tree for years, but suddenly it became so vividly familiar he blinked to assure himself he really saw it. Its memory had stayed in his mind all this time. He wished it hadn't.

I have been here, growing, enduring, the tree seemed to say. And what have you been doing, all these many years? With yourself? With your life? What have you become? Anything? Or nothing more than you were?

The cedar presided like a grandfather over the smaller trees and the scanty seedlings just sprouting. Cactus, too, grew up here, stunted but stubborn. Century plants thrust up, rooted in the hairline cracks of the stone.

"I'll be," Grady muttered, walking toward the tree. Del skipped along beside him, and Lono came panting up to them, winded by a chase after some real or imaginary animal. Grady was conscious that Tara was purposely keeping behind them.

For the moment he was glad. Nostalgia was foreign to Grady. But this isolated place brought memories surging

back the way no other place in Crystal Creek had. He had
flashes of himself as a child, not much older than Del, trailing after his cousins Cal and Tyler. Flashes of himself,
growing up, with his younger brothers trailing him.

It was eerie—a procession in time, a progression of boys
learning to make this journey by following their elders.
Boys moving upward, as if climbing toward manhood. And
this time it was Del he was leading.

"What is it?" Del bounced in excitement beside him.
"What is it?"

Grady moved to the ancient tree and lay his hand on its
trunk. "I forgot."

"Forgot? Forgot what?"

Tara moved up next to Del and put her hand on his fair
hair. "Del, honey, let me have your canteen. Lono's thirsty.
He needs a drink."

Del shucked off his canteen and offered it, hardly looking
at her. He was too interested in what had caught Grady's
eye. Grady felt another alien emotion, something close to
shyness. Tara crouched down to pour water into the palm
of her hand for the dog. She was so close, she must have
seen the way he'd touched the bark.

His life had changed at this spot. He'd made a fool of
himself over a girl and vowed it would never happen again.
He'd lost himself in work, and when that threatened to no
longer keep the demons at bay, he moved on, took up something else, worked hard again.

It became so much his second nature he'd almost forgotten the demons, loneliness and the fear of settling for too
little. Now he was back where he'd started and found he
was asking himself questions he didn't like. His life seemed
like a half-made crazy quilt, patches of this and that, but
without pattern or design.

He shrugged off his self-consciousness. He pointed at a
set of marks on the tree trunk, marks he had made years
ago. He pretended they meant little.

But he'd cut them deep, and they were still clear: G M + B T.

Del squinted at the letters. "What's that say? What's it mean?"

"Aw, nothing. I carved that years ago. Because I liked a girl."

Del stuck out his tongue in disapproval. "Yuck."

Grady watched as Tara lifted her gaze and studied the letters. She smiled, almost to herself. "G. M.—that's you. Who was B. T.?"

Grady stuck his thumbs in his belt and cocked one heel in mock chagrin. "Beverly Townsend. I got her up here once. I was trying to impress her."

Del had lost interest. "I think I see another eagle feather! Caught on a cactus over there." He sped off to a clump of prickly pears, followed by a bounding Lono.

And although Del and the dog stayed in sight, Grady realized that he and Tara were, in a sense, alone. He was amazed to find himself almost as tongue-tied as he'd been with the unattainable Beverly, all those years ago.

TO BREAK THE SILENCE, TARA SAID, "Beverly Townsend? Isn't that Lynn and Cal's cousin on the other side? The beauty queen?"

Grady looked almost bored. "Oh, yeah. Every inch the beauty queen."

He sat down on a slab of limestone and leaned back against a lichen-speckled boulder. He said, "Pass that canteen, will you?"

She handed it to him and took off her backpack, laying it on the slab. Then she sat down, too, with the backpack like a small barrier between the two of them. She settled against the same boulder as he had and let herself steal a look at him.

He tilted his head and took a long pull from the canteen. He wiped his mouth with the back of his hand. What was he remembering? What had he and Beverly done on this lonely summit?

"Well," she found herself saying, "did you impress her?"

He gave a short, self-mocking laugh. "Hardly. She gave me the classic 'I'll always think of you as a friend' speech. She's married and living in Denver now. All settled down."

He recapped the canteen and handed it back to her. She took it, careful not to so much as brush his fingers. *All settled down,* she thought with a pang. *The way a man like you will never be.*

She turned her gaze from him to Del and Lono, playing farther down the slope. "You said you wanted to talk to me about my son. Well?"

He shifted, and she sensed an odd discomfort in him. He said, "It's just—"

"Mom! Grady!" Del came running toward them. "I found four-leaf clovers. Look!" The dog loped ahead of him, tongue out, tail wagging.

Del waved a fistful of greenery.

Lono reached their resting place first. He flopped down in the shade of the big cedar tree and sniffed the breeze, savoring all its scents. Del was upon them a moment later, holding his prize.

Breathing hard, he thrust the stems out proudly. "Look what we found—four-leaf clovers—a bunch! Look!"

The stems held mostly large, three-leaf formations, but a few had four leaves. Tara didn't want to ruin Del's delight, but she didn't want to lie to him. These weren't *real* clovers, and she searched for a way to tell him so.

But Grady nodded. "You sure did. That's what we call low hop clover. I never did see any four-leaf ones, though. You've got a good eye."

Del smiled. "I found one and then another, then another with two of 'em on it. It must be a special lucky plant, huh?"

"Must be." Perhaps Grady read something in Tara's expression that told him she was dubious. He held her gaze and added, "There's many a kind of clover in Texas. Another name for this is field clover. The deer and rabbits eat it. It's got yellow flowers in the spring."

"You know a lot about clover," Del said.

"When you grow up in the Hill Country, you know wildflowers. Springtime's famous in the Hill Country. People come from all over to see the flowers. Why, it looks like Texas turns into a great big rainbow. You'll see, when spring comes."

Del looked both intrigued and doubtful. "I don't think boys were supposed to like flowers. *Girls* like flowers."

Tara folded her arms, leaned back against the rock and watched Grady. *All right, hotshot, you can answer everything. How do you answer that?*

Grady rubbed his chin. "Cowboys are tough. But I've seen the toughest, orneriest old cowpoke ride out just to see those flowers. And he can name 'em, same as me. It's what you do in the Hill Country."

"Will you teach me the names?" Del shoved aside Tara's backpack and sat between her and Grady.

Grady's face went unreadable for a moment. "I probably won't be here. Your mom can teach you. She can get a book."

Tara knew Del wouldn't like the idea of Grady going away, so she tried to sidestep the topic. "Del, don't you want to ask about Robber's Ridge? About the horse thief?"

"Oh, yeah, the horse thief. That's a good story." Grady didn't miss a beat. "Let me see. You know what the Civil War was?"

"No," Del admitted, "but why do you have go away? You could stay—"

"We should eat something," Tara interjected, rummaging in her backpack and pulling out the thermos of cold cider.

"The Civil War," Grady began in a voice that promised a tale of high excitement, "happened way back when..."

GRADY STARTED TO TELL THE STORY much as his great grandpa Hank used to tell it. Hank was a fine spinner of yarns, and he spun them with art, wit and a high sense of drama. Grady intended to use all the old man's embellishments and throw in a few of his own.

During the Civil War, a Yankee deserter from the battle of Palmito Hill made it on foot to the upper branch of Crystal Creek. There he came across a small, hard-scrabble ranch.

"That ranch was run by a little bitty woman, Francina Travis," Grady said. "Her husband had gone off to war.

"She had six children to look after, and times were hard. She had one horse, a little old donkey and an old half-blind mule. The rest of her livestock had been whittled down to four scrawny chickens."

"And the guy robbed her?" Del looked uneasy at the thought.

Grady nodded. "Yup. He wanted money and food. And he wanted that horse. So, he waited until night, then he sneaked up on Francina and the children at bedtime. Pointed his big old rifle at 'em and robbed 'em."

"He took their money?" Del asked warily.

Grady shook his head. "Francina didn't have any money. So he took her wedding ring and a silver thimble that had belonged to her grandma.

"Then he made her saddle up the horse for him and load all the food on the donkey that it could carry. He took the last of the family's ham and sausages, two pillowcases full of beans and a small jug of whiskey she kept for doctoring purposes.

"He wrung the necks of the four chickens and hung them over his saddle horn. Yep, he meant to take just about all they had."

"That was *mean* of him," Del said, his lower lip starting to tremble. "How would the children *eat?*"

Tara put her arm around him to comfort him. She shot Grady a warning look. "This is not going to be too

S-C-A-R-Y, is it? Remember what I you about the *N-I-G-H-T-M-A-R-E-S?*''

Grady saw such protectiveness radiating from her, that he decided he'd better tone down the tale. He'd seen that same expression on his own mother's face when she felt her children needed safeguarding.

So he left out the part about the deserter throwing a lighted lantern at the little house, setting it aflame. He left out the part about Francina and her terrified children beating at the fire with blankets and dousing it with water from the creek.

He carefully watched both their faces, as he went on. He said, ''Another woman might have sat down and cried, but not Francina.''

Grady leaned forward as if confiding a secret. ''That robber thought he'd left them helpless. What he didn't know was that Francina had a big old pistol hidden away. Her husband had left it there for protection.

''So Francina said to her oldest child, a girl of twelve, 'Ella, watch the little ones. I'm going to get back our horse, our food and our valuables.'''

''But the robber could *shoot* her,'' Del protested, upset, ''and then they wouldn't have a mama anymore.''

Grady put his hand on the boy's shoulder. ''Naw. He was just a stupid, mean robber. And she was a smart, good woman. So she took that gun, she got up on that old, nearly blind mule, and she went off after that thief.''

Tara now seemed interested in spite of herself. Grady said, ''Even with the best horse, a man can't travel far at night if he doesn't know the land. But a woman who does know it, why, she can go as far as she has to, even on a limping old mule.

''That robber got to the top of the ridge and made camp. He'd been drinking from that jug of whiskey and it made him stupider than he already was. So stupid that he built a fire to roast two of those chickens.''

Del understood. ''She saw the fire?''

"Exactly. As soon as she saw it, she knew. At the bottom of this hill, she tied the mule and started up on foot by light of the moon.

"Just at dawn, she found that fool robber. He was snoring and sleeping off that whiskey. So Francina just took back all her things, and she took his rifle, too."

"Good for her!" cried Del.

Grady narrowed his eyes. "Not only that, he'd kicked off his boots before he wrapped himself up in his blanket. So she took his boots, too. No way that robber could come after her barefoot when he woke. Not in this rough country.

"Francina got on the horse and led the donkey down the hill, and left that old robber snoring. He didn't know that now *he* was the one that was helpless and left with nothing."

"Ha!" crowed Del.

"She was back home to her children by noon. A patrol of soldiers came along later in the week and captured that deserter. He couldn't walk anymore—his feet were too full of cactus spines."

"Serves him right," Del said with satisfaction.

"The war ended and Francina's husband came back. When he heard what she'd done and saw that outlaw's rifle, he said, 'You're the bravest gal in the world, and from now on I'm calling you Two-Gun Frannie.'"

"And so she was known for the rest of her days. And that," finished Grady, "is the story of Robber's Ridge. That old deserter camped right about—" he pointed at a stretch of limestone under a small ledge "—there."

Del's eyes were round and full of awe. "Right there?" He stared at the spot as if he could see little Francina stealing up on the outlaw.

"So said my great-grandpa Hank," Grady affirmed. "And if you go to the Crystal Creek cemetery, you can see her gravestone. It says 'Here Lies Francina Louise (Two-Gun Frannie) Travis. She Lived To Be 101 Years Of Age And Then Went Home To Her Lord.'"

"Wow." Then Del frowned. "Did the robber stay in jail all his life?"

"Yup," Grady said cheerfully. He hadn't told the boy how the story had really unfolded, and he'd had to omit his favorite part, Grandpa Hank's grisly remarks about buzzards.

"My father used to have both those firearms," Grady said. "Francina's pistol and the deserter's rifle."

"He did?" Del asked, clearly fascinated. "Why?"

"Because Francina was—let's see—my great-great-great-great-great-grandma. And a mighty fine one, too."

Tara blinked in surprise, but her expression was questioning.

Del, though, was excited. "Can I *see* them someday?"

"We'd have to go to Austin. He gave them to a museum there. Now wipe your chin. It's got peanut butter and jelly on it."

Del obediently scrubbed at his chin with a paper napkin.

Grady watched him. "There's a moral to this story. The bravest person in the world is a mother protecting her children. Yessir."

"My mom takes care of *me*." Del looked at her with pride.

"Yes." Grady took her in, her cheeks pink with the breeze, her bright hair stirring. "She's some gal, your mom."

But Del's mind was already skipping to other things. He looked at his clover stems, carefully arranged in the empty cider thermos. "I'm going to go look for more four-leaf clovers. I'm going to find a whole lot. Then we'll be really lucky—all of us. Come on, Lono."

He ran down the slope, the dog leaping before him.

Grady set down his empty thermos cup. "You look like you've got something on your mind. Do you think that story was too *S-C-A-R-Y?*"

"I think it was scarier than you let on. You didn't tell him everything, did you?"

"No. I left things out."

"What things?"

"The guy tried to burn down their house. And that by stealing the horse, he was sentencing them all to death. Back then, in this country, stealing a horse was the same as leaving you to die in the wilderness."

"Francina really took back all her things without waking up the man?"

"No," Grady said. "He woke up, all right. He was sleeping with his carbine. He drew on her. She blew his brains out and left him for the buzzards to eat."

"My God," she said. "She *killed* him?"

"It was self-defense. Think about it. You've got six helpless children trapped in the wild with nothing to eat. Some bastard's taken everything that makes their survival—and yours—possible. You go to get it back, and he draws on you. If you die, your children are probably going to die. What would you have done?"

She stared down at the stony ground. "What she did. If I had the courage."

"You don't lack for courage." He knew that was true.

She kept gazing at the ground. "But it is a scary story. I don't know why you ever considered telling it to a child."

"Hey," he said with exasperation, "I toned it down. I got your signals. And it happened here. It's part of the history of your home."

She shook her head. "Even toned down, it was violent. I hope it doesn't give him dreams."

He bristled. "No more violent than those videos he watches all the time."

Her head snapped up. Sparks danced in her eyes. "I beg *your* pardon. *Bob the Builder* isn't violent—"

"Look at *Peter Pan.*" He made a gesture of disgust. "It's full of people fighting with knives and swords and cannons. A crocodile eats a guy's hand, for God's sake. Pirates make a little girl walk the plank."

"But it's only a cartoon."

"It's still violent. Look at *Pinocchio*," Grady argued back. "He's sold to a sadist. He's swallowed by a whale. He *drowns*. And Del loves it. How many times have you let him watch it? Four? Six? Ten?"

Her cheeks flushed a hotter pink. She jutted out her chin. "Is *that* what you wanted to talk to me about? You think my child sits in front of the TV too much? You're *right*. But I can't send him outside to play by himself. We're strangers here. And this country's *wild*."

She looked both defiant and vulnerable. Her chin quivered slightly. Tears glittered in her eyes, but she blinked them back fiercely.

Grady had hit a nerve, and his irritation fled. He didn't like quarrels, and he hated himself for making her sad.

He shook his head. "I'm sorry. I guess I got my back up 'cause I thought you were criticizing my dear old two-gun granny."

Something like a smile flirted briefly at the corners of her mouth. She blinked again. The tears were gone; she'd conquered them.

He leaned forward and looked her in the eyes. He made his voice as kindly as he could.

"Look, what I wanted to say to you, in all sincerity, is that if he wants to help me paint, I don't mind. It'd probably be good for him."

She began to pack up the leavings from lunch. "He'd make a mess."

"If he does, I'll clean it up. It wouldn't take much."

She didn't look convinced. *Lord,* Grady thought, *she is one stubborn woman.*

She buckled up the knapsack and laid it aside again. "He'll get bored. He'll do it for five or ten minutes and see it isn't fun."

"That's fine. What does it hurt? At least he got to try. Little guys like to try to do what the big guys do."

He'd hit a second nerve, he could tell. She looked down

the slope at Del crouched among the weeds, searching for more clovers.

She murmured, "He needs a man to look up to." She seemed almost to be saying it to herself.

"Yeah. Boys need that."

She turned to face him, the challenge back in her eyes. "I don't want him getting too attached to you because you're not going to stick around. I have visions of you riding off into the sunset while he runs behind, yelling for you to come back, like—like that old cowboy movie—whatever it was."

"Shane," Grady said. "It was *Shane.*" Grady had seen that movie on television when he was a kid, bedfast with flu. He'd hated that scene; it had made him feel terrible.

"It wouldn't be like that," he said. "He'll know plenty of people by then. And your brother—won't he be coming?"

"Yes. He will." She tried to smooth her blowing hair, but it would not be tamed.

"And Cal's going to be moving back, be your neighbor. He's got boys almost Del's age. Del knows Cal, doesn't he?"

"He loves Cal. Cal's a lot of fun with kids."

"See?" Grady smiled. "Nobody'll miss me."

She glanced down at the limestone slab, caressed it with the flat of her hand. "You don't know that for sure."

He stared at her hand. He saw that one knuckle was bleeding slightly.

He frowned. "You're hurt."

She pulled her hand back, clenched it into a fist and hid it in her lap. "It's nothing," she said. "When Del's clovers blew away, I scraped against the rock catching them, that's all."

He remembered. He knew he shouldn't do it, but he reached for her hand. "Let's see."

She clenched her hand more tightly. "There's no need to."

"I've got some bandage strips in my wallet. And antiseptic wipes."

She looked unconvinced. "You do?"

"I'm always fixing stuff at your place and sometimes I get a scratch or a blister. You don't believe me?"

With his left hand he drew his wallet from the back pocket of his jeans and flipped it open. He showed her that it contained a few bills and half a dozen bandage strips and as many alcohol packets.

"See?" His smile was half-taunting. "So show the doc your ouchie."

She shook her head as if in frustration, but she smiled back and gave him her hand. "Do you also carry splints and slings?"

"Nope." He tore open an alcohol wipe. "But I carry a jackknife. I can make both if I have to."

His tone was joking, but now that he held her hand in his, something was happening. A wave of desire surged over him, making his head light.

He wiped her knuckle gently, savoring the warmth of her flesh against his. Then he stroked his thumb over the back of her hand. "The reason it's bleeding is you've worked your hands raw. I meant what I said. They're nice hands. You should take care of them."

His breath stuck in his chest, choked by his own need for self-restraint.

When she spoke, her voice sounded as strained as his. "They're not nice. I've got two broken fingers. They're all crooked."

"You're a piker," he said. "I've got seven." He held his hands up next to hers to show her. His fingers were long and strong, but the injured ones were as crooked as hers or more so. They were a worker's hands, and they made hers look like those of a princess who has done a bit of scullery work.

Her lips parted slightly. His breath locked more tightly in his chest.

But he struggled to act efficiently, to seem as clinical as an M.D. He used his teeth to help tear the cover from the bandage. He fastened it over her wounded knuckle and smoothed it out.

He should have let go of her then. Instead he looked into her eyes. He thought he could get lost there. He leaned nearer.

She did not draw away. She seemed, instead, to move her face infinitesimally closer to his.

He stole a quick glance down the slope. Del sat, picking through the clover plants, facing toward them. When the boy saw Grady looking in his direction, he waved enthusiastically.

Grady thought, *This is plumb crazy. I can't kiss her with him watching.*

He turned back to Tara. He squeezed her hand and let it go.

But he let his eyes tell her what his lips couldn't say. *I want to make love to you. And I would be good to you. So good.*

She kept her face raised to his. But her gaze had gone wary, full of doubt. *No,* it said. *I can't allow it. It's not going to happen.*

She rose and slid the backpack's straps in place. She pretended nothing had passed between them. "We need to get back," she said.

He stood, too. "Fine. You call the shots. You set the pace."

Once again the color flared on her cheeks. She understood, all right.

She stepped away from him and started down the slope. She called, "Del—heads up! We're going home."

Grady looked at her straight, stubborn back. He watched as she took the boy by his hand, and the dog danced around the two of them.

An odd emotion struck Grady. He hadn't experienced it since he was a boy of seventeen. He hadn't wanted to. And a new, less familiar feeling was there, too. He felt a growing tenderness for Tara and her son. So much it dismayed him.

I should have never come back to Crystal Creek, he thought.

CHAPTER SEVEN

DEL WAS PROUD OF HIS CLOVERS. He'd found eight. Eight—
what luck he and his mother and Lono were going to have!
And it was because of *him*.

As proof of his luck, Del got to paint with Grady. He
used a brush and dabbed around a taped windowsill. He
splotched only a few globs on the wood, and Grady got
them right off.

Del even used the roller, which was fun because the paint
smoothed onto the wall in a wide, neat stripe, like magic.
It was hard to get the paint squished onto the roller just
right, but Grady helped.

Painting, however, was hard work, and Del decided to
quit after he'd done it quite a long time (almost fourteen
minutes!). Grady helped him wash the paint off his hands
and get it out of his hair.

He and Lono rucked up a kind of a nest in the tarpaulin
that covered the slate floor. Del lay on his stomach, his
elbows on a pile of newspapers and his chin on his fists.

He watched Grady roll the milk-colored paint on the wall.
Grady's arms had great big muscles that changed shape. Del
wanted great big muscles when *he* grew up.

"Did you live in Texas when you were old as me?" Del
wriggled his feet back and forth.

"Yup. It's a good place to grow up."

Del's eyebrows drew together. "I *had* to move here. My
mom made me."

"I understand." Grady dipped the roller in the paint pan.
"I had to move with my folks. To Idaho."

"Did you like Ida—Idadoe?"

"Um. Well. Idaho. They grow a lot of potatoes there. Have you ever heard of Idaho potatoes?"

Del didn't like to admit he hadn't. "I've heard of mashed potatoes. French fried potatoes. Baked potatoes. And—those kind they make at McDonald's for breakfast."

"Hash browns. You're well-versed in potatoes."

"What's that mean?"

"Well-versed? It means you know a lot."

"Did your family go to Idaho to grow potatoes?"

"Not potatoes. Cattle. Cows."

Del hesitated. This was a grown-up conversation, so he struggled to sound as grown-up as possible. "Are you well-versed in cows?"

Grady, climbing a stepladder, grinned down at him. "Absolutely. But I like horses better."

Del sat up and scratched his stomach. "Me, too. You can't ride a cow. I got a pony. I miss him, but he'll be here soon. Do you have a horse?"

"Not now. My dad does, though."

"My dad doesn't have a horse anymore. Horses make his new wife sneeze. Her nose swells up and gets red."

Grady threw him a glance. "Is that so?"

"Yeah," Del examined a small but interesting scrape on his stomach. "But my uncle Gavin's gonna have horses here. Lots. He's my mother's brother. He used to be in movies."

Grady looked interested. "Your uncle's a movie actor?"

"No." Del spit on his finger and rubbed the scratch to see if it would come off. "He fell down for money. He used to fall off horses a lot. He fell off buildings, too. And cliffs."

"He was a stuntman?"

"Yeah, that's it." Del lifted his shirt higher and pointed. "Look. I don't know how I got this scratch. Do you think a bug bit me?"

"No. I think you rolled around in the weeds and got a cocklebur."

"What's a cocklebur?"

"A scratchy seed. Why doesn't your uncle fall off horses anymore?"

Del pulled his shirt back down and began to pet Lono. "Uncle Gavin got rich. Mom said he played the market. Not like the supermarket. It's a market where people sell each other pieces of paper. I don't understand it."

"I don't, either." Grady shook his head. "Never could."

"So he bought *this* place," Del explained. "And we came out here to fix it up. And you're helping us. Do you want to see me stand on my head?"

"That would be quite a sight." But Grady's eyes weren't on Del. He was staring into the living room where Del's mother was washing windows. Del noticed that Grady did that a lot, stare at her.

"How come you keep looking at my mom?"

Grady's gaze jerked back to Del. "She's pretty. Don't you think so?"

Del put his head and hands on the tarp. "Yeah. Look, I'm *almost* standing on my head. I just can't get my feet up in the air."

"That'll come in time. You got the first part down fine."

Del did a somersault. "What are we going to do when we're through painting?"

"Wash the outside of the windows."

"We've got a lot of work," said Del, trying to stand on his head again. "Know why?"

"Why?"

"Because we're the *men* of the house. You and me." Triumphantly he succeeded in getting his legs in the air. It was almost a second and a half before he fell over.

ALL AFTERNOON TARA WAS conscious of Grady's presence. Too conscious. She would glance at him and find his gaze on her. Quickly she would break eye contact. Was it too late to tell him not to come to Lynn's? Would it be better to have a moment of awkwardness now than a whole evening of it?

She was relieved when he went outside. But, even so, her emotions were tangled. Del trailed after Grady like a puppy. And Grady didn't seem to mind; in fact, he acted as if he truly *liked* the boy's company. He accepted it with the same easy grace he brought to everything.

He let Del try the window scrubber and the squeegee, showing him the right way to use both. He kept the boy from soaking himself, and he seemed to listen to him as intently as he would to an adult.

But Del soon grew tired of the task and began to play in the dirt, gathering pebbles. Tara went outside to bring him in, but Del sulked and didn't want to come.

She held him by one grubby hand, and he tried to free himself. "I want to stay with Grady. We're talking."

Yes, and I worry about what you're saying. Del could be spilling out their life story, for all she knew. "Come inside." She led him away firmly. "Grady isn't paid to babysit you."

"I'm not a baby." Del dug in his heels. "He doesn't mind. He likes having me around. Don't you, Grady?"

Grady kept scrubbing and didn't miss a beat. "You're mighty good company. But mind your mother."

"Yes," Tara told the boy. "You need to lie down. Take a break."

"Sure thing," Grady agreed. "Store up some energy. You'll need it for the party tonight."

Del's eyebrows rose in happy surprise. "Party? Will you be there?"

"Yup. Your mom said I could come."

Damn! Tara thought. Now she couldn't ask him to back out. She flung him a look of resentment. He didn't seem to notice.

Del glowed with excitement. "Will we have cake? With ice cream?"

"Could be. We'll see," Grady said.

Tara gripped Del's hand more tightly. "Come along. You need to rest."

"I don't want to rest. I'd rather be out here with—"

Grady turned and gave him a surprisingly stern look. "You mind your mother, hear?"

That single glance, those few words, made Del change his tone. "Yessir," he said. But his shoulders slumped as Tara led him into the house.

He looked back in longing. "Grady was teaching me to wash windows. He used to be a real window washer. In Seattle. On skyscrapers."

Good Lord, Tara thought in exasperation, washing windows on a skyscraper. She supposed it would impress any little boy—and it should set off alarm bells for any woman with a grain of sense. The man had done everything—and stuck with nothing.

She ushered Del into the house and patted his bottom. "Wash up. Then get some picture books. You can lie on my bed while I scrub the walls."

"I'd rather talk to Grady."

"You can talk to me."

"We were talking guy stuff. He knows all kinds of things. He knows about the slime creatures. He saw the *whole* movie."

"*You* shouldn't have seen any of it," Tara said. On one of the few times Del had visited Sid and Kylie, they'd left him alone in the den watching television. Del watched part of *Revenge of the Slime Creatures,* and it had scared him so badly he'd gotten nearly hysterical.

Tara still couldn't forgive Sid for that. There was much she couldn't forgive him for. But the worst was that he'd turned his back on Del and then, to add to Del's sense of rejection, he'd adopted Kylie's young son.

At last Tara got Del to settle on her bed with a stack of picture books. But he quickly grew bored and wanted to watch a video. He whined so much that Tara finally relented.

"*Star Wars,*" Del insisted as he pulled his beanbag chair in front of the screen. *Star Wars* was the only part of the trilogy she allowed him to watch. Tara feared the part about the villain turning out to be the hero's father might disturb Del.

Now Del said, "I'm like Luke Skywalker. He doesn't have a dad, but he's got a buddy. Han Solo. Grady's like Han Solo. He's my buddy."

She tried not to flinch. "You have a dad."

Del's face went stubborn. "He doesn't want me. And I don't want him. I don't need him. I got a buddy." He sank into the chair and pulled Lono into his arms, hugging him tightly.

"Del—" She wanted to tell him that his father still loved him in his own way. It was a lie, but she believed it was a lie he needed. He was too young to deal with the truth.

But he must have read something in her face. He thrust out his lower lip and put his hands over his ears. "No! Don't. I just want to watch my movie."

Stung, Tara put on *Star Wars.* The thrilling theme music welled up, but her heart, instead of rising, sank.

What were her choices? To let her son sit like an automaton in front of the television screen? Or let him fall even further under Grady McKinney's spell?

For Grady could cast a spell, a strong one. She was close to being snared herself. Del was clearly starving for a man's company. And so, perhaps, was she.

LYNN'S HOUSE, LIKE LYNN, was warm, friendly and utterly without pretension. She'd cajoled Bret into visiting many times since he'd come to Crystal Creek. For a Sunday dinner, a family supper or just a cup of coffee.

He'd always felt easy and at home at Lynn's. Until tonight.

To Bret, the house was growing uncomfortably full of

people. Every five minutes somebody else arrived. Some of the crowd he'd once known—almost twenty years ago. And tonight he felt the weight of all those years.

When he'd left the Hill Country, he'd been a hotshot young ranch manager with a future full of possibilities. He was on his way up and out of backward little Claro County. He'd had a faithful, funny, adoring wife and three boys he intended to lead into manhood and independence.

Well, he'd finally made it to the top in Idaho. He'd managed the kind of spread folks called a "Rolex ranch," so massive it was like managing a corporation. The absentee owner wasn't a person, but an agribusiness giant interested only in profit. Bret's job was to make that profit, and he did. But after Maggie died, he no longer had any heart for the place.

So here he was, back in Hill Country, and he'd been glad to come. But tonight, it struck him that he'd traveled in a long, futile circle. His future was full of marking time. His funny, adoring wife was gone. And he obviously hadn't led his sons to either full manhood or independence. Two were living with him again, and the third might soon join them.

Bret nursed his mug of beer and pretended to leaf through a coffee-table book so he wouldn't have to talk. He was conscious of being in a house full of people who had managed, unlike him, to make sense of their lives.

Jonah wouldn't come tonight, of course. Not all of Lynn's wheedling could lure him into a crowd of milling people. Grady hadn't shown up—and Bret hoped he wouldn't.

Grady had once been one of the most promising kids in Crystal Creek, yet what was he now? A drifter who lived on luck, and whose luck had run out. No, Bret didn't feel sociable tonight.

Then a stir rippled through the knots of chatting people, and he looked toward the entrance. Lynn, standing at the opened door, called out, "Hey, everybody, our guests of honor. The new neighbors!"

Lynn drew a woman inside, and Bret felt a quiver of

attention run through the room. The woman held a small blond boy by the hand. The boy was shy. He put his hand over his face and peeked through his fingers.

The gesture caught Bret's heart and he found himself staring at the boy, overwhelmed with remembrance. Lang used to do the same thing when he encountered strangers, splaying his fingers into a protective mask.

Jonah had been worse; he'd hidden behind Maggie, or clung miserably to Bret's leg, burying his face against it. Grady, of course, from the time he could walk, swaggered into the midst of things, hell-bent on having fun.

Then Bret raised his eyes from the boy to the woman, whose face he could not yet see. She was tall and dressed in a black pantsuit. Lynn led her into the living room, pausing to introduce her first to this knot of guests, then that.

"Hank," Lynn called to her ten-year-old son, "Del's here. Take him into your room and show him your trains."

Lynn leaned over to whisper something to Hank, and at that moment, the tall woman turned her head. Bret's idle gaze met with a pair of gray eyes like none he'd ever seen.

Good Lord, he thought. *She's a beauty. A thoroughbred beauty.*

He was not a man to ogle at young women; he did not gape at pretty girls. But she had taken him by surprise, and he remembered what he'd said, off-handedly, about her and Lang.

Bret scrutinized her more closely and saw it was true. *This* was the right sort of match for Lang. Not the hopeless, helpless Susie, with her giggling and weeping, but Tara Hastings, who bore herself with dignity and could take on a job as challenging as the old Kendell spread. She just *might* be the one. He felt the rightness of it clear to his marrow.

TARA COULD SEEM FEARLESS about many things, but a party full of strangers was not one of them. The people smiled, and their eyes held kindness, but also curiosity. She felt on display, and she knew that she was being measured—and yes, judged by these people.

And so *many* people. Lynn introduced her to person after person. Identities began to melt together. Faces got separated from names, and the names formed an untidy, meaningless heap in her memory: Trent, Blake, Gibson, Slattery, Munroe. Camilla and her husband arrived from next door, with their son, Jamie.

But only one name leaped to life in Tara's ears: McKinney. And only one person stood out in her mind: Bret McKinney.

His dark eyes and dark hair recalled Grady's. Like Grady, he was tall and wide-shouldered, and he carried himself with the loose-hipped ease of a cowboy. He had the same bronzed skin and distinctive black eyebrows.

Yet father and son were different. Tara sensed an aloof loneliness in Bret McKinney. He didn't smile like Grady; he barely smiled at all. He had a formal courtliness that she liked, but a natural sternness that she did not.

He scrutinized her so closely that she felt as if he had an inner tote board on which he was scoring her. He practically grilled her about her background with horses. Lynn rescued her. With a teasing look at Bret, she drew Tara away. "You'll have plenty of time to talk to her, Big B. You live right next to her. Tara, come on. I want you to meet some more Gibsons…"

Tara edged closer to Lynn. "You said this was a *small* get-together."

Lynn gave her an aw-shucks grin. "It is small—for Texas."

"Who turns up for a big one? The Queen of England?"

Lynn glanced at her watch. "Glad you reminded me. She's late again. I've got to have a talk with that girl."

Tara gave her a friendly swat on the arm.

A faint furrow appeared across Lynn's brow. "The one who's really late is Grady. I thought he'd come with Big Bret. He'd better not stand me up."

Tara glanced over her shoulder at Bret. "They're not much alike, really, are they?"

Lynn tugged her forward to yet another introduction. "No. That's always been the problem."

LYNN LIFTED HER WINEGLASS. "To our new neighbors—Tara and Del."

A feast of barbecue was set out on the long oak table. The other guests gathered round the buffet murmured roughly the same toast, their voices tumbling together.

But in that friendly babble, Tara was conscious of one voice, close to her ear, unexpected but familiar. *"Recepción, vecino bonito."*

The words were Spanish and flirtatious, "Welcome, pretty neighbor."

And the voice was Grady's. The warmth of his breath on her ear made her skin tingle as if brushed by the softest of feathers.

She turned and looked into his eyes. He smiled. A flutter stirred her stomach, and her bones suddenly seemed without strength, soft as warmed candle wax.

He touched his glass to hers. "I drink to you. And your son. Happiness to both of you." He sipped the dark wine.

She struggled to gather her scattered composure. "When did you get here? Lynn was afraid you weren't coming."

"I got a late start. I drove into Austin. Bought some stuff that'll lift that graffiti right off your limestone. It's good stuff. It'll do the job."

Her back stiffened. "You didn't have to do that. I didn't ask you to."

He shrugged. "You mentioned you didn't know how to do it. I do. You just need the right cleaner. Aren't you going to taste your wine? That toast was in your honor. It's Texas wine. From my cousin's vineyard. Second cousin really, but 'round here we don't fool with that distinction."

She took a sip, more to steady her nerves than to be

polite. "You didn't have to go to Austin. I'll reimburse you. For your time and mileage."

"Consider it a housewarming present." He nodded toward their glasses of ruby wine. "Like it?"

The taste lingered on her tongue, rich and haunting. "It's lovely. But I *will* reimburse you."

His gaze slid to her lips. "We'll see."

Her breath locked in her chest. "Why all the concern about the graffiti?"

"The boy shouldn't have to see those words every day."

"The boy can't read."

"He can tell they're ugly. Ugly to look at. Ugly in spirit. I don't like that you have to look at it, either."

She felt a rush of relief when Del appeared, tugging at her hand. "Mom, fix me a plate, will you? Us kids got our own special table."

"Excuse me. Duty calls." She turned from Grady, conscious that more than one set of curious eyes had been on them, watching their exchange.

She moved to the buffet and busied herself asking Del what he wanted and fixing his plate. Lynn's spread was down-home, but sumptuous.

Platters steamed with stacks of beef ribs slathered in barbecue sauce. Halved duck breasts, grilled crispy brown, lay wrapped in bacon slices. German meatballs simmered in their gravy in a yellow Crock-Pot.

There were bowls of potato salad, coleslaw, pasta salad and a three-layer strawberry salad. There was an array of breads, fresh from the oven, cheese bread, corn bread, apple pecan bread and buttermilk biscuits. And there was a boggling range of desserts, pecan pies, two German chocolate cakes and twice-frosted brownies.

Even Del, who was picky, wanted a full plate. Tara settled him at a table in the kitchen with Hank and Jamie and a little boy named Josh, who was related to the Gibsons. She was tempted to pull out a chair and eat with the children, avoiding the crowd of adults—and Grady.

But Lynn found her and pounced, taking her by the arm again. "No hiding back here. I want you to mingle with people over ten years old. Come on, get a plate. I saved you a seat."

Tara gave her a look of mock reproof. "All that food. You must have killed yourself getting this ready."

Lynn waved her hand dismissively. "Everybody helped out. Sam did the barbecue and grilling. I only did some of the breads. You've got to try Mary Gibson's meatballs. Nora Slattery does that killer strawberry salad. And Bret's housekeeper, Millie Gilligan, sent the pecan pie—grab it while you can. It's going to vanish. The men are inhaling it."

"I'm going to inhale you, beautiful. How you doing, skunklet?"

It was Grady again. He grinned down at Lynn. She whooped with glee and threw her arms around his neck. He kissed her on both cheeks, then her nose. She kissed him back, a big, smacking buss on the chin.

"Grady! I'd given up on you. Oh, God, let me look at you." She stepped back, clamping her hands on his shoulders. "You look wonderful."

He did look wonderful, Tara thought, tightness knotting her throat. He wore a shirt so dazzlingly white she wondered if it was brand-new. It set off his tan and matched his smile.

Grady's hands almost spanned Lynn's waist. "You're a sight for sore eyes. Give me a real piece of sugar." He pulled her back to him, pressed his lips to hers in a brief but affectionate kiss.

Tara couldn't help herself. She wondered what it would be like, being embraced by those strong arms, held fast against that chest, tasting that mouth shaped for laughter and seduction.

"Mmm," Grady sighed as he straightened and gazed down at Lynn. "You don't ever get any older. Just prettier."

"Same old Grady." She touched his cheek.

Bret appeared beside Grady. Lynn said, "Look who I found."

Bret seemed unamused. He looked Grady up and down, his brow furrowed. "You're late."

The way he said it put a chill in the air. His disapproval was palpable. But Grady seemed unconcerned. "I had things to do."

Bret gave him a scornful look.

Tara turned away with the uneasy feeling that she was spying. In those few seconds she'd seen the tension between father and son, a current of lasting conflict between two men who didn't see eye to eye and probably never would.

AND YET BRET MCKINNEY could be charming in his way.

Lynn had set up card tables in the living room dining room, and sunroom. By chance more than choice, Tara found herself sitting with Bret and an attractive couple in their fifties, Carolyn and Vernon Trent.

The Trents lived on the Circle T Ranch, the second largest ranch in the county. Their borders touched those of both J.T.'s spread and the land belonging to Three Amigos.

Carolyn was still a beautiful woman, blond, with aristocratic cheekbones and a mischievous smile. Her husband was a jolly-looking man with curling gray hair and a kind expression. All of them were politely curious about the plans of the Three Amigos.

"I honestly don't know all they've planned," Tara confessed. "It's going to be what's called a 'conservation community.' At its center will be an equestrian section. But as for details—it's not even named yet."

Bret's expression was philosophical. "Then we shouldn't try to pick your brain. You're an expert horsewoman. You might be interested to know that Carolyn here's got the most beautiful black Arabian in the state."

Carolyn nodded. "It's true. You'll have to come see him."

Tara smiled, grateful that Bret had helped her to switch conversational tracks. Carolyn was so clearly enchanted with the Arabian that the topic might last through dessert.

But just as Bret went back to the buffet table, his cell phone rang. From her chair, Tara watched him frown, then turn so she could no longer see his face. Vernon Trent was saying, "Both of Bret's two older boys are good with horses. Grady's supposed to have a fine way with horseflesh. But Lang's the better."

Carolyn tossed her head. "Piffle. Grady's every bit as good as Lang. I've watched them both since they were kids."

"I won't argue," Vernon said amiably.

Tara saw Bret McKinney put his phone back on his belt, then go to Lynn and Sam's table. They sat with Grady and a man named Zack. Theirs had been, until now, the group with the most laughter.

When Bret spoke to them, faces that had been merry went solemn. *Something's wrong,* thought Tara. Uneasiness prickled her spine. Bret shook Sam's hand and kissed Lynn's cheek. He was leaving.

"Uh-oh." Carolyn was watching over the rim of her wineglass. "Must have a problem at the Double C. Oh, the joys of ranching."

Bret stopped on his way out. He said, "There's a—situation. I need to get back."

Vernon rose to shake his hand in goodbye. "Nothing serious, I hope."

"I hope the same." Bret made a stiff sort of half bow to the women. "Good evening, Caro. Miss Hastings, I hope to see more of you soon. A pleasure to meet you."

He left, and Carolyn said, "Well, that was mysterious."

"You know Bret," Vern said. "He's not one for gibble-gabble."

Carolyn gave him a teasing swat on the arm. "Meaning I am?"

"No, my love," said Vernon. "You're totally perfect." He took the hand that had struck at him and kissed her on the knuckles.

It was a gesture so rich in affection that Tara was moved.

This was a marriage full of real love, still touched with humor and flirtation.

Carolyn smiled at him and purred, "That's better." Then her face sobered and she stared at the door through which Bret had left. "I wonder if it's about Lang. He's worried about Lang. Lynn squeezed it out of him. He doesn't think this reconciliation with Susie's going to work."

Vernon took a sip of wine. "From what I've heard, he's probably right."

"Oh, I know." Carolyn sighed in frustration. "It's too bad. It'll never work. Lang needs to find another woman. One more his type."

Her eyes settled on Tara, and a speculative gleam rose in them.

No, Tara thought with something akin to panic. *No matchmaking. No, no, no.*

GRADY KNEW PARTIES. He had an intuitive understanding of them, and he could tell this one would break up early.

Many of the couples were older, like the Trents, the Blakes and Bubba Gibson and his wife, Mary. Their nights of owlhooting were over. The younger guests were mostly married ranchers. They all had to rise by dawn tomorrow, for as surely as the sun rose, chores would be waiting.

Grady admitted this wasn't his kind of party; it was full of people who were settled—settled to a fault. They all belonged in Crystal Creek, and they were there for good. Their lives were tied down with routine, tied up with duties, orderly and predictable.

Except for him. And Tara, to whom everything here was still new.

So he looked about for her, wanting to get to her before she escaped. She was getting ready for it; he could sense it coiling up in her, the desire to flee. He watched as she said her goodbyes to the Trents.

God, but she was a lovely thing. Maybe she'd worn simple, dark clothes so that she could fade into the background, but it didn't work. In black, she was leggy and sleek, a column of grace. To him, she was as emphatic as an exclamation point.

The loose black blouse, of some silky material, nearly hid the curves of her breasts. And somehow, because they were so well-disguised, he imagined them all the more vividly.

Her neck was so graceful that he imagined nibbling it, tasting it. She had that burnished hair pinned back, but he remembered what it was like loose and tousled, and he yearned to pull the pins out, one at a time. Her eyes were alert and wary, making him wonder what they'd look like, heavy-lidded in desire.

She held a glass only half-full of wine, and he knew as soon as she finished it, she'd make her break for freedom. He picked up a bottle, filled himself another glass, then moved close to her and topped hers off.

She gave a start. "I didn't want any more. I have to drive home."

Lynn, closing the door after the Gibsons, made an impatient little wave. "Oh, for goodness' sake. You've been nursing that same glass all night long. I've been watching."

Tara looked as if she felt trapped. She'd probably intended to grab Del as soon as the Trents were gone and head back to the safety of her house.

"Did you keep track of everybody's drinks?" Grady lifted a mocking eyebrow at Lynn.

"As a matter of fact, yes. It's my job as hostess to see nobody gets behind the wheel pie-eyed. You're on your third, so that was last call, hotshot. Then I'm cutting you off."

"Oh, hell, Lynn. I can hold my liquor. It won't affect me."

"Exactly what Cal said just before he set the piano on fire in that bar in Bandera. But *I* don't have to drive anywhere—hand over that bottle."

She took it from Grady's grasp and filled her own glass nearly to the brim. She took a hearty pull from it and exhaled in satisfaction. "I may hate myself in the morning, but my God, that tasted good."

Grady chucked her under the chin. "You earned it."

"I really should be on my way—" Tara began.

"Nonsense." Lynn tilted her head toward the hall. "The kids are still going strong. Let Del enjoy himself."

From Hank's bedroom came laughs and giggles. Tara hesitated. Grady could tell she was torn. "Then let me help you tidy up," Tara offered. "It's the least I can do."

"You were the guest of honor. You're not supposed to lift a finger. Besides, I've got Sam, and Camilla said she'd stay and help."

But Tara insisted and Lynn finally relented. "Okay," she sighed. "You can check the sunporch for me. I think there are some cups and glasses left out there."

"I'll help," Grady volunteered. "I can fold up the tables and chairs."

"That'd be great." Lynn beamed up at him and gave his shoulder an affectionate cuff. "It's good to have you home, big guy. Does it feel strange to be here?"

"No." He looked at Tara. "It feels just right."

CHAPTER EIGHT

Tara had the illusion of walking into a tropical garden on a mellow night. Lynn's glassed-in porch was lush with greenery. Hanging baskets overflowed with ivies, pothos and the long airy tendrils of spider plants. They stirred in the night breeze that floated through a set of louvered windows.

On each of the four tables, candles were burning low in votive glasses. The light glowed golden and unsteady, making shadows play on the leaves.

Grady moved to her side and stroked the frond of a maidenhair fern. Awareness of him skimmed over Tara's skin in a sensual tickle. He said, "It's like Eden out here."

Eden made her think of temptation—and sex. She shrugged off his remark and began to gather up the empty glasses scattered around the room. "Your father left early. I hope nothing was wrong."

Grady lifted a wooden chair and folded it shut. "Jonah called. There was an accident. Mrs. Gilligan, the housekeeper, fell down the attic stairs."

Her gaze flew to him in concern. "Was she badly hurt?"

He leaned the chair against the wall and took up the next one. "Wrenched her back. She was hurting, so Jonah called old Doc Purdy. Then he let Dad know."

Tara set a tray of empty glasses on the white wicker stand next to the matching love seat. She started moving the candles, too, to the same table.

The light grew more concentrated, became an island of flickering brightness. It gilded the planes of Grady's face and turned his white shirt to shifting shades of copper. The far corners of the room fell into darkness, which made it seem cut off from the rest of the world, private and mysterious.

Tara tried to ignore this sense of intimacy. "Mrs. Gilligan must have been hurt seriously if your father left."

"No." Grady shot her a glance that seemed jet-black by candlelight. "Dad's just that way. He wasn't in a party mood tonight anyway."

"Someone said he was worried about one of your brothers."

She said it hesitantly, as if unsure she had the right to bring it up.

"Lang. His marriage may be breaking up. It'll be hard on him if it does. He expected to stay married forever."

"I can understand that."

He cocked his head in interest. "Can you? Is that how you felt? That you'd be married forever?"

She wished she hadn't spoken. She tried to concentrate on folding a tablecloth. "I—suppose. I mean, of course. That's why a person makes vows."

He added another chair to the stack that leaned against the wall. Then he stopped and gave her a long look. "You don't seem like the type who'd break a vow."

Her spine stiffened and she held the folded tablecloth against her breasts, an instinctive gesture of self-protection. But she held his gaze and didn't flinch. "I didn't."

"Then he must have been the one who did."

She looked away and said nothing.

"Then I'm right. And you know what?"

He hooked his thumbs in his belt, his hands splayed against his jeaned thighs. The silence stretched out so long that Tara imagined she could hear her heart thudding.

Grady's voice was quiet, but full of conviction. "If he cheated on you, if he treated you badly in any way, he's crazy."

"That's kind of you." She tried to keep control in her voice. "But I don't want to talk about it."

"It still hurts too much?"

"No." That was true. The worst of that pain was over. She'd had a husband, she'd lost him. She'd accepted the reality of it. It was what he'd done to Del that still throbbed like an open wound.

"You might as well tell me." Grady's voice held something close to a taunt. "If you don't, somebody else will. This isn't L.A. It's a small town."

"Nobody here knows." She lifted her chin at that small triumph.

"Then they'll make it up. Nature hates a vacuum."

He set the table on its edge, folding its legs. When she didn't reply, but kept on working instead, he said, "Cal knows what happened, right?"

She exhaled in frustration. "Yes."

"You think he never told his wife?"

"Serena? Of course. They both know. They've been— good friends."

"And you don't think that either of them is ever going to tell? That it's some kind of state secret they'll never mention, even to their own family?"

"Cal and Serena are *not* gossips."

He propped the folded table against the wall and put one fist on his hip. "I didn't say they were. But you've moved next door to his family's spread. You're just a few miles from his sister. You're a neighbor now. You're also the strange lady in town. People are going to ask about you. It's human nature."

She swept the last cloth from its table and folded it, almost angrily. "Let them ask. I don't care."

"Then tell me just one thing."

"What?" She was glad the light was dim; her cheeks burned and a vein in her throat jumped crazily.

"The reason you don't want to talk about him—is it because you still love him?"

The question caught her unaware. She took such a deep breath it dizzied her. "No. I don't love him."

"Good." He nodded in satisfaction. "I thought maybe you wore black because you're still mourning for him."

"I wore black because I like black."

"And I like you in black."

She didn't trust herself to listen to such talk. It confused her and awakened feelings she'd laid to rest. Dangerous feelings.

She made her face blank, her movements brisk. She stacked the tablecloth with the others and picked them up, along with a bunch of napkins. "I'll take these to Lynn and come back for the glasses and candles. You should be done by then."

"Don't you like to be complimented? I said I liked you in black."

"Thank you. Compliments are nice. But they're only words."

She started to turn her back to him, but as she did, the breeze gusted. The leaves rustled and the hanging plants rocked lazily. Just as lazily the breeze plucked one of the napkins Tara carried, wafted it to a corner, and then, as if suddenly bored by the prank, dropped it into the shadows.

Tara moved to retrieve it, and Grady, closer to the corner, moved, too. They both dropped to their knees at the same time to pick it up, their heads nearly bumped and their hands went grasping after the fallen napkin.

Tara captured it, but by accident, his fingers closed over hers.

A bolt of pure sexual awareness speared through her. She looked at his face. It was so close.

I should move away. I can't move away. I don't want to move away.

His grip on her hand loosened. "Oh. Sorry."

Then it tightened again. "No." His voice was husky. "I'm not sorry."

He drew her nearer.

No, no, no. But her hungry body made her change her mind. *Maybe. Maybe…*

She raised her lips to meet his.

Yes.

FOR THE SPACE OF TWO HEARTBEATS, Grady's face hovered above hers.

Slowly he lowered his mouth. *Trouble,* he thought. *This could start God knows how much trouble.*

He clenched his teeth and asked, "Do you want me—to stop?"

She sucked in her breath in a quiet gasp, then let it out noiselessly. The warmth of it feathered against his lips. It made him slightly crazy with desire.

"Is silence consent?" he whispered.

Again she said nothing, but she was so close, so irresistibly close, that he could not bear it any longer.

His fingers gripped hers more possessively. His other hand rose to clasp her silk-clad shoulder. He marveled at its softness, its smoothness and the feel of her body, maddeningly near, beneath it.

He kissed her. Her mouth was moist and supple beneath his.

It was a mouth formed for loving and being loved. But it was also shy; it trembled with reluctance that made him feel both wild and tender.

His lips explored the ways he and she could fit together. All of them seemed to work. He liked each one better than the last, so he kept trying new ways, teasing her, pleasuring her, trying to tempt her further.

He put both arms around her, his hands sliding up and down her slender back, glorying in the planes and curves of her body.

She didn't touch him back. But her mouth became more lively and questing, and she was no longer passive, but kissing him back, and he was aroused by her growing excitement.

His hands closed on her shoulders, pulling her nearer, pulling her deeper into the spell that had fallen on them both. Grady's head felt full of the weight of wanting, and his groin pulsed with it.

Then she touched him. She put her hand to his chest and drew back, trying to push him away at the same time. She twisted her head and shook it no. She was breathing hard, but not half as hard as he was.

"No," she panted. "Don't. I'm sorry."

"There is absolutely nothing to be sorry for." His jaw taut, he tried to pull her back into his arms.

She resisted and crossed both arms over the folded linens. "This is crazy. Let me go. This isn't the time or place—"

He softened his grip on her shoulders but didn't release her. "Does that mean there is a time and place?"

"No!" She said it with such emphasis it was like being doused with cold water. But even in the shadows, he could see how contrite she was. She knelt there, her arms crossed, her head ducked down as if she was doing penance.

She started to rise. He wanted to keep her, hold her, love her. But he let her go. He got to his feet with a weary sigh. He reached down and picked up two more napkins that had fallen. He offered them to her. It seemed a gesture as ridiculous as his hope to have her.

"Thank you. Now let's forget this ever happened."

She started to step away but he couldn't stop himself. His hand shot out and seized her by the arm.

"Forget it ever happened? Why? Because I'm the hired man?"

She flashed him a glare of resentment. "That's got nothing to do with it."

"Then what does?"

A strand of her perfectly restrained hair had come loose, and she pushed it back from her face. "You said it yourself. I'm the strange lady in town. I—I came here to make a new home for my son and me. A fresh start. I have to watch my step. Be careful.'' She bit her beautiful lower lip. ''Of my reputation. I *have* to be. Forgive me. That's the way it is.''

Grady swore inwardly. His hand dropped away, freeing her. ''I understand.'' He did understand. He just didn't like it.

He shoved his hands into his front pockets so he'd keep them off her.

He gave her a sideways look that was half glower. ''You should have told me to stop. I gave you the chance.''

''I'm like anyone else. Only human.''

''Are you?''

''Good night.'' Disgust edged her voice. He imagined most of it was for herself. She was that kind of woman.

She turned and headed for the French doors. Over his shoulder he called, ''You should get on home. Tell Lynn I'll bring in the glasses and candles. I'll just spend a few minutes out here till you're gone.''

''Thanks, Grady.'' She sounded sad. He watched her go. He went to the candles, and one by one he blew them out. Then he stood for a long time, staring out a window at the moonlight, silver and lonesome.

ON THE WAY HOME, Del clutched a paper bag, something Lynn or Hank had given him, Tara supposed. He rambled on in happy weariness of all he'd done. ''And then we played cars, and I had the fire truck and the ambulance, and Hank had two dump trucks...''

Tara smiled and nodded at his recital, glad he'd had a good time.

But inwardly, she was kicking herself, repeatedly and hard. Why had she let Grady kiss her? Lynn had given her and Del a beautiful party. But Tara had ruined it for herself, by necking among the potted plants. Was she crazy?

She ticked off the reasons she'd been a fool.

You hardly know him.

He's only a drifter.

He's a flirt.

He works for you, for God's sake.

Does his job include giving you sex? Did you make him think so? Are you that pathetic, that desperate?

She gripped the steering wheel more tightly. Del yawned. He stopped talking. He was winding down at last.

She returned to her argument with herself. She'd done nothing wrong. A few kisses? On the sin scale, it didn't even register, it was a zero, a joke.

And she did know him—sort of. They'd spent two full workdays together and an evening. Good grief, there were people who slept together after less time.

Oho. So are you one of those people?

She winced. No, she wasn't promiscuous. She hadn't been with a man since Sid left her. She'd refused to act out any of the clichés: taking a lover to spite Sid, taking a lover to prove she was desirable, taking a lover on the rebound, out of loneliness.

But the loneliness got to you tonight? Ah, poor thing. Poor Tara.

Grady'd caught her in a weak moment, that was all. And she'd—well, she'd admit it—she had wondered what kissing him would be like.

And it was fabulous, you loved it. It was scrumdiddly-delicious. You wanted to rip off his shirt and run your fingers through his chest hair...

Mentally she shoved such thoughts into a vault and locked them up tight. But she could sense them beating on the walls to get out. "No," Tara whispered from between her teeth. "Absolutely not."

"Mmm?" asked Del. "What?"

"Nothing, honey. We're almost home."

She turned onto the bumpy lane that led up to the house. She parked the truck and led Del inside. Lono danced around them so frantically that Del giggled sleepily.

Tara helped him put on his pajamas and tucked him into bed. He insisted on keeping the paper bag close to him. "What is that?" she asked. "A present?"

''A secret,'' he said, and lay down with his arm around
it. She shrugged, kissed him good-night, plugged in his
night-light and switched off the overhead. She went to her
nearly empty bedroom. Its air reeked of a combination of
must and antiseptic.

Just like your love life, she taunted herself. It was an idea
she wanted to ignore, but she succeeded only in setting off
a train of unpleasant thoughts.

She flexed her fingers. She still wore the bandage Grady
had put on her earlier in the day. Her hands looked terrible,
and she knew why: she'd purposely neglected them. She
didn't want to look attractive because she didn't want to
attract anyone. It was that simple.

She looked in the bureau mirror. It was cloudy and spotted with age, but it reflected her as she was—a woman who
allowed herself no vanities, a woman who dressed as Grady
said, as if in mourning.

In truth, she *was* mourning. Not the end of her marriage,
but the end of innocence, the betrayal of trust. Not just her
own, but Del's.

A year and a half ago, Sid confessed what she'd suspected
for months. But what Tara hadn't suspected was how hu-
miliating the truth would be.

Yes, Sid admitted, he had a mistress. She was a starlet,
twenty-one years old, with a two-year-old son. He'd tried
to break it off with her, but he couldn't. He was possessed.
He had never known what real sex was until now. Until
Kylie.

Kylie. The name still made Tara feel as if she'd swallowed poison.

Sid said he loved Kylie. She wanted to marry him. He
wanted to marry her. His life with Tara was a sham, and he
hated it. He wanted out. He moved into a condo with Kylie
and her son, Presley. At first he made a show of taking Del
on the weekends, but Kylie didn't like it; she was jealous.
So Sid stopped picking up Del. He stopped phoning. He

stopped sending child support payments. He didn't send so much as a card for Del's birthday or for Christmas.

He didn't fight Tara for custody. He didn't object when she sent word that she and Del were going to Texas.

Once Tara realized she could leave California, she'd been fired with determination to get away, start a new life. But during the divorce, she'd found a strategy to cope with having her family torn apart by a bimbo like Kylie. She made herself into the anti-Kylie.

She threw out her cosmetics, took her best clothes to a resale shop and vowed she'd never embarrass herself again by trying to seem alluring.

A man had almost destroyed her emotionally. She would not be hurt the same way twice. She never again needed the delusion of being in love.

But now her divorce had been final for a year. Against her better judgment, she *was* looking at a man. The man was sexy, flirtatious—and rootless.

She'd been foolish to think that she could switch off her sex drive as if it was a mechanical thing. It wasn't mechanical, it was biological. And biology, repressed too long, was rising up in rebellion. A great, seething rebellion.

She could not be in the same room with Grady without acute physical awareness of him. She'd been aware of men before, but never like this. But her brain knew what her body liked was wrong.

She'd told Grady the truth. She had to guard her reputation. If she dallied with someone like Grady, and Burleigh found out, he'd vilify her as much as he could. And Burleigh would make it his business to find out every questionable thing she did.

She had to be prepared to fight Burleigh, and she would be a fool to give him ammunition to use against her. If part of the fight meant sexual abstinence, then abstinence it was.

She turned from the mirror and began to take off her clothes. Yet, it had been exciting to feel like a woman again.

It had been wonderful. But touching him, being touched, must never happen again.

She ached with the remembering of it.

GRADY DROVE TOWARD the Double C, simmering with conflict in mind and body. To distract himself, he switched on the truck's radio, only to hear Bruce Springsteen growling about his head being on fire with a bad desire.

Grady didn't need that. He gritted his teeth and punched the button for a different station.

But that gave him Clint Black, moaning about not getting any younger and freedom being a lonely prison. That was worse. Grady snapped the radio off with an angry flick.

He listened to the thrum of the wheels on the blacktop and felt the too-hard beating of his heart. Why wouldn't his blood stop pounding?

All he'd done was kiss Tara. Hell, why did he feel so jittery and frustrated that it was like being seventeen again? He was a grown man, a man of considerable experience. But tonight he didn't feel experienced; he felt like a green kid who's found himself on the edge of uncharted territory.

He wondered what would happen tomorrow. He'd told Tara he'd come to work on Saturday. Would she revert to her ice-princess mode and tell him to go away and stay away? Had he blown everything for a few stolen kisses? And what in blazes did he mean by the word *everything?* He didn't even know. Maybe he didn't want to know.

She wasn't like any woman he'd ever met. She was strong, but beneath her strength lay great vulnerability. She built walls between herself and people—not just him, everyone. He'd watched her do it tonight. She was polite, even genial, but she wanted no one to get close to her.

Except the boy. With Del she was different. With everybody else she was not so much aloof as elusive.

She was so emotionally private that being with her sometimes made him feel as if he was with an elfin queen and they were under a spell that needed to be broken.

So kissing her was exceptional. It wasn't trivial; it wasn't a favor she easily granted. It was a true intimacy. That both intrigued Grady and spooked him. He'd avoided intimacy for years, yet there he'd been, indulging in it and wanting more.

He felt relieved when he reached the ranch house. Back to a solid, four-square reality. A man's world. Except, of course, for Millie Gilligan. Grady parked behind a strange car and got out.

Then, like an apparition of the moonlight, a silvery man appeared. He was elderly, and his age made him spare, but not yet fragile. His white hair shone like platinum.

The silver man carried a black bag and stopped, statue-still, when he saw Grady. A grin split his face. "Grady," he said and held out his hand.

Grady grinned in return, clasped the other man's hand and pumped it. "Doc Purdy."

Nate Purdy had practiced medicine in Crystal Creek before Grady was born. In fact, he'd practiced medicine *while* Grady was being born; he'd delivered him. And Lang and Jonah, as well.

Nate couldn't stop smiling. Even by moonlight Grady could see how many wrinkles time had engraved on the familiar face. He threw his arm around the Nate's shoulders. "How's my favorite sawbones?"

"Son of a gun." Nate's voice was as creaky as an old door. "I heard you were here. How're you doing?"

"I'm fine. How's Mrs. Gilligan?"

"She'll live. Fell and threw her back out of whack. Herniated a disk, I'm pretty sure. But your dad's going to bring her in for an X ray tomorrow morning. Want to make sure that's all she's done."

Grady stepped back and looked him up and down. "And you're still doctoring. Even making house calls."

Nate's expression grew wry. "I'm a relic from another century. Don't remind me. I'll be retiring soon. Rose is starting to nag. As a rash young whippersnapper, I promised her we'd go to Capri someday. She says she's waited fifty years and she's beginning to think I'm not a man of my word.''

Ah, Rose Purdy. Grady remembered her with pleasure. Brown-eyed, pixyish and trim, she'd made the best damned cinnamon rolls in the known universe. He doubted even Millie Gilligan could do better.

"Tell Rose hello for me."

"Come over and tell her yourself. Pay a visit. That's the doctor's order. Come see us before you go off rambling and roaming again."

"Yessir. I'll do that."

Nate looked up at the moon. "Full moon tonight. Strange things always happen on a full moon. Shirley Jean Ditmars accidentally swallowed a bottle cap tonight, a 'possum bit Sheriff Jackson on the thumb and Mrs. Gilligan fell out of the attic. I hope this is the last of the craziness. I need my beauty sleep.''

Grady laughed and slapped Nate's back. They said their goodbyes, and as Grady climbed the stairs, he heard Nate's car pulling out.

The back door was open, so he stepped into the kitchen. His father sat at the kitchen table with Jonah. Both had shot glasses and a whiskey bottle was set in the middle of the table.

Bret's expression was grim. "Home so soon? I expected you to party till the last dog died."

"It wasn't that kind of party," said Grady. "How did Mrs. Gilligan fall out of the attic?"

Bret made a face. *"Arrgh."*

Jonah picked up his shot glass and looked at Bret mildly. "She didn't fall out. She just fell down the last three stairs."

Grady went to the cupboard and got a glass of his own. "What was she doing in the attic?"

"Making potions," growled Bret. "Grinding up toads and bats."

Jonah shook his head. "I was reading. She came and asked me if this house had Christmas decorations. I said it used to. She asked where they'd be, and I said that I guessed in the attic. The next thing I heard was *whump, whump, whump!*''

Grady sat down and poured himself a shot. "Did it knock her out?"

Jonah regarded the play of light on his whiskey. "Nope. She looked up at me and said, 'Why can't you have an out of the body experience when you need one?'"

"Whatever the hell that means," Bret grumbled. He cast a displeased glance at Jonah. "Why'd you call Doc Purdy? Why didn't you call an ambulance to come and take her away?"

Jonah shrugged. "She said, 'My pain is considerable. Call a physician.' So I did."

"Pah." Bret downed his whiskey in a single swallow.

Grady didn't understand. "What's the problem? Nate's a good doctor."

Bret refused to reply. Jonah lifted his eyebrows in an expression of helplessness. "Dr. Purdy says she might need up to six weeks of bed rest."

Grady frowned. "Six weeks? That's kind of extreme. I hurt my back in Vegas and they had me up and moving in a couple of days."

"You're young. She's not," Bret snapped. "Nate says nothing works as well for a sprung back as old-fashioned bed rest. And the bed she'll rest in will be *here.*" Bret stabbed the table with his forefinger for emphasis. "In this house. With us.

"She's got no place else to go," Bret said. "She gave up her apartment in Fredricksburg to come here. This is now her place of residence. She was injured on the job, and I don't want her to get in a huff and sue."

Grady whistled. "I see. So now we keep house for the housekeeper. But who keeps house for us?"

Bret rose to his feet and slammed his empty shot glass on the counter. "She insisted on calling somebody named

Rhonda. Rhonda—somebody. A niece or something. She's agreed to come.''

"Mrs. Gilligan was really upset that she couldn't work," Jonah said. "So Nate said let her make the call. And after he did he shot her full of muscle relaxant. She's out like a light.''

"I wonder who Rhonda is," Grady mused.

"Probably a member of her coven," Bret said.

"I've got to hit the sack. I need to get up early." Jonah pushed away his half-filled glass and got up.

Grady nodded good-night and watched him go. He heard his footsteps fading down the hallway. He squinted at Bret. "What's with the whiskey? You're not much of a drinker."

The line of Bret's mouth grew grimmer. "I needed a stiff drink by the time Nate got out of here. It's going to be a long six weeks.''

"Anybody hear from Lang?"

"No. God knows what's going on."

Grady shrugged. "In that little girl's room I feel like I'm bunking in a candy box. Can I move into his room since he isn't here?''

"No. He might show up yet. He will if he has any sense. I met that Tara Hastings tonight. I was right. *She's* the kind of woman he needs. She's got backbone and sense. She'd make a rancher a real wife.''

Grady went cold. The hand holding the shot glass suddenly felt numb, unmovable. It wasn't so much that Bret was mentally marrying Tara off to Lang. It was simply the thought of Tara as a wife. A *wife*.

Good Lord. The idea was staggering.

Bret scowled at his empty shot glass. "What about you? Have you heard anything about getting reimbursed for your truck?''

Grady shook his head, still feeling stunned. "No. I talked to the lawyer late this afternoon. Looks like I have to go to court. It could last a long time. Till it's decided, nobody's giving me a dime.''

Bret made a sound of disgust. "That must be hard on you. Being stuck in one place. You'll be stir-crazy."

"I'm fine." Grady spoke with more calm than he felt.

Bret's expression said that he doubted it. He probably thought Grady would get so restless that he'd spend his first paycheck on a bus ticket and vamoose. He probably hoped it.

That's how he sees me. That's how he's always seen me. But it's not the way I am.

Bret finished his whiskey and pushed away from the table. "I'm going to bed."

He turned and left the room without saying good-night. Grady looked after him. He didn't say good-night, either. He stared at the whiskey bottle and resisted pouring himself another drink.

He thought. *A wife. He's right. Tara isn't the kind of woman a man has a fling with. She's the kind he marries.*

The realization made his chill sink deeper, worming its way into his spine. He'd always figured he'd settle down someday, maybe when he was forty or forty-five. But now? *Now?*

This was an awful time to think of such a thing. He was a nobody in this town, and he had nothing to offer her. She'd spoken of reputation. He suddenly wished he'd given a damn about his own.

CHAPTER NINE

THAT NIGHT BIOLOGY MADE another attack on Tara. She dreamed about Grady: long, sensual dreams. Explicit dreams of his naked skin against hers as they tangled in the sheets, mouth to hungry mouth.

She woke herself making small noises of pleasure in the back of her throat. Her body was pulsating. "Yes," she'd been trying to say, "yes."

No, she thought, sitting straight up. *No! This is insane!*

The first grayish light of dawn peeked through her makeshift curtains. The room was cold, but her flesh was warm, her blood thrumming through her in phantom excitement. The dream of Grady had even made her nipples achingly taut.

She crossed her arms over her flannel-covered breasts. She gave herself a hard, unloving hug and shook her head to chase away her dreams and their tingling effects.

What she needed to do was tell the man to leave and not come back. If she welcomed his loving in her sleep, did it mean she might welcome it in her waking hours? She could not allow such a thing. She would not.

She couldn't fall into bed with the first man who drifted into her life.

For Del's sake, for Gavin's, and her own, she had to establish herself as a solid, responsible member of the community. Her name should be spotless, not the stuff of gossip and dirty jokes. And certainly not a name that Burleigh Hastings could tarnish for his own ends.

Tara rose from her guilty bed and slipped into the bathroom. She took a punishingly brisk shower to wash the memory of Grady's touch from her body, to scrub haunting thoughts of him from her mind.

Her family had always lived in rural areas. She understood how rumor worked in such communities, how reputations were ruined. Besides, Sid had created enough scandal to last her and Del a lifetime. She needn't add to it.

So she would tell Grady to go away, that she didn't need his help after all. She would do it nicely, with a reference letter and severance pay. But she would do it.

She stepped from the shower, cleansed and relieved. She could find other able-bodied workers. They couldn't be off repairing the flood damage in Baswell forever. She would import help from Austin if she had to.

As for Grady, he was skilled, he was capable. Let him find work elsewhere. And let him find other women to flirt with. He would have no trouble doing either, she was sure.

She wrapped herself in a bath sheet and was toweling her hair dry when the phone shrilled, echoing through the big house.

She ran to scoop up the receiver before the ringing woke Del. She was slightly out of breath when she answered.

"Is this The Ranch With No Name?" asked a man. "I want to talk to long, tall Tara."

With pleasure she recognized Cal McKinney's voice. "Cal! How are you? Where are you? Still in Mexico?"

"I'm fine as wine, babe. And we're back in L.A., but have to go to Mexico again soon. Serena says hello. And to give that Del boy a hug."

"The same to her. And hugs to the twins."

"So how's it goin' there? Wait—not a fair question. It's probably hardly goin' at all yet, right?"

Tara glanced around the kitchen. Although the furnishings were shabby and the old fridge wheezed, the walls shone, pristine and flawless.

Del's room, too, was bright with fresh paint. The windows sparkled, cleaned inside and out. The roof was patched and the temporary paddock and stalls stood in place.

Not a quarter of this could have been done without Grady.

She bit at her lower lip and pulled the towel more securely around her naked body. "Um...actually...um... we're a lot further along than you'd expect."

Cal laughed mischievously. "Yeah, Lynn told me you hit pay dirt. That second cousin of mine showed up, the old Gypsy Rover himself."

"Yes—he—he's been a great help." Tara couldn't stop staring at the perfect walls. It was as if they, in combination with Cal's voice, had hypnotized her.

Cal said, "He helped move a whole house once. My grandpa Hank's from the oil fields to the Double C. Took it apart and put it back together again, stone by stone. He wasn't more than a teenager. Amazin'. Yes, ma'am. You're one lucky lady."

I don't feel lucky, Tara thought darkly. *And last night I wasn't much of a lady.*

But Cal, ever lighthearted, sailed on. "I told Gavin you're in good hands. Grady can do anything. Might make us a good project manager. He needs a decent gig. Lynn says he's down on his luck. And, hell, I'm not above nepotism."

Tara's face burned. She couldn't complain about hiring from within the family. Three Amigos had taken her on, hadn't they? They had every right to do the same with Grady.

Carefully she said, "He's very good, but I get the impression he won't stay here long."

"Shucks, honey, he's just got that McKinney ramblin' streak. I had it myself. It took Serena to settle me down. So—how's my baby sister? She been helpin' you out?"

Tara welcomed a different subject. "Lynn? She's been my guardian angel. Really, I can't tell you how much she's done. I don't know how to even start to thank her."

"I got something in mind for her. It's got four legs, a mane and a tail. But don't give away the surprise, okay?"

"Cal, you're wonderful," she said with real affection.

"Naw. But Lynn is. I knew you and her would hit it off. Don't you worry, sugar. Us McKinneys'll watch out for you."

Us McKinneys.

Grady's image flashed through her mind. The easy way he moved. The intimate way he smiled. His laugh.

His smile and laugh, she suddenly realized, were much like Cal's. How could she tell Cal the truth, that she'd just been vowing to *fire* Grady?

And what, after all, was Grady's sin? She found him attractive. She couldn't fire him for that, not in the face of all the McKinneys' kindness—she'd be an ungrateful hypocrite.

"I called because I wanted to be the one to tell you the news," Cal said. "We finally got a name for this here project. I won."

He said it with such satisfaction that Tara smiled. The partners worked well together, but one thing they couldn't agree on was what to call the development at Hole in the Wall. They'd squabbled for months.

"And how'd you win this marvelous triumph?" Tara teased. "Draw a name out of a hat?"

"We figured we weren't ever gonna settle on what to call it. So we made a bet. We each predicted the final score of the U.T.—Texas Tech game. The other two tried to reason sensible-like, which was a fool thing to do. So *I* won. And *you* are no longer at the No Name Ranch."

"So where am I?"

"It's a name that probably won't mean a thing to you. But I always did like it—Francina Hills."

Tara sucked in her breath. Francina—the woman in the story that Grady had told her and Del. That woman from so long ago, so determined to protect her children. A lump rose unexpectedly in Tara's throat. "I think it's a wonderful name. Just wonderful."

"Then you got more sense than Spencer. He wanted to name it Audubon Park, for God's sake. And your brother—ha! He wanted to go all geological and call it 'Balcones Fault Environmental Estates.' Which has all the poetry of a cowpie going 'plop.'"

Tara smiled. "You're right. 'Francina Hills' is best."

"Good. You want to tell that to Mr. Tin Ear himself?"

She wasn't sure she'd understood him. "What?"

"Your tone-deaf brother. Want to talk to him?"

"Gavin's there? With you? In L.A.? I thought he was still in Hawaii—"

"Nope. I'll let him explain. Here he is."

She heard Gavin's voice. "I do not have a tin ear. Hi, kiddo. How're you doing?"

Puzzlement changed to delight. "Gavin? I thought you were still overseeing construction at Waimea."

"Nope. We put Isaiah Chan in charge. He can handle the finishing touches. Spence has to stay in Switzerland, Cal's going back to Mexico, and we need somebody to stay stateside. So I'm back."

"Back?" Her heart leaped. "For how long?"

He sounded purposefully vague. "We'll see. However long it takes." His tone grew gentler. "How's Del? Is he adjusting to the move?"

"As well as can be expected." She wiped a damp strand of hair back from her cheek. *Better than could be expected.* After all, he thought he had a "buddy." She thought of Grady McKinney again, and as if in self-protection, she pulled the towel higher over her breasts.

"That's good." Gavin was deeply fond of Del and protective of him. "Does he mention his father?"

Tara swallowed. "Yes. He doesn't understand. It's hard for him."

"Hell, I don't understand. Sid's nuts. He let Hollywood

get to him. Forget him. How is it, being a stranger in a strange land?''

"It's fine," she said. "I *like* this kind of work. I've missed it. It's like when we were growing up. Sometimes I expect to turn around and find you there, smelling like turpentine, your mouth full of nails."

"How'd you like to have me really there—for a while, at least?''

"You're kidding," she said, so joyful that she almost bounced on her bare tiptoes.

"Not kidding," he said. "I've got to tie up some loose ends here, then go to Austin on Monday. And from Austin straight to Crystal Creek."

"Austin?" she echoed. "Then *here?*''

"Yep," he chuckled. "Monday night if I'm lucky. Could you stand to have company? I've got a new sleeping bag to test for Spence. I could test it there."

The news seemed too good to be true. "You're teasing."

"Nope. Things are going faster than we hoped. We got a call from Meyers and Meyers in Austin. They had a schedule change. We've been bumped up a place. We don't have to wait until March. We're going to start platting all three projects. I'm going to Austin to consult with their engineers and architects. They'll probably be in Crystal Creek Tuesday, hanging around for a week or so. Then we bring in the preliminary crew."

"This is wonderful. Del's going to be *so* excited."

"The Meyers people'll stay at the hotel in Crystal Creek. But I'll bunk with you and Del—if that's okay."

"It's more than okay. It's the best thing that could ever happen."

"I'll need a sofa bed or something for the guest room. Meyers, Sr. may want to come, stay there, get the feel of the place. And don't worry about expense. We're preselling in Hawaii like you wouldn't believe. We're making money hand over fist. We're going to pull this off, kid."

Her throat knotted with happiness for him. He deserved

to pull it off. They all did. They'd showed vision, dedication, and above all, guts.

"Whoops," he said. "Damn. Call on another line. If it's from Switzerland, it'll last forever. Look, I'll call you again tomorrow. Take care, Tara. I worry about you, clear out there on your own. But I'll see you soon. I love you. Give Del a kiss."

"I will," she said, her throat tightening. "I love you, too."

They said their goodbyes. Tara hung up and shook her head in pleased disbelief. Her damp hair stirred against her bare shoulders, reminding her of her nakedness.

She was not only glad that her brother was coming, but she was also profoundly relieved. As long as he was there, he would stand between her and all the forbidden longings that Grady had awakened.

WHEN GRADY PULLED UP in Tara's driveway, the sky was such a bright, cloudless blue that all nature seemed to be beaming welcome to him.

He doubted that Tara would do the same.

After a restless night of thinking, he had it figured out. She'd hand him his walking papers, and maybe that was best. He could get a construction job down at Baswell, put some distance between them. Then she could keep her honor, and he could keep his sanity.

But he'd no sooner stepped from his borrowed truck than a small figure hurled out of the house and wrapped himself around his right leg. *Somebody* was glad to see him. And he realized, with an odd pang, he was just as glad to see Del. The kid was getting under his skin.

"Grady!" Del cried, hugging his knee, "Guess what we're going to do today?" The boy wore only one sock and no shoes.

Grady swooped him up and set him on his shoulder. "I don't know what all, champ. I told your mom I'd clean up those garage doors."

"No," Del said excitedly. "We're gonna paint inside more. Know why? Because my uncle's coming to see us Monday!"

"Your uncle the stuntman?"

"Yeah, the stuntman." Del grinned. "Maybe we can get him to fall down for us."

Then the front door flew open, and he felt the pull of physical desire and an emotional yearning such as he'd never known. Tara appeared, her loose hair like dark fire.

Suddenly he wanted to see that autumnal hair spread against the whiteness of a pillow, to feel his fingers lacing through it, press his face into its silkiness, breathe its fragrance. He might want it on a regular basis and for a long time.

Her eyes widened when she saw him and pinkness flared in her cheeks. But she whipped her gaze from him to Del. "Del," she said. "I didn't know where you went. You don't have your shoes on—there's dew on the grass."

"It's okay," Grady said. "I got him."

He shifted the boy to his arms and carried him inside and set him on the floor. Lono danced around the three of them in doggy celebration. Well, Grady thought, the dog liked him and the kid liked him.

Two out of three wasn't bad.

"My sock feels icky," Del said with a frown. "I think a worm got in it."

"Then go change it," Tara said.

Del hopped away. "If it's a worm, I'll name him Wilber. Come on, Wilber." Lono, ever loyal, followed him and the alleged worm.

Tara was barefoot herself and carried a hairbrush. "I—didn't hear you drive up. I had the radio on."

"I'm early," Grady said.

And he was glad he was early. He liked seeing the way she tried to tame her hair with the brush and the graceful line of her neck. She reached into the pocket of her yellow flannel shirt and pulled out a barrette. She flicked it open

smoothly and fastened it into place with a soft click. The
hair, imprisoned, fell into place, but rebelliously.

Her feet were naked on the blue-gray slate of the kitchen
floor. They were white, narrow feet. He imagined them rubbing against his bare leg, up and down.

She sat at the rickety table and pulled on a pair of gray
socks, then her boots. "There's coffee on the counter," she
said, "Please feel free to help yourself. And sit down. I want
to have a talk with you." Her tone was formal.

Ah, he thought, she did mean to fire him. Over coffee—
very politely, of course. Very civilized.

He opened a cupboard scantly furnished with mismatched
dishes. He took out a blue plastic mug with a picture of Han
Solo. He smiled as he filled it. "I remember these. Didn't
they used to come in boxes of breakfast food?"

"I don't remember. I wasn't into space warriors. Just
horses." Her voice sounded strangely tight. "How's your
father's housekeeper?"

"She should be fine."

Yep, Tara was leading up to his firing courteously. But
of course, she would; she was a lady. He sat across from
her, trying to hide his fatalism with an air of nonchalance.
She didn't look at him, only stared into her own coffee mug.
He supposed she was polishing her farewell speech. He decided to help her out.

"Del says your brother's coming to visit Monday. Does
that—change work orders?"

There. He'd given her an opening. All she had to do was
take it and say Yes, it did. She wouldn't be needing him
anymore.

He knew it was coming, and his heart skipped a beat,
maybe two. He had the disturbing hunch that more than a
job hung in the balance. And more than an affair with a
pretty lady. Far, far more.

A fine blue vein pulsed in her temple. Her hands tightened
around her mug. "Yes. I want to fix up his part of the house,

the west wing. I know there isn't time for us to get it perfect—but we'll do what we can.''

His heart started beating again, so hard that his blood
pounded in his ears. *Us,* she'd said. *We.* Good God, there
was still a chance.

But he gave his most don't-give-a-damn smile. ''We can
try. I'll put in extra hours. I don't mind.'' He let an edge of
invitation slide into his voice to see how she'd react. ''If
you need me, I'm ready.''

She raised her eyes. The expression on her face looked
as wary as he felt. ''That won't be necessary. I just want
some painting done in the other wing. All I need—''

She stopped speaking, as if she might reveal too much.
She rose and went to the sink, emptying her coffee cup and
rinsing it out.

He stretched out his long legs, crossed his booted ankles.
''All you need is what?'' he asked in lazy challenge.

She dried the cup. ''For his part of the house to be as
nice as possible. That's all, really…''

''You want to show him you're grateful.'' It was a guess,
but he knew it was right.

''Yes.'' She turned to face him. ''He'll be staying with
us. I don't know for how long. For quite a while, I hope.''

For quite a while. Now Grady understood why she'd keep
him on. Grady would no longer be the only other adult with
her out here in this lonesome place. Now she had a shield
to protect her—and to make him keep his distance.

She pushed back a stray strand of hair, as if she was
smoothing away all her difficulties. ''Some planners will be
here, too. And he'll be bringing in a crew sooner than we'd
thought.''

''I see.'' He'd be reduced to a face in the crowd, one of
many. He'd have small chance of seeing her alone anymore,
and she'd find safety in numbers.

''Yes.'' She folded the dish towel and set it aside. ''This
project's about to really take off. Oh, and I talked to Cal,

too. He said they've finally named this place. Francina Hills.''

Grady gave her a small, mocking smile. "Appropriate. Named after a woman who could hold her own against any odds.''

"I've got to get to work. This gives me another set of walls to scrub down. I'm sending you to town for more paint. There's a list of what I want on the counter.''

She nodded at a square of paper beside the ancient toaster. "So—you'd better be on your way.'' She started to turn from him.

Grady could see beyond her to the living room. Del was sitting on the beanbag chair, struggling to fasten his shoes. He already had turned on the video player, as if the habit was automatic. On the screen Beauty was running from the Beast.

"I had an idea," Grady said.

She turned back to him, giving him an unreadable look. "What?''

He rose from the table and tilted one hip, thrusting his thumbs into his front pockets. "A fence. I thought about a fence.''

She looked at him questioningly. "Yes?''

"If you want, I'll get some fencing, make a play area for Del. So he could be outside more.''

Her chin shot up. "There's painting to be done.''

She apparently took his suggestion as criticism. This gave him perverse pleasure. He said, "You're scrubbing down the walls? It'll take a while for them to dry.''

"I just don't think you'll have time for a fence, too.''

"I'll make time. If not today, tomorrow.''

"Tomorrow's Sunday.''

"I can work Sundays. It makes me no nevermind. December's coming. There might not be many more good days to play outside.

"A fence'd be good for the dog, too. He's feisty, but there are coyotes around here. Predators.''

"Yes," she said, her gaze holding his. "I'm well aware of predators."

"You want to hold them off, don't you?"

"Most certainly." Her words had warning in them.

"So? Fencing? Or no fencing?" He quirked his mouth thoughtfully and looked beyond her to the child slouched in front of the television screen.

She saw the shift in his gaze. Her tone grew even more aloof. "Fine. Get fencing. Put it on my account. But you can't be here tomorrow. We won't be here. Lynn and I have plans."

"It's okay. Somehow I'll work it in."

"Whatever." She went to Del and knelt to tie his shoes.

Grady put his hand to his hat brim in a sardonic salute that meant, *Whatever you say, Boss Lady.* She didn't see it.

She was back in charge.

Grady picked up her list and prepared to do her bidding. But inside, he was smiling. She hadn't sent him away. And he, a man always ready to move on, was satisfied to stay put. More than satisfied.

By the time Tara had both of Del's shoes securely fastened, Grady was in his truck, pulling away. Only then did Del notice he was gone.

"Where's Grady?" He jumped up and sprinted into the kitchen. He heard the already fading sound of the truck's engine. He ran to the screen door and looked out, his face suddenly forlorn. "He's *gone.*"

Even Lono seemed disappointed. He stood with his paws on the screen, his usually lively tail hanging down straight as a plumb line. Tara put her hand on the boy's shoulder. "He's going into town to buy paint. So we can paint Uncle Gavin's room."

"I have something to tell him."

"You can tell him later."

"I could have gone *with* him."

"No. You need to stay with me."

Del's tone went petulant. "He didn't even say bye."

"You were watching your video."

"Not *really*. I just turned it on to help me tie my shoes."

Tara didn't know how to refute this childish logic, so she didn't try. She squeezed his shoulder. "He'll be back. Now come on. We've got to clean Uncle Gavin's room. You can help me dust before I scrub. I'll let you use the feather duster."

He shook off her hand. "Dust makes me sneeze. I'll watch my video."

Lord, Tara thought, her child was turning into a couch potato. Or would be, if she had a couch. Grady was right about the fence. Blast him.

"Nobody ever died of sneezing," she said and took Del by the hand. She started to lead him to the west wing. He tried to resist.

"I might be the first." He let out a loud, dramatic, and completely manufactured, sneeze.

Tara was unimpressed, but she was curious. "What did you want to tell Grady?"

Del's face went more stubborn than before. "It's a secret. Just between guys."

BRET SCOWLED WHEN JONAH came in from the stable. He'd hoped his son had eaten and would be gone until noon at least. But Jonah went to the counter and poured himself a cup of coffee. "I'm starved," he said. "I didn't have any breakfast."

"Then you better start cooking. I can't," Bret said. He didn't mean it unkindly; it was the truth, pure and simple.

Jonah sipped the coffee and grimaced. "This tastes like mud."

"I can't help it. Why can't J.T. have a plain, old-fashioned coffeepot? That thing looks like it belongs to Flash Gordon."

Jonah squinted at the machine and coffee can on the marble counter. "Dad, you used espresso coffee. What are you doing in here, anyway?"

Bret glowered at the dishwasher. "Trying to figure out how this blamed thing starts."

Jonah sighed and stepped to his father's side. "I'd try hitting the button marked Start." He pushed it, and immediately the panel lights glowed red and a swishing noise began.

"It has all those—those controls and everything," Bret said defensively.

"Mrs. Gilligan probably has them all set. How is she?"

"She's sleeping like a baby. Nate gave her enough pills to knock out a horse."

Jonah rummaged in the cupboard, found a box of cereal and filled a bowl. He got the milk and poured it over the cereal. He began to eat standing up. "When's the other one coming? The niece or whatever?"

"How do I know? Maybe she's a figment of an opium dream."

Jonah tried another sip of coffee, made a face and pushed the mug away. "When do you take Mrs. Gilligan to see Nate? Maybe she's really not hurt all that bad."

"I've already done it." Bret opened the freezer and stared into it helplessly. "He won't change his mind. Six weeks of bed rest. My God, look at this stuff. She's marked everything in code. How'm I supposed to know what's what?"

Jonah shrugged. "What are you looking for?"

Bret kept staring fiercely at the freezer packages. They all had cryptic marks on them, as if Mrs. Gilligan used a private alphabet. "I'm looking for lunch. Supper."

"Try peanut butter." Jonah finished his cereal and poured another bowl. "That's why God made it. For men who can't cook."

Bret closed the freezer door in defeat.

"Have you heard from Lang yet?" Jonah asked.

Bret shook his head. He feared Lang was going to go back to his pretty little nitwit of a wife. He feared it because he believed the marriage was hopeless. He knew they would just break up again. She was wrong for him, just wrong as hell.

He remembered Tara Hastings from·last night. Now *there* was a woman, Bret thought. A woman of strength, character and good looks. By God, if he were twenty years younger, he might go after her himself…

The idea not only startled, but shamed him. It was wrong for him to think such thoughts.

He turned to the cupboards and opened one, pretending to search for sustenance beyond peanut butter. He looked at the perfectly lined rows of cans and frowned.

"Good Lord, what's this? Cream of celery soup? Who'd eat such stuff? She's got a dozen cans of it. And a dozen of mushroom soup. *Ecch.* Cream of asparagus? I've never touched any of this glop in my life."

Jonah's voice was sardonic. "Yes, you have. She puts it in casseroles and stuff. You've eaten it over and over."

Bret refused to believe it. "Bah." He opened another cupboard.

"Dad?"

Bret saw approximately a hundred cans of beans, some suspiciously foreign. What in hell were canelli beans? These alien beans put him in a worse temper. "What?"

"There're *suds* coming out of the dishwasher. Something's wrong."

Bret spun around. Thick white froth oozed from the edges of the dishwasher's door. It was as if the machine had gone rabid and its square mouth was foaming.

He swore and opened the door. All he could see was more foam. It bulged out of the dishwasher and spilled across the tiles. He swore again and rummaged for a towel. He found only a small, ineffectual one embroidered with bluebirds.

A knock sounded at the door. He hardly heard it. Suds inched across the floor, and he felt like the Sorcerer's Apprentice, confronting a rising tide he couldn't control.

"I'll get it," Jonah muttered, gingerly making his way around the creeping suds. He swung open the door.

Bret heard a woman's voice say, "Hello. I'm Rhonda Cole. I'm Millie Gilligan's niece. She asked me to help you out while—"

She stopped. She must have seen the flood bubbling out of the dishwasher.

"I guess I came just in time." She laughed. It was such a throaty, rich laugh that Bret looked up in surprise.

She stood in the doorway, a short, voluptuous woman in her forties. Her hair was light-brown and fell in soft waves halfway to her shoulders. Her eyes twinkled with good-natured merriment and were as green as glass.

Bret McKinney met her gaze as the soap suds stole around his booted feet. She smiled what must have been the sweetest smile in Texas.

And he thought, *This is the woman coming to stay with us?*

Omigod. Oh. My. God.

CHAPTER TEN

TARA HAD PLANNED TO AVOID GRADY. She found she couldn't.

As soon as he came back from town and Del heard about the fencing, he was bewitched—especially when he learned Grady had rented a portable cement mixer. Del itched to be near this marvel.

Grady had carried the cans of paint inside and was about to unload the fencing. Del wanted to follow, his heart was set on it. He tugged at the hem of Tara's shirt. "Can I? Can I go with Grady?"

Grady kept his face innocent, but his eyes challenged her. He made clear that his interest in her was intense—and stubborn.

But she also saw a disconcerting kindness in his look. It was as if beneath the teasing and innuendo, there was true concern. That confused her even more. She was torn, but she hated to forbid Del to join him. The boy was excited, and, what's more, he wanted to be outside.

"All right," she said. "As long as you mind and don't make a nuisance of yourself."

"He won't be any trouble." Grady kept his eyes on hers. She felt a feminine tremble deep within her body.

"If he is, send him back inside."

He pushed the brim of his hat up in a lighthearted salute and grinned, nodding his agreement. "Your wish is my command." Her heart pounded, and the inner tremble shook harder.

"Come on, champ," he said to Del. He went out the back

door, and Del and Lono followed him as if they'd been born to do so.

All morning long, Tara found herself stealing glances outside. She'd opened the windows of the west wing so that the walls would dry faster.

A warm breeze wafted in from the yard. When the rumble of the cement mixer quieted, she heard snatches of conversation between the man and boy.

Her ears pricked up when Del said earnestly, "I told Mom you and I are buddies."

"I'd be proud to be your buddy." Grady's drawl was kindly. The sound of it made her feel as if butterflies danced along her backbone.

Del spoke again. "Want to shake on it?"

"Sure, champ. Glad to."

She peered out and saw Grady kneel on one knee. His thigh muscles flexed, straining the tight denim of his jeans. Solemnly he shook Del's hand. There was no mockery in the gesture. He wasn't condescending or merely humoring him. His way was serious, man to man. *Damn. Why does he have to be so good with my son?*

She moved into the west office and was dusting when she heard Del ask a question that made her cringe. "How come you don't have a little boy?"

She found herself holding her breath, listening intently for the answer.

"I haven't got a wife."

"Why not?"

"I guess I never met the right lady."

"Oh." Silence. Then Del's voice again. "My mom's a lady."

"She certainly is."

"You said she was pretty."

"She is. Mighty pretty."

"Well—" a moment of hesitation "—she doesn't have a husband anymore. He went away."

Tara squeezed her eyes shut, gritting her teeth. She

wanted to lean out the window and cry, "Del, no!" But she couldn't do that. It would only prove that she'd been eavesdropping. She changed her wish to a prayer.

Please, please, God, don't let him say any more.

Del plunged on. "And I don't have a dad. Maybe you could be—"

Grady cut him off. "I don't think you should talk like this, champ."

"Why? See, he left us. But you could be my—"

"Talk like that might embarrass your mom." Grady's tone was firm. Tara started breathing again.

"Why?" Del demanded.

"It's personal."

"What's 'personal' mean?"

"Private stuff about your family. You don't talk about it with other people."

"But we're buddies," Del protested.

"Right. So we have to stick to the gentleman's code."

"What gentleman? What coat?"

"Gentleman's *code*. It's like a set of rules so you're always polite. You want to be one of the good guys, don't you?"

"Yes. Are you a gentleman?"

This time it was Grady who was silent for a moment. "I'm trying to be.

"Let's talk about something else. Have I told you about the bull that stuck his horn into me?"

"Wow! A big bull?"

"Way too big. Want to see the scar?"

Blessing Grady for once, Tara opened her eyes and edged again to the window. He'd stripped off his work shirt and hung it on a fence pole. Now he pushed up the right sleeve of his T-shirt to bare his shoulder. A ragged scar gleamed like a pale epaulette on the hard, brown flesh.

Del gazed up, his face radiant with hero worship. "When I grow up I'm gonna be just like you."

Grady's expression went serious. "Thanks, champ. Thanks a lot."

BRET KNEW IMMEDIATELY that Rhonda Cole was no ordinary woman. Her first glimpse inside the house had shown her the kitchen floor disappearing under a sea of suds.

She hadn't hesitated. She'd kicked her shoes off on the porch's welcome mat, rolled up her jeans and shirtsleeves and taken charge. She switched off the dishwasher and asked Bret where she could find a mop, a pail and old towels.

Of course, Bret didn't know. She gave an understanding smile that made her nose crinkle. "That's all right," she said and located everything herself—how? Superior logic? Woman's intuition? Magic?

When the floor was mopped and the dishwasher bailed, she dried her hands on a paper towel and offered him one to do the same. Then she thrust out her hand. "Like I said, I'm Rhonda Cole. Millie's niece. She asked me to come help."

Her hand was plump and warm and soft. That was how Rhonda seemed all over: plump and warm and invitingly soft. She was a bit heavy-set, but on her it looked just fine.

Her face was kindly and pretty. Although she must have been in her mid-forties, she hadn't a wrinkle. Her skin was flawless, smooth as cream.

The green eyes that made Millie Gilligan look like a sorceress were, in this woman's face, gently merry. She had an engaging mouth, full and wide, and when she smiled, dimples winked in her cheeks.

She said, "And you'd be Mr. B. McKinney?"

"Bret McKinney. Bret." Ruefully he gazed at the damp floor and the gaping dishwasher, which still had fangs of suds in its mouth. "This isn't the best introduction, I'm afraid."

She laughed. "Don't even think about it. I'll wager you

put in the wrong soap, that's all. It happens to folks all the time.''

"I'd offer you a cup of coffee." He found it strangely hard to get the words out. "But I didn't do too well at that this morning, either.''

She turned toward the counter. "Ah." Her dimples appeared. "I see your problem. I'll make you a fresh pot.''

She began rinsing out the coffeemaker. Though still barefoot, she didn't seem self-conscious. Her rolled up jeans revealed slender ankles and smooth, sturdy calves.

Her behind was generous, but nicely so. She wore a green plaid cotton shirt and a green sweater vest. Her bosom was also generous, *very* nicely so. Her every moment was quick and sure. The coffeemaker from outer space held no mysteries for her.

This was a woman who, by God, knew how to *do* things.

Who would have thought the strange, wizened Mrs. Gilligan would have such a full-bodied and sweet-natured niece?

Jonah had disappeared, but Bret hardly noticed. He said, "Your aunt's sleeping. It's what the doctor thought—a herniated disk.''

Rhonda clucked in sympathy. "Ah. The poor woman. She's done it before. It'll take her a while to mend. She's such a little bit of a thing.''

Bret felt another surge of gallantry. "She's welcome to stay here. And so are you, of course.''

"Well, I don't know about that." Her expression went shy and she ducked her head. "Millie mentioned it, but I'm not sure. I have a little apartment in Fredericksburg. I can drive back and forth.''

Bret feared that he'd barged over some line of impropriety. For the first time in years, he blushed. "Excuse me—I thought your aunt said—''

A frown creased her smooth brow. "On the other hand, she's modest. She'd rather have a woman taking care of her personal needs. If she has to get up in the night. Things like that. You know.''

''Er—yes.'' So far Millie Gilligan had been able to get to the bathroom and back by herself, although Bret knew it must pain her. He had a horrific vision that, one of these times, she would be unable to rise from the commode, and he would have to rescue her. Even thinking of it made his face get redder.

Rhonda gave him a smile of understanding that crinkled her nose again. ''We'll play it by ear.'' She glanced down at her feet. ''Goodness. I better get my shoes on. I'll check on Millie and then get to work.''

Yet she paused a moment and raised her eyes to his. ''Millie said you're a good man. That you've treated her mighty fine. I appreciate your kindness. A lot of people think she's—you know—eccentric. But she's a good soul. I'm glad she found such a compassionate family.''

Bret was struck speechless.

She smiled her bashful smile and said, ''I think compassion is just about the most important quality a person can have. Don't you?''

''Oh, yes,'' Bret managed to utter. ''Absolutely. Yes.''

TARA MOVED FROM ROOM TO ROOM, sweeping, dusting and airing closets. She heard Del laughing and, curious, peeped out a window. Grady, too, was chuckling. Her heart knotted strangely at the sight.

Then Grady looked up at the sky, grimacing and wiping his neck. The sun, high in the sky now, blazed down. The back of Grady's T-shirt was damp and clung like a second skin to his back.

Lono stretched out in the sun panting, his ears laid back. Del, still giggling, crouched on the ground and poked in the grass with a stick. Grady took off his hat and hung it on the same post as his work shirt. He lifted his T-shirt and pulled it off, baring his upper body.

Oh, why did he have to do that? Tara sucked in her breath.

He had an absolutely gorgeous upper torso: wide shoulders, a hard chest and sculpted abs. Dark hair, shaped like a pair of wings, shadowed his chest and ran in a narrowing stripe downward, disappearing into jeans so low-slung they showed his navel.

He put his Stetson back on, pulling it low to shade his eyes. He inserted a white post into a corner hole, squaring and plumbing it. His biceps bulged and the muscles in his back shifted in a display of power.

She clenched her hands, wondering what it would be like to clasp those shoulders. To feel the ridge of his scar beneath her fingertips, to touch the moisture of his film of sweat.

Stop thinking like that. Don't look at him any longer.

Quickly Tara turned from the window. But the image of his half-naked body wouldn't go away, nor would it leave her in peace.

Ha, ha, ha, sneered biology.

BRET MADE A PRETENSE OF WORKING in his office, but he was conscious of Rhonda Cole coming, going, moving quietly about the house. He heard the murmur of feminine voices coming from Mrs. Gilligan's room; the older woman must have awakened. He no longer worried about her. He had a peaceful sense that, from here on out, Rhonda would take care of things.

Later, he heard the opening and shutting of kitchen cupboards. He smelled the delicious aroma of something frying, bacon? Onions?

She knocked at his open office door. "Lunch is ready. Do you want me to bring you a tray or would you rather eat in the kitchen?"

Bret looked at her, appreciating her manner, the fetching combination of friendliness and diffidence. He also appreciated her soft curves.

"Will you be eating in the kitchen?" He tried to keep from sounding foolishly hopeful that she would.

"I'm taking a tray in to Millie. I'll eat with her."

"Oh." Why should he feel disappointed? "I'll just have it in here."

"Whatever you like."

She brought him a tray with a beautiful omelet. It was fluffy, golden and studded with bits of bacon, pepper and onion. There was a piece of Texas toast, the butter still melting into it, and a mug of black coffee. There was flatware perfectly arranged on a white napkin.

"Nothing fancy," she apologized, setting the tray on his desk. "Today I'm just kind of making it up as I go along."

He thanked her and stole a look at her as she left the room. She seemed to be making it up mighty well. If only she could cook half as fine as little Millie Gilligan. That, he thought with a sigh, was too much to hope for. He unfolded his napkin and speared a forkful of omelet.

He tasted it and had something akin to a divine experience. Her cooking wasn't half as good as Mrs. Gilligan's. It was better.

He was astonished to find tears rising in his eyes. He found himself actually bowing his head in humility. *Dear God,* he thought, blinking back the tears. *I don't deserve this. I'm not a good enough man to deserve this.*

TARA MADE DEL COME INSIDE for lunch. Impatient at being separated from Grady, he gulped down his food. "Don't gobble," she cautioned.

"We got men stuff to do," he told her. He still gobbled, but more slowly.

She stifled a sigh and managed to get him to wash his hands. Then he burst back out the door to rejoin Grady and the wonders of cement.

Shaking her head, she began to clean the lunch dishes. As soon as she finished, she headed for Del's room to gather up his sheets and dirty clothes for the laundry.

But before she reached the hall, the phone rang. She was cheered by the thought it might be Lynn.

"Hello, there," a man's raspy voice growled. "I got your letter. Did you think you'd get away with this? You won't. This is war."

A chill seized Tara, a cold, bone-deep dread. She knew that bullying voice too well: Burleigh Hastings. Tara had prayed for a respite from Burleigh, but here the man was already, seething with spite and bellicose with threat. Her muscles stiffened.

"Did you think you could take my grandson and just run off like this?" Burleigh hissed. "Steal off like a thief, kidnapping him to Texas?"

"I didn't kidnap him." Tara spoke from between clenched teeth. "I have custody of him, and I moved out of state to a new job."

"You didn't ask my permission," Burleigh accused. "You didn't inform me until it was done. He's my grandson. You violated my rights. You did this behind my back. You *will* pay. You will pay *dearly*."

Tara put her hand to her forehead. Burleigh was in one of his imperial rages. They were cold and poisonous, meant to frighten his opponent into submission.

"I sent the letter from California," countered Tara. "I told you we were moving."

"You knew how long it'd take to reach me, you scheming bitch. While I'm over here in this hellhole, you skip California with *my* grandson."

Tara closed her eyes, trying to calm herself. "Burleigh, I'm sorry it happened that way. But I needed to take this job. We're here, and we're staying here."

"You didn't even give me a phone number—and no address but a rural route. You're not only a sneak, you're vengeful. And stupid. Did you think you could keep me from finding out this number?" He laughed unpleasantly. "Did you think you'd outsmart *me?* Did you?"

"I didn't have a phone yet when I wrote the letter. That rural route *is* our address."

"When I get back to the states, I'm taking you to court," Burleigh threatened. "Neither you nor Sid is fit to raise that child. I won't just have visitation rights. I'll get custody."

Burleigh had threatened such things before, and it was always insufferable. Tara's temper flared. "You can't take him. No court in the land would let you have him."

"I'll prove you're unfit," Burleigh said with deadly calm. "You broke his arm. There are hospital records."

This was a new charge from Burleigh, and so unfair that Tara saw a red mist before her eyes. "He fell off his pony and broke his arm."

"You were negligent. You let him get hurt. He could have been killed."

"It was an accident," Tara shot back. Del had been riding the pony in the outdoor ring. A gust of wind sent a sheet of newspaper flapping over the rail and into the pony's face. Blinded and frightened, it reared, and Del had lost his seat. He'd gotten a hairline fracture, a break that quickly healed.

"You bloodied his nose more than once."

"He fell down the front stairs, Burleigh. He fell out of a tree. He ran into a stall door. He's a *boy,* for God's sake."

"That's your story. I'll get witnesses. I'll have you in court. This is the last straw. I'll teach you to come between me and that boy. You're *unfit.*"

"This is insane," Tara cried. "I won't listen to this."

"You're negligent. You consort with thugs and drug-users. You keep dangerous company."

"I had special needs students," Tara retorted with passion. "I wasn't consorting. I was teaching, dammit."

"You deliberately associated with people with criminal records and mental problems. You tore that child from where he's always lived and dragged him to some godforsaken place that probably doesn't even have a private school or decent medical care.

"I could provide him with the best of everything. You

took him there to keep me from helping him and to cheat me out of my visitation rights. I'll prove you're vindictive, unfit and a liar. I'll prove you're a danger and—''

Tara slammed the phone down and yanked the plug from the wall. Her heart hammered so hard that it hurt, and she couldn't get her breath.

Burleigh had been blustering and overbearing before, but never as hateful as this. Rationally she knew that Burleigh could never get custody of Del, she also knew he could make endless trouble. He could twist truths and spew lies. He was rich enough to buy witnesses. He could smear her with accusations, and even false accusations could do painful damage.

Tara sank into the desk chair and put her head in her hands. Burleigh had shaken her so badly she felt faint.

THE REST OF THE AFTERNOON, she kept going to the window to check on Del. She feasted on the sight of him. She barely noticed Grady, and she didn't want to. An irrational whisper of paranoia told her that perhaps she was being punished for desires and dreams that had to do with anything other than her son.

She went to Del's room, forcing herself to keep working, not to let Burleigh stymie her. But in Del's room, she found something puzzling.

Beneath his bed was a small, ordinary matchbox. It sent a dart of fear into her. Was he playing with matches? What if he started a fire? Lord, he could hurt himself, burn the house down. And what utter hell Burleigh would raise…

She drew the matchbox out and opened it. In it was a packet of salt, the sort that restaurants provide. Perplexed, she put it in her shirt pocket, meaning to ask him about it. Shortly she found a second, identical matchbox under the dresser beside his door. A third was on the floor of his closet behind his hamper. A fourth was on his windowsill, hidden behind a curtain. Each contained a packet of salt.

Tara frowned, tucking them all into her pocket with the

first. What was Del thinking? What strange notions flourished in the minds of children? Where had he got the salt, and what had he done with the matches?

It was one more thing to worry her. Should she confront Del now, or wait until she was calmer? Burleigh's call had rattled her until she couldn't think straight.

THE EARLY AFTERNOON SUNLIGHT glowed down on Grady's bare back, its heat pleasant across his skin. The breeze carried the aroma of the late-blooming bee-bushes up the slope.

Grady's task was more than half done; the fence's white posts and bottom rails were almost all installed. He'd built a crude support for the framework from scrap as he went.

He snapped the last lower rail into place, and started propping it with old boards he'd brought from the scrap heap. His muscles surged and swelled to the work; he liked the feel of blood pumping hard through his veins.

The kid, worn out, no longer played at helping. Del sat beside the wheelbarrow of scrap, running a toy car up and down an old two-by-four. Since morning he'd been out in the open air, and he'd finally run out of energy. He yawned.

Grady figured Tara would be along any minute to fetch the boy inside to take a nap. She'd stayed out of sight since lunchtime, but he knew she would be keeping an eye on Del. He glanced toward the house to see if he could catch a glimpse of her.

What all did she do in there? Did she ever stop working? Did she think about him as much as he thought about her?

A trickle of sweat ran down his temple. He took his hat off, hung it on the corner post and wiped his forearm across his eyes.

Just as he did so, Del let out a shriek. He began to cry, a frightened and desperate sound. *He's hurt.* Grady whirled. Del had tried to pull another board from the wheelbarrow, although Grady had warned him not to.

Now the boy sat, one hand clutched to his forehead and

covering his eye. A trickle of blood welled from between his fingers.

Alarmed, Grady was at Del's side in a flash. He knelt beside him and made him move his hand. Grady swore under his breath.

The board must have slid from the wheelbarrow and struck the boy in the forehead. Del had a red scrape that bled, but the worst part was a long splinter embedded half an inch above his eyebrow.

"The board *bit* me," Del said between sobs.

"It's a splinter, pal. I told you not to touch those boards."

"I—I just wanted one more. To make another r-r-road for my c-c-car."

He blinked against the blood dripping into his eye. Grady dug his handkerchief out of his back pocket and gently wiped the blood away.

Then Tara was flying out of the house, the screen door slamming behind her. She ran to Grady and Del, her face pale. "What's wrong? Is it his eye? Not his eye—oh, *not* his eye—my God—what?"

She dropped to her knees beside the boy, taking his face between her hands. "Splinter in his forehead," muttered Grady. "His eye's fine. Hold on, champ. We'll take care of you."

Del's mouth quivered and tears spilled down his cheeks. He started to grope at his forehead. "It *hurts.*"

Tara seized his hand so he wouldn't force the splinter deeper, and she didn't seem to notice that her knuckles grazed Grady's. She winced as she examined the wound. "Oh, *honey.* Oh, my love."

Del closed his eyes and cried harder. The splinter, brown and ragged, was at least an inch long. Fully a third of it was embedded in the skin over his eyebrow. Grady dabbed the remaining blood from the scrape and mentally damned himself for taking his eyes off the boy for a minute.

"Take it out," Del pleaded.

Tara, holding his hand, leaned forward and kissed his

tearstained cheek. "Love, we'll have to go inside and use the tweezers. I'm sorry."

She tried to pick him up, but Del struggled to escape her. The idea of the tweezers scared him. Grady rose to his feet, lifting the boy. Tara reached for him, but she looked too shaken to carry him.

"I've got him," Grady told her. "Where to?"

"The kitchen. Oh, honey, don't cry. We'll get you fixed up, I promise."

But Del kept sobbing, and Grady could see how the child's pain and helplessness twisted her heart. "Come on, kid." He made his voice both firm and gentle. "We'll have you patched up in no time."

Del pressed the unwounded side of his face against Grady's scarred shoulder. Grady rubbed the kid's back. The bones felt small and fragile beneath his hand. "There, there. You'll be okay."

Grady carried him into the kitchen and to the sink. He held him while Tara washed the scrape as best she could. Grady helped her dry it, then set Del on a kitchen chair. Lono had slipped in with them and stood staring up at them, whining in sympathy.

Grady crouched beside the boy, holding him by the upper arms and talking to him as Tara raced into the bathroom. She came scurrying back with the first-aid kit and almost stumbled in her haste.

She looked in shock. Her hair had come undone and spilled around her bloodless face. She washed her hands frantically, then switched on a front gas burner. When Del whimpered and gave a shaky sob, her body stiffened as if she'd been shot.

Grady watched Tara fumble in the first-aid kit until she found a long, silvery needle. She tried to hold its point in the flame, but her fingers shook too badly.

Grady went to her side and moved against her so that she yielded her place to him. He gestured for her to turn the needle over to him. "You sit at the table with him. I'll do this. My hands are steadier."

She went to the chair, took her son into her arms and sat down, hugging him tightly to her. She leaned her cheek against his, and she looked so disconsolate at the boy's hurt that she seemed more wounded than he was.

Grady slipped her a concerned glance as he washed his hands. She clung to Del, her body rocking back and forth. Grady was surprised and puzzled; she didn't seem the sort to come apart in a simple crisis. Far from it. A swell of protectiveness swept over him. It was so strong that it astonished him. *My God,* he thought. He looked away and steadied himself.

He cleaned the soot from the needle, then pulled a chair up in front of Del. He held the needle in his right hand and steadied Del's head with the other. Tara clamped her lips together in shared pain.

Grady looked into the boy's eyes. "I'm sorry, champ. This'll hurt a little. I'll make it fast."

Then his eyes locked with Tara's. *Hold him tight,* he tried to say to her silently. *It'll be harder on him if he fights it.*

He saw her struggle against her own desire to protect her child from hurt of any kind. She held him fast and gripped his chin to keep his face still. Her cold fingers were pressed beside Grady's strong, sure ones.

Frowning in concentration, Grady loosened the splinter.

"No!" Del tried to wriggle free, Tara hugged him closer. Lono whined again, more sharply.

Grady's motions were precise and economical. "This is sort of how you get a tattoo. Pretend you're getting a tattoo."

"I don't want a tattoo," Del wailed. Tara grimaced. Grady picked up the tweezers and with one deft movement, drew out the small spear of wood.

He whistled. "That's a lunker. You're mighty brave."

Del blinked back tears, his shoulders slumping with released tension. "I am? But I cried."

"Brave? Absolutely. I'd have cried myself." Grady held the splinter up, admiring it, then set it aside. "You might want to save this. Put it in a box so you can show it to people if they don't believe how big it was."

He put his hands under Del's armpits. "Come on. Let's wash it again. Don't want any germs camping out in there."

He carried Del back to the sink. Tara stayed close by his side, her shoulder and hands sometimes brushing Grady's as she tried to help. Grady tried to ignore how her touch made the nerves blaze up and down his arm.

"Antiseptic," he said tonelessly.

"Right," Tara breathed. "I'll do it."

Grady took Del back to the table and sat down, settling the boy on his lap. "Okay, let's wipe out those germs for good." Lono, sensing the worst was over, wagged his tail.

Still tremulous, Tara sat down and took out the antiseptic. She applied it to the puncture and the scrape then gave Del a cotton ball to hold on the wound. "It may still bleed a little. That's all right. The blood helps clean it. And now, I think you should lie down and rest."

"Don't want to," Del sniffled. But already his eyelids were fluttering with fatigue. He was exhausted, and there was no real fight left in him.

"I'll carry him," Grady said. "Lead the way."

She nodded and went to Del's bedroom. Grady followed, the boy in his arms. Tara drew back the bedspread, plumped the pillow.

Grady lowered Del to the bed and watched as Tara unlaced his shoes and took them off. "Lie down now." Del started to object, but yawned instead. He stretched out with a sigh. Lono leaped up beside him.

"I'll stay with him until he's asleep." Stroking the boy's hair, Tara looked up at Grady. Such complexity swam in her eyes it half dizzied him. He felt like a man at the edge of a precipice. He struggled to step back from it.

"Sure." He turned to go. He paused in the doorway and

looked over his shoulder. Lono stretched out protectively beside the boy, his chin on his paws.

As for Tara, she didn't look at Grady at all. She had eyes only for her son.

CHAPTER ELEVEN

GRADY WENT BACK OUTSIDE to finish propping the fence.

How Tara had acted made no sense to him. All his instincts told him she was strong. But seeing her kid with a splinter had turned her to jelly. Anybody who worked with horses saw injuries to humans and animals all the time. Nobody queasy about blood could handle such a job. It was impossible.

What had gone on in her head? Her heart? This couldn't be her usual reaction. Del had told him about breaking his arm and proudly said his mother "knew just what to do." She'd splinted the fracture, put a cold compress on it and driven him to the emergency ward. "I wasn't scared 'cause Mom wasn't scared."

But this afternoon, she'd been terrified. Why? Head wounds bled profusely, and Grady'd been wiping the boy's eye with a handkerchief already scarlet with blood. That was the first thing Tara saw, and she'd feared he'd injured his eye—that was natural.

But quickly she'd seen his eyes were fine, that the problem was only a splinter. A big one, but still just a splinter. Boys got dozens of splinters in the course of growing up. She had to know that.

So why had she nearly come undone? What brought on this baffling change in her? *Something else must have happened.*

He shook his head. She'd been alone in the house. But it was hard to be really alone in this technological age. She had a telephone. She had a little computer so she could probably get e-mail.

He reckoned she'd got a message, and it had shaken her badly. He remembered that Del had said something vague about a troubling grandfather. "My dad's got a dad, but he's far away. We hope he doesn't come back. He gives me presents, but he scares me. He's mean to Mom."

"Scares you how?" Grady had probed. "How's he mean?"

"Just…scary and mean," Del had answered. "Want to see the scar on my knee? I fell on a piece of glass. I got a *stitch.*"

Grady had asked no more. The kid clearly didn't want to talk about the old man. But Grady could add two and two. He guessed the grandfather was capable of harassing Tara. He doubted if she'd tell him, but Lynn might know something. He didn't like to pry, but this was different. When something bothered Tara that deeply, he took it personally.

After he'd finished propping the fence, he carried the tarps inside. Going back for the painting supplies, he passed Del's room. The door was ajar, and Grady looked inside.

Tara lay curled on the bed, drowsing, one arm thrown over Del—even in sleep she protected her son. Grady had meant only to take a casual look, but the sight of her stopped him. She was so lovely. Her hair spilled around her face, a wonder of brown and red and gold.

Her legs were bent at the knee, and he marveled at their slimness and their length. The swell of her hips formed such a sweet curve, and beneath the thin fabric of her shirt, he could see the shape of her breasts.

She sighed in her sleep, and the sigh made her breasts shift. He swallowed hard. Had she been conscious of how often she'd touched him when they were tending Del? He didn't think so.

But he knew; he'd been hypersensitive to her nearness. Each time their arms met, their fingers brushed together, awareness had pricked him like a stab of fire. At one point, her loosened hair had skimmed his naked shoulder like a kiss of silk. He could still feel it, a kind of sensual ghost, tickling on his bare skin.

He had never seen her as vulnerable as she had been with her child hurt. Something wrenched within him, a primal urge to guard them both.

Sleeping beauty, he thought and wondered what would happen if he kissed her the way she needed to be kissed. He gritted his teeth, knowing he shouldn't be looking at her this way. He forced himself to stop, to move away from temptation.

WHEN TARA WOKE, HER EYES snapped open in alarm. Good Lord, she'd wasted time! She sat up in bed, quietly, so as not to disturb Del. She glanced at her watch and was appalled to see that she'd lost half an hour.

She rose and left the room, keeping Del's door ajar so she could hear him when he woke. She hurried to the kitchen to put away the first-aid kit and get back to business.

Preoccupied, she almost ran into Grady, who stood by the counter. She came so close to the lean expanse of his chest, she could feel his body heat, inhale the scent of his fresh sweat.

Startled, she sprang backward. The frail composure she'd just regained spun away; she was like a swimmer overwhelmed by an unexpected wave.

She'd forgotten Grady was stripped to the waist. Now, her guard down, his half-nakedness caught her unprepared.

"You're still here?" She realized her words, pinched by nervousness, sounded more like an accusation than a question.

He was cleaning the tweezers with an alcohol wipe. For the first time she realized he was hatless. A lock of hair slanted across his forehead.

He gave her a bemused sideways glance. He placed the tweezers in the first-aid kit and snapped the lid shut with a metallic *click.*

"I'm letting the cement set. I put down the tarps in your brother's room and taped the trim. The walls are dry enough to paint. I was going to check on the cement. On the way back out, I noticed this."

He tapped the first-aid kit with his knuckle. "Thought I'd help pick up."

She was conscious of the narrow hips and sleek waist, the winglike marking of dark hair on his chest. She didn't mean to notice him this way, God knew, but she couldn't help it.

He leaned toward her, a frown line deepening between his brows. "Are you all right?"

She pushed her hand through her hair. She turned slightly, so her vision wouldn't be filled with the sight of him.

He seemed perfectly at ease being half-clothed. It must seem natural, even ordinary to him. But it didn't to her. For much of the day, she'd tried to ignore it. Now she could not.

He bent closer. "I said are you all right?" Concern tinged his low voice. She struggled not to be touched by it.

"I'm fine," she lied. She knew her resistance was especially weak now because of Burleigh's call and Del's accident. And because of her stupid dreams this morning. But no number of reasons could excuse how she felt and didn't want to feel.

"I didn't think you'd be the excitable sort." His tone stayed maddeningly gentle. "In an emergency."

"I'm generally not." This was true. She'd coped with accidents before, far more serious ones. She'd done it with calm and determined control. But today everything had been different.

Grady kept searching her face. "You're protective of him."

She shrugged and groped for her barrette, so she could gather her hair back. She couldn't find it; it must have come loose. She'd lost control of her hair, her thoughts, her urges, her common sense.

He said, "I mean, mothers are supposed to be protective. It comes with the territory."

Oh, hell—why couldn't he leave her alone? Why did he have to be like this, complicating her life when it was complicated enough?

She jerked up her chin defiantly. "Aren't you supposed to be working?"

It was a rude and condescending thing to say, and she said it with the cold, flicking sharpness of a razor.

He blinked at her tone, his body stiffening. He straightened, restoring the distance between them.

Her harshness shamed her. "I—I didn't mean that the way it sounded. We both need to get to work." It was an inadequate apology, but the best she could manage.

She reached to pick up the first-aid kit, but he laid his fingers lightly on her arm. The touch coursed through her like electricity. She jerked her head about to face him, her eyes flashing in challenge.

His face was serious, the frown still on his face. "Do you blame me for what happened to him out there? I told him not to play with those boards. But maybe I should have watched him closer. I guess I should have. I'm sorry."

His apology took her by surprise, sent her emotions skittering off in yet another direction. She looked into his eyes and was perplexed to see contrition.

"No," she breathed, looking away from him. "I don't blame you. No matter how closely you watch, accidents... can happen."

"I'll be more careful."

"Thank you." She wanted to add, *Thank you for helping me when my boy was hurt. You were so kind, so good, so much help. Thank you.*

But she couldn't get the words out. She shrugged as if there was really nothing more to say. He seemed to understand. He drew his hand back, but slowly. As if he didn't want to.

RELUCTANTLY GRADY LEFT TARA, went back outside. He told himself he should be glad to escape.

When she'd nearly run into him, all his senses went on high alert. He'd been aware of her with every atom of his being. He desired her, but he was concerned for her. Somehow his concern provoked her.

What was a man to make of such a woman?

And yet, he thought he was starting to figure it out, figure her out. In the meantime, he was perturbed in both mind and body. Work was the only cure—hard work. He picked his hat off the corner post and jammed it on his head as if it could stop him from thinking about her.

It didn't.

TARA HEARD HIM COME BACK INSIDE the house to paint Gavin's bedroom. She busied herself in the neighboring room that would be Gavin's office. She dusted it from top to bottom, cleaned the closet, then the built-in oak cabinets. Mice had nested in the cabinets, creating a mess.

Well, she'd mucked out horse stalls, so mouse dirt should be easy in comparison. She supposed she deserved an odious task to pay for her odious behavior to Grady.

The longer she worked, the worse she felt for snapping at him so haughtily. He hadn't been flirting with her or pursuing her. She'd nearly bumped into *him,* and had been as flustered as some adolescent in the throes of puppy love.

Worse, he'd tried to be kind. He'd even apologized for Del's injury when it wasn't his fault. And she hadn't thanked him properly for his help with Del. It was Grady, not she, who'd taken charge of the situation.

By the time the penance of mouse filth was finished, she was certain she should apologize. It was mid-afternoon. He would not be near her much longer. Tomorrow was Sunday, and she wouldn't see him. Monday, Gavin would arrive, and she would be safe.

She washed her hands and smoothed her hair into even more strict control. She'd pinned it back severely again. For a moment she wondered if she should put on a touch of lipstick. No. She wouldn't do a thing to make herself seem attractive. Not one thing.

She made her way down the hall. The house smelled of fresh paint and, with the windows open, clean country air. She paused at the doorway and rapped on the frame, briskly, formally.

Grady had his T-shirt back on, for which she was thankful. His back was to her, wide-shouldered and tapering down to his narrow cowboy's hips.

He cast her a look over his shoulder. "Do you need me for something?"

He didn't put a flirtatious spin on the words. She was grateful for that, too. "I just wanted to talk to you for a minute."

"Sure." He set the roller in the paint tray and turned to face her.

She'd chosen a warm, pale sand color for Gavin's bedroom, and Grady was already finishing the second wall. How did he *do* it? She'd never seen a man who could work so swiftly, yet cleanly.

"I can get this done today, then finish the fence," he said. "I wanted to cover that graffiti, too. I could stay late if you want."

The last thing she wanted was for him to stay late. It was hard enough being with him in broad daylight. Night was too—intimate.

"No," she said. "It can wait."

"I'd hate it to be the first thing your brother sees when he drives up." Grady shrugged one shoulder. "That's all."

"He knows about it. He's seen it before."

"It'd be nice if he didn't have to see it again."

"It can wait." She took a deep breath. "That's not what I wanted to talk about."

He raised an eyebrow in curiosity.

She exhaled between her teeth. She forced herself to keep

meeting his eyes. "I was very rude to you. I'm truly sorry. I had no right to speak to you that way."

He raised his chin, as if doubting what he heard.

"I mean it," she finished humbly. She dropped her gaze to the tarpaulin. "My acting that way was a sin of commission. I also made one of omission. I didn't thank you for all you did for Del. You were—very good with him. I was—pretty worthless, I'm afraid."

She pretended to be interested in the multicolored paint stains on the old tarp. He said, "Worthless? No. Not you. Upset, yes."

She made a gesture of impatience and frustration. "I didn't *used* to be this way. I mean it was just a sliver. A big one. But just a sliver."

"It looked worse than it was." Again the kindness in his voice surprised her.

"I've dealt with slivers before. And worse. With my students, every thing from crushed toes to broken noses. Horses? I've helped get them untangled from barbed wire. I've fixed their gashes, delivered their foals and drained their hematomas. Blood? I've seen buckets of it."

"It's different when it's your kid, I'd imagine."

Yes. Very different. She set her jaw and said, "I just can't stand to see him hurt. In any way." Her voice trembled when she said it, and she cursed herself for showing weakness.

"Life is going to hurt him," he said in the same quiet voice. "It hurts everybody, one way or another."

"Not the way that it's hurt him," she said, then clamped her lips tightly together.

"You mean his father?"

She nodded but could say no more. *God,* she thought, *if I talk about this, I'm going to cry. And I won't do that. I will not do that. I will not let him see me cry.*

"I—had an upsetting call right before Del got hurt," she managed to say. "Very upsetting. And when I saw him holding his eye and the blood, I thought—I thought the

worst. Look, I just wanted to tell you that I'm very grateful
to you. And I'm sorry that I didn't show it better.''

She wheeled around abruptly and left him standing there.
Her heart knocked in her chest. She went back to Gavin's
study and began to wipe marks from the wall. Her hands,
she was chagrined to see, were unsteady, and she still felt
tears smart her eyes.

Why did he have to be so nice about it all? Why couldn't
he have been his old smart-assed self?

And then, she nearly laughed. How ironic: when he was
bad, he was very, very bad. But when he was good, he was
impossible.

THE MORE TROUBLED GRADY WAS, the harder he worked.
He was working like the very devil.

He finished painting the walls in the master bed and bath
and strode outside, glad to escape into the open. The house
was so quiet that he could hear the soft sound the paint roller
made, the whisper of the paintbrush.

He could also hear Tara moving about: her light footsteps,
the hiss of a spray cleaner, the whisk of a broom, the splash
of water. A rustling here, a pattering there; all these phan-
tomlike noises reminded him too vividly that she was tan-
talizingly near.

Outside he breathed deeply, inhaling the fragrance of pine
tree and bee bush instead of the chemical scent of paint.
The sun was moving down the western sky. If he worked
hard and fast, he could get almost everything done.

He started work on the fence, trying to force Tara from
his mind. He snapped the crimped top rails into place. He
installed the steel supports in the corner posts, then filled
them with concrete. She stayed in his thoughts. He worked
more furiously.

It was her apology that did it. The sight of her fighting
tears had damned near undone him. For once, her lovely
eyes no longer seemed otherworldly. Their pain, their frustration had been so human it cracked his heart.

Once again he'd been bushwhacked by the contrary urges of protectiveness and desire.

He needed to call Lynn when he got home. Maybe even Cal, if he could track him down. He'd been right about Tara getting a message. Now he needed to find out if he was right about who had upset her so deeply.

THE SUN WAS BEGINNING ITS DESCENT toward dusk when Tara heard Grady's knock. She was in the kitchen, starting supper. Del was drying off from his bath.

Through the screen door she saw Grady. He'd slipped back into his work shirt but hadn't buttoned it. His T-shirt, showing from beneath, was smudged with dirt. Streaks of cement dust smeared the thighs of his jeans.

She moved to the screen door to unhook it. If he felt any fatigue, he didn't show it. He stood just as tall and straight as he had this morning.

His hat was pushed back at the same jaunty angle.

"Almost done out here. I'll soon be on my way." His tone was cheerful and friendly. It was as if the events of the afternoon had never happened.

But he couldn't be done. Was he back to his old self, teasing her? "Done? No. It's not possible."

She cast a skeptical glance past him into the backyard. She'd avoided looking out at him since her apology in the bedroom. Now she saw the fence rails and pickets in place. The fence stood shining and straight in the afternoon sunlight.

He smiled at her surprise. "I installed the post rebars in the end posts and put in the rest of the concrete. I can cap the pickets and posts later. But it's basically ready."

She was impressed in spite of herself. "It looks—wonderful. He'll love having a place to play."

"It'll do for a while. Is it okay if I come in? I'm pretty dirty. That cement mixer was harder to get back on the truck than get off. I'll take it back to the hardware store. They're open late tonight."

She nodded and opened the door. She edged back carefully, so that they would not touch each other. He reached into his back pocket and drew out a new padlock and key. He offered it to her. "I thought you might want this. To make sure he doesn't get the gate opened. I put it on your bill, too. I hope that wasn't out of bounds."

She held out her hand, which seemed small compared to his. He dropped the padlock into her palm, a hard, solid weight, warm from his touch.

"No," she breathed. "It wasn't out of bounds. It was very—" she didn't want to say *thoughtful;* it seemed too personal, so she lamely finished "—very forward-looking of you."

"Could I clean up? I tried to use the hose, but some of this needs soap and a real scrub." He glanced critically at his hand. Grime darkened the seams of his knuckles, framed his fingernails.

A spatter of cement spotted his jaw, just below his ear. She resisted the impulse to raise her hand and try to rub it away. He had a smear of dirt on his chin, right underneath his lower lip.

I know how his lips feel on mine. How they felt last night.

She stepped to a cupboard and distracted herself with searching for a bar of soap. She set it on the table. "Go ahead. I put a few towels in the west wing linen closet. You can use one of the bathrooms on Gavin's side."

"Thanks. Then I'll paint the trim in that master bedroom."

She felt her expression grow dubious. She looked at her watch. "It's late. It's almost four. You've done more than a day's work. Wash up, then I'll write you a check for the week and you can go home."

"I'd rather stay." He said it simply and with finality.

She stared up at him. The look in his eyes jolted her with its glint of hunger.

But his voice, calm and not flirtatious, belied his gaze.

"It's just that I don't like to leave a job undone. It's what you wanted done today."

She shut the cupboard door uneasily. "No. You got that fence up—"

"It was my idea to do that. I said I'd make time for everything. I can. His room was the first thing on your list. Let me get you back on schedule."

Uncertainty made her hesitate. "But you wouldn't get home until seven—or later."

He shrugged as if it hardly mattered. "They don't need me for anything. Let's get this done before your brother comes."

He started to pick up the soap and saw four match boxes ranged beside it. He gave her a questioning look. He seemed to wait for her to say something, but she had no idea why.

She said, "I found these hidden in Del's room. I thought he was playing with matches. I had visions of him burning the house down. That was when I was—upset. I need to ask him about them."

"But they don't have matches in them," Grady said. "They have little packages of salt."

She blinked, mystified. "How do *you* know?"

"I slipped 'em to him at the party last night."

She stared at him with greater puzzlement. "But why?"

He looked slightly chagrinned. "I asked him about the nightmares. He told me about the slime creatures. I saw that movie on TV. The way you get rid of slime creatures is salt. They won't come near salt."

"Oh…" It was all she could say. She looked at him as if seeing him clearly for the first time.

Grady said, "He wanted to keep it secret. Pride, I guess. Maybe he thought you'd laugh. But he said that it worked. No slime creatures last night. Sorry if it gave you a start. He never had any matches, if that's what worried you. I didn't mean to add to your troubles."

She could scarcely speak. "I—no. I should thank you. That was very thoughtful. What do you suppose…"

The question trailed off, but he seemed to understand it.

"I suppose you just could put the boxes back where you found them. Since they seem to work."

She stared first at them, then at him. She nodded.

He grabbed the bar of soap. "Thanks." He smiled.

The flash of his smile sent a frisson of pleasure shuddering through her.

But it was more than sensual pleasure. There was gratitude mixed with it, and admiration.

He turned and went down the hall, whistling in his carefree way.

THE MOON, just beginning to wane, hung midway to the zenith of the dark blue sky. Stars glittered, looking larger than they ever did in the city.

Grady pulled up to the ranch house of the Double C and saw a car he didn't recognize. It was a dark little Ford, an older model, but so well-maintained that it gleamed like new in the moonlight.

He didn't think much about it. His mind was on other things and in another place. In his wallet, in his back pocket, was a check from Tara.

He needed the money, God knew. But he hadn't liked taking it. It made it official: he was her hireling.

He wouldn't see her tomorrow. She and Del would be gone until evening. It would be a hell of a long Sunday. And a lonesome one.

He climbed the back stairs, shivering slightly. The temperature had plunged since moonrise. Maybe winter was truly beginning.

He knocked at the door. His father hadn't given him a key, and he hadn't asked for one. He jammed his hands into his pockets and hunched his shoulders against the cold. He waited. He knocked again.

At last the porch light flared on, and the door swung open. His father stepped back and waved him inside, but there was something almost grudging in the gesture. "We didn't hear you,'' Bret muttered. He was wiping soot from his hands with a paper towel. ''I was trying to help Rhonda get the damned fireplace to work.''

Grady cocked an eyebrow. ''Rhonda?''

At that moment a woman entered from the living room. She wasn't so much plump as she was very well-rounded. She gave Grady a smile that was both sweet and shy. Her brown hair was as soft and neat as the rest of her. Grady swept off his hat, because she seemed like that kind of lady.

Bret nodded in her direction. ''This is Rhonda Cole, Mrs. Gilligan's niece. She's helping us out. Rhonda, this is my oldest son, Grady.''

Her smile widened, making dimples twinkle in her cheeks. She stepped up to Grady and took his hand in a hearty shake. ''Pleased to meet you.''

Unlike most people, those words seemed to mean something to her and to be sincere. ''The pleasure's mine, ma'am,'' he said. He liked the look of her—warm and comfortable.

''I didn't know if you were coming home or not,'' Bret said, regarding Grady's dirty jeans and wrinkled shirt. ''Thought you might've gone out bar-hopping or something.''

''I worked late.''

''You've been working till *this* hour?'' Rhonda asked. ''Have you had any supper?''

''No, ma'am.''

''Well, let me rustle you up something,'' she said, going to the pantry.

''He can dig around and find something for himself,'' Bret said. ''He's a grown man. And you just finished putting the dishes away.''

''Oh, pshaw. It's no trouble. It's what I'm here for.'' She took an apron from its peg and tied it around her ample waist. She smiled at Grady. ''I'll have you something in a jiffy. While I'm at it, maybe you could help your father figure out that fireplace. I never saw anything like it.'' She shook her head in wonder.

Bret scrutinized Grady's soiled shirt and jeans. ''You ought to clean up.''

Rhonda laughed. ''My husband was a construction worker. I don't mind a little dirt from an honest day's work.''

''Let's see that fireplace,'' Grady said.

Bret led the way to the den. A little oak TV table was set up in front of the leather couch. The table held a white mug and a plate with cookies arranged on it.

Grady sniffed the air. ''I smell cider. Spiced cider.''

''I was in here reading *The Cattleman's Journal*,'' Bret said defensively. ''She brought me some cider and cookies. I didn't ask her to.''

He glowered at the fireplace. ''She said there was a chill in the air. She was right. She offered to start the fireplace. But she didn't know how. I think the damned thing's disconnected or something. There's no place to turn it on.''

Grady narrowed one eye and studied the offending fireplace. The grate held artificial logs with gas jets.

Bret grumbled, ''Who'd want a gas fire, anyhow? I don't know why J.T. doesn't have a real fireplace.''

Grady shrugged. ''Gas is cleaner. And faster to start.''

''It's not faster to start if you can't start it.''

Grady grinned, slow and wicked. He couldn't help it. ''This is a top-of-the-line fireplace. I've helped install a couple of these.''

''I wouldn't have one. I *like* throwing a log on a roaring fire. Well, Mr. Genius, how does it work?''

Grady walked to the media center. He studied the collection of remote controls that turned on the TV, the video players, the CD player. He picked up one and went to stand beside his father.

Bret looked at him in disbelief. ''You've got to be kidding.''

"Nope." Grady aimed the remote at the fireplace. "Behold my powers. Rise up, oh, fire."

He clicked the remote and cheerful flames leaped up, gold and blue and capering. Grady handed the remote to Bret. "Just push the buttons to create the conflagration of your choice."

"What a gimmick," Bret muttered, but he couldn't keep himself from playing with the remote.

Rhonda Cole came in. "I've set out some supper for you— Oh! You got it figured out. Millie *said* you were handy. Now you go eat. I'm taking some cider and cookies in to Millie."

Grady said, "How is Millie? Better, I hope."

Rhonda looked pleased that he'd asked. "She's getting along. She's got her little television and her books. And I try to keep her company."

She ushered Grady back into the kitchen, sat him down and poured him a cup of coffee. Then she took a tray from the counter and bustled out.

Grady took a bite of meatloaf. *Damn!* He couldn't believe it. He tasted the scalloped potatoes. This woman was every bit as good a cook as Millie Gilligan. It must run in the family's genes or something.

He ate hungrily, finishing with a piece of pumpkin pie. He rinsed his dishes off and put them in the dishwasher. He wandered down the hall and saw a strip of light from under Jonah's door. The kid stayed in every night, sitting at his computer pecking away on his dissertation. Grady didn't know how he stood it night after night.

At the far end, Millie Gilligan's door was ajar, and light spilled into the hall. Grady could hear the low sound of women's laughter. It gave him an odd pang.

He went into the pink, ruffled bedroom, stripped off his dirty clothes and stuffed them in the hamper. He took a shower in Jennifer's pink bathroom. Her shower curtain was pale pink with dark pink ponies dancing across it. He dried himself with a thick pink towel, slipped on a clean pair of jeans, then sat on the edge of the bed and started to shine his boots.

A knock sounded at his door. ''What?'' Grady answered, hoping it wasn't Rhonda Cole, because he didn't want to put on a shirt again.

''It's me. Jonah. Can I come in?''

''Sure enough, little bro. Come in and pull up the poufy-chair or whatever that thing is.''

Jonah entered with a shy grin. He wore jeans and an old University of Nebraska T-shirt. He flopped down on the chair to Jennifer's dressing table. He said, ''You know, I like seeing you with all this pink around you. I think it's your color.''

Grady cheerfully told him to perform an anatomical impossibility.

''I didn't know you were here until I heard the shower.'' Jonah crossed his arms and tilted the chair back on its hind legs. ''You work late?''

Grady pretended to concentrate on polishing his boot. ''Yeah. A lot to be done over there. Did Lang call today?''

''Nope.''

Grady wondered if Lang really was going to patch things up with Susie. ''Hmm,'' was all he said.

Jonah said, ''Did you meet Mrs. Gilligan's niece?''

''Yeah. Seems nice. Hell of a cook. Is she going to stay here? Live here, I mean?''

''She'll stay tonight and see how it works out. She brought a little suitcase. Mrs. Gilligan has one of those sofa things you can sleep on. A photon.''

''A futon,'' Grady corrected and kept polishing. ''A photon is a subatomic particle. You ought to know that. You're the one with the college education.''

''I know cattle. I don't know furniture or physics. But I know another thing.''

''What?'' Grady put down his boot and picked up the other one.

Jonah said, "I think Dad's taken with her. With this Rhonda."

Grady looked up and stared at his brother. His dark brows drew together. *"What?"*

"He's taken with her. And you know what?"

"What?" Grady asked warily.

"I think it's good." Jonah nodded and gazed at Grady with blue eyes so much like their mother's. "He's been miserable since Mom died. Mighty lonely. It's what makes him so edgy. He's the sort of man who needs a woman. It's—natural."

Grady was surprised that Jonah, of all people, would say such a thing. Yet the kid's words made Grady view their father in a different light. Not as grudging and hard to please, but as a solitary man who hated his solitude, a man comfortable with being married, who had lost what he'd loved most.

Still, he gave Jonah a sardonic smile. "If it's so natural, how come you haven't picked yourself some pretty little filly?"

Jonah shrugged. "The right one hasn't come along."

Grady's grin grew more cynical. "Yeah, junior? Well, how you gonna *know* the right one? What if you pick the wrong one?"

But Jonah, with his seraphic eyes, looked sure of himself, almost serenely so. "I'll know her when I see her. It'll be like Mom and Dad. He said he knew she was the one as soon as he laid eyes on her."

"You've been listening to too many soupy songs on the radio," Grady said. "I don't believe all this 'I was born to love you' bunk."

"Believe what you want," said Jonah.

"Ha." Grady picked up his shoe brush and wielded it almost fiercely.

But the words that had come from his own mouth haunted him. *I was born to love you.*

Could a man look at a woman and know those words were true?

But he didn't want to admit such a thing to Jonah, so he shook his head, and said "Ha" again. He spit on his boot and polished harder.

As soon as Jonah left, however, he picked up the receiver of the pink phone. He called Lynn. She knew a little of Tara's problems with her father-in-law, but not much. She gave him Cal's number in Mexico.

He called Cal and asked questions for an hour. Not about Tara and her ex-husband. About other matters, ones he'd pondered since late afternoon.

CHAPTER TWELVE

LYNN HAD ENTICED TARA into spending all day Sunday in Austin.

"First, Sam's willing to baby-sit," she'd said. "And Camilla's going to help. So Del will have somebody to play with."

Lynn said they'd start by going to church in downtown Austin. "This'll give us the spiritual strength to endure a hard day's shopping," she'd teased.

Besides, she said, her friend Moira had just been ordained as a Methodist minister, and Lynn had been promising to go to a service.

"And," reasoned Lynn, "this is the perfect day to go to the city. Because there's a huge antique show. And a crafts show. All handmade furniture. Sam hates shopping—but it's practically your *duty* to go."

After all, Lynn said, Tara wasn't just supposed to get the house back into shape. She was also supposed to furnish it. She might as well get a jump on it. And while they were in Austin, Lynn would show her some of her favorite shops, as well.

So they did it all, an early church service, then brunch in the penthouse restaurant overlooking the lake and the skyline of Austin.

At the antique show, Tara found a wonderful oak desk that she knew Gavin would love and a bookcase that matched it. She'd been worried about Gavin's money, but he kept swearing he was flush now, and he'd given her a generous allowance for furnishings. "Do the job right," he'd told her.

At the craft fair, she found a furniture maker who worked with native woods. She commissioned a dining room table and chairs and a bed and dresser for Gavin. Lynn ordered a rocker as a surprise for Sam's birthday.

"Classic is great," Lynn sighed, closing her checkbook. "But for hip and funky, we want Sixth Street. Onward and upward!"

Sixth Street was crammed with bars, boutiques, galleries and restaurants. Antique stores jostled against tattoo parlors, and windows filled with kitsch vied with those displaying real art. Sixth was the center of the Austin music scene, and it was alive with an electric sense of things happening.

Tara bought Del a set of wildly colorful picture books and an antique map framed in gold for Gavin's office. Lynn splurged on sexy lingerie and mischievously tried to incite Tara to do the same.

"Oh, come on. Live a little. You haven't bought one thing for yourself yet. I love naughty underwear. It reminds me that I'm a woman—even if I do have to muck out stalls and worm horses."

She held up a set, skimpy black panties and a bra. Tara was surprised to find herself almost tempted. For the first time in over a year, the silkiness and sensuality of these garments seemed attractive again.

But to wear them would be to invite silky and sensual thoughts. And who would ever see them? Grady's image came to her. Not only the physical man, but the kind, smart, funny one, as well. She blushed and shook her head.

From Sixth Street they went to Lynn's favorite mall. She and Tara both bought jeans for their sons, and Tara found a Buzz Lightyear T-shirt that Del didn't have. She collected fabric samples for drapes and purchased throw rugs for the bedrooms and a Persian carpet for the front room. She picked a large leather sofa bed for Gavin's guestroom, as he'd asked.

She ordered a new bed, dresser, armoire and nightstand for Del, a good set of oak furniture that he could grow up with.

"What about you?" Lynn asked while the clerk wrote up the order. "You need a bed, too, you know."

They were surrounded by beds, too many beds: canopy beds, four-poster beds, beds of every sort of design, from sleek Scandinavian to Art Deco and Art Nouveau. There were those with headboards of metal, rattan, wood of every sort, and even leather. All looked lushly comfortable.

Tara told herself that she did not need a lushly comfortable bed. She might be tempted to share it. She remembered her dreams of being tangled in the sheets with Grady. The more attractive he became, the more she knew she couldn't. Burleigh would lick his chops in glee if she did such a thing.

"My bed's fine for now. Besides, I don't really know what I want."

Lynn rolled her eyes. "But they've got anything you could want. Well, I don't see one shaped like a swan, but they could probably special order it."

"Mine's fine." The words came out almost as a whisper.

Lynn, sobering, gave her a long, strange look.

THE SUN HAD SET BY THE TIME the two women headed back toward Crystal Creek. The hills hunched blackly against the darkening sky.

Lynn switched on the car's heater. "Ah. Shopping is like sex. If you do it right, it wears you out, but you feel great."

Tara smiled in spite of herself. "I'll take your word for it."

Lynn threw her a speculative glance. "Nobody's said much, but I get the impression that my cousin Lang may not show up, after all. He may work things out with his wife."

"Good. It's terrible when a marriage doesn't work out."

A moment of pensive silence hung between them. Lynn

said, "Tara, what about you? Are you healed from it yet? From the divorce?"

"I'm getting closer." Tara hoped it was true. She was no longer pained by what Sid had done to her. Only by what he'd done to Del. And what Burleigh might do.

Lynn reached over and squeezed her shoulder. "Good. I'm glad."

There was another interlude of silence. Then in a careful voice she said, "And what do you think about Grady?"

Tara's body tensed. She could not tell the whole truth, so she told part of it. "I don't understand him. He's talented. He's skilled. He can do the work of two men. He's smart. He's got a…pleasant enough personality…I guess. He could have made anything of himself. But he just drifts from place to place, from job to job. Why?"

"Grady's philosophy is that he'd rather be free than rich. I think it bothered him that Uncle Bret took that job in Idaho. It was a huge job, high-paying, but all-consuming. It owned him. Grady wanted experience, not money. He's not irresponsible. But he doesn't want to be owned."

Tara stared into the night and said nothing.

Lynn said, "Some of the men in the family have a rambling streak. Grandpa Hank did when he was young. So did Cal. So does Grady."

"I guess some never settle down."

Lynn shrugged. "Some just settle late. Once Grady wanted only to come back to Crystal Creek. He hated it in Idaho. So he just took off and bummed his way back. But when he got here—it wasn't the same. Things had changed. So he moved on. And kept moving."

Tara sensed there was more to the story. "Why wasn't it the same? How had things changed?"

Lynn hesitated before speaking. "He had a bad case of puppy love when he went to Idaho. On a Crystal Creek girl. He stood it there for five months before he lit out.

"It took him another month to make it back to Crystal Creek. And when he got here, she told him he shouldn't have come. Her feelings for him were platonic. She told him that she'd always think of him as a friend. That sort of thing.''

Tara remembered Grady on the stony plateau and the initials he'd carved on the cedar tree so many years ago. She frowned slightly. ''Was this your cousin Beverly?''

Lynn nodded. ''Cousin on my mother's side. A gorgeous girl.''

Tara shifted uncomfortably. There seemed to be hidden depths in Lynn's story, unspoken complexities. ''He mentioned her. The beauty queen?''

''Many times over. She was first runner-up for Miss World once. She was winning pageants from the time we were in eighth grade. And, unlikely as it sounds, she and I were best friends.''

Lynn smiled wryly. ''We were born only twelve days apart. We knew each other from the cradle. Our ranches were next to each other. We learned to ride our ponies together. My brothers persecuted us together. Grandpa Hank spoiled us together because we were the only little girls.''

''But that was a terrible thing she did to him,'' Tara said. ''It must have destroyed him.''

''I think he took it really hard. He tried not to let it show. But it changed him, all right.''

Tara thought such a crushing rejection could put a man off love for the rest of his life. ''Didn't you resent it? Did you stop being friends with her?''

Lynn gave a sigh tinged with both laughter and sadness. ''For a while. But you've got to understand Beverly. All the boys were gaga over her.''

She paused, as if searching for a way to explain. ''You remember that scene in *Gone With the Wind* when Scarlett's in her green-sprigged dress at the party at Twelve Oaks, and every available man's gathered around her? That's what it was like for Beverly—except she wasn't manipulative like Scarlett. She was actually rather sweet.''

"A sweet Scarlett O'Hara? Isn't that a contradiction in terms?"

Lynn tried to put it differently. "Sweet but spoiled. She was *used* to boys thinking they were in love with her. But she didn't take these things seriously. She didn't set out to hurt Grady. They'd had a few dates, a couple of kisses. She cried when he left—for about five minutes. She wrote to him. She liked getting mushy letters from him."

She paused and shook her head. "She didn't think in a million years that he'd leave Idaho and come back for her. She wasn't ready for a relationship like that. Grady was one of a dozen boys who thought they were in love with her. It never occurred to her to take him more seriously than the others. She wasn't heartless. Just young and unthinking."

Tara wasn't convinced. "Still, she broke his heart. In a way she ruined his life."

Lynn gave her a curious look. "None of us was the most mature person in the world back then. We were kids. The emotions burned hot, but so hot they finally burned out. Yes. She broke his heart—temporarily. He hung around for about a year—"

"A year seems like a long time at that age," Tara interjected.

"True. But he got to see Beverly for what she was. A beautiful, flirtatious girl who was light-years from growing up. But he was growing up—fast."

Fresh curiosity pricked Tara. "What did he do that year? Why didn't he go back to school?"

"He thought he'd lost too much time. He hadn't finished his first semester in Idaho. He got here too late to start the semester in Crystal Creek. He cowboyed a little. Then he went to work for Orly Mannix, a stone mason. Daddy hired Orly to move Grandpa Hank's house onto our land.

"Orly hurt his back. But Grady was a kind of genius at fixing and building and solving problems like that. He's got a very analytical mind; he figures out how to do things. He did that job almost single-handed."

"Cal said that, too."

"It was quite a feat for somebody his age. A man in the Panhandle heard about it and hired him to go out there and work on the same sort of project. He went. But he was too restless to settle down to one thing yet. After that he went on the rodeo circuit."

"Like Cal," mused Tara.

Grady and Cal were alike in many ways. They were both handsome, easygoing, and liked to sweet-talk. They'd both been prodigal sons who'd rodeoed and loved seeing the world.

But there the likeness ended. Cal was a businessman who shouldered more responsibility than most men dared. He was married to a woman he adored, raising a family and getting ready to come back to Crystal Creek to settle for good.

Cal had moved on from his days as a bad boy and a rover. But Grady hadn't. Maybe he couldn't.

The headlights caught the sign that stood at the edge of town, Welcome To Crystal Creek Population 7017.

"Ah," Lynn said with satisfaction, "almost home. But it's been a fun day, hasn't it?"

"Yes." A glow spread through Tara, a kind of contentment she hadn't felt for months. For too long her life had been complicated and topsy-turvy. Going shopping with a friend was a simple act. But it felt good. It felt wonderful.

Maybe Lynn's words were right for both of them. Maybe she, too, was almost home, at last.

DEL HUGGED HER, and she hugged him back hard. "I missed you," she said, buckling him into his car seat. "Did you miss me?"

"Yes," he said dutifully. "We played in the sandbox with Thomas the Tank Engine and Power Rangers. Jamie's mother made us tacos for lunch. Hank's daddy took us to see Dr. Turner. He took us to his hospital. It's for animals. He's a vet-vet-vetranian—"

"Veterinarian," Tara supplied.

Del hardly heard her. He was too intent on recounting his adventures.

"Dr. Turner has a skunk. But he fixed it so it don't stink."

"*Doesn't* stink."

"Its name is Sweetpea. I got to pet him. He put his face up to mine and tickled me with his whiskers. Dr. Turner's got a parrot and a ferret, too. The parrot talks. The ferret doesn't. The parrot sat on his shoulder. The ferret tried to run up his pants leg. I want a ferret and a parrot and a skunk. I'm going to ask Santa Claus. Then we went to the movies, and we saw…"

He chattered so enthusiastically she thought he must not have missed her much at all. That was good, because she didn't want him to be a mama's boy. She had to raise him to have friends of his own, to be open to experience, to have a life beyond the walls of his house.

He babbled on, recounting the entire plot of the movie, which concerned a young frog who went on a journey to save his pond.

But he was punctuating his story with yawns when they reached the lane to their house. "I had a fun time," he said sleepily.

"I'm glad." She pulled up into the drive and reached to hit the button of the garage-door opener.

Then she noticed the house looked different. Her hand froze midway to the button. The graffiti on the limestone next to the garage doors was gone, cleaned away. The doors had been painted. It was as if the obscenities and insults had never existed.

Grady, she thought, emotions tumbling through her, making her chest feel too tight to hold her heart. *Grady came here and did this.*

Then she realized that next to the garage, the new fence also looked different. It looked complete. He must have installed the picket and post caps. He'd been here to work on his day off, unasked.

She was not sure how she felt about his doing this. Grateful? Resentful? Flattered? Wary? All of these at once? She parked the car in the garage and unbuckled Del. He was fading fast, so she carried him inside, into the kitchen.

"I want Lono," he said sleepily. "He's been out by himself all day."

"I'll let him in." She opened the back door and the dog bounded in, nearly hysterical with joy. He kicked something lying in the doorway.

He ran round Del, wagging his tail wildly, and he jumped up, putting his paws on the boy's chest.

Tara leaned over to see what Lono had kicked. The feeling in her chest grew tighter. She picked up a bouquet of pink and lavender carnations, ornamented with fern and wrapped in cellophane.

Grady had left her flowers. She looked down at them and tears stung her eyes. It had been years since a man had given her flowers.

Too many years, she realized, far too many.

A note was taped to the cellophane. "Sorry to disobey orders. Didn't like sitting around doing nothing. Apologies if this is out of line."

She shook her head helplessly. What was she to make of this paradoxical man?

MONDAY AT THE DOUBLE C, Grady was the first man awake and stirring. But Rhonda Cole was already bustling at the stove, and he smelled the aromas of brewing coffee and baking cinnamon buns.

When he walked into the kitchen, he found her humming as she ironed a freshly laundered shirt, the one he'd worn yesterday. She threw him a smile. "Morning. Aunt Millie said you'd be the first one up."

Rhonda wore gray slacks and a bright pink sweatshirt.

The color set off her pink cheeks and made her eyes seem a deeper green.

She looked mighty nice, and she looked right at home. Or maybe she was just the kind of woman who made anyplace seem homey. Grady thought again of what Jonah had said, that their father was smitten.

Bret had always claimed to be a one-woman man. He'd sworn after his wife's death that he'd never marry again. He wasn't the sort who changed his mind or his ways—ever. Yet now Grady found himself wondering if such change was possible.

Rhonda put his ironed shirt on a hanger and hung it from the pantry doorknob. "Let me switch off this iron. I'll rustle you up some breakfast. Sausage and eggs and hash browns okay? There are cinnamon buns, too."

"Coffee and buns are fine, ma'am. I can help myself. And you didn't have to do my laundry."

She poured a mug of coffee and gestured for him to sit down. "My aunt's got firm ideas about how things should be done. She said you'd be on your last set of clean clothes today. When she runs a house, she wants her folks to go out looking respectable. To her, that means washed and ironed. Even if they're going out to muck stalls or brand."

Grady grinned. "I've done a lot of jobs in my life, but ironing wasn't one of them."

Rhonda chuckled. "Millie said *that* was obvious." She opened the refrigerator, took out a package of sausage and a carton of eggs. "And she insists that a hardworking man needs a full-size breakfast. She says you're a hard worker. She can tell."

Grady had taken the coffee, but he hadn't sat down. "Is she awake?"

"Oh, yes. If you want, go in and say hello to her. She'd like that."

"I will." Yesterday, after getting back from Tara's he'd stopped in to chat with her. She was strange, but she intrigued him.

He carried his coffee down the hall and rapped at the door. "Come in, Grady McKinney," called Millie Gilligan.

Grady blinked. How did she know it was him? Did she have X-ray vision? He pushed open the door. She sat up in bed, with a pillow behind her back. She was a small woman, and the large bed made her seem as slight as a child. She wore an old-fashioned bed jacket, dark blue. It was pinned together at the collar with a silver brooch shaped like an owl.

On her lap was a bed tray, and she was shuffling a deck of cards on it. Her radio was on, playing classical music. "Morning, Mrs. Gilligan," Grady said. "Feeling better today?"

"The matter is that sometimes I can't get my mind over matter, and I mind it. Ah, well. No matter. Never mind."

"Yes, ma'am." Grady couldn't unravel what she meant, but he was interested in spite of himself.

"So I took a pill," she said, cutting and shuffling again. "But eventually I'll transcend that. Have patience and you'll have thrushes for a farthing."

"Er, that's an interesting way to put it." He nodded at the cards. "Playing a little solitaire?"

Mrs. Gilligan spread the cards out expertly, fanning them across the tray. She turned one over. It was a tarot card that showed a woman in a flowing Renaissance gown.

"Ah, you again," she said to the card. "The High Priestess. The anima, you know. Primordial feminine wisdom. Been turning up a lot lately."

Grady squinted at the card. "You tell fortunes?"

"Only fortune itself will tell fortune. I read what the cards say. Would you like me to read what they say about you?"

"Sure." In truth, Grady didn't believe in tarot cards, but his curiosity was aroused.

"Sit down. Please pour me a cup of tea. Then cut the cards." She stacked and shuffled them again. Grady refilled her cup with a strange-looking tea that smelled like seaweed and mint.

He sat in the wooden chair at her bedside. She gave him a long, measuring look and smiled knowingly.

"Rhonda's surely making your breakfast, so I'll do a short reading. Pick three cards and turn them over in front of you. In a row. If they're upside down, leave them that way."

Grady picked up the deck, pulled three cards and placed them on the tray. Mrs. Gilligan looked at them and scratched her chin. "Hmmmph. Ah. There's a surprise here, I'll warrant, or dogs eat stones."

Grady peered at the cards. "A surprise? Where?"

She pointed a bony finger at the card on the left. "Not here. This is your past. The six of swords. You've had many travels. You've journeyed by water. Explorations. Expeditions. Here and there. Thither. Yon."

"Right." Grady nodded, but he wasn't impressed. He had a reputation for roving. She probably knew it.

She took a sip of tea, then pointed at the center card. "Nor is the surprise here. This is your present. The Empress. A very fine woman to preside over your present. She can initiate you. She can lead you to a culmination of action. She offers growth, development."

Grady tried to smile, but it came out crooked. Mrs. Gilligan was handing out the usual sort of fortune-teller blather. Glittering generalities, vague and lofty utterances. But they made him think of Tara.

"It's a good thing she's showed up." She fixed her eyes on him again. "How old are you?"

"Thirty-five."

"Well, learn what she's got to teach. You haven't much time. A fool at forty is a fool indeed."

Grady almost winced. He hadn't expected such a pointed remark. But she smiled, screwing up one eye in a sort of canny wink. "And here's the surprise." She laid three fingers on the card on the right. "This is your future. Or it can be. The Queen of Cups."

Grady stared at a woman in a long green dress, sitting on

an ornate throne and holding a golden goblet. Her hair was the same rich brown, shot with red and gold as Tara's. "The Queen of Cups," Millie Gilligan repeated. "Success. Happiness. Pleasure—great pleasure. A good mother. A perfect spouse."

Grady swallowed uncomfortably. A spouse? A *wife?* A good mother. *Children?* He'd been thinking such things lately. Did it show?

Then Mrs. Gilligan frowned. "Are you sure you didn't turn the card? Because if it was really upside down, well, it would mean something completely different. A shallow life of self-deception. Fickleness. A poor grasp of reality."

Grady was almost certain he hadn't turned the card. And what if he had? He told himself again that he didn't believe this supernatural bull.

"And if you reversed the Empress," she mused, "that's worse than a bat in a velvet bag. You'll probably die alone and unloved, completely out of harmony with the universe."

She picked up the cards and shuffled them back into the deck. "Well, don't worry about it. I watched you like a hawk, but, of course, my brains are addled with painkillers. Go now. Your breakfast is ready."

She didn't have to be psychic for that, Grady thought. He could smell the aroma of sausage wafting down the hall. He rose and picked up his coffee mug. "And I'm ready for breakfast. Thanks for the reading. See you later, Mrs. Gilligan."

"When the moon comes over the mountain," she said. "And thank you for the flowers."

Grady, who hadn't blushed in decades, felt his face grow warm. He'd brought the old woman a bouquet last night. The same sort he'd left, God knows why, at Tara's door.

"I was glad to do it," he told her, easing toward the door.

"They want you to tell their sisters hello," she said. She reached over and stroked a frond of fern.

He paused to stare at her. "Excuse me, ma'am?"

"The flowers," she said, then covered a small yawn.

"You bought more than one bunch. These say to tell their sisters 'hello.'"

He nodded, forcing a smile. "Sure thing. You take care."

"Just let me know if you want another reading," she told him. "I can do much more complete ones."

"I sure will." He left the room and headed for the kitchen. He would not ask her to read those damned cards again; it was too spooky and unsettling. He shook his head in wonder. How had she known he'd bought two bunches of flowers? How *could* she have known?

CHAPTER THIRTEEN

TARA GAVE DEL BREAKFAST, then sent him outside to play with Lono in the newly fenced yard.

She set about putting the house in order for her brother's arrival. She laundered the new towels she'd bought, hung the gold-framed map in his study, put down the throw rug in his otherwise empty bedroom, placed hangers in closets. She cleaned the west wing bathrooms and stocked them with supplies.

But it was not Gavin who kept her mind occupied. It was Grady. She hadn't known what to do with the bouquet he'd left her. She'd found an old pressed glass pitcher to use as a vase. But where to set the pitcher?

To put it in the kitchen might seem too dismissive, as if the bouquet was only good enough to sit beside the rattling refrigerator. But to put it on her desk might seem too personal, as if she wanted it near her. To hide it by putting it in one of back rooms and not mentioning it seemed cowardly.

She compromised by setting them on the sill of the living room window that overlooked the valley. The flowers were humble ones, and although the big window framed them, it also dwarfed them.

She thought then that she was prepared for Grady, but when she heard his truck wheeling into the driveway, her heart knocked so hard she felt it in her throat. Going to the screen door, she saw him get out of the cab. He wore his usual blue work shirt, immaculately pressed. The black Stetson was pulled down to a rakish angle.

"Grady!" cried Del, running to the gate, Lono behind him, wagging and bounding. Del tried to open the gate, but it was locked.

Grady merely put one hand on a railing and leaped the fence as agilely as a stag. He laughed, gave Lono's head a quick rub, then picked up Del and whirled him around.

Tara heard Del giggle and say, "Grady! I missed you."

"I missed you, too, champ. Did you have fun in town?"

Grady settled him into the crook of his right arm. Del nodded.

"Mama and Lynn went to Austin. Mama bought me some books and some jeans and some new underpants. I'd rather have a new truck than underpants."

Grady nodded sympathetically. "I know the feeling."

He tossed a grin toward Tara, still standing in the doorway. His dimples flicked into being like dark punctuation marks framing the white smile.

Del was still recounting his day. "And we saw a movie about a frog…"

Grady seemed deeply interested, but his eyes kept moving to meet Tara's. She stood as still as if she were bewitched. He stepped onto the porch. She opened the door.

He swept in, doffing his hat to her. He set Del down. Del's face had grown concerned. "I gotta go pee-pee," he said, holding his crotch. "I'll be right back."

He raced down the hall, and Tara managed to say, "Thank you for what you did yesterday. Finishing the fence and covering the graffiti."

He shrugged. "My father didn't need me. Thought I might as well make myself useful."

The way he looked at her made her feel as if tiny fires rippled beneath her skin. She drew a long breath to keep her voice steady. "I hope you kept track of your hours, so I can figure it into your next paycheck."

"We can talk about that when payday comes."

She refused to draw out the matter. "Thank you also for the flowers. It was a nice gesture. But unnecessary."

He shrugged more cavalierly. "It was nothing. I bought some for Mrs. Gilligan. Got a second bunch half price. No big deal."

He treated the subject so casually that he again threw her off guard. If he was telling the truth, she shouldn't have obsessed about the gift.

He put his hat back on, the brim pulled down. "Hear from your brother?"

She went to the desk and toyed with the fabric samples. "I don't expect him until late afternoon. But I have to get ready. Del and I are going into town to put in supplies. I'd like you to paint the hall in my brother's wing. Also as much of his guest room and parlor as you can."

"The colors you talked about?"

"Yes."

His eyes traveled her body again, from head to toe and back. "I had an idea."

Her throat went dry. "Yes?"

He cocked his head toward the backyard. "Del's got a fence now. But not much to do. Later, I could build him a sandbox. A swing set. I've done it before."

A wave of unwanted gratitude, almost tenderness, swelled in her breast.

Why did he have to be so considerate? So good-hearted? To always have something to offer that would make her child happier?

"That would be...great." She cast her gaze down at the floor, no longer trusting herself to face him.

"But I'll do your painting today." His voice was matter-of-fact, yet beguiling. "I can do the sandbox next week. Or whenever you want."

"I—I'll think about it." She was saved from saying more by Del, pounding down the hall and skidding to a stop.

"I went pee. I washed my hands and everything. I even used soap."

"A good habit," said Grady. "Always do that."

The phone rang, a fresh distraction. Tara seized it, praying it wasn't Burleigh again. "Hello? Tara Hastings speaking."

Gavin's voice was teasing. "Shouldn't you practice saying 'Francina Hills. Tara Hastings speaking'?"

"Gavin!" she said happily. "When will you be here?"

"I'll leave Austin around five. Shouldn't take me much more than an hour to get there. Tomorrow, the others will show up. The place is going to be overrun. Architects. Landscapers. A landscape historian. Are you ready for the horde to descend?"

She thought of Grady, standing only a few feet away. She could sense his presence, and it made her spine tickle, the fire under her skin flicker and spread.

"The more the merrier," she said as brightly as she could. The more people milling around the ranch, the more obstacles between her and Grady.

When she hung up, she felt a sense of liberation. She looked cheerfully at Del. "That was Uncle Gavin. He'll be here by suppertime. And tomorrow, all kinds of people are coming. You and I need to go shopping and get ready."

"Can Grady come shopping?" Del asked.

"No," Tara said. "He can't. I need him to stay here."

"But why?" Del asked, disappointment keen in his voice.

Tara squared her shoulders. "It's what he's paid to do. It's his job. Isn't it, Grady?"

His eyes gleamed with challenge, but he said, "I have to do what I'm told, champ. You do the same."

Del took her hand when she offered it, but he looked sulky. "It'd be more fun with Grady. Everything is."

Tara pretended she didn't hear.

GRADY KNEW TARA WAS A WOMAN he couldn't chase hard, and he knew the time he had alone with her was running short. He needed to use it well.

So, when he heard her truck return that afternoon, he wiped his paint-flecked hands on a rag and went out to help her haul in her bundles and bags.

She couldn't refuse help, of course. So he joked with the boy and took the heaviest grocery sacks from her. She must have bought out half of Crystal Creek, he thought. He hauled in more bags, and she was putting away things: cans, fresh fruit and vegetables, a ham as big as his thigh.

He lugged in a box of cabernet and one of riesling from the Double C's winery, and a case of German beer. She'd bought two new coffeemakers, one for regular brew, one for espresso. Snacks, soft drinks, sparkling water, fruit juices, fresh breads and pastries from the German bakery.

She seemed intent on provisioning herself to wine and dine not only her brother, but his army of experts. Most of whom, Grady thought darkly, would be men who were well-to-do, professional and established. Men who, if they had brains in their heads and testosterone in their systems, would look at Tara with sharp interest.

Today she was especially interesting to look at. To go to town she'd worn a pair of thigh-hugging black slacks he hadn't seen before and high black boots.

A snug, pale yellow T-shirt just skimmed the top of her belt. The shirt had a rose embroidered in gold satiny thread on the front. The rose was placed just between the peaks of her breasts. When she breathed, its petals moved gently.

Never, thought Grady, had a flower rested in a more tempting place. He tried to distract himself by unpacking a bag of canned vegetables for her.

"How many people are you planning to feed?" he asked. He stood just close enough to her that she'd notice but couldn't object. She smelled lovely today, like exotic spices. She must have allowed herself the indulgence of perfume.

"As many as I have to." Deftly she stacked the cans in the pantry. "Gavin's a generous man. Those men will be spending a lot of time here. It'll be easier for them to eat and snack here, not drive into town all the time. And he wants them to eat well."

He eyed two jars of gourmet mushrooms suspiciously.

"And you're supposed to be the hired gal and cook. Serve them all?"

She plucked the jars from his hands and shelved them. "I'll keep things simple. It's like being camp cook. I've done it before."

He shrugged and passed her the canned asparagus. "So have I. If you need any help, just whistle."

She shot him an exasperated glance. "Don't tell me. Sometime in your checkered past you were a master chef. I should have known."

"Nope. Just a cook. But a good one. I was first mate on a chartered yacht. I did all the meals. You should try my lobster thermidore or my mahi mahi Tahitian."

She raised one eyebrow and turned back to her work. "Fresh mahi mahi's in short supply in central Texas."

He edged an inch closer to her. The spices of her perfume teased his nostrils. "Just offering," he said, almost in her ear. He gazed at the graceful curve of her neck, so perfect for nibbling kisses.

She edged an inch away. Her voice was brisk as a cold shower. "There're another two sacks in the truck. Also some doormats from the hardware store. Would you please bring them in? Then, if you'd like to get back to painting…"

She let the sentence trail off, and he recognized it as an order tactfully given. From the truck bed he took two more brown paper bags from the grocery. The scent of carnations wafted from one; he frowned and stared inside. She'd bought six more bouquets, almost exactly like the one he'd left at her door.

His body stiffened in displeased surprise. The other bag gave the muffled clink of wrapped glass. He stole a glance: cheap vases. What the hell?

But then he smiled in self-mockery. She was trying to reduce any power his bouquet had by filling the house with other flowers. His would be one bunch of many, just as he would soon be one man of many.

TARA FINISHED storing groceries. Then, coolly and skillfully she arranged the flowers in their identical vases and placed them around the house.

Del, no longer wanting to play outside, tagged after Grady. From the west wing, Tara heard their voices mingling. Del said, "The lady at the store said Mom looked like the Yellow Rose of Texas. What's that?"

"It's a Texas song," Grady said. "And she's got a yellow flower on her shirt."

"Can you sing it?" Del asked.

"Sure," Grady said. "I'll teach it to you. You've got to know these things if you live here."

Then she heard Grady's strong baritone:

"There's a yellow rose in Texas

"I am going there to see,

"No other fellow loves her,

"Not half as much as me…"

Tara glanced self-consciously down at her breasts, at the embroidered yellow rose that moved with her breathing. At the second chorus, Del's voice, uncertain and piping, joined Grady's.

"You may talk about your Clementine,

"And sing of Rosalee,

"But the yellow rose of Texas

"Is the only gal for me…"

He's doing that on purpose, she thought, narrowing her eyes. But then the sound of tires on the gravel outside captured her attention. She raced to the back door and saw the antique dealer from Austin. He'd come to deliver Gavin's office desk and bookcase.

The dealer was a tall, broad-shouldered man, but approaching old age. His hair was silvered, his back stooped and his big hands crooked with arthritis. He pulled down the truck's ramp, hobbled up it and folded the moving blanket that had covered the desk.

The desk seemed larger than she remembered; formidably

large, the size of a bull hippopotamus. "I can handle it," the dealer assured her. "Been doin' it forty years."

Yet the man strained so hard trying to place the desk on the dolly that Tara was ready to go to his aid, no matter how little help she might be. Then Grady was there, moving past her. Two strides took him up the ramp.

"Let me give you a hand," he said to the dealer. He picked up one end of the oak desk and took the bulk of the weight from the older man. He settled the desk on the dolly, expertly lashed it in place with a set of moving belts, and wheeled it down the ramp.

He pretended the old man was helping him, but Tara could see by the tensing of his muscles that it was Grady wrestling the weight of the great thing.

"We almost got it," he said between his teeth, getting the dolly up the back steps. He gave the dolly a superhuman heave so that it cleared the last step and was even with the door.

"Young feller," said the dealer, puffing, "you've done this before, ain't you?"

"Yessir. Used to deliver antiques in Los Angeles. For Sotheby's."

He gritted his teeth harder as he angled the big desk through the door. The dealer whistled. "Sotheby's. That's la crème de la crème of this trade. You ever want a job you come see me. Hiram T. Heckathorn of Austin. I'm gonna give you my card."

"Thanks, sir. But I got more than I can handle right where I am."

He cast a pointed look at Tara and wheeled the desk inside.

TARA STAYED MERCIFULLY BUSY the rest of the afternoon. Other delivery trucks came. The furniture store delivered Del's bedroom suite; Grady, unasked, helped the wiry little driver unload it and put it in place.

Next a scarlet panel truck came chuffing up the lane.

Grady helped the two deliverymen carry in the large, rolled Persian rug and lay it in the living room before the fireplace.

At three o'clock a second furniture store truck arrived with a leather sofa bed and matching chair for Gavin's guest room. Once more, Grady lent a hand.

Moving the chair didn't prove difficult, but the sofa bed was heavy and awkward to handle. One of the two deliverymen stumbled on the back steps. His grip on the sofa slipped, and it knocked Grady halfway down, pinning him against the frame of the back door.

Del, who thought moving men were almost as interesting as cement mixers, cried out in alarm. "Grady!"

One of the men swore. "Help him!" yelled the other. "Don't let it slip!"

Tara's heart took a sharp, terrifying tumble. The sofa had rammed against his body like a big log breaking free from a jam. He grimaced in pain, he seemed trapped, but somehow he'd kept hold of the thing. He exerted himself to push it away so it wouldn't crush his ribs.

Her hand flew to her mouth. But Grady, twisting, struggled to regain his footing, and taxed his strength to keep more weight from heaving against him. The other two men hauled at the piece, until it tipped the other way.

Grady swayed, but managed to keep his balance. He was free, and the three men fought the sofa inside.

But the back of Grady's T-shirt was torn, a long crescent-shaped tear across the shoulder blades. He was bleeding, and a bright red line curved along the skin beneath the ripped cloth.

Del sprinted to his side. "Grady! You're bloody!"

Grady, his forehead beaded with sweat, shook his head, signaling him to get back. "I'm okay, I'm okay. Just let us get this thing in place. Stand back, champ."

"But you're *hurt*," protested Del.

Tara, too, had run toward Grady, but she saw the determination in his face. She clutched Del by the shoulders, pulling him safely out of the way.

"Grady?" Her voice trembled.

"I'm fine. Just let us get this sonuvabitch where you want it." He winced. "Excuse the language. Sorry, Del."

Tara tightened her grip on Del. The men toiled to get the piece through the kitchen door and into the hallway. There was more sweating, more grunting and hoisting and wrestling. There was more swearing, but not from Grady. Tara covered Del's ears.

As if powerless to resist, she and Del followed, keeping at a safe distance. Finally, standing in the doorway, she saw the three men maneuver the thing into place. The taller of the deliverymen went to Grady, clasped his shoulder. "Sorry, buddy. Really sorry. Them stairs are crooked. My foot caught—"

Grady's skin looked greenish white under his tan. "It's okay. It was an accident. Knocked the wind out of me, that's all."

"Good Lord, man," said the other, "I thought we were gonna squash you like a bug. Break your back and kill you dead."

Grady managed a sickly grin. "Only the good die young."

The first man turned to Grady, stared at his back, and shook his head. "You got a cut there, buddy."

"Just a scratch." He turned so his back was hidden. "I've had worse."

The second man's expression was jittery. "Lady, will you sign this receipt? Then you better take care of him. Do you need help?"

Numbed, Tara remembered how the sight of Del's blood had thrown her into a panic. She wanted to show Grady that she could handle an emergency, that Del's case had been special.

"I can handle him fine. Give me the receipt."

The man yanked a pad and pen from his shirt pocket and offered them to her. Hastily she scribbled her name and thrust the receipt back at him. The men, eager to be gone, hurried down the hall.

Tara turned to Del. "Get me the first-aid kit." The boy scurried away. "Grady, turn around. Let me see the damage."

"I can take care of myself." He stepped toward the office's bathroom, his gait not fully steady but stubborn.

Just as stubborn, she followed and stood, arms akimbo, in the doorway so he couldn't shut her out. "Take off your shirt," she ordered.

He turned his back to the mirror and pulled his shirt over his head.

She sucked in her breath. Beneath his pectoral muscles, a great bruise crossed his ribs like a mottled band.

"Good grief," she breathed, reaching out to touch the purpling flesh. "You must have broken ribs."

He flinched slightly but let her rest her fingertips against his bare skin. "No. I know what broken ribs feel like. I've had my share."

"You're sure? Maybe I should drive you to the doctor—"

Her hand moved along the hardness of his stomach, trying to feel his ribs. He let her. "They're not broken," he said again. "But I'm about to bleed on your floor. Let me clean my back. I can do it myself."

Her hand still stroking across his ribs, she looked over his shoulder, at his mirrored image. His back, too, was bruised and a cut shaped like the narrowest of new moons slashed across it. Blood ran in tiny trickles down the muscles of his back.

Her hand flattened against his chest in shock. Her other hand flew to his bare upper arm, gripping it as if she needed to support him. This wound didn't unnerve her as Del's had done, but she stared at his mirrored back in horror.

"How—"

Grady looked down at her hand on his chest. He spoke out of the side of his mouth. "I landed against the lock's catch. I got shoved along it. I skidded against a sharp edge, that's all.''

''Del,'' she called, forcing her voice to stay calm, ''bring me some clean towels.''

''I don't need towels. I'll use my shirt.'' He turned from her and began to run water on the wadded T-shirt. She saw that the cut did not look deep and it was narrow, its edges close together. Grady wrung out the shirt, and Tara held out her hand for it, but he shook his head. ''I can do it. It's minor. It looks worse than it is.''

He tried to reach the cut, but couldn't. Not from over his shoulder, or reaching around behind. He swore in frustration. Tara touched his arm again. ''Let me. It needs to be cleaned.''

Sighing harshly, he relinquished the shirt and braced both hands against the sink. She laid one hand on his scarred shoulder and with the other swabbed the cold cloth over his back. Although the laceration was shallow, it kept bleeding.

She rinsed the shirt and pressed it to the wound again. Del appeared, carrying the first aid kit and dragging a pair of new towels. His face was full of worry. ''Is he going to be all right?''

Grady threw him a strained grin. ''Heck, yes, pal. It hurt a little at first, that's all.''

Tara said, ''Put the first-aid kit on the sink.''

Del looked more upset than before. ''But it goes clear across your back. And it's still bleeding.'' He touched his scraped forehead. ''I didn't bleed that much.''

''It'll stop in a minute,'' Grady said. ''You go outside and play. Let your mom do her job here.''

Tara took the towels from Del. She bent and kissed his cheek. ''He's right. Go out and watch to see if another truck comes, all right? I need a lookout.''

Del seemed relieved. When he was gone, Grady said, ''I've got a hunch he's not going to grow up to be a surgeon or work in a blood bank.''

Tara wet the shirt again. ''Let's face it. You look gory.''

"Yesterday you couldn't handle a splinter. Now you're Florence Nightingale."

"It does make a difference when it's your *child* that's bleeding."

"Ah. Outsider blood doesn't count."

She ignored the gibe. "And this shirt's not doing the job. It's no better than a rag." She tossed it into the tub and wet a fresh towel with cold water.

"Hey," he said, frowning as he straightened. "Don't ruin a good towel on me."

Firmly she pushed him to brace against the sink again. "Stay put. You bleed less in that position. And you're more important than any *towel*."

"I am?" he asked in mock wonder. "That's the nicest thing you've ever said to me. When I'm dead and gone, that's what I want on my tombstone. 'Grady McKinney—more important than a towel.'"

"Oh, hush." She pressed the towel against the cut. It was far more absorbent and effective than the thin cotton of the shirt. She held it in place.

Glancing up, she saw him watching her in the mirror.

He must feel better. Mischief glinted in his eyes. "I could get to like this treatment. I'll have to have sofas fall on me more often."

Her cheeks grew hot. "You're lucky you didn't break something. I had visions of broken ribs and punctured lungs. Have you had a tetanus shot?"

He quirked an eyebrow. "I've had a shot. Nothing's broken. All that's punctured is a little line of skin. And my pride."

She pressed harder on the towel. The bleeding was slowing. "You could have been badly hurt."

He kept his gaze on her face, and she saw the question in it: *Would you have cared?*

"Turn around and hold still," she ordered.

He smiled, but kept watching her in the mirror.

WHEN TARA WAS SURE THE BLEEDING had stopped, she led Grady into the guest room and made him sit on the sofa. She sat beside him, the first-aid kit at her feet. "Let me put on some antiseptic."

He angled his body so his back was to her. She squeezed the cream onto her fingertips and began to smooth it onto the cut. His back was marred by the bruise that framed the long cut, but it was still a beautiful male back. "Am I hurting you?"

"Not at all," he said in a low voice.

She rubbed the cream on the thin red streak across his back. His muscles contracted slightly at her touch and his shoulder blades shifted subtly.

She skimmed the bruise where it was darkest, at the cut's left edge. "Does it hurt to be touched here?"

"Not the way you do it."

She exhaled sharply. His skin, feeling her breath, twitched in response. Realizing how close they were, she snatched her hand away and drew back.

"I—I'm going to tape you now." Hastily she reached for the roll of sterile tape. She snipped a six-inch strip. She was forced to lean closer to him again to place the tape precisely.

By willpower, she kept her voice businesslike, almost natural. "This is a very thin cut. The edges are close together. There shouldn't be any problem with it healing. You're lucky."

As she stroked the tape firmly into place, he said, "I'm very, very lucky."

She cut a second strip and put it on the middle section of the cut. "Tell me if this hurts."

"I told you. You've got a wonderful touch."

She needed both hands to get the tape placed right and pressed flat. This was the trickiest section of the cut, the curve between his shoulder blades, where it crossed his spine. She felt the bulge of his vertebra, the striations of his muscles.

He glanced over his shoulder. "Is that tight enough? It feels like it might come loose when I move."

Setting her jaw, she pressed both hands against his back. The tape felt angular and artificial in contrast to his body's warmth and strength. "Better?" she asked from between her teeth.

"Good. Um. Very good."

She busied herself with the scissors. "One more strip and we're done."

"You're very—expert."

"I'm pretending you're a horse," she said tartly. "I'm used to patching them up."

Quickly she pressed the last piece into place, making sure it was tight.

"There. Done. You should go home now. Rest. You're going to be sore."

He changed position to face her. Her gaze fell to his bruised chest. There was a dark bruise at the edge of his left pectoral. Nearly hidden by his chest hair was a reddened scrape.

"Oh," she breathed. "Oh, dear. Do you need that bandaged?"

"No. But maybe some of that antiseptic."

"Um. Yes. I should clean it first."

More flustered than before, she tore open an alcohol wipe and unfolded it. She had to use the fingers of her left hand to part the crisp dark hair on his chest to see the scrape. She dabbed at it timidly.

He laughed, so near that it stirred her hair. "Go ahead. Don't be afraid of hurting me."

She took him at his word and gave the abrasion such a scrub that he flinched. "Sorry." She bit off the word as she reached for the antiseptic.

"It's okay."

Lightly she spread the cream, watching her hand move against his skin, the dark, curling hair.

Suddenly his hand rose to cover hers and press it against

his chest. The movement was so swift it left her breathless with surprise. She could feel the pounding of his heart. She could feel the pounding of her own.

Her gaze rose to meet his. He leaned nearer. He said, "Tell me. Tell me what the real difference is."

"I—don't know what you mean." She knew she should free her hand from his and pull away. But she did not.

"Why did you nearly fall apart Saturday, when Del was hurt, but not today? What's the *real* difference?"

She seemed mesmerized, powerless to move away. "I told you. He's my son."

"You'd panic if he was really hurt? You wouldn't be able to help him?"

She shrugged in confusion. "I told you. I'd just had an upsetting call. I overreacted. That's all."

He brought his face closer to hers. "What could upset you that much? I have a good guess. But I want to know."

"Don't do this to me," she begged.

His free hand rose and stroked a wayward strand of hair from her face. "Don't do what?" His hand settled lightly on her cheek, his thumb near her lips.

"That." Fiercely she tried to shake his touch away. "Don't touch me that way. Don't look at me that way. Don't—say the things you do."

But he would not be deterred. He cupped her chin and raised her face to his. "Why? And what's it got to do with how you acted Saturday?"

Her head spun. He was going to kiss her if she didn't stop him. She didn't want to stop him. But she had to. And perhaps the truth would make him draw back.

Her words came stumbling out. "Del's grandfather called. My ex-husband's father, Burleigh. He accused me of trying to keep Del away from him. He said he'd take me to court, try to get custody."

A knot constricted her throat so tightly it hurt. "He said I've neglected Del, that I've let him get hurt. He said that he'd have me watched and charge me with being unfit and he'd prove it. So the next thing I know, Del's got a bloody hand over his eye—my God, I thought he'd been blinded. I thought my child's blind and Burleigh will take him away and—I just—I just—I lost it.''

"I'm sorry." His voice was gruff. Slowly he moved his hand from her face. She was both glad and sorry. His touch had felt good, it had felt right.

But he kept her hand clasped against his chest, and she was more conscious than ever of their beating hearts. They beat nearly in unison.

Her eyes filled with tears. "I can't have a casual affair with you. I *won't* have a casual affair with you. If he found out, he'd throw that at me, too.''

He raised his hand to her chin again, and again he tipped her face toward his. "Who said it'd be casual?''

He kissed her long and hard and deep.

CHAPTER FOURTEEN

GRADY FEARED HE HAD ALREADY LOST her, so he held her more tightly. He feared that kissing her was a fatal blunder, so he kissed her for all he was worth.

Her mouth beneath his was so warm and so sweet he was intoxicated, crazy with wanting more of it, more of her. Yet he sensed such conflict in her that conflict rose in him, as well, a drowning tide of it. It made him more desperate.

Because he shouldn't kiss her, he couldn't stop doing it. It should have hurt, holding her against his bruised chest. He felt no pain except that of longing.

She was slender as a sylph in his arms. If he released her, she might vanish like some otherworldly creature that no mortal could follow or claim. But if he held her as he wanted to, he sensed there was a spell upon her that he just might have the power to break.

For a few dizzying seconds, she was as responsive as he was hungry. But then her hand, so rightly placed over his heart, tried to push him away.

Her other hand pressed against his bare shoulder, and she struggled to lever her body away from his.

''Don't!'' she said against his mouth. She said it with such anguish that he hated himself for wanting her so much. ''Don't—please.''

He drew back, but he didn't let go of her. He bent and nuzzled her neck. ''Don't be afraid of some controlling old man thousands of miles away,'' he begged her. ''He doesn't want you to be happy or human again. Don't let him have that power.''

She tried to wrench free. "This wouldn't be right, even if he didn't exist. What would people think? I came here to build a new life for me and my son. I won't end up starting a—a fling the first week I'm here. With the first man I meet."

He gripped her by her upper arms. She looked so abject he could have shot himself. A faint smear of red marred her yellow shirt. It was his blood.

He leaned nearer to her, willing her to look into his eyes. "It isn't like that, you and me. I care for you. And Del. I'd do anything for you. I'll help you in any way I can."

She wouldn't meet his gaze. "Then let me go. And never do this again."

He tried to pull her closer, but she resisted. He said, "You call it a fling. I call it a…love affair."

There. He had said it. He'd said the word "love," and it was alien to him, so he plunged on past it. "We'll see where it takes us. And we'll be discreet. Nobody would have to know."

He saw immediately it was the wrong thing to say. Her head jerked up and her eyes flashed. "Somebody *would* know. *I'd* know that I was gambling with my child's happiness. Maybe you don't care about reputation—and security—but I do."

The words hit him like a slap because they were partly true. Not completely, but true enough to sting harder than the cut on his back. All his adult life, he'd flaunted what most people called reputation. He'd bothered with no one's security but his own. He was broke, he had no prospects, and his past, which once seemed so free, now felt like an imprisoning chain.

This time when she pulled away, he let her. She stood and glared at him.

"And if this is your idea of being 'discreet,' necking in the middle of the day—with my child likely to walk in any second—then you're hopeless. I can't get involved with anybody. And I won't."

She turned her back to him, crossing her arms as if trying to contain her shame and anger.

He rose and stood behind her, but he didn't touch her. He knew full well that she could get involved with someone. But it would be a serious affair with a serious man. And it would end in marriage.

Her brother would arrive today, trailed by all sorts of likely suitors for her. And Grady would be shut out, unable to offer her any of the things she needed: steadiness, stability, a distinguished past, a secure future.

He didn't have a thing in the world to offer her. Except love. He had to admit it, he loved her. He found the words forming in his mouth to tell her. *I love you.*

But she wouldn't believe him. He could hardly believe it himself.

"I reckon you're part right. You're not the kind of woman a man fools around with. He marries you or nothing. So, if you want, I'll keep my distance. And you can keep your good name."

She whirled to face him, hugging herself more tightly. Her lips parted in disbelief. He remembered the taste and feel of those lips.

"What?" she demanded.

He felt suddenly self-conscious of his paint-flecked jeans, his bare, bruised chest, his empty pockets and his aimless future. But he crossed his arms stubbornly. "I meant you're the kind of woman a man marries. That's not exactly an insult, you know."

She made a furious, futile gesture. "I didn't come to Texas on a husband hunt."

He shrugged. "I didn't say you did. But you'll find one. Or he'll find you. Even though you're playing hard to get."

She clenched her fists at her sides. "I'm not playing hard to get. I'm not *playing* anything."

He cocked his hip and shook his head. "You pretend. You're pretty, but you try not to be. Pulling your hair back, letting your hands go, wearing no makeup. It doesn't work. Men notice. I did. I couldn't help it.''

She squeezed her fists so tight that the knuckles went white. ''Well, you could certainly help yourself from getting touchy-feely. There was no call for—''

Grady resented this. ''*I* got touchy-feely? You're the one who had your hands all over me. Touching me like that, driving me half-wild. And you knew it. You could tell.''

She tossed her head and her hair came partly undone. It spilled in waving strands down to her shoulders. ''Oh! I only took care of your back because you couldn't reach it.''

He gave her a jeering look. ''I could have reached my chest just fine. See?'' He lifted his hand and jabbed near the spot with his thumb. ''But there you were, practically sitting in my lap. Rubbing me. Putting cream on my chest. So close I could feel your breath on my skin.''

Her cheeks burned a darker pink, and her chin went stubborn. She looked mad enough to spit railroad spikes at him, but she said nothing.

She said nothing because she knew he was right, and she was honest enough not to deny it. Her breasts heaved in a way that made him stare at the yellow embroidered rose going up and down.

He swallowed and said, ''I got a spot of blood on your shirt. I'm sorry.''

She looked down and in a small voice said, ''Oh.'' She put her hand across her breasts, shielding them from his view.

He raked his hand through his hair and said, ''And I shouldn't put the blame on you. I don't think straight around you. I—''

''Mom!'' cried Del from the yard. ''Mom! Grady! Somebody's coming. It's not a truck!''

Tara, startled, jerked her attention to the window. Grady's gaze followed hers. A milk-white Cadillac was gliding up the lane.

''It can't be Gavin,'' Tara whispered, almost to herself.

"He said he'd call first. That he wouldn't be here until after dark, probably."

Grady moved closer to her, then wished he hadn't. He sensed her nearness too keenly; it penetrated his body like thousands of tiny pinpricks.

The car pulled to a stop, its door opened, and a handsome man with waving brown hair got out. He waved cheerfully at Del, and Del jumped up and down at the sight of him. Lono ran and put his paws against the fence, his tail wagging in greeting.

"I'll be damned," Grady said in a low voice, staring at the familiar face. "Cal."

"Mom!" Del called. "It's Cal! He's here!"

Tara's face lost its tenseness and her mouth curved into a smile. Without saying anything, she turned and ran from the room. Grady heard the screen door slam.

Cal McKinney, his cousin, the golden boy. Grady glanced down at his bare chest and knew he needed to put his shirt on. But he paused long enough at the window to see Tara unlock the gate and throw herself into the other man's arms. She gave him a long, enthusiastic kiss on the cheek.

"CAL," TARA SAID WITH PLEASURE, putting her hands on his shoulders. "Nobody said you were coming."

He grinned down at her. "It's a surprise. Figured since Gavin was coming, I would, too. Just to look in. And how are you, long, tall Tara? You're the only gal I know half as pretty as my Serena."

She smiled. "Did Serena come?"

He shook his head. "No, she ran off without me. She took the twins to Napa Valley to see Tyler and Ruth."

Del was clamoring for attention, so Cal swooped him up and held him. "How you doin', squirt? You like this house?"

"It's getting better," Del said. "I'm helping. I painted. I washed windows. I helped put up this fence."

Cal whistled. "Woo. You done worked up a storm. Done a fine job, too."

"How are Tyler and Ruth?" Tara asked.

"Workin' too hard. It's a tough year for wineries in California. I reckon that—"

He broke off as Grady came out the back door. He'd put on his work shirt but hadn't buttoned it all the way. Tara could see a triangle of his golden chest shadowed by dark hair.

As Grady crossed the yard, the two men grinned at each other, and Tara was struck by their resemblance. Cal was built more leanly, and his hair and eyes were lighter than Grady's. But both men had the same laid-back way about them, the same high-hearted careless ease.

Wealth had polished Cal. His tan Western-cut shirt was tailored, so were his darker tan slacks. His boots were works of art. His hands were not callused from work like Grady's. His aftershave lotion did not come from the drugstore.

Still, Cal was anything but snobbish. He set down Del, grabbed Grady and gave him a bearlike hug. "Dang. It's good to see your ugly face."

"Ooph," Grady said and fought against wincing.

"Grady hurt himself," Del said, tugging at Cal's pants leg. "A sofa hit him. There was blood all over."

Cal drew back and studied his cousin. "You were wrangling a sofa?"

Grady looked rueful. "Trying to help the deliverymen. It threw me and stomped me. I hit the door latch."

"He bled. He's real bruised, too," Del said in admiration. "It just happened a little while ago."

Cal clasped his cousin's shoulder. "Hell, buddy, I'm sorry. Hope I didn't hurt you."

Grady shot him a crooked smile. "I've been hurt worse. And so have you. I remember the time you got hung up on the bronc in Waco."

Cal shook his head. "Thought I was knockin' on heaven's door. Like you that time in Taos."

Grady shrugged it off. "Where's your better half? Your *much* better half?"

"She didn't feel like any more flying this week. Been havin' collywobbles." Cal put his hand over his stomach. "In the morning, if you get my meanin'."

"Another child?" Tara asked. He grinned like the Cheshire cat and nodded. "That's wonderful," she said and hugged him again.

Yet Tara felt a pang of yearning. What would it be like to have a happy, growing family? Without realizing it, as she drew away from him, she lay her hand on her flat stomach.

Grady laughed and punched Cal's shoulder. "Another kid? When?"

"About eight months. And I get down on my knees every night and pray it *ain't* another set of twins. I swear I don't know where those boys get their devilment."

Grady and Tara stole glances at each other and smiled in spite of themselves. The twins didn't get an ounce of deviltry from Serena; Cal's own hell-raising genes had come back to haunt him, and everybody knew it.

But then Tara forced her eyes away from Grady. Sharing secret looks and knowing smiles with him was not safe. Nothing about Grady was settled or safe.

She turned to Cal. "So where's my brother? Why isn't he with you?"

"He's still in Austin, talkin' to all those planners. He's good at it. I ain't. So I drove out to see Lynn. I just came from her place. I was on my way to call on Big Bret, and she told me to stop off and see y'all." He nodded at Grady, then Tara. "My no-count kin here, and you and Del. Serena sends her love."

"Send ours in return." Tara shook her head in wonder. "And our congratulations. Another baby. I can't still can't believe it. Congratulations." But the yearning, the emptiness in her midsection didn't go away.

Cal's mouth quirked into a self-mocking grin. "Must

mean it's finally time to stop rovin'. I'm holdin' out about four hundred acres for myself. Over yonder, on the west. Borderin' Daddy's place.''

Grady's eyes narrowed, looking westward. ''Some mighty pretty spots over there. I remember.''

Del, tired of listening to the grown-ups talk, seized Cal by the hand. ''Come see my room. Today I got new furniture. Grady helped move it. It's like a real room now.''

''Sure thing,'' Cal said, his brown fingers tightening around the boy's. ''Let's see how things are shapin' up.''

With his other hand he reached for Tara's. ''You show me, too.''

She led Cal toward the house, Del still clinging to his other hand. Grady followed a few paces behind.

Cal glanced at the garage and the cleaned limestone. ''I see you got that damned graffiti off. Must have been a job.''

''Grady did it,'' Del piped up. ''He put up my fence, too. And fixed the roof. I can't go up on the roof until I can grow whiskers.''

''Good policy.'' He glanced over his shoulder at Grady. ''You've been busy, old son.''

Grady thrust his hands into the back pockets of his jeans. ''Keeps me outta trouble.''

''You not in trouble? That'll be the day.''

To Tara's humiliation, she blushed.

Cal gave her a long, sideways look. He studied her tousled hair, then his gaze fell to her yellow shirt, where her left breast was marked by Grady's blood. He said nothing, but an odd, knowing smile quirked the corner of his mouth.

GRADY WATCHED as Cal toured the house, marveling at how much had been done in so little time. He stared approvingly at Del's bedroom. ''That's one fine-lookin' place,'' he said. ''Do you know my boys got curtains just like that at our California place?''

Del nodded. ''We played there. Last time you came to

stay in Los Angeles.'' He frowned up at Cal in perplexity.
''Are you really going to move *here?*''

''Yep. We'll build a house. You and the boys'll be neighbors. Full time.'' He ruffled Del's fair hair. He looked the
bright walls up and down, then put a hand on Tara's shoulder. ''Your brother said you were a wonder. It was one sad
mess when we looked at it after the rains.''

Del said, ''Grady made a paddock and a stall for my
pony. I miss him. But he's coming soon. And Mom's, too.''

''A paddock *and* a stall. Woo!'' said Cal.

Grady was conscious that Tara's eyes turned to him. In
a low voice she said, ''I couldn't have done half of it without him. Not a quarter.''

Grady blinked in surprise, but kept his face impassive.
She'd said it of her own accord. She could have waited,
taken Cal aside, and complained about Grady to him. Was
it possible that, in spite of what had just happened, she still
wanted him around?

Cal walked to Del's window and fingered the curtains
with their colored cartoon figures. His face was uncharac-
teristically serious. Maybe he was thinking of his own boys,
now in California, or of his third child, yet to be born. He
stared out across the western range of hills, to the land he'd
claimed as his.

''A lot of building to be done,'' he said. ''Good, strong
building, meant to last. *Homes* meant to last.''

He turned to Grady, hooking his thumbs into his tooled
belt. ''Gonna need men to build 'em, cuz. Gonna have a lot
of jobs. If you'd want to stick around—for a while.''

Caught off guard, Grady hesitated. ''I—I may be stuck
here for a spell.''

Cal's serious expression fled and his grin flashed. ''Yeah.
Your truck. You may have a long, white beard before you
get any money settled on that. Canola oil. Good Lord. Lynn
didn't know whether to laugh or cry when she told me. Hell,
I didn't know whether to laugh or cry.''

''Me, either,'' Grady said with honesty.

He thought of his crumpled truck, hauled off to the garage, a wreck growing more worthless every day. He thought of his cousin's rented Cadillac parked outside. And he thought, *How in the hell did I get to be thirty-five years old and have so damned little?*

But Grady said nothing. Now it was Tara who stared pensively out the window, as if this conversation did not affect her. Del had lost interest in the adults' words. He crouched on the floor, intently coupling and uncoupling his wooden train cars.

Cal's eyes roved up and down Grady's figure. They weren't judgmental, and they contained neither pity nor any suggestion of charity. He was just being Cal, who was as generous and loyal as he was lighthearted.

He gave Grady a smile. "Think about it. We'll need good men. Experienced. You don't have to answer now. Just mull it over."

Grady nodded and muttered that he would. But his attention was not on Cal. It was on Tara, gazing out the window in her unconcerned and unfathomable way.

Cal glanced at his watch. "I better get movin' if I'm gonna make it to the Double C and back to Lynn's in time for supper. I'm staying with her."

Grady, still conscious of Tara's profile, her air of distance, was surprised. "You're not staying at the Double C?"

Cal shook his head. "It's near full up. Cynthia's having the guesthouse re-done so your daddy can live in it when she and *my* daddy get back. No. Lynn's got a mighty comfy guestroom. I'm stayin' there."

Tara came out of her reverie. "I'll walk you to your car."

She took his arm. Cal patted her hand. "Both of you walk me. I think Del's more interested in Thomas the Tank Engine down there."

But Tara tapped the boy's shoulder. "Get up, Del. Cal's leaving. Come and say goodbye."

"But you just got here," Del protested to Cal, almost poutily. But he stood, minding his mother.

He was a good little kid, thought Grady. A fine little kid. How could his father just let him go? How could a man do such a thing?

He realized that a week ago he would never have asked such questions. Now they haunted him without ceasing. Wordlessly he strolled with Tara and Del to escort Cal back to his car. Tara looked at the Cadillac and said lightly, "I guess you guys *aren't* worrying about money any longer. Here you are, renting an Elvismobile."

Cal deepened his voice to Elvis range. "I'm a hunka hunka burning tycoon."

She smiled. "You're crazy."

"Like a fox." He kissed her, chucked Del under the chin, pumped Grady's hand. "If you're not doin' anything later," Cal told him, "come over to Lynn's. Chew the fat. We can sit up late and tell each other lies, just like old times."

Grady thought about it. He and Cal had talked on the phone a long time, but Grady still had questions, lots of them. "I just might do that," he said.

The three of them watched him drive off. Del rubbed his forehead where the board had hit him. He frowned.

"I forgot to tell Cal about my ouch."

"You can tell him later," Tara said. She grasped his shoulder to guide him back inside. Del gazed thoughtfully at her hand.

He said, "You had an ouch, too. It's almost gone."

"It's healing," she said.

"I'll go finish painting that wing," Grady said.

Tara opened her mouth to say something, but Del spoke first. "And Grady got an ouch today, too. A big one. We're like the Ouch Family. All of us got hurt."

His face brightened at the revelation, and he giggled, finding it funny. Grady smiled dutifully, but he thought of what Millie Gilligan had said. *Many an accident happens, and many an accident will.* Maybe the old woman really could see into the future. He thought of what she'd read in the cards.

But Tara ignored Del's remark. She shot Grady a look that had no warmth in it. She said, "Tomorrow you can start working down at the lodge. I won't need you around the house anymore. My brother can give the orders from here on out. You can report to him."

It was happening. She was sending him into exile where he belonged.

GRADY LEFT JUST BEFORE SEVEN O'CLOCK. Tara knew he wanted to speak with her alone, probably to apologize for the kiss. She didn't want it mentioned again. She wanted him on his way, to be free of his troubling presence.

Yet his absence was just as troubling. The house seemed empty without him.

When Cal had asked him if he wanted a job, she'd listened, her pulses skipping, for his answer. But he hadn't committed himself. That, of course, was the story of his life, and after what had happened between them, what had she expected?

She was relieved and gladdened when the phone rang and it was Gavin.

"I'm on my way, kid," he said. "I'm in the car now. Meetings ran long. I should be there in half an hour."

"I'll have supper waiting," she promised. "And the wine open."

"Shouldn't I be taking you out? Aren't you dying to get out of that place by now?"

"I want to serve you your first meal in your new home. It won't be fancy—"

"I never much liked fancy. And it's your home, too. I'll only be there now and then."

"The sofa bed came today," she said. "You won't have to test that sleeping bag."

Guilt prickled, making her think of Grady, his bare arms around her, his mouth claiming hers. She supposed it would be months, maybe years, before she could think of that damned sofa without a twinge of shame.

Gavin laughed. "I don't want a sofa bed. I told you. Spence gave me a new sleeping bag to try out. I'm an official tester."

Spence Malone, the third partner, had family money. The Malones had built an empire on camping and travel equipment. Spence was the only person she knew who'd been both to the North Pole *and* the South Pole.

"Let Spence test his own sleeping bag. I bet you've traveled until you don't know what time zone you're in. You need a bed, not a floor."

"We slept on plenty of floors when we were kids. It'll seem like the good old days."

"Along around three in the morning, your bones won't feel like a kid's. You're a grown-up now."

"The hell I am. If I was an adult, I wouldn't be palling around with clowns like Cal and Spence."

Nervously she said, "Yesterday I went into Austin and spent a lot of your money on this place."

"Don't worry about the money. We're fine. More than fine."

"I hope so. And I hope you'll like how I'm fixing things. Especially your section."

He chuckled. "I trust you. You know what I like. And you've got taste, style. Have you—"

Static crackled, his voice grew fainter.

"Gavin?"

"I'm getting interference on this phone. I'll see you soon, babe. In no time at all."

"Hurry," she begged. "There's nobody I'd rather see come walking through that door."

But as she hung up the phone, her own words troubled her. What if she had to choose between who would come into this house tonight, Gavin—or Grady?

Gavin, she told herself sternly. Of course it would be her beloved and protective brother. Gavin.

AFTER SUPPER AND AFTER DEL had been tucked into bed, Gavin built a fire in the fireplace. Tara and Gavin lay on their stomachs on the Persian rug and watched the flames dart, the sparks fly upward.

They sipped the last of the wine. Gavin turned to her and smiled. "You've done a hell of a job, Tara. It's unbelievable."

Propped on her elbows, she stared down into the ruby depths of her wine. "I had good help." She hoped he wouldn't ask about Grady.

But he did. "Cal's cousin? Or second cousin? Grant?"

She kept her gaze on the wine and her tone noncommittal. "Grady. Second cousin."

Gavin nodded. "Grady. Cal said he was a good worker. Superior, in fact. And versatile."

"Yes. He is."

Gavin sipped his wine. "Sounds interesting. You like him?"

The question made her heartbeat skitter. "He's all right."

She stole a glimpse out of the corner of her eye and saw Gavin regarding her questioningly. "What? Something about him bother you?"

"No. Not really."

He nudged her in the ribs with his elbow. "Hey. This is *me*. Your big brother. Cal wants to keep him on here. Is something wrong with him?"

She shrugged. "I wouldn't count on him staying, that's all. He's restless. Doesn't settle long in one place."

"That's what Cal said on the flight out here. But he thinks he'd stay on here for a while. He says he's got a hunch."

No, she thought, trying to ignore the hopeful speeding of her blood, the swooping sensation deep inside her.

"No," she said, then had to add, "Why would he stay?"

Gavin stared at the restless flames. "Why not? To everything there is a season."

She remembered Cal's offer to Grady, and that Grady hadn't taken it. She shook her head stubbornly. "He won't stay long. He gets tired of things. He lives for change. He's not a man you can count on that way."

Gavin put his elbow on the rug and leaned his cheek on his fist. His eyes searched her face. "Is that what you're looking for? A man you can count on?"

"I count on you and Del. That's all I need."

"Is it?" His tone was kind. "Are you going to be on the rebound from Sid for the rest of your life?"

She raised her chin and stared straight ahead. A log broke, collapsing into red coals. "I'm over Sid. I don't miss him."

"Good." He kissed the tip of his forefinger and placed it against her cheek. She dropped her head and gave him a smile.

He didn't smile in return, and the firelight played on his face. "Are you over Sid's father?"

She suppressed a groan. "Why can't he just leave us alone?"

He frowned. "Is he after you again already?"

"Yes." She said it through gritted teeth. "The same day you called, he called. That afternoon."

Gavin shook his head in disgust. "Still making the same threats?"

She nodded unhappily and told him what Burleigh had said.

"What?" Gavin's expression was of angry disbelief. "You're a good mother. You're a wonderful mother. Who does he think he is?"

"Del's grandfather, that's who. And under the law, he has the right to see Del and be with him. He'll push those rights to the limit. It's his way."

Gavin reached over and put his hand over one of hers. "Tara, you don't have to fear this guy. He's got no case, and you know it. If he's bullheaded enough to try anything, I'll hire lawyers who'll tie him in knots he'll never untie."

She looked at him with both regret and gratitude. "I know you would. But I don't want it to come to that. You've done enough for Del and me. To give us this chance. To trust me

with this job—which I love. To let us live in this house
You don't have to do more.''

He frowned. ''Don't be so damned independent. You're
my sister. Del's my nephew. If you need help, I want to
give it. Hell, even Cal's concerned.''

''Cal? Why?''

''Because he likes you and Del. He was asking about this
mess on the plane. About Burleigh, I mean.''

''He shouldn't concern himself. I've got a good lawyer.'

''Cal knows some of the best.''

She tried to act nonchalant. ''Look, let's not talk about
Burleigh unless he actually makes a move. Let's change the
subject.''

''All right. New subject. You look beautiful tonight,'' he
said. ''Like your old self. Is it just for my benefit? Are you
still trying to play Plain Jane? Because of Sid?''

He'd caught her out. Before he'd come, she'd changed
her clothes again, donning a pale pink blouse with a scooped
neck. She'd brushed her hair out, long and free, and put on
lipstick, the only makeup she'd kept.

She couldn't look him in the eyes. ''I haven't had time
for froufrous. You hired me to do a job, remember?''

His hand tightened on hers. ''You said you're over Sid.
Don't be afraid to be yourself. You're a lovely woman. Stop
trying to hide it.''

''I'm not,'' she lied. But she was not a good liar, had
never been.

''You'll fall in love again one of these days.''

''I don't want to.'' That, at least, was the truth.

''This is a new place, a new life,'' he said. ''Look the
way you used to. For me. It makes me happy to see you
look this way again. Do it. For me.''

She said nothing. She gazed down at the intricate pattern
of the carpet.

''For me,'' he repeated. ''Okay?''

"Okay," she whispered. But she didn't want to. Oh, how he didn't want to.

He picked up her hand and kissed it. "Good girl," he said, affection thickening his voice.

CHAPTER FIFTEEN

GRADY AND CAL SAT ON THE CUSHIONED wicker sofa on Lynn's sunporch, nursing beers and watching the moon ascend the sky.

Lynn had set votive lights on the wicker end tables. They threw their separate colors into the night and made the shadows play. Grady tried not to think of being on this same porch, in the same sort of darkness, with Tara.

Sam and Lynn had gone to bed, leaving them to drink and catch up on old times and fresh news. Cal took a sip of beer and cuffed Grady's shoulder.

"So you're here because of a canola oil spill and a lawsuit. Damn, that's strange."

"And you're here to build a house and become respectable," Grady said sarcastically. "*That's* strange."

"No," Cal returned. "I'll define strange. Your callin' me last night. Why're you so interested in Burleigh Hastings?"

Grady had known the question would come. He tried to sound rational and detached. "I told you. He's hassling Tara. Over the kid. I wondered how he could get away with it."

Cal shrugged. "It's like I said. Legally speakin', this whole grandparents' rights thing is a can of worms. 'Specially in California. What's it to you? You sweet on her?"

"Hell, no," Grady lied. "I just felt bad for her. She wouldn't say much about it. I wondered if anything could be done, that's all."

"Yup, you're sweet on her," Cal said, locking his hands behind his head. "I knew it soon as you asked the first question. You know, settlin' down ain't half-bad, old son. You ought to try it. It grows on you.''

The remark's irony stabbed through Grady. ''I don't reckon it's for me.''

''Suit yourself. But like I said, if you want to hang around here—for whatever reason, the female sort or not—the job offer's open.''

''When I get this mess about the truck settled, I move on. I meant to stay here a day or two and be on my way. Dad's bummed out, having two of us home again. And maybe Lang on the way.''

Cal shifted, crossing his foot over his knee. ''Speakin' of your daddy, I met that new lady workin' for him. That Rhonda. She's an appealin' sort. I don't usually like a woman that's roundish, but on her it looks good.''

''You're ogling my dad's housekeeper? She's twice your age. Does Serena know you've got this kinky streak?''

''She ain't twice my age. And I wasn't oglin'. I was merely observin'. I observed that your daddy was also observin'.''

''Dad?'' Restless, Grady stretched out his long legs. ''Yeah, he kinda seems to have an eye on her.''

Cal leaned back more lazily. ''Never thought I'd see him lookin' at another woman. I don't mean no disrespect, but your daddy took being single as a *vocation*. Like he's a monk.''

''Looking's one thing. I don't think he'd marry up again.''

''That's what I thought about my daddy. Figured he'd spend the rest of his life bein' a bereaved old grouch. But time passed. Along came Cynthia. Ding dong. Wedding bells.''

''Aren't you being kinda premature?'' Grady demanded. ''That woman hasn't been in the house but two days.''

''I'm talkin' about sexual vibrations. I can *perceive* 'em. I have a gift.''

"Oh, bullshit." Grady reached for his beer and took a long swallow.

"I perceive 'em vibratin' away between your daddy and Rhonda. Take my word for it."

"My dad's set in his ways. Stubborn. You think he's going to change like *that?*" Grady snapped his fingers contemptuously. "Sheesh. Two days. He courted my mother for two *years*."

Cal gave him a pitying look. "And how long did it take him to fall for her? We all grew up hearing that story. Two *seconds*."

"It doesn't happen that way," Grady protested. But he knew it had with his parents, and he knew the strange thing happening to him, so he added, "Very often."

"It did to me," Cal countered. "I had no more mind to get married than I did to grow tail feathers and eat worms. And then, there she was. Serena."

"What she saw in you, I'll never know," Grady grumbled.

"Me, either," Cal said cheerfully. "I was as sorry a case as you are."

Grady scowled. "Me? Leave me out of it."

"I can't," Cal said, picking up his beer bottle. "I look at you and see me. As the wretch I used to be. I once was lost, but now I'm found. Saved by the love of a good woman. But you know what? I was ready. Deep down I was tired of my ramblin' ways."

Grady shook his head. "When you shovel it, you pile it high and deep."

"I do go at it with a certain art, don't I? But those sexual vibrations? I also perceive 'em betwix you and the fair Tara."

"She's not my type," Grady muttered. This was both a lie and the truth. She was not the type to be seriously interested in *him*.

"Yeah, she'd need somebody more steady than you,

that's for sure, after what that SOB of an ex-husband done to her.''

Grady let a few beats of silence pass, but he couldn't resist. "Okay, what happened? You started to tell me last night.''

"Yeah, and then one of the twins whopped the other over the head with a saucepan. The screams are still ringin' in my ears. Yi-yi-yi.''

"I heard,'' Grady said dryly, but again could not resist. "But her husband. Her ex-husband. He threw her over for somebody else, right?''

Cal's lip drew up in a sneer. "Sid Hastings ought to be horsewhipped. He impressed Tara because he was 'an artist.' He was 'an intellectual.' Hell, he even taught college. Taught film producin' or something.''

He took a pull from his beer. "He met Tara when he was makin' this TV documentary about using horses to help disadvantaged kids. She did that kind of work. She was good at it, too.''

He sighed in distaste. "So he taught at the university, part-time. But he always had a hand in other projects. Like everybody else in Hollywood. He came from a family with money, so he had a little more leverage than most.

"Tara and Gavin didn't grow up poor, but not rich, either. She was fresh out of college. They'd just lost their folks. Killed in a plane crash. So she was real vulnerable when she met this snake.''

He gave Grady a sidelong glance. "She's one gorgeous woman. She tries to downplay it since the divorce. Well, she can downplay it, but she can't hide it. You noticed—unless you're dead, and I'm talkin' to a ghost.''

"I guess,'' Grady said as casually as he could. "She's okay. But aloof.''

"Ah, that's a front,'' Cal muttered. "Anyway, this Sid is making this film and he sees her, this tall, drop-dead beautiful girl—and she's poetry in motion on a horse. He's gotta have her. He chases her big time.''

He made an exasperated gesture. "She's dazzled. He's got all these degrees. He's got all these *plans*. He writes, he directs, he produces—never has much success, but she's got faith he's gonna make it."

Grady felt an unpleasant curiosity. "Was he any good?"

"Gavin knows the business. He says no. But in Tara's eyes he was Mr. Brilliant Talent. Then he gets involved in producing this cheesy B-movie. You know, *Amazon College Girls on Mars,* some crap like that."

Grady said nothing, waited for him to go on.

Cal shrugged. "And he meets this twenty-year-old girl. By this time, he and Tara have been married for four years, have a kid. But Sid's smitten with this bimbo. He has a hot affair. Tara finds out. He's under this girl's spell by now. He moves in with her."

Grady had to know. "The girl. You ever meet her?"

"Naw. Gavin did. He says she's a slut. Slept all over town. She had a little kid by some porn director. Gav says everything about her is phony. Her nose, her lips, her cheek-bones, her boobs. Nothing real but her sex drive. And that, they say, is legend."

Grady swore. "He left *Tara* and his own kid for some piece of trash?"

"He's obsessed with her. She's jealous of Del, so she doesn't want Sid to be around him. She wanted him to adopt *her* kid. And he did."

Grady felt slightly sick. "How could he do it?"

Cal slouched deeper on the sofa, looking contemptuous. "Gavin's heard rumors that more than sex is involved." He held an imaginary rolled paper to his nostril and pretended to inhale. "Nose candy."

Grady stood up, wanting to hit something. He pushed his hand through his hair in frustration. He wanted to swear, but he held back. "You think it's true?"

"Probably," Cal muttered. "Sid's actin' too loco. Gavin got word that one night at a party, they jumped in the swimming pool, stripped down and did it in front of everybody. Nice, huh?''

Grady paced to the porch's end and wheeled around. ''If I'd have been Gavin and heard that, I'd have gone and beaten the bastard silly.''

Cal nodded. ''Yeah. I've had to sit on him a time or two to keep him from doin' it. Which ain't easy. He's a strong guy.''

Grady wasn't appeased. ''Why'd you stop him?''

''Why should he dirty his hands? He'd get arrested, get his picture in the tabloids—that wouldn't help Tara and Del. Do you think it would?''

Grady tried to swallow his anger. He gazed at the floor, feeling both vengeful and stymied. ''No. I guess not.''

Cal rubbed his upper lip reflectively. ''Now I told you about Sid's daddy. Gav says he's a bad piece of work. He'll have his way or bust a gut tryin'. Threatens to try to take Del away. Old bastard.''

Grady watched the candlelight playing hide-and-seek on the floor. ''But he can't do that. You said so, right?''

''Gavin's sure he can't. Still, the old goat *does* have his rights, so he can always make trouble. That hangs over Tara's head. She worries.''

Grady stared into the shifting shadows, his emotions in tumult.

Cal said, ''But you asked some interestin' questions last night. You always did have a good head on your shoulders. So I made some phone calls. I got you some answers. And some names.''

He reached into his shirt pocket and drew out a dozen or so index cards. ''For what it's worth,'' he said, handing them to Grady.

Grady took them, a strange mixture of hope and fatalism stirring in him. Cal said, ''You told me you were askin' all this stuff just to be helpful. And because you were interested in the—what?—of the problem?''

''The technicalities,'' Grady said defensively. ''Just like

any problem. You wonder ways to solve it.'' Grady thrust the cards into his own pocket. "That's all."

Cal smirked. "I don't buy that. On account of my super-powers, namely perceivin' sexual vibrations. I think you want that lady, but you're worried you can't get her."

Grady's muscles tensed, and he felt caught out. He said nothing.

Cal said, "How do I know? 'Cause I been in that very spot myself. Serena wasn't about to have anything to do with a footloose cowboy like me. So what I had to do was not give up. Convince her I was bent on stayin' the course. And that's what you're gonna have to do."

Grady ground his teeth and still said nothing.

"'Course if you ain't got the grit," Cal observed, "you can just walk off. And let somebody else get her."

Grady sat and sulked. He should have known he couldn't fool Cal. Suspiciously, he said, "You didn't come here because of my call, did you?"

"No," Cal said, throwing him a lazy glance. "You exaggerate your importance in my life if you think that."

"Because I called—is that why you offered me a job?"

"I'm offerin' you a job because I know you're a workin' fool. I like gettin' my money's worth. Keeps me in Cadillacs."

Grady sat, trying to stare a hole through the darkness outside. At last he said, "I don't know when I'll get any money for that sorry-ass truck. You offered me a job. Tell me more about it."

TARA SAT ACROSS FROM GAVIN at the breakfast table. Del, still groggy with sleep, lay on the rug in front of the fireplace playing with his cars.

Tara put her elbow on the table and cupped her chin in her hand. "I can't believe you slept on the floor last night, Gav. You're a very weird person, you know that?"

Gavin gave her the smile of a satisfied man. "I *wanted*

to sleep on the floor. Like old times. To feel the floor. To feel the house. To hear it talk.''

She laughed at his eccentricity. ''You still think that? That houses talk when they think people are asleep?''

He refilled his glass from the orange juice pitcher. ''I don't think it, I *know* it. The trick is you have to learn the language.''

She remembered this theory from their childhood. He claimed a house would speak at night. It spoke in creaks and soft groans, by the way the wind touched it and the way the air moved in it; it even spoke with its scents and dust.

As a child, she'd been fascinated by his stories. It was lovely to know he still told them. ''So what,'' she asked, ''did the house have to say?''

Playfulness gleamed in his slate-colored eyes, but his face was serious.

''The house is breathing easier. It was scared. It thought it was dying. Now it feels almost safe.''

She raised an eyebrow. ''Almost safe? What's it need?''

''To be a home. It doesn't know you well yet. It knows Del better.''

She tilted her head and studied him, wondering how long he could do this with a straight face. She said, ''And it knows you best of all. Because you sleep on its bare floor.''

''The better to hear its heart beat.'' He seemed to be only half teasing.

''Hmm. And you translate its whispers. I hope it's not speaking to you with a forked tongue.''

''Mock away,'' he answered. ''I have an instinct about places. Always have. That's why I know this project can work.''

''That's what I like. The sound, scientific base to your reasoning. How was Spence's sleeping bag?''

His mouth quirked to a thoughtful angle. ''On a scale of one to ten about an eight. Excellent for a synthetic-fill bag. Packs big, though.''

''What did the house say about it?''

He reached over and tugged a strand of her hair affectionately. "Nothing. You look pretty this morning. Know that?"

She ducked her head self-consciously. Although she wore her usual jeans and boots, she'd put on one of her few colorful pieces of clothing. It was a coral-colored T-shirt with three-quarter-length sleeves and a ballet neck.

Coral had been one of her favorite shades. She knew it set off the color of her eyes and brought out the highlights in her hair. For Gavin's sake, she wore her hair loose, falling to her shoulders in a waving cascade.

Today she'd also put on a pair of simple gold hoop earrings. The only jewelry she'd kept was that given to her over the years by Gavin. She supposed she could wear one item at a time without seeming vain, but she still felt odd, like a woman who had long gone veiled and was now letting the world see her face.

She heard tires coming up the driveway and fought against cringing. Grady was even earlier than usual. She would introduce him to Gavin, who would be giving the orders from here on out, and then she would keep out of his way. And that would be that.

But when she moved to the window, she did not see Grady's borrowed truck. Instead three long cars, one behind the other, pulled into the driveway. They gleamed as richly as newly minted money. Doors opened, strange men got out, doors slammed.

Tara gripped the window frame more tightly. "Who—?"

Gavin had moved to her side. "It's the crew from Austin. Come out and meet them. They're quite a bunch."

Tara, her heart pounding with shyness, let him usher her outside. There were five men in all. Two were in suits and one in a shirt and tie. A fourth wore jeans and a dark leather jacket. The fifth was clad in suede pants, a tie-dyed cotton gauze shirt and designer boots.

They all had the aura of money and the subtle swagger of success. They carried themselves with the confidence of experts, men who have important knowledge and do important things.

Gavin began the introductions, and Tara struggled to keep their names, titles and jobs straight. Two of them, one in a suit and the one in suede, eyed her with frankly sexual interest.

She felt that her jeans and coral shirt did not really cover her. She felt as vulnerable as if she was naked. But she smiled and nodded and one by one shook their hands.

GRADY'S BORROWED TRUCK shuddered and made little bucking spurts as he drove up the slope. What fresh hell was this, he wondered. He'd check the motor when he got to Tara's.

He squinted through a haze of gravel dust. Somebody had climbed this road not long before him. They'd raised enough dust for a caravan. He and Cal were supposed to meet here at eight; had Cal beat him?

When he pulled into the driveway, he saw three strange cars, but none was Cal's rented Cadillac. The cars were long and sleek, their polish only faintly dimmed by the dust they'd raised.

And he saw Tara, standing by the first car. She was surrounded by men. The men were like their cars, radiating sleekness and fine-tuned power. And she—oh, Lord, his heart turned over slowly and painfully—she'd never looked lovelier.

She wore some little top of coral and her striking hair was loose, moving and dreamlike, on the morning breeze. Gold flashed at her ears. She looked like a long-stemmed rose to him. And at least two of the men eyed her as if they saw the same tall flower and wanted to pluck it.

A feeling of hopelessness cut through him, and he felt the emptiness of a man recognizing the odds against him were impossible. He parked far behind them and took his time getting out of the truck. Then he opened the hood and pretended to fiddle with the motor. He'd wait until the crowd around Tara thinned—if it ever did.

He took the tallest of these men, the least flashily dressed, for her brother. He had her height and clean-limbed build, and the man's longish hair was a sandy, less vivid version of hers.

Grady was putting a spark plug back in when he heard the sound of another motor. Cal's Cadillac came gliding up the hill. Cal parked, got out and ambled toward him. Grady wiped his hands clean on a scrap of rag.

"What's the matter, Cinderella?" Cal asked with a sardonic smirk. "Why you here all alone? Didn't you get invited to the ball?"

"Oh, shut up," Grady muttered. "They're having some kind of meeting or something. I wasn't about to horn in."

"Why not? You know this piece of land better'n any of 'em. Except me. And you're lookin' mighty sharp. Like you just stepped out of a band box. Who pressed that shirt? It wasn't you."

"Rhonda." Grady slammed down the hood of the truck.

Cal looked him up and down and whistled softly. "She is some woman. You look downright respectable."

"Looks are deceiving." Grady was in a dark mood, and he didn't feel like letting anyone lighten it. Especially Cal, who was only egging him deeper into this mess.

Cal clapped him on the shoulder. "Come on. I'll introduce you. That feller with the beard thinks I'm a real goober, but last time I was in Austin I won four thousand dollar off'n him playin' poker. When it comes to cards, he ain't worth a bucket of warm spit."

The two walked toward the loose knot of men with Tara at its center. She flashed Cal a smile that seemed nervous, but when her eyes met Grady's, her expression became guarded and even more tense.

Cal's arm went around Grady's shoulders in a masculine embrace. "Howdy," he said to the group. "This is my relative, Grady McKinney. He's been helpin' Tara put the house back into shape. He's both a craftsman and an expert construction worker.''

Grady resisted giving him a sidelong look that asked, *Have you no shame?*

''Grady, this is my partner, Gavin Chance, Tara's brother. Gavin's staying on here a few months while we get the groundwork laid.''

Gavin and Grady shook hands. Grady looked deeply into the other man's eyes, wondering if he'd see suspicion in their depths. There was none. His glance seemed to take Grady's measure, yet at the same time he seemed genuinely friendly. ''You've done a great job,'' he said. ''Good to have you on board.''

''Thanks. Pleasure to meet you.''

Cal made a gesture that indicated the remaining men, who looked at Grady with expressions ranging from mild curiosity to condescension. ''As for these other hombres...''

Cal introduced them. Their names were Plotkin, Berringer, Dabchick, Forbes and Cahill. They were mostly architects, and they had a bewildering number of titles and specialties: master planner, design developer, landscape architect, equestrian architecture, conservancy developer.

Grady concentrated on keeping them straight, which was difficult with Tara standing there, her hair stirring around her face like a celestial corona. He shook their hands. He repeated their names. He memorized their faces. He logged their specialties into his memory. He decided who would chase Tara and who would not.

But even as he measured them, both as men and as possible rivals, he sensed Tara readying herself for escape. She shifted her weight uneasily and brushed her hair from her eyes. She murmured, ''Very nice to meet you all. You won't be needing me. I'll get back to my son and leave you to discuss what needs discussing.''

She paused and gave Grady a glance that seemed sad.

Then she turned on her heel and strode to the house. Grady tried to pretend she wasn't dragging his heart behind her like a cheap toy on a string.

THE MEN, LED BY CAL AND GRADY, walked down the slope to the deserted lodge. Grady had been looking it over from his first day on the job, and he thought he knew what its main problems were. Cal remembered the building in its heyday, and added what he thought its advantages and drawbacks had been.

Plotkin, Berringer, and company looked about with sharp eyes and asked questions, many questions, some hard, some easy—and a few stupid ones.

Dabchick, the dude in the suede pants and gauzy shirt, asked the stupid ones. His haircut was trendy and the blond streaks in it had come from a salon, not the sun. He was the sort of guy who was unshaven because he thought it made him look more masculine.

He was the equestrian architect and had been the one who'd looked most flirtatiously at Tara. He was about thirty-eight, had teeth as even as a movie star's and wore a necklace of small earthenware beads. Grady decided that he hated him.

Grady and Cal managed to answer most of the questions between them. Then the five architects and designers drifted apart, inspecting this, poking at that, stepping outside to regard the lay of the land.

Gavin was about to go outside with the boyish Cahill and the bearded Plotnik, when Cal drew him aside. "Can I talk to you a minute?"

"Sure," Gavin said. Cal led him to the fireplace of lodge's main room, where Grady stood, looking critically at its mortar. Cal rested his hands on either side of his belt buckle and asked Gavin, "Did we answer your questions about this place?"

Gavin nodded his sandy head. "Absolutely. It's worth saving. Plotkin saw it right off. You did a good job." He nodded to Grady. "Both of you."

"All right for a couple of hicks, eh?" grinned Cal. "You've seen Grady's work, and you've seen him *at* work. What do you think?"

Gavin smiled crookedly. "I think for once in your life, you didn't hand me a load of Texas B.S."

"He meant that as a compliment," Cal said to Grady. "To both of us." He turned back to Gavin. "So how about we make him a kind of on-site project foreman, like we talked about? He's got experience in a lot of different areas. And he knows the land."

Gavin's face grew serious. "Cal's told me some of your qualifications. You've pretty well been everywhere, done everything."

"Pretty near," Grady said, his throat going strangely tight.

"The thing is, are you willing to stick around here? Sign on for up to a year? A year'll just see us getting started on the main construction."

Grady's throat grew tighter. He thought of a thousand reasons not to do this. And he thought of one pair of disturbingly beautiful eyes. "I could probably guarantee you three months. I could do that."

Cal's eyes narrowed. "What about twelve? We need you for at least twelve. It'll be worth your while."

Grady's lips clamped into a grim line. He didn't want to stick around if Tara would have none of him. But he saw the challenge glinting in Cal's eyes and muttered, "I'll think about it."

"Ha!" crowed Cal and slapped his back.

He shook hands with Cal and Gavin, a hearty shake, full of strength and determination. But his mind was asking in alarm, *What have you done? What in hell are you doing?*

"You did what?" Tara's eyes widened.

"We offered ol' Grady a year's contract," Cal told her. He and Gavin stood in the kitchen with her. "To be a sort of a foreman."

Her hold on the coffeepot nearly slipped. But she held herself steady and filled the men's mugs without so much as a tremor. She set the mugs on the table with such a perfect imitation of calm that she amazed herself.

"In the movies, he'd be a cross between a gaffer, a gofer and a best boy," Gavin said, sitting down.

"A kind of informal wagon boss," Cal offered. "A top hand who can ride point or flank. An all-around sort."

Tara tried to keep her breathing regular as Cal, too, sat. "Do you really think he'd stick around that long?" She made the question sound light.

Cal picked up his coffee mug. "If he signs a contract, he'll stick to it. He's done it before. Besides, it's a good job. Worth his while."

A year, she thought. It seemed a long time, forever. It also seemed short, the blink of an eye.

"He knows things about these parts I don't," Gavin told her. "He does good work, and he can think on his feet. He's got connections here. And it'd be good to have a man around when I can't be here." Then he gave Tara a sharp glance. "Why? You have a problem with him?"

She tossed her head. "No. But I'm running this house and the stable when it's done. For everything else he reports to you. He's your—gofer-gaffer-point man. Understand?"

"I understand." Gavin sipped his coffee laconically. "Well. I'm glad. Good help is hard to find."

Cal frowned. "We ought to have a name for this job. Like 'semiexalted dogsbody.' Or 'grand poobah.' Something with a nice ring to it."

Del came in from the backyard. "Where'd Grady go?"

"He had to show the city slickers around," Cal said. "And I've got to get goin'. I gotta catch a plane to California. A mighty pretty lady is waitin' for me."

He rose from the table. Gavin scooped up Del in his arms, and Tara went with them to walk Cal to his car. Cal kissed Tara goodbye, hugged Del and gave Gavin an affectionate squeeze before he drove off.

Del watched the car disappear, and his small face grew sad. "I don't like it when people go away." He tightened his arms around Gavin's neck. "You won't go away—will you?"

Gavin held him closer and spoke against his cheek. "Sometimes I'll have to. But I'll always come back. I promise."

Tara looked at her brother and fought the absurd urge to mist up and cry. She knew she could always depend on Gavin, just as Cal's family could always depend on Cal.

She thought of her ex-husband and Grady. Real men, she told herself, weren't frightened of promises. Not of making them, and not of keeping them.

CHAPTER SIXTEEN

IN THE FOLLOWING DAYS, Tara threw herself into dozens of tasks. She worked at coordinating the house's interior. She knew Gavin's taste as well as she did her own, and she knew what she wanted.

She ordered new appliances for the kitchen and laundry room. She was refining her furniture plan and making decisions about textures, patterns and upholsteries.

The architects came and went, singly, in pairs, in packs. Mr. Myers, Sr. often spent the night in the guest room. Politely friendly, she offered these men hospitality, but she didn't involve herself with them. Gavin dealt with them. The equestrian community as a whole was his baby. The house was hers.

The only architect who kept seeking her out was Daryl Dabchick, he of the suede trousers and unshaven jaw. His specialty was design for the horse industry, and he pestered her with details about the stable and riding arena plans.

Tara and Gavin agreed on how they wanted the stable done. Yet Dabchick tapped at the door every few hours to offer her a new idea, a different option, a finer refinement. She liked none of his suggestions, but smiled and said she'd discuss them with Gavin. Gavin hated them all.

As for Grady, Tara was relieved to let Gavin deal with him, too. But to her chagrin, the two men got on well. In fact, they got on *too* well. Gavin came to think him invaluable.

Grady helped scout locations. He knew the land's secrets and he could translate them into builders' language. He could read exactly how much damage the flood had inflicted on the valley. He understood what was good about the lay-out of the original riding trails of the dude ranch and what was weak.

When Plotkin wanted the attic of the lodge crawled in preliminary inspection, Grady crawled it. When Cahill needed the lines of the lodge's septic tank located, Grady located them.

When Berringer wanted to know if there was a spot he could use as a landfill, Grady pinpointed two. When Forbes asked about the site of the first house on the property, built in 1882, Grady led him straight to it.

"He's a born problem-solver. He's got good ideas," Gavin told Tara on the sixth day of what she thought of as the Invasion of the Architects. "Oh—he said he'd like to build Del a sandbox and swing set. Why didn't you take him up on it?"

Because I want to keep him as far away as possible, Tara thought.

"Because there's so much else to do with all these hot and cold running consultants," she said.

"All the planners meet in Austin tomorrow," Gavin said. "I've got to be there, too. We've got to talk to state water commissioners, conservationists, some transportation peo-ple. Grady could put up the playground equipment while we're there."

Tara's mind spun, going nowhere. She could not think of a rebuttal. And she could not escape; she had to stay at the house. A consultant from Austin Window Treatments was coming and the kitchen appliances were due to arrive.

"Besides," Gavin went on, "Del really likes him. I think he's done the kid a lot of good."

Grady made a point to see Del every day. He brought him cookies and brownies from the Double C. He had cop-ies made of the photos of the guns Francina Travis had owned, and he let Del keep them. He found two arrowheads in the creek bed and gave them to the boy.

Tara fidgeted with the coffeepot. She told Gavin, "Del may like him too much. I don't want him getting too attached. Grady McKinney could up and leave in a minute."

Gavin's sandy brows drew together in a frown. "Tara, the guy's not running off in a couple of days. He's signing a contract to stay on a year."

She lifted her chin in challenge. "Has he signed it? No." She'd heard from Lynn that perhaps the matter of Grady's truck might be settled out of court, after all. Tara thought as soon as his pockets were jingling again, he'd be off.

Gavin didn't agree. "Cal's local lawyer's under the weather. Grady's contract's not finished. But we'll get it to him soon enough."

But Tara wasn't convinced. He hadn't signed it yet.

LATER THAT AFTERNOON, Bret struggled with a secret.

He found Rhonda Cole devastatingly attractive. He thanked his lucky stars he could conceal his feelings. He'd hate for his sons to suspect such a thing. They'd think him a lecherous old fool.

He found himself watching the fetching roundness of Rhonda Cole's hips when she walked away. Bret's Maggie had tended toward plumpness after the boys were born. Bret had liked it. He'd relished her curves and softness and warmth in bed at night.

He found Rhonda's firm, generous breasts impossible to ignore. They lodged in his consciousness so that he thought about them when he was awake, and dreamed about them when he was asleep.

He had a powerful dream censor, so he could never clearly remember these dreams of snuggling and fondling. But it wasn't powerful enough to obliterate the memory completely. He awoke feeling ashamed for imaginary acts that he couldn't quite recall.

He might have ignored such ample charms in another woman. But it was Rhonda's sweet nature that made the rest of her irresistible. She did not have an atom of meanness in her.

Her smile pleased him so much he found himself trying to make it appear just for him. He'd begun making little jokes. He didn't think he'd joked with a woman since Maggie had died.

He found himself searching for small acts of courtesy he could perform for her, bits of domestic gallantry. If something heavy needed moving, he moved it. If something unwieldy needed to be carried, he carried it. He stopped scattering his newspapers all over the study floor and leaving his half-empty coffee cups about.

Did she notice this awkward chivalry? She acted grateful for any kindness. She would smile and thank him, and say things like "Bless your heart." But she seemed to treat him with no special deference.

Indeed, he thought she might like his sons more than she did him. She recognized Jonah's shyness and was gentle with him, even protective. With Grady she was open and natural. Grady could make her laugh because he was the only one bold enough to tease her, and she admired him because he could fix anything.

Bret brooded on this. Did she not notice *him?* Or was she conscious that he watched, thought about her, and tried to please her? One part of him thought that she must, but she was sending a message that she didn't want to see him as a man, only as an employer.

Another part of him wondered if she was so genuinely innocent that she did not see his interest—or recognize it for what it was.

She did a multitude of little things that touched him. She set a table that felt homey to sit down to. With Millie Gilligan, the food was fine, but she'd served it with intimidating military precision. As for Rhonda's meals, everything she made tasted as if it was cooked with love.

He liked the way she ironed his shirts and folded his underwear. He opened his sock drawer and was smitten by

her comforting gift for order. How she cared for his under-
shorts made him blush and think of cold showers.

He realized he had become a man who'd kept too much
to himself. He struggled to be more outgoing with Jonah
and even to Grady. He even began paying courtesy visits to
Millie Gilligan. She no longer seemed quite as strange to
him. How could she, when she had a niece as kind and
unspoiled as Rhonda?

When Rhonda had said, yes, she thought she could stay
on in the house until Millie recovered, Bret's heart leaped
with pleasure. He felt giddy. He wanted to thank her, but
he didn't know how.

Yet he was terrified that anyone would see these emotions
rioting in him. He was most terrified that she would see—
and think him a fool.

This afternoon she had gone grocery shopping, and the
house seemed hollow and lifeless without her, as if it had
lost its heartbeat. Jonah was out gathering the bulls to pasture them separately for the winter. Grady was off working.
Only Bret and Millie Gilligan were in the house.

Bret had accounts to do, and later in the day he would
ride out with Ken Slattery to check a troublesome waterhole.
But he was restless and thought it might please Rhonda if
he paid some attention to her aunt.

Millie Gilligan took to convalescence better than he'd expected. She watched her little television, she listened to the
classical music station on her radio. Rhonda had brought
her a stack of library books, and she had knitting and cro-
cheting projects.

When he knocked on her door and entered, her radio was
playing something with lots of groaning organ music. She
wore blue flannel pajamas with pictures of the moons and
stars all over them. The moons all had grinning faces.

To Bret's dismay, he saw the woman had a tray across
her lap and was dealing out cards. Tarot cards. Although he
dismissed fortune-telling as a parlor trick, he had to admit
that tarot cards gave him the creeps.

She smiled crookedly at him and looked him up and down. He wondered why her green eyes seemed sharp as broken glass, and Rhonda's were peaceful as forest pools.

"I just took out my deck," she said, shuffling the cards. "Sometimes it whispers when the time is right. Did you hear it?"

Bret stiffened as if challenged. "Of course not. I don't believe that stuff. I just stopped in to say hello. And see if you wanted anything."

"Rhonda has seen to my comforts. I'm happy as a calmed low tide."

What? Bret asked himself in frustration. He fought not to grit his teeth, but she still must have read his puzzlement in his face.

She frowned slightly. "Or do I mean happy as a clam at high tide? Whatever. She's attended to my earthly needs. She's a pearl of pure heart. I think she's happy here. Good, because who gets from here to there without a bridge?"

Bret nodded, but his mind had fastened on only one of her statements. "She's happy here?"

"Mmm. Needs to be among people, that one. Alone too long will do you wrong. Sit if you're going to chat. You're putting a crick in my neck."

Bret lowered himself to the bedside chair. "Er—Mrs. Cole has—"

"Rhonda," she corrected him.

"Yes. Rhonda has been alone for a while? I mean I take it she's a widow, but she's never said much about her past."

"Ask her," Mrs. Gilligan said briskly. She fanned the cards out on the tray.

Bret was taken aback. "I didn't want to pry."

"Then ask your eldest son. He doesn't pry. He knows things because he makes friends. He talks to her. And me." She pointed a bony finger at him. "But he doesn't talk as much to you. You don't let him. I hope you're not like the fox who ate his own bright tail for spite."

"Wh-what fox?" Bret sputtered. "Ma'am, excuse me, I

don't mean to be rude, but your words don't always make sense to me."

Her face was bland with unconcern. "They do to me. Anyway, he's not the one your heart worries about. No, not him."

He stared at her confounded. It was true he worried more about Lang than Grady, but how did she know? Lang and Susie had been quibbling for days. Today he'd phoned. The marriage seemed as good as dead. Bret sensed that Lang had her out of his system at long last.

"Pick three cards," she invited.

Bret tensed with suspicion. "Why?"

"You have a question. I can tell, sure as a hawk's not a hacksaw."

"No, I don't," he lied. He did have a question, an important one that troubled him, but he wasn't going to share it with Millie Gilligan.

"You want an answer about something. It stands out like eyebrows on an egg. So ask," she wheedled. "You don't even have to say it out loud. Keep it under your hat, like a turtle."

"I told you, I don't believe in that stuff."

She patted the cards and sighed. "I see. You're afraid."

"I'm not afraid of a pack of pasteboard."

"Then ask a question. Pick just one card. What can it hurt?"

Bret shrugged. He'd humor her, then get out. But his question was about Rhonda, not Lang. Was there a chance on God's green earth that she'd return his interest? That his loneliness might come to an end?

He picked one card and slapped it down on the tray. It showed a woman in a bower of roses. She sat in a chair with a cupid carved on its back.

Mrs. Gilligan squinted at it. "Hmm. The Queen of Pentacles—or coins, some say. She holds a key to the future. She is a woman of generosity and a guardian of the home. She provides solace, security and happiness. A key, a key is what I see. I sense things locked up that could stay locked forever. What good is a key not touched?''

Bret's skin prickled with a chill, but he only cleared his throat and muttered, "Interesting."

She raised a wispy eyebrow. "Would you like to ask another question? Or have me give you a longer reading about yourself? About what your future holds? I sense your worry about your sons…''

A superstitious dread welled up in him. "No. Certainly not. Have to get back to my accounts. No worrying. No wondering. None at all. I'll drop in another time, Mrs. Gilligan.''

He rose, turned to go, and was astonished to see Rhonda standing in the bedroom doorway. She wore a green coat, and her cheeks were pink with cold. Her hair was a soft cloud about her face.

Bret's heart turned over in his chest, and his knees felt almost watery. "Oh," was all he could utter.

She smiled. "I just got back. I'm sorry. I didn't mean to startle you.''

"No, no," Bret said, flustered. "You didn't startle. We were just having—eh—a nice talk. Didn't hear you come in, that's all.''

"We were talking about his future," said Millie Gilligan, folding her pack of cards back into a deck.

Rhonda chuckled. "Oh, Millie. You're not saying things like that again? That you can see his future?''

Millie tapped her deck against the tray. "I can see it as clear as I can see you standing there," she said slyly.

GRADY WAS MILDLY SURPRISED when his father came to his room that evening.

"I'd like to speak to you man to man," Bret said, his voice gruff.

Grady sat on the bed, putting a new cord on Millie Gilligan's hair dryer. The old cord was so frayed and patched with tape that Rhonda had asked him to replace it.

"Sure." Grady nodded at the little chair with the pink velvet cushion. "Have a seat."

Bret sat on the delicate little chair, his big hands on his thighs. "Is there a lot of work over there? At that Francina Hills place?"

Grady wondered what this was about. "Enough to keep me busy," he said evenly.

Bret sat stiffly, as if posing for a portrait. "I got a call from Lang. Things aren't working out with Susie. He may be coming here after all."

Grady looked up from the cord. "I'm sorry. That it's not working out, I mean. When's he coming?"

"He's not sure. Probably soon." He cleared his throat. "Things are slow around here. I got more men than work. I was thinking of sending Lang over there to help out. At Tara Hastings's. Just to be neighborly, you know."

Grady carefully connected a wire. "Her brother's got construction crews coming in starting next week. It's not Lang's kind of work."

"Those horses of hers are coming soon, aren't they?" Bret asked. "She'll need a hand with them. That's his kind of work."

Grady gave him a level look. "I can take care of horses. So can she."

"Well, he's expert at it," Bret stated. "And she'll be putting up a new stable. He knows all about that sort of thing."

"So does she. So does her brother. They know what they want. They've got plans."

"I'm sure they'd appreciate his opinions. His experience." Bret tapped his fingers nervously on one knee. "I'll send him over. After all, you probably won't be staying on there long. It's not your style."

Grady felt grimness settling into his face, but fought against letting it show. He said nothing.

"When Cal called here, he said something about offering

you a contract,'' Bret muttered. ''You never mentioned a contract to me.''

''I haven't signed one. I haven't seen one.''

''Doesn't sound like you to me,'' Bret said, ''sticking around here. You'd be bored out of your mind in a month. I know you.''

Grady raised his head and looked his father in the eye. *Do you?* He wondered. *Do you know me at all? Have you ever?* Then he turned back to the dryer and tightened another screw.

Bret made a harumphing sound and kept tapping his thigh. ''That woman. Tara. She seems like a nice woman. Respectable woman. Is she?''

''She's nice enough. She's respectable. Mighty respectable.'' *So respectable she's nearly killed me with it. She's damned near brought me to my knees.*

''Thought she and Lang ought to meet. They've got a lot in common. Lang could handle a contract like that. He could be a big help to her.''

Grady's hands went still. Then he connected another wire. So his father was still playing matchmaker for Tara. Wasn't it bad enough watching that ninny, Daryl Dabchick, chasing her? Berringer and the younger Meyer of Meyer and Meyer were giving her the eye, too. His father's remarks grated like hell.

''Lang hasn't left Susie yet,'' he said as coolly as he could.

''It'll happen. I've felt it all along.'' Bret sat even straighter. ''I didn't used to approve of married couples splitting up. One man, one woman for good, that's how I saw it. With Lang, I—understand better.''

Grady raised his eyes. ''One man, one woman for good. Yeah. That's what you always said.''

Bret stopped tapping. ''A man can have a change of heart. If he's wrong, he should admit it. That's how I see it.'' He paused. ''What's that thing you're fixing?''

"Mrs. Gilligan's hair dryer. The cord was wearing out. It worried Rhonda."

Bret folded his arms over his chest. "It looks a hundred years old. She should buy a new one."

Grady held it up to the light. He took a rag and began to polish it. "Rhonda says she's partial to it. It's got sentimental value to her. Rhonda's mother gave it to her one Christmas."

Bret frowned. "You and Rhonda are mighty chummy."

Grady shrugged. "She's a friendly woman. We sit and talk in the kitchen some nights. You could join us if you wanted. But you're always holed up in your study or something. She thinks you work too hard."

"I wouldn't want to intrude," Bret said righteously. But then his tone softened. "She said that? She thinks I work too hard?"

Aha, thought Grady. *It's true. He's sweet on her. Maybe he's not all dried up inside after all. And maybe that's why he's talking about this change of heart. He's talking as much about himself as Lang.*

Grady began to choose his words with care, even with cunning. "Yeah. Her husband died. He worked all the time, too, worried too much. Then one day—boom. Heart attack. Fell over right in front of her eyes." He shook his head. "Terrible shock. Happened two years ago. In Waco. Left her alone in the world. Except for one son."

Bret looked thoughtful. "I knew she was a widow. Didn't know the details. She's from Waco, eh?"

"No," Grady said. "They moved around a lot. He worked for a construction company. Specialized in bridges. Went from job to job. She never really got to settle down. Shame. She seems the settling sort."

"You think so?"

"Sure enough," said Grady. "She would have liked more children. But there was just the one. Too bad. She's the kind that likes to take care of people. She reminds me of Mom that way."

Bret stiffened, his expression almost disapproving. "Your mother? Why do you say that?"

Grady laid down the dryer and made a guileless gesture. "She's sweet like Mom. Really modest. Always thinks the best of people. Needs people. Needs family."

"You think so?" Bret said again.

"Yessirree. That's why she just moved here. To be close to Millie. That's her only kin, except the son. But he's a geologist. He goes all over the world. He's in—let's see—Manchuria, I think."

"Manchuria! He might as well be on the moon."

Grady nodded sagely. "Those are the very words she used. 'It seems like he's on the moon.' She misses him. So she likes to stay busy. Keep her time filled. She has her little hobbies and interests."

"Hobbies?" Bret repeated, leaning forward. "Interests?"

"Gardening. Preserves. Stuff like that. Course she's never had much chance to. The family didn't stay put. Too bad."

Bret seemed lost in thought. Grady paused. "Know what? She ought to find a nice man and get married. I ought to see if I can fix her up with somebody."

Bret snapped back to alertness. "What?"

"Well," Grady said innocently, "it's like you said about one man, one woman. That's fine, but what if a person has that, but then gets left alone? You said Lang should find somebody he has things in common with. So should Rhonda. Yessirree. You fix up Lang. And I'll find somebody for Rhonda."

Bret came close to sputtering. "Who do *you* know?"

Grady shrugged nonchalantly. "I meet a lot of folks over there at Francina Hills. There's this one engineer, a widower. About your age—"

He stopped and gave his father a thoughtful look, as if just struck by a startling idea. "A guy your age. You know, Dad, *you* could ask her out. Take her to a movie, buy her a nice supper. Lord knows she's always doing for us. Of course, I realize you probably don't have the nerve—"

"Don't have the nerve? Me? Short on nerve?"

Grady looked innocent. "Anyway, it's not your style. You'd never do something like that. Though, Lord knows, she's a mighty fine woman. Shapely, too."

"Who says I'd never do something like that?" Bret challenged. "I would if I wanted. But you and your brothers would never approve. Me, paying attention to a woman not your mother?"

"Why would we disapprove? Jonah really likes her. So do I. Lang wouldn't object—he knows what it's like to be lonesome. Now that I recall, Cal even kind of suggested it—back when he was here."

Bret looked stunned. "Well," he said finally. "It's an idea that never crossed my mind. I'll have to think on it. Maybe I'll consider it."

He stood and crossed the room. He put his hand on Grady's shoulder. "I'm glad we had this heart-to-heart, son. It's come to me I should talk to you boys a little more. I've never told you this, but I've come to accept your rambling ways. There are men who stay put, and there are men who can't. I respect your independence. Even if it seems shortsighted to me sometimes. To each his own, eh?"

He gave Grady an awkward pat and left the room.

After he was gone, Grady stared at the door. He shook his head to clear it. He wasn't sure if they'd had a conversation or a contest, and if it was a contest, he didn't know who'd won.

A moment later, the pink phone on the night table rang.

Night after night he'd holed up in this room making calls, too many to count. Some were local, some were long distance, and he'd talked to so many different people it was hard to keep them straight.

He had no idea who was phoning him. He picked up the receiver to find out.

THE NEXT MORNING, TARA SAT at the kitchen table, poring over a furniture catalog. She had stacks of specialty catalogs, her graph paper, and her laptop. She worked in the kitchen so she could hear Del if he called from the backyard.

She knew he was waiting for Grady, excited to have him working close again. And she, too, was waiting for him, excited in a different way, and frightened of her own emotions.

All week Gavin had kept him occupied elsewhere. But she and Grady saw each other. They exchanged looks that seemed freighted with too much meaning. They exchanged simple information about practical matters, but every word vibrated with a significance that had nothing to do with practical matters and everything to do with the two of them.

She was conscious of him even when he wasn't there. When he was there, she became so keenly aware of his presence that her mind buzzed like a hive of bees.

But Burleigh's warning haunted her. Her lawyer, John Clarkson, had phoned from California, telling her that Burleigh's attorneys were threatening to take Tara to court. Burleigh had decided that he wanted custody of Del during the summers.

Burleigh's reasoning was that by moving to Texas, Tara had tried to deprive him of his visitation rights. He would make her send the boy to him and take all his visitation at once. It was, of course, merely a ploy to get partial custody.

The thought literally sickened Tara. Clarkson assured her that Burleigh couldn't win, but reminded her that the old man could still visit Del and perhaps get limited weekend custody.

"Tara," Clarkson had said, "the grandparents' rights issue is one of the most complicated in family law. It's in flux in California. We can try to get a restraining order against him. But it won't be easy."

Tara had to stay poised and ready for this fight. And she meant to keep her reputation squeaky clean. It would be stupid and reckless to have an affair with Grady, even if she secretly longed to be closer to him. She supposed, like a fool, she had let herself fall in love with him.

Now she heard the sound of a distant engine growing closer. Her heartbeat sped, and her fingers tightened around her pencil. Then Del cried, ''Grady's here! Mom! Grady's here!'' Lono barked an excited greeting.

The pencil fell from her numbed fingers, and she rose to go meet him. Today, with Gavin gone, she should have reverted to her plainest clothes, pulled her hair back, left her lipstick untouched.

But she hadn't. She wore her fitted yellow T-shirt with the embroidered rose. She'd pushed her hair back behind her ears but left it free and flowing. She'd colored her lips lightly with coral lipstick.

She knew she would be sending Grady mixed signals again. How could she help it? She sent mixed signals to herself. Did she want him? Yes. Did she dare to act on it? No.

She went outside, reluctant to see him, yet eager at the same time. She stood at the gate with Del as Grady parked the truck and leaped out. He was dressed as usual, in jeans and a crisply ironed chambray shirt. The black cowboy hat was pushed back to the familiar carefree angle. She expected his usual jaunty smile.

But for a moment, he stood still, just staring at her. His face was serious, almost solemn. His eyes met and held hers, and for a long, tremulous moment, she had the sensation of being drawn out of her body.

But Del, hyper, jumped up and down, and jiggled the padlock so that she'd undo it. The key was in her hand. She squeezed it, as if assuring herself that the key—and she—were real.

Then Grady's white smile flashed, slightly off-center. The dimples deepened in his cheeks, and he looked her up and down appreciatively. ''Howdy,'' he said. ''Are you going to let me in? Or keep me locked out?''

''Let him in, Mom.'' Del gripped the gate as if he'd climb over it if she didn't open it. She managed to keep her movement steady and brisk as she unlocked the gate and swung it open. She stood aside to let him pass.

She hadn't returned his smile, but his was still in place. Del whooped and jumped, and Grady caught him, swinging him up toward the sky. Grady laughed.

"Will you build my sandbox and swing today?" Del asked, still suspended above Grady's head.

"You want me to?"

"Yes!"

Grady gave him a mocking frown. "I didn't hear the magic word."

"Please," Del supplied. "Pretty please?"

"Pretty please with cream and toads on it?"

"Yes—cream and toads. Please?"

"Then I will. You can help. If your mom says it's okay."

He braced Del against his shoulder, holding him with one arm. He turned to Tara. Again his eyes met hers, and his face grew serious, searching. "Okay if he helps me out?"

"Yes." Her voice was almost a whisper. "Fine. I'll be in the kitchen.

"Del, let me know when the people come to help with the drapes."

She was ready to escape back to the kitchen, but Grady, his gaze on her lips now, said, "Your brother's gone, isn't he?"

Her throat was dry. "Yes."

"Gone all day?"

"Yes." Gavin had said he might not be home until late, perhaps not until after midnight.

Grady's mouth said nothing, but his eyes told her that he relished being near her again. Her own gaze hardened and sent him a silent message. *Nothing's going to happen between us again. Nothing.*

A slow, almost bitter smile curled his upper lip. It sent a message back. *I'm not quitting. I'm not backing off. Not yet.*

CHAPTER SEVENTEEN

ALTHOUGH TARA MANAGED TO STAY out of Grady's way most of the morning, she kept tabs on him through the kitchen window. It was a cool day with a gray sky full of long, low clouds. Not only did Grady keep his shirt on, he donned a denim vest lined with sheepskin. She looked at him in it and thought, *It makes his shoulders look even wider. Damn.*

She called Del inside to put on a heavier jacket and a cap. She hoped he might want to stay in the warm house, but no, Grady offered delights beyond a small boy's resisting: hammers, nails, saws, a level, an automatic screwdriver, a whole toolbox of treasures. Besides, Del loved Grady's company. He worshiped the man.

Oh, why did Grady have to be the way he was? Perfect, except that he didn't believe in permanence.

Shortly after one, Del called, "Mom, somebody's coming!"

The drapery consultants, at last, Tara thought. There were enough windows in the house to keep her busy with them all afternoon—and she was still waiting on the arrival of the kitchen appliances.

But it was not the van from the Austin Window Treatments nor the appliance truck. It was an unfamiliar car, a black BMW. It stopped by the fence, and the driver got out.

She was a stunning woman in her thirties, with strawberry-blond curls heaped atop her head. She was tall, and her silvery-gray wool suit hinted at an hourglass figure. Tucked under one arm was a manila envelope.

Tara didn't know her, but Grady obviously did, and she knew him.

"Grady McKinney, you haven't come to see us at all, you worthless thing. I shouldn't even talk to you. Open this gate and let me in."

"Billy Jo," Grady answered with a slow grin. "I didn't recognize you. You look almost respectable."

"So do you," she said with a toss of her head. She held up the envelope. "I've got something for you. And your 'employers.' Would they be about?"

Tara then realized who the woman must be: Billy Jo Avery, the much-younger wife of the town's senior attorney. Lynn had told her that Billy Jo had once been the wildest girl in town, but marriage to Martin Avery had tamed her. She must be bringing Grady's contract.

As Tara threw on a jacket, she was surprised to see another person get out of the BMW from the passenger side. It was Lynn, and next to the statuesque Billy Jo she looked tiny and tomboyish.

Grady opened the gate and gave each woman a hug. "Mercy," teased Billy Jo, "if I'd have known you'd clean up so nice, I might have waited for you."

"You'd still be waiting," he tossed back.

Tara felt a sting of jealousy at Billy Jo's flirtatiousness. But it vanished when Lynn introduced the two women. Billy Jo's handshake was firm and genuine, and all playfulness disappeared from her face.

She was, Tara realized, worried. "I'm sorry not to get this to you sooner. Martin isn't well. He would have brought it himself, but—I—wanted him to rest. There are copies of the contract for both parties. If you have any questions, feel free to call. But at home, not the office."

Tara took the envelope reluctantly. It felt unnaturally heavy. If Grady signed these papers, he would stay another year. And if he didn't...

Lynn turned to Grady. "Well, Grady, are you really going to sign this thing?"

He showed his dimples and said, "I haven't read it yet, have I?"

"You'd better be careful," Lynn said with a sidelong glance at Tara. "You might get to like it around here."

"There's a big world out there," Grady said. "I haven't seen it all yet."

Billy Jo sighed. "I should get back. I have prescriptions to pick up."

Lynn squeezed her arm. "Oh, come on, worrywart."

Billy Jo hoisted her cheery facade back in place, said something sassy to Grady, patted Del's cheek and shook hands again with Tara.

Grady locked the gate and watched the car cruise down the driveway. Tara did, too. Del, bored with grown-ups, sat on the edge of the sandbox, playing with the carpenter's level.

Tara stole a look at Grady's profile. His expression was serious, almost grim. She said, "What's wrong with her husband?"

Grady tapped his fist against his sternum. "His heart. Lord, it's hard to believe, him and Billy Jo. I hardly recognized her. She's so—different."

Tara had heard both he and Billy Jo had been reckless as teens. She wondered if they had been lovers, reckless together. But she could not ask such a thing. She said, "She really seems concerned."

"That's what's so different." He paused, watched the dust settling in the empty road. "She used to act like she hadn't a care in the world."

Tara clasped the envelope to her chest. "I suppose you want to look over your copy of this."

He kept staring after the vanished car. "Not yet. Later, when I get this done."

"Whenever." She nodded with a briskness she didn't feel and started back toward the house.

"Grady," Del said, "aren't you going to put any sand in my sandbox?"

"Just getting ready to, champ," she heard Grady say. "Want to give me a hand?"

Tara went inside and hung up her jacket. She sat down at the table, her planning and figuring forgotten. She opened the envelope and began reading the contract.

If he signed, what would that mean? What would happen if he did?

But there was no time to think about it. A pair of deliverymen arrived, bringing in the major appliances, still in boxes. Then the electrician who was to put them in place and connect them phoned to cancel until next week. The drapery people came.

They stayed until dark. Winter was deepening and dark fell early.

BY THE YARD LIGHT GRADY LOADED his truck. The window people were gone, and Tara'd called Del inside for supper. She'd barely spoken to Grady. She didn't mention the contract again. Did she expect him to drive off and settle it later with Gavin? If so, she thought wrong.

He put the tool chest into the truck bed. He thought again about Billy Jo. In high school, she'd been flashy and fast, and a lot of boys panted after her. He hadn't. He'd had eyes only for Beverly Townsend. Still, he'd half admired Billy Jo for her sheer audacity.

Grady had been cynical when he'd heard Billy had married Martin Avery, an older man, staid and prosperous. It had never occurred to Grady that she might actually love someone like Martin.

But it was clear: she did. Now she feared losing him, and it hurt. He slammed the tailgate of the truck shut and thought about it. That's what love did to you. It made you vulnerable to hurt. The deepest hurt. The sort he'd spent his adult life avoiding.

He walked to the back porch and knocked on the door. Tara answered. "Going home?" Her voice was a bit too chipper. He saw Del behind her, dancing around in his underpants, getting ready for his bath.

Grady pulled his hat down to a serious angle. "Nope. I'm going to town, get a bite to eat. I'll be back when the boy's in bed."

Del was tired, he'd played outside in the cold all day. Grady figured he'd be fast asleep in another hour. He couldn't see Tara's expression because the light was behind her.

She shook her head, so that her hair moved like a darkened cloud. "No. It'll be too late."

He held his ground. "I need to talk about the contract. Just you and I. No interruptions."

She shook her head more stubbornly. "Talk to Gavin. Tomorrow."

"I have to talk to you. Not him."

"But he's the one in charge, and I—"

"Gavin's not in charge of what I have to say to you. I have questions only you can answer. I have to see you alone, Tara. I'll be back. In an hour. I *need* to talk to you. Please."

He didn't give her time to argue. He turned and strode out past the new sandbox, the new swing set. They smelled piney and fresh in the cool air.

SHE'D REHEARSED WHAT SHE HAD to say to him.

When he knocked, she swung open the back door. He loomed on the little back porch, blocking her view of the moon-silvered clouds. She glared up at him, her jaw set. "You know, this is kind of presumptuous—"

"Yes. It is. Will you please let me in? I want to talk about this contract." He held up the envelope in his right hand.

"I told you to talk to Gavin. The contract has nothing to do with me."

"Tara, it has everything to do with you. It has from the start. My signature is on this paper. It means I work for

Three Amigos, specifically for your brother. And your brother's 'agent.' That's you. So this is official business.''

Her spine stiffened, and she gripped the edge of the door harder. "You signed it?"

He took a deep breath. "Yes. But before I hand it over, I need to talk to you. Will you let me in? Or do I have to stand out here like Romeo doing the damned balcony scene?"

She hesitated, but sensed an unsettling urgency in him. What could he have to say that was so important? "All right." She opened the door and told a white lie. "My brother may be back at any time. If you want to talk to me alone, you'd better make it fast."

He came into the kitchen, bringing the chill of the night with him. He still wore the denim vest that made his shoulders seem so broad. He paused, taking off his Stetson. "Could we go in the living room?"

She nodded. She'd built a fire in the fireplace. The only other light was the gleam of her secondhand desk lamp. But the living room, so large and scantily furnished, seemed safer than the crowded kitchen, which was filled with appliance boxes.

She swept past him, and he followed her, hat in hand. She went to her desk and stood behind its chair, gripping its back. It was a barrier between her and Grady, and it kept the two of them inside the lamp light's safe circle.

She made her voice even. "You can put the contract on the desk. I'll see that Gavin gets it."

"No." His eyes seemed to be trying to read her face, discover some important message there. "I'm not sure I'm taking the job."

She clutched the chair more tightly. "What? But you said you signed the contract."

He nodded, tapped the envelope on the edge of the desk. "I signed it. But it's made of paper. I can tear it up." He glanced toward the fireplace. "Or burn it."

She felt as if he'd knocked her breath from her body. "Why would you do that?"

He held the envelope between his forefinger and thumb, as if to emphasize how fragile it was. "Because of you," he said.

Her breath caught and her heart pounded, making her feel light-headed. "What about me?"

"I'd stay for you," he said in a low voice. "I want you. I want you more than I've ever wanted anything or anybody. But if you won't have me, I'll be on my way."

She looked at him in shock. "What is this? A proposition? My God, do you think I'm—I'm a job perk?"

He gave a short, unhappy laugh. "It's not a proposition. It's a proposal. I want us to get married. Right away."

She stared at him in disbelief. *"What?"*

"When I first came to your door, I didn't have much in the way of prospects. Wasn't looking for any, either. And then—I saw you."

Stunned, she realized that his usual glibness had deserted him. He chose his words slowly, almost laboriously.

He tapped the envelope against his open hand. "There you were. And by the end of the day, I started to understand. Understand that I could stay in one place—for a woman like you. The road stopped calling me. Its voice just went—away. But—"

He stopped, frowning, a muscle in his jaw twitching. She took a deep, ragged breath and held it, waiting.

He set his jaw harder. "I had nothing to offer you. Or your son. Now I got a check for forty thousand dollars in my back pocket. My lawyer called last night. The tanker company offered a settlement on the truck. I've got a contract from Three Amigos for a good job. By your standards, that's probably not much. Not much at all."

He shook his head almost angrily. "But I'm a good worker. A hard worker. I can make good on this job. I can make myself damned near *indispensable* to this place."

He spoke through teeth clenched in determination. "But only if I'm indispensable to you. And Del."

She stared at him, her hand pressed over the rose embroidered on her breast. She blinked back a mist of tears.

He looked at her, exasperation etched into his face. "So—" he said "—how about it?"

"How about it?" she repeated, feeling like someone in a dream. "You're really proposing to me, and you say 'How about it?'"

He flung up a hand in frustration. "Well, hell, I don't know how to say it. I've never done this before."

Her heart beat so hard that she could hardly speak. "You mean that you love me?"

"Good Lord, yes. I love you. I love you more than I can tell you. Do you love me back?"

She could not speak. But her mouth formed the word yes.

He threw the contract on the desk, dropped his hat, jerked the chair from between them and swept her into his arms.

She raised her mouth to his, and he took it in a kiss so impassioned that her head swam. She wrapped her arms around his neck and pressed closer to him. They feasted on kissing, on holding and touching each other.

He had a warm, pliant mouth that could be demanding or giving, tender or wild, almost out of control. His hands moved over her hungrily, exploring her back, the curve of her ribs, the flesh of her arms. His fingers cupped her face, then tangled in her hair.

His tongue teased her mouth to open more intimately, to let her tongue flirt and dance against his. He closed one hand over her clothed breast and with the other cradled her bottom, drawing her pelvis closer to his.

At his touch, her nipples hardened and throbbed, aching for more. She could feel his arousal thrust against her, igniting her own. He pulled her still more tightly against him.

He was strong, irresistibly strong, and she loved the feel of his power. She loved the hardness of his chest, the coiled force in the muscles of his arms playing under her palms.

His thighs, long and sinewy, pressed against hers. She slid her hands under his denim vest, to feel the brawn of his back.

He shuddered with pleasure, his mouth moving to her jaw, to the exciting spot beneath her ear, down her throat and then his lips kissed first one breast, then the other. She could feel the heat and moistness of his breath through the thin cloth.

His hands circled her waist, then moved upward, under her shirt, against her bare skin. She swayed, dizzied by desire, against him.

"Grady," she panted, "we've got to stop this while we *can* stop it. What if Del wakes up?"

"He won't wake up," he murmured, pressing his mouth to her ear.

"He *might*," she insisted. "If we keep at this, we'll be tearing each other's clothes off and going at it on the floor."

"Sounds good to me." He nuzzled her more seductively.

But there was a clicking sound on the slate floor, and Lono came strolling into the room, his ears perked up, his tail curled like a question mark. He glanced idly at Tara and Grady, as if what they were doing was of no interest to him. Instead, he made for the kitchen.

"He hears something," Tara said, putting her hands on Grady's chest to force distance between them. "Somebody's coming. Maybe Gavin. He said he'd call when he was on his way, but—"

Lono let out a low "woof," a neutral bark that meant he hadn't decided if friend or foe was approaching. Tara heard the muffled rattle of tires on driveway and saw the flash of headlights beaming through the kitchen window.

Grady swore under his breath. Tara tried to step away, but he kept one arm around her. She heard the garage door go up and knew Gavin was home early.

"Oh," she said helplessly. She felt like a naughty teenager who was about to be caught. "Well, we'll just have tell him."

Grady, breathing hard, scowled. "Do I have to ask him for your hand or his permission or something? I swear all this is new to me. I never studied the protocol."

She smiled up at him and leaned her head against his shoulder. "I think what we ask him is if he'll baby-sit."

He gave her a one-sided smile. "While we go where?"

She played with a button of his shirt. "Someplace we can be alone."

"Excellent idea," he said, pulling her to him and kissing her again.

And that was what Gavin saw when he came in. He stood in the kitchen doorway, staring.

When Grady came up for air, he grinned at Gavin. "Your sister just said she'd marry me."

Gavin's expression was one of dawning comprehension. "Hellfire," he said under his breath. "I felt this was coming on. That's why you called last night, asking what you asked."

"I admit it," Grady said. "I hope you approve."

Gavin studied the happiness on Tara's face. He smiled. "Yeah," he said. He gave a satisfied nod. "I approve. And Del's going to be one very happy kid."

GAVIN SUGGESTED GRADY AND TARA take his car, as a sort of diversionary tactic, just in case, and check into an inn in Fredricksburg. Tara, starry-eyed and flushed, agreed, but insisted they would be back by the time Del woke in the morning.

She packed a small bag, and Grady borrowed a change of clothes and some toiletries from Gavin. By nine o'clock, he was driving Gavin's rented Corvette toward Fredricksburg, only forty minutes away.

Fredricksburg was a quaint town in one of the most beautiful parts of the Hill Country. It was also a frequent destination for honeymooners, lovers and couples who wanted a romantic interlude. It had beautiful inns and over two hundred bed and breakfast places, some exquisite. Grady'd phoned ahead to one of the best and, because November was off season, got a reservation.

The car glided through the darkness, and Grady's heart thudded in anticipation. He steered left handed and with his right gripped Tara's hand. It seemed dreamlike that she was with him, this way. He thought if he kept hold of her, the dream might not vanish.

He could still not quite convince himself she had really said yes. But he was a man who thought things through ahead of time and did it thoroughly. He squeezed her hand. "I have some ideas about how we could get married. Tell me what you think."

She gave him an affectionate look. "Ideas? You were so sure I'd agree, you had a *plan?*"

"Hell, no, I wasn't sure," he said, still scared at the thought she might have said no. "I had a plan, too, if you turned me down."

She chuckled, like a purr. "And what was that?"

"I'd tell Gavin some things that could help you. Then I'd hit the road, never come back. And I'd spend the rest of my life loving you in vain. That was Plan B."

She cocked her head in curiosity. "And what's Plan A?"

He swallowed. "I think we ought to get married as soon as possible. Tomorrow."

Her mouth dropped open. "Tomorrow? We can't. It's too soon—I have to tell Del. I have to prepare him for this."

He nodded. "I know that. But the sooner we get married, the less time your ex-father-in-law can meddle or raise hell. So here's what we do."

Tara's face went painfully serious at the mention of Burleigh Hastings.

Grady said, "I figure what we do is get married twice. Tomorrow you and I and Gavin and Del fly to Arkansas."

"Arkansas!" Her eyes went wide.

"Hear me out, Tara. Please. This makes sense. In Texas there's a waiting period between buying a license and getting married. Three days. There's none in Arkansas. We'll fly from Austin to Little Rock. Like we're taking a day off, that's all.''

She shook her head in confusion. "I don't understand."

"Trust me. Different states have different laws, and that's why all this'll work. The sooner we get married, the sooner I can apply to adopt Del.''

"Adopt?"

"Absolutely. While we go off to get married, Gavin takes Del to the Children's Museum there. They've got a good one.''

"How do you *know* these things?"

"I've been a lot of places. Anyway, while they do that, we get a license and get married. But we don't tell anyone but Gavin—and a judge and lawyer here. We don't even tell Del.''

"I can't lie to Del," she objected. "I can't suddenly marry and not even *tell* him.''

She tried to draw her hand away, but he held it fast. "What we tell him, what we tell everybody, is that we're *going* to get married. And when Del's used to the idea, and he's ready, we get married a second time, with him there. But in the meantime, you quietly apply to transfer your divorce from California to Texas.''

"Transfer the divorce? I never heard of such a thing. Why?''

"Like I said, state laws are different. In all kinds of ways. Why not in divorce? And why not in visitation and custody rights? So I called Cal, and he got me some lawyers' names and basic information.''

"But a transfer? I still don't understand."

"It doesn't have to be done publicly. We go to a judge here in Texas, and ask for it. If Sid agrees, it can be done in a day. One day, Tara.''

She looked more puzzled still. "Why would Sid agree?"

"Why wouldn't he?" Grady countered. "You could nail him to the wall for child support if you wanted. His wife doesn't want you around—or Del. And Sid probably wouldn't mind spiting his father. I wouldn't blame him."

"Grady, you're making my head spin. What's this got to do with Burleigh?"

"Honey, in California, a biological grandparent can make a claim on a grandchild. In Texas, he can't. If Sid agrees to transfer the divorce, the divorce gets interpreted according to Texas law. Burleigh no longer *has* automatic visitation rights. Especially if I adopt Del. That'll cancel them out double. He'll be my son, not Sid's, a McKinney, not a Hastings. Texas law will recognize only *my* dad as his grandfather."

She blinked, stunned.

He shook his head in concentration. "Last night I asked Gavin about Sid. From what he said, Sid won't fight. He can't. He's all but abandoned Del. So Del's going to be *our* little boy. And I'll be as good a daddy to him as I can."

"When Burleigh finds out..." She couldn't finish the sentence.

"He won't have a leg to stand on. If he tries to fight it, he's got to fight the two of us—and the whole state of Texas. In the meantime, we can get this adoption in total privacy. And done in a week or less. Burleigh's hog-tied before he knows the rope's even been tossed."

She repeated what she said before. "How do you *know* these things?"

"I called lawyers. Sometimes they had me call other lawyers. But bit by bit it came together. Last night, after I found out about the settlement on the truck, I knew I could leave this place. But, Lord, I knew I didn't want to. I called Gavin. I phoned Cal. I called lawyers to double-check. I looked up stuff on the Internet."

She laughed with chagrined surprise. "You use the Internet?"

"Hell, yes," he said, almost defensively. "You think I'm just a strong back and a weak mind?"

She laughed again, laying her head on his shoulder. "I

think maybe you're the smartest man I ever met. And the most unexpected.''

''Right now, I'm thinking what any smart man would think.''

''What's that?'' Her voice was low and playful.

''I need to get you to that room in Fredricksburg fast as possible.''

He put his arm around her shoulders and dropped a kiss onto the top of her head. Her hair tickled his lips and drove him half-mad with longing.

THE BED-AND-BREAKFAST SUITE in Fredricksburg was designed for sensual pleasure. It was expensive, but Grady didn't care. He only intended to get married once in his life.

He unlocked the door, then picked up Tara and carried her over the threshold. Her arms flew around his neck in surprise. He grinned.

The sitting room was cozy, yet lavish, furnished with Victorian antiques. The carved wood was dark and polished. But the fabrics and textures were in shades of sky-blue and white.

Snowy drapes covered the windows, and the cream-colored carpet was thick and rich. A sofa and love seat were upholstered in white velvet and accented with tapestry pillows of blue and white. A matching rug of blue and white ornamented the floor. The lamps alight on the end tables had shades of pale blue silk and their bases were cut glass.

Grady looked at it and hoped it would please her. It was lovely, he thought, but not half as lovely as she was. She was the most beautiful thing in the room.

''Oh, Grady,'' she breathed, embracing him more tightly.

He refused to release her. Still holding her, he said, ''There's supposed to be a bedroom somewhere.''

He carried her across the room to a white door that stood slightly ajar. It led into a darkened room. He stepped inside, using his elbow to switch on the light. A delicate chandelier flared into life, illuminating another room of white and blue.

In the center stood a huge bed with gleaming brass posts. It was curtained all around with gauzy white material swept back and fastened with blue satin rosettes. In the muted light, a quilted satin bedspread gleamed like pearl.

"Oh, Grady," she said again, pressing her face against his neck. "I don't even have a nice nightgown to wear."

"Then don't wear anything," he said, his voice tight. He realized he had never seen her naked except in his imagination. His groin hardened.

But he said, "I smell like sweat and sawdust. I'm going to take a bath."

He set her on her feet. He wanted to take her to bed then and there, but he forced himself to let go of her. Another door led to a bathroom that was old-fashioned except for the large whirlpool tub.

He turned on the water, hoping a bath would cool him down enough so that he could make love to her the way she deserved, with long, intricate foreplay that would pleasure her again and again.

But he hurt all over with wanting her. His head pounded as he dropped his clothes to the floor. He was about to step naked into the tub, when she appeared in the doorway, barefoot, unbuttoning her blouse.

He saw the shadowy cleft between her breasts, and his erection, which he'd hoped to tame, just got wilder. She saw, but she didn't look away. "We could take a bath together," she said in a soft voice.

Then her clothes were in a heap beside his on the floor, and she stood before him, so beautiful in her nakedness that he almost got tears in his eyes.

She was tall and slender, with small, perfect breasts. Their tips were a warm and delicate pink that made his mouth water, wanting to close over them.

Her long legs were a marvel. He took them in hungrily and was hypnotized by the silky russet curls between her thighs. He clenched his hands into fists to control himself.

"You get in first," he said.

She stepped into the big tub and slid down into the water. It came up just beneath the curves of her breasts. Gritting his teeth, he reached for one of the guest soaps and unwrapped it. It was as pink as her taut nipples.

He knelt beside the tub and dipped the soap into the water. Then he rubbed it between his hands and began to stroke the foaming bubbles onto her body.

First, slowly, savoring the feel, he moved his hands over her shoulders, which were faintly freckled and smooth as satin. She sighed deeply, leaning her head back, and her hair fanned out against the white porcelain.

His breathing labored, he soaped her breasts, beginning with their outer roundness and moving to the tender centers, fondling and teasing them, loving them with his hands.

She closed her eyes and threw her head farther back. "Oh, *please* get in here with me."

He rose and looked down at her gleaming body. "Please," she said again. She parted her long legs. He stepped into the tub and lowered himself, facing her. She raised herself so that his legs could slide beneath her hips.

His erection was pressed against her, only inches away from entering her. His heart slammed in his chest like a mad thing.

Her eyes opened, those mysterious eyes whose depths could always suck away his soul. Now mischief and desire mingled with the mystery.

"Hand me the soap," she whispered.

CHAPTER EIGHTEEN

MORNING AT THE DOUBLE C STARTED off fine, just fine. Bret walked into the kitchen and found Jonah polishing off a plate of Belgian waffles.

Rhonda was at the counter, peeling an orange. She wore a pants outfit of dark pink, and she looked like a million dollars. Bret took in her full figure and thought, *Great Scott, she's got a proud bosom.*

He hadn't thought of the term "proud bosom" for thirty years, but it might have been coined just for her. She gave him that shy smile of hers. "It's a special breakfast this morning. We're celebrating."

Bret's heart softened, almost melted, at her smile, but he had no idea what she was talking about. "Celebrating?"

She smiled and nodded proudly at Jonah. "Somebody finished his dissertation last night."

Bret forced his gaze from her and looked at Jonah. The boy stared at his plate, blushed, and stuffed a forkful of waffle into his mouth.

Bret's back straightened in unexpected pride. He'd known for weeks that Jonah was supposedly near the end, but he had been resigned that the end would never really come.

"You're finished?" he asked.

"Umph." Jonah nodded.

"Isn't that something?" Rhonda said, looking at Jonah with something akin to awe. "He's written a whole book. I know how much work that is. My son did it, too. I was so proud."

"That's wonderful," Bret said to Jonah. "You're finally done?"

Jonah's blush deepened. *"Umph."*

"Sit, sit," Rhonda told Bret. "I'll make you a waffle."

Bret sat across from Jonah. "So now what?" he asked him. "What's the next step?"

Jonah raised his startling blue eyes. "I'm going to drive to Nebraska. Give it to my dissertation director. Go over it with him."

Bret blinked in surprise. "When? Soon?"

"Yessir. Soon as you can spare me."

Bret thought about it. Most of the work of readying for winter was done. He could work with a skeleton staff until spring, and Jonah must know this.

Bret saw hope in the boy's expression.

"Work's light," he said gruffly. "Go when you want. I know you're eager to get this done."

"Yessir. I thought—since Lang can take my place—maybe I could leave today?"

This was sooner than Bret had expected, but he understood. Jonah had been working over two years on the dissertation. He'd come to the Double C to do the final draft. This son had traveled a long and difficult road. He'd almost reached his destination, and he was eager for journey's end.

Gratefully Bret took a mug of coffee from Rhonda. It gave him time to pull his thoughts together. "Today? If you want. Sure. No problem."

Jonah nodded. "Great." He finished his waffle and smiled his thanks to Rhonda. "That was wonderful. I'm going to go pack."

He rose and left.

And that, Bret thought, numbed, was that. His quiet son was leaving. He realized the Double C would seem different, incomplete.

Rhonda beamed. "Isn't that something? Your son's going to be *Doctor* McKinney."

"It sort of slipped up on me." Bret shook his head. "I

didn't know he was that close. There's been so much going on lately. And he never says much. You have to pry things out of him.''

''Not this morning,'' she said, putting a waffle topped with ice cream before him. ''I heard that printer in his room going on into the wee hours. I *thought* something was up. And this morning, when I saw his face, I knew. I asked, and he told me. He was downright talkative.''

Jonah talkative? Bret looked up at her gentle face. *Rhonda, you're a wonder,* he thought. Then he tasted the waffle and had the sudden insight of what heaven was like.

But shortly after Jonah finished packing his car, mumbled his goodbyes, and took off, Bret came crashing back to earth. Jonah's departure gave him an unexpectedly empty feeling.

Then Lang phoned.

''Where are you?'' Bret asked. ''If you're coming, you've missed Jonah. He finished his dissertation and took off out of here like a bat out of hell.''

There was an ominous pause. Lang said, ''Dad, I'm not coming. Susie and I are back together.''

Bret's heart plummeted. He did not truly believe that Susie could make Lang happy. He stammered, ''But…I…had plans for you here.''

''I'm sorry, Dad. I can't explain it. It's just that we're going to give it another try. Here in Santa Fe. She thinks she'll be happier if we're close to her folks.''

''But ranching,'' Bret said, stunned. ''What about ranching?''

''There's a riding school here that needs an instructor. I'm applying. I'm pretty sure I can get it.''

A humble riding school. Bret knew Lang was meant for more important things, a happier fate. He thought of Francina Hills. He had been able to *see* Lang running that place. He could envision it in his mind's eye. And Lang and Tara Hastings…

''Dad, I love Susie. So I'm staying here. Wish me luck.''

All of Bret's handsome fantasies crumbled. They were not to be. He knew they'd been fantasies, mere pipe dreams, yet it pained him to let them go. He was an adult; he let go anyway.

"Good luck," he said, then added, "son."

"Thanks, Dad. And congratulate Jonah for me."

When Bret set the receiver back in the cradle, he felt stranger and more vacant than when Jonah had left. He sat at his desk, staring out the window at nothing in particular.

The phone rang again. He picked it up mechanically.

"Hello." It was Grady, sounding both cheerful and wary. "I suppose you noticed I didn't come home last night."

Once again Bret was caught by surprise, unpleasantly so. He hadn't, in fact, noticed. At first his attention had been focused on Jonah, then on Lang. Now, God only knew what Grady'd been up to.

He must have met some fast woman and spent his night tomcatting. Bret hoped it was no worse than that, but he wasn't optimistic.

"Nothing better have happened to that truck you borrowed," he said, warning in his voice. "That truck is J.T.'s property, and if you—"

"The truck's fine, Dad," Grady assured him. "It's why I called. It's parked over at Francina Hills. By Tara's house. I'm going out of town today, and I'm going to leave it here, if that's all right. Otherwise, could you send somebody here to pick it up? I'll leave the keys under the floor mat."

Bret felt a small wave of relief. "Nobody's going to need it."

"Dad," Grady said, "I've got some news for you. It may come kind of unexpected. I signed the Three Amigos contract. I'm staying on here."

He was staying on? Grady, his wayward son? He would be the one in Crystal Creek? Bret wanted to pinch himself. Maybe he was having some strange and illogical dream. He needed to wake up from it, now.

Grady said, "There's another thing, Dad. I'm engaged. To Tara Hastings. And I'm going to adopt her boy."

"What?" Bret said tonelessly. "You're what?"

"I'm marrying Tara. And adopting her boy."

Bret's head began to whirl dizzily. He put his hand to his brow to steady himself. "When?"

"As soon as possible. I finally found the woman for me, Dad. And I think Mom would approve. I think she'd be happy."

Yes, yes, Bret thought dizzily. Maggie *would* be happy that Grady was settling down at last. And with a woman like Tara Hastings? Maggie would certainly approve. It was the sort of thing she'd always hoped for.

"So what do you think, Dad? You're going to be a grandpa."

Grandpa. Ye gods. "I don't know what to think," Bret said truthfully.

Grady laughed. "I'll tell you more when I get back. There's business I've got to attend to. Tara and I have to go to Little Rock…"

When Bret hung up this time, he put his elbows on his desk and his face in his hands. He'd had too much news to digest. Grady staying? In a responsible position? Married? With a child? *Grandpa?*

Rhonda, passing by the door, must have seen him. He heard her say, "Oh, goodness. Is something wrong?"

"I don't know." Bret kept his face buried in his hands. "I just don't know."

She came to him, putting her hand on his shoulder. "Are you all right?"

He didn't move except to shake his head in bewilderment. "Did you ever have a day where the whole world turned inside out and upside down? And it felt like somebody put your brain in the blender?"

"I—I'm not sure what you mean." She bent nearer, clearly concerned for him.

Haltingly he told her about first Lang's call, then Grady's.

She squeezed his shoulder. "But it's good," she said earnestly. "Surely it is. A marriage saved. And a marriage made. Grady's a good man, I can tell. He'll make a good husband and father. He'll be a credit to you. And a little boy around? Why, that's just the best thing I can think of."

He put his hand atop hers. "You're a wonderful woman, Rhonda."

"Is there something I can get for you? Coffee? Something stronger?"

"No," he said, grasping her hand more tightly. "Just stay with me."

He rose from his chair. He looked into her lovely, caring eyes. "Stay with me," he said hoarsely. "Please."

He put his arms around her.

One thing led to another. And another.

In her bedroom, Millie Gilligan gathered her cards into a deck and set them aside on the nightstand. She removed the tray from her lap. She put her hands behind her head and leaned back against the pillow. She stared upward and smiled to herself in satisfaction, like a woman who has done her job well.

GAVIN NODDED. He said Grady's plan, to marry secretly, then publicly, was good. "It'll work. You'll outmaneuver Burleigh. He won't know until it's too late to do anything."

Tara looked worried. "He'll still make trouble."

Gavin frowned in disgust. "Tara, then get a restraining order against him. Clear back in California you were steeling yourself to do it. Let him be decent—or keep his distance. And it's not just your fight anymore. Grady's beside you—and so am I."

She nodded, and Grady squeezed her hand.

Gavin insisted he would pay for the trip to Arkansas and back; it would be part of his wedding present to them, he said.

Del was puzzled by the trip. But he was too pleased to be traveling by plane to question why they were going.

Gavin took him to the children's museum, where Del played in delight with model trains, blew bubbles, climbed on the indoor gym, and pretended to drive the antique car.

Grady and Tara were married by an elderly justice of the peace in his cottage home. He performed the ceremony in his living room, with his silver-haired wife as the official witness. The unofficial witness was a blinking calico cat that lay draped across the top of the old upright piano.

After lunch, Gavin went his own way for a time while Tara and Grady took Del for a walk beside the river. They walked with him between them, each holding him by the hand.

Tara stopped and knelt down beside her son. "Del," she said carefully. "I like Grady a lot. And he likes me. We love each other. He wants to be your daddy."

Del's gray eyes widened. He looked at her, then up at Grady. "You want to be my daddy?"

Grady, too, knelt beside him. He put his hands on the boy's upper arms. "Yes. I want to love you and take care of you and your mother. I want to marry her. And for you to be my little boy."

Tara's heart seized up in her throat. She watched the emotions play across Del's face. She knew he adored Grady, but what would he say to this news?

His little face looked puzzled and thoughtful and glad all at once. He swallowed and cocked his head. He stared solemnly at Grady and asked, "Do you mean it?"

"I mean it, champ. With all my heart."

He spoke with such sincerity that tears rose, hot and prickling, in Tara's eyes. She bit her lip.

Del's gaze held Grady's. He took a deep breath. "I been needing a daddy. Mine went away. You won't go away will you?"

Emotion touched Grady's features, a deep and grave emotion. When he spoke, his voice was rough with feeling. "I won't go away. Ever. I will love you as long as I live."

He himself seemed almost stunned by his words. Gruffly he said, "So give me a hug, okay?"

Del threw his arms around Grady's neck. Grady embraced him. Then he picked him up. "I think I'll carry you for a while. I like holding you. Let's go meet your uncle Gavin. And then let's go home to Texas."

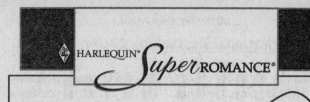
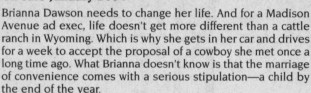
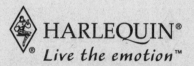

National Bestselling Author

brenda novak

COLD
FEET

Despite the cloud of suspicion that followed her father to his
grave, Madison Lieberman maintained his innocence...*until* crime
writer Caleb Trovato forces her to confront the past once again.

**"Readers will quickly be drawn into this well-written,
multi-faceted story that is an engrossing, compelling read."
—*Library Journal***

Available February 2004.

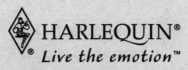

HARLEQUIN®
Live the emotion™

Visit us at www.eHarlequin.com

**Sea View House in Pilgrim Cove offers
its residents the sea, the sun, the sound
of the surf and the call of the gulls.
But sometimes serenity is only an illusion...**

Pilgrim Cove

Four heartwarming stories by popular author
Linda Barrett

The House
on the Beach

Laura McCloud's come back
to Pilgrim Cove—the source
of her fondest childhood
memories—to pick up the
pieces of her life. The
tranquility of Sea View House
is just what she needs. She
moves in...and finds much
more than she bargained for.

**Available in March 2004,
The House on the Beach
is the first title in this
charming series.**

*Available wherever
Harlequin books are sold.*

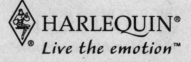

HARLEQUIN®
Live the emotion™

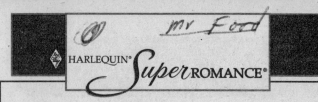

mr Ford

HARLEQUIN *Super*ROMANCE®

Alouette, Michigan. Located high on the Upper Peninsula. Home to strong men, stalwart women and lots and lots of trees.

NORTH COUNTRY *Stories*

Three Little Words
by Carrie Alexander
Superromance #1186

Connor Reed returns to Alouette to reconnect with his grandfather and to escape his notorious past. He enlists the help of Tess Bucek, the town's librarian, to help teach his grandfather to read. As Tess and Connor start to fall in love, they learn the healing power of words, especially three magical little ones....

Available in February 2004 wherever Harlequin books are sold.

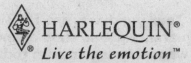

HARLEQUIN®
Live the emotion™